MARKED

I think Richard's got mind mages or enchanters working to sway the crowd, I said. *He's going to prime all of those adepts out there for violence, then when the Keepers arrive he's going to whip them into a frenzy. If I can find the mage working the spell and shut it down, there's a lot less chance of another massacre.*

Shit, Luna said. *It's like the demonstrations last year, isn't it? He wants to have the Council fighting adepts again, just on a bigger scale.*

Best guess, yeah. Let's make sure that doesn't happen.

By Benedict Jacka

BENEDICT JACKA

MARKED

orbit

www.orbitbooks.net

ORBIT

First published in Great Britain in 2018 by Orbit

1 3 5 7 9 10 8 6 4 2

A CIP catalogue record for this book is available from the British Library.

ISBN 978-0-356-50721-7

Typeset in Garamond 3 by Palimpsest Book Production Limited, Falkirk, Stirlingshire
Printed and bound in Great Britain by CPI Group (UK) Ltd, Croydon CR0 4YY

Papers used by Orbit are from well-managed
forests and other responsible sources.

MIX
Paper from
responsible sources
FSC® C104740

Orbit
An imprint of
Little, Brown Book Group
Carmelite House
50 Victoria Embankment
London EC4Y 0DZ
An Hachette UK Company
www.hachette.co.uk

www.orbitbooks.net

1

The factory hadn't changed much in five years. The building was the same shade of brownish grey, grime on brick, and the rusted coils of razor wire still gaped atop the walls. From my position on the rooftop I could look down into what had been the car park, and into the windows of the factory itself. There were no signs of movement, but that didn't matter: I knew what was inside. Off to the right, the skyscrapers of Canary Wharf rose into the night, yellow-white pinpoints glittering off the dark waters of the Thames, topped by the double strobe of the pyramid-shaped tower. The hum of a boat's engine blended with the deeper rustle of the waves, all of it merging into the sounds of London.

It was June, but the night wasn't a warm one. The breeze off the water was keeping the air cool, enough so that my armour was comfortable to wear. My armour is plate-and-mesh, an imbued item, alive in its own way, and if I focused on it I could feel its presence, guarded and watchful. There was a second imbued item tucked into my pocket – a dreamstone – and a third hidden in that factory. Of the three, my armour was the only one I was glad for. It might not be the strongest of items, but it was one I'd come to trust, and its reactive mesh had saved my life more than once. It could deflect a knife or bullet, maybe even a spell from a battle mage.

Assuming the battle mage didn't have time to study the

armour beforehand and figure out exactly how much power he'd need to pierce it.

A voice spoke from behind. 'Hey.'

'Correct term of address, please,' I said absently. Normally I go by Verus to colleagues and Alex to friends. As of eight months ago, I'd picked up a new title.

The man behind me grimaced, thinking I couldn't see him. He was young, with close-cut hair and a narrow face, and he'd been staring at my back for the past few minutes. His name was Chimaera, and he was the newest and youngest of the three Keepers assigned with me to this job.

'Councillor,' Chimaera said grudgingly. 'We going?'

'Patience,' I said. Sergeant Little was due to call, but it wouldn't be for another two to five minutes. So I'd gone up here to admire the view, and to see if Chimaera would make a move. So far he hadn't, but I'd seen flickers of possibilities where he did, enough that I was continuing to stand with my back to him, waiting to see if he'd give in to temptation. I wondered whether Chimaera had volunteered, or whether someone had put him here. I could look into it, if I had the time.

Standing here made me think of the first time I'd come to this factory. I'd been hunting a barghest, and once it was over I'd met Luna up on this rooftop and warned her that the Keepers who'd been working with us today might be our enemies tomorrow. I'd thought I was experienced; with hindsight, in my own way, I'd been as naïve as her. Back then I'd thought of the Council as a single block, something to work with or distrust. But it wasn't a single block: it was a thousand individuals, each one with their own motivations and agenda. Trust didn't come into it; you work with the tools you're given.

My communicator was about to ping, and the short-term futures were quiet. Chimaera wasn't going to try it. *Pity.* I waited for the voice in my ear to say my name before answering. 'Verus.'

'We're ready,' Sergeant Little's voice said.

'On my way,' I replied, and turned. 'Time to go.'

Chimaera nodded. I could feel his eyes on my back all the way down.

The men were already assembled when we arrived. There were twenty Council security, armed and armoured, led by a compact, tough-looking man with sharp blue eyes called Sergeant Little. Of the two Keepers, I only knew one, a tall veteran with a long face who went by the name of Ilmarin. The other, Saffron, was a heavily built woman whose communication consisted mostly of grunts.

'Our target's in the factory,' I said. 'Both him, and the people he's suborned. Sergeant, pick out enough men to cover the exits. The rest of us will go in through the front door.'

'ROE?' Sergeant Little asked.

He meant the rules of engagement. It was a good question, and one with no good answer. 'Non-lethal where possible. Remember, these are civilians.'

The sergeant nodded slowly, though I could tell he was doubtful. One of the other men wasn't so reticent. 'All due respect, sir, but that's going to be a bit hard if they're shooting at us.'

'I'll be on point,' I said. 'Keepers Saffron and Ilmarin will assist. We'll disarm as many as we can.'

'What about me?' Chimaera said.

'You're rearguard.'

'Why should I——?'

'Because Ilmarin and Saffron can subdue non-lethally,' I said. Ilmarin was an air mage, and Saffron a mind mage. 'You can't. Unless you were planning to burn them *half* to death.'

Chimaera scowled. Fire mages are notoriously bad at using less than lethal force, and they don't respond well to criticism, either. 'You're going to prove something by going first?'

I saw the faces of the security men shift, and several looked at Chimaera with expressions that were a little too neutral. The Council has a habit of using its security forces as screening units, and if someone needs to be first through a door, then it's usually a Council security man who gets the job, in much the same way that one might poke a suspicious object with a long stick. Sometimes the object turns out to be a bomb, which is hard on the stick. The men (and it's almost entirely men) on the Council security forces know the risks of the job, and they're paid well, but no one likes to be reminded that they're expendable. Ilmarin shot Chimaera a sharp glance, which the younger mage didn't notice.

'Is this the kind of discipline Keepers are taught nowadays?' I didn't raise my voice, but I didn't take my eyes off Chimaera either. 'You were assigned to my command. If you have a problem with that, get lost.'

Chimaera glowered but didn't answer. I waited a second, then turned back to the others. 'Primary objective hasn't changed. Remember, there isn't any limit on the number of thralls this thing can maintain. It takes it a certain amount of time to bring someone under its control, but once it's got them, it keeps them. That means the longer we leave this problem, the worse it's going to get.'

'What about the bearer?' Sergeant Little asked.

'No restrictions,' I said. 'Take him down any way you

can.' I would have liked to take the guy alive, but I was asking enough from the men as it was. I looked around. 'Any questions?'

The group looked at me. No one spoke. 'Okay,' I said. 'Move out.'

Up close, the factory loomed like a monstrous shadow. Orange radiance from the street lights lit up the upper walls, while the ground floor was shrouded in gloom. 'One on the gate,' Ilmarin said quietly into my ear.

I nodded. I could have crept up and taken him down, but we could afford to take things slowly. 'Saffron?'

Saffron leaned around the railings, staring into the shadows surrounding the front door. I could feel the spell working, a kind of rhythmic pull. Mind magic is hard to detect; it's not easy to make out the details of a spell even when you know what to look for. Thirty seconds passed, a minute, then I saw a dark shape slump to the ground. The futures in which the alarm was raised vanished.

We moved up, the security men trailing us. Once we reached the door I clicked on my light, shining it down. The beam revealed a kid of maybe seventeen or eighteen, dressed in dirty clothes. He was fast asleep, breathing slowly and steadily, and on his head was a silver mesh cap.

'That's how it controls them?' Sergeant Little asked quietly.

I nodded. The Council records on this thing had been thorough, and they'd contained drawings of similar devices. The cap was made of metal, crudely soldered, and it was clamped around the boy's skull. 'How long would it take you to get it off?' I asked Saffron.

Saffron shrugged.

Which meant I couldn't count on her to do it fast enough.

'Cuff him and move him back to the perimeter,' I said. This one hadn't been carrying a gun; that would change once we got inside.

Little's men removed the sleeping boy while Ilmarin worked on the door. It opened quickly and we moved in.

We picked our way through dark corridors. Junk and rubbish littered the floor, making it hard to find a path, and every now and then there'd be the crunch of something being crushed under an unwary boot. Each time it happened, Little would shoot a glare at the offending person, but I didn't turn to look; all my attention was focused on the futures ahead.

There were signs that the factory was in use — footprints in the grime, splinters of wood and brick that had been kicked out of the way — but there had been no attempt to make the place more hospitable. There was no power, and judging by the smell, no plumbing either. Even if there had been, I didn't think anyone would want to live here. The factory had an unwholesome feel to it, malignant and cold.

There was a metallic skittering, something small bouncing away down the corridor. 'Hold up,' Ilmarin said quietly. He put a hand to the wall. 'Sergeant?'

'I see it,' Sergeant Little said, frowning at the scratches and pockmarks in the concrete. 'Looks like an AP mine.'

'They've got the place trapped?'

'No,' I said absently.

Behind me, I felt Ilmarin and Little exchange glances. Little bent down, picked up a ball bearing, sniffed at it. 'It's not new.'

'You sure?' Ilmarin said. 'If there are mines here . . .'

'This is years old,' I said.

Ilmarin gave me a thoughtful look. He'd been with me the last time we'd come here, and there hadn't been any mines. 'He's right,' Little said. 'Too much dust in the scorings.'

'You hear that?' one of the other men said.

We stood still, listening. After a moment I could pick it out: a steady throbbing sound. 'Generator?' Little asked.

'I think so,' Ilmarin said.

'All right,' I said. 'Little, have the men do their final checks.'

'You're still planning to be the first one in?' Ilmarin asked me.

'You don't approve?'

'I don't mind backing you up, if that's what you're asking,' Ilmarin said dryly. 'But I have a shield.'

'Well, I don't,' Saffron announced, 'and I'm not going in first.'

'Stay and cover the door,' I told her. 'You can pick them off from there.'

'And Chimaera?' Ilmarin asked.

The young Keeper was at the back of our procession, far enough away to be out of hearing for the conversation. 'I meant what I said,' I told Ilmarin. 'I want these people alive.'

'You do make life difficult for yourself,' Ilmarin murmured, but his lips quirked in a smile. 'Well, then. Shall we?'

I looked at Little and got his nod. 'Let's go kick the hornet's nest.'

The main factory floor had been mostly cleared. The old machines, too heavy to be moved, still squatted like rusting statues, but the concrete around them had been swept clean, the rubbish piled untidily in the corners. In the centre of the floor were a pair of splintered wooden tables, and a dozen people were clustered around each, sitting on broken chairs and old packing crates. They were young and old, male and female, and they were all hunched over, working with feverish intensity. All wore the mesh headpieces that we'd seen on the boy outside. Above, catwalks ran from wall to wall. Yellow lights around the room threw off a dull glow, and in one corner a petrol generator was rumbling away with a steady *chug-chug-chug*.

Ilmarin and I walked out onto the factory floor. With the sound of the generator drowning out our footsteps, no one noticed us at first. Then a woman at the end of the table saw us out of the corner of her eye and looked up.

There was a moment's pause, then every other person in the room looked up in eerie synchronisation. Twenty-four pairs of eyes stared blankly at us, then as one, they rose to their feet and began moving forward.

'Well, we have their attention,' Ilmarin said. 'What's step two?'

'Step two is to take out the ones with guns,' I said. I'd been hoping that their reaction to two apparently unarmed men would be to capture, rather than shoot. It seemed to be working, at least so far, but three at the back had pulled out pistols. If I wanted to avoid any dead bodies, I needed them disarmed.

The thralls had closed to within a few feet. Their arms came up, reaching to grapple. 'Go,' I said, and darted forward.

For an instant they hesitated, but an instant was all I needed. I slipped the attack of the first, knocked the breath out of the second, tripped him and threw him under the feet of the third. They tried to press around me and grapple, acting in unison. Against most people it would have been effective, but here it was the reverse. Normally it's uncertainty that's my biggest enemy in combat, the chaos and confusion cutting the range of my divination to a bare few seconds. But here I wasn't really fighting a crowd, I was fighting a single entity that was using the thralls like fingers and toes, and I slid away from their attacks, using their numbers against them.

There's a rhythm to battle, a cadence, almost like a dance. Every move has its counter, every strike its timing. Once you understand it, it doesn't feel as though you're attacking at all: you just do what's natural. Dimly, through the press, I was aware of Ilmarin hammering thralls with fists of air while they beat uselessly at his shield. A man swung at me with a broom handle. I like sticks, especially long sticks. The staff came out of his fingers as I twisted it, and a blow to his head put him on the ground.

Felling him opened a gap in the crowd, and I sprang onto a packing crate and up onto the table. Grasping hands reached for me but I ran down the table, kicking aside bits of metal and unfinished headpieces, then jumped down in front of the trio with guns. They had their pistols levelled but I could see in the futures that they weren't going to fire, at least not yet. My stick cracked the wrist of one of them, sending the pistol skittering off across the concrete, and I kicked the second hard enough to make him fold over. The third backed up, still aiming the gun, and I closed, spun, took his ankle out from underneath him, then stunned him with a blow to the head.

The futures changed. There was gunfire, now. *Time for step three.* 'Little,' I said out loud, hearing the communicator in my ear chime. 'Go.'

There was a rush of footsteps and the Council security came charging in. Caught between us and the reinforcements, the thralls hesitated before turning on the security men, but the Council security waded in with batons and tasers, focusing the thralls down one at a time.

The thralls on my side of the room ran for the fallen guns. I caught one before he could reach it, tripping him then cracking him over the skull as he tried to rise. 'Ilmarin!' I shouted, and the air mage threw out a hand; the other two pistols went flying up and over the mêlée, falling behind the Council security.

One more man tried to grab me from behind; I threw him over my shoulder and drove the stick into his stomach, and all of a sudden the fight was over. The last of the thralls were being wrestled to the ground and handcuffed by the security men. Not a shot had been fired. I strode across the room, heading for a small metal door on the north wall, dropping the stick and pulling out my stun focus. Chimaera appeared through the crowd, looking belligerent. 'You need—' he began.

'Get out of the way,' I snapped. I pointed to two men in line with the door. 'You and you. Back off.'

The two security men obeyed. Chimaera didn't. 'You're supposed to—'

The door was yanked open. On the other side was a woman with fat cheeks, dirty blonde hair and a gun held in both hands. 'Get out!' she screeched. 'Get out or I'll kill you all!' She started firing without waiting for an answer.

Twelve bullets in the gun; ten steps to the woman. The first two shots went wild, then her eyes focused on me and she aimed for my chest. I sidestepped to make the next two miss, then reversed direction, letting the next three go past on the other side. Only five steps left, but the closer I came, the harder it was to dodge. The eighth shot breezed by my head, but the ninth would have taken me in the stomach and I had to spin; that threw my balance off and I had to halt my advance and dodge the other way to avoid the next two. I twisted sideways, jerked my head out of the way as another bullet barely missed my neck, then I was square on and the pistol was pointing right at my chest. The woman's eyes never changed as she pulled the trigger.

The gun clicked as the hammer fell on an empty chamber. If the woman had been directing her own actions, she probably would have looked surprised. Instead she pulled the trigger again, and again: *click click click* went the gun and then my stun focus took her in the stomach and her eyes rolled up and she slumped to the floor.

I turned around to see Chimaera and at least half the security men staring at me. Some of the thralls were still struggling, but every member of the detachment not occupied with them seemed to be looking in my direction. Chimaera's mouth was slightly open. 'What are you all staring at?' I said, picking up the empty gun.

Little rounded on the men. 'All right, enough rubbernecking! Get them secured!'

'Something's coming,' Saffron said. She'd taken so little part in the fight that at some point she'd actually found the time to get a stick of gum and start chewing.

'I saw,' I said. The futures were converging to a single track. 'Little! We've got sixty seconds. Get as many of these people out as you can, then have your men fall back. Nothing more you can do here.'

Little nodded. Some of the younger men in his profession, the ones who have something to prove, will ignore warnings like that. The ones that survive to Little's age don't. 'You heard the man. Move out!'

The security men fell back in good order, dragging thralls off the factory floor as I assembled in the centre of the floor with the other mages. 'I assume that lethal force is back on the table,' Ilmarin said.

'Yeah, I think we've reached the gloves-off stage,' I said. Now that I got a better look, I could see that the thralls had been running a mass-production operation with those headpieces. One person had been filing rods, another wiring caps together, another treating them with some sort of liquid and so on. A dozen completed models were piled in a cardboard box, though I couldn't sense any magic. Probably they needed to be infused. I pointed up to the catwalks. 'He'll be coming from there.'

'Finally,' Chimaera muttered.

'Saffron, focus on shielding,' I said. 'Ilmarin and Chimaera will handle offence.' Saffron gave a nod, still chewing.

Footsteps sounded from above and a figure appeared on one of the catwalks, his shoes ringing on the rusted metal. He was no more than a boy really, twenty or twenty-one years old. His clothes looked to have been good quality once, but now they were dirtied and rumpled as though they'd been slept in. Resting around his brow was a thin silver crown set with black stones. 'So,' he announced from above us. 'At last you've come to face me.'

'Sorry about the wait,' I said. 'It's been a busy month.'

'You take me for a fool?' the boy said. 'You think I didn't know about your spies? I bent them to my will and now they serve me!'

I sighed. 'We didn't send any spies, David.'

'Don't call me that!' David snapped. 'That person is gone. Now I am—'

'Your name's David Winslow, from Hackney,' I said,

interrupting him. 'You developed adept abilities in secondary school, and while you were at the London Met you fell in with a couple of adept groups. Somehow or other, you got in touch with Morden's people, and you were able to get your hands on that crown you're wearing now. At which point you stopped being David Winslow, and became its latest thrall.'

'I'm no thrall. But you're about to be.' David swept his arm across, gesturing to the room. 'I'll have you rebuild everything you've destroyed. Then you'll become the first of my new servants.'

'Do you ever wonder why you're doing that?' I said. 'Why your entire life suddenly revolves around acquiring "servants"?' I pointed to the crown on David's head. 'That thing is called the Splinter Crown and the Council have records on it going back hundreds of years. Every single time it's allowed to possess a new bearer, the first thing it does is make him find a base of operations, then it starts capturing thralls. The thralls are used as slave labour to capture more thralls. Sometimes it takes a few weeks, sometimes a few months, but sooner or later the bearer ends up holed up in some fortress, trying to raise an army.' I glanced from left to right. 'Well, maybe not a fortress, but I guess this was the best you could find. Seriously, stop and think for a second. Before all this, you were a third-year studying English literature. You were living in a shared house and you had a girlfriend. Now you're a slavemaster living in an ugly, decaying factory. Did you ever think about how that happened?'

I saw doubt flicker in David's eyes for a moment, then his expression firmed. 'You Council mages just want to control us. You can't stand the thought of anyone else with power.'

'How long are you going to keep wasting time with this guy?' Saffron said.

'I'm afraid I have to agree,' Ilmarin said. 'The item's bonded at this point.'

'Don't ignore me!' David shouted, and lifted a hand.

I felt a surge of power, something rolling down towards us, trying to crush and squeeze . . . and failing. Saffron stared up at the catwalk, chewing away on her gum. I could vaguely sense the domination effect, but it wasn't reaching us.

'Like I said,' I told David. 'We have records.'

David concentrated, and I saw sweat beading on his forehead. I felt the spell brush against my mind, and shrugged it off. The Splinter Crown was powerful, but I've had a good deal of practice at resisting mental attacks, and I was pretty sure I could handle this thing even if it were free to attack me at full strength. With Saffron shielding us, it had no chance at all.

'Can we just kill him?' Chimaera demanded.

'Kill me?' David shouted. 'You think you can kill me?'

From all around us, objects rose into the air. Sticks, knives and pieces of jagged metal floated up from where they'd been lying scattered on the floor, then darted towards us.

A bubble-shaped shield of air came up. The pieces of debris slammed into it and bounced away. 'Okay,' I said. '*That* wasn't in the records.'

'David Winslow was originally an air adept, if you recall,' Ilmarin said.

'Oh right,' I said. 'This thing has some amplification abilities too, doesn't it?' The projectiles picked themselves up off the floor and hurled themselves at us again, with a similar effect. 'Nice shield, by the way.'

'Yes, although as I understand it, that may simply be

an alternate use of mind magic. There's always been a theory that proper use of mental spells can take an existing talent and—'

'Screw this,' Chimaera announced, and lifted a hand. Flame roared upwards.

David disappeared in fire, but as the spell ended, he reappeared, unharmed. With my magesight I could see a tightly woven shield of air around him; it wasn't as strong as Ilmarin's, but it had been enough. 'I won't be defeated!' David shouted. 'Not again!'

'Can we hurry this up?' Saffron asked.

Chimaera sent another blast of fire up at David with the same result as the first. Another volley of projectiles bounced off our shield in turn. Air magic tends to be a lot better at defending and evading than it is at attacking; fights between air mages can take a long time. 'That shield looks like it'd soak up kinetic strikes as well,' I noted to Ilmarin.

'It does, doesn't it?' Ilmarin agreed.

'You've crossed my path for the last time!' David shouted. 'I'll take all of you! You hear me? I'll—'

Ilmarin wove a spell, sending a hammer blow of hardened air curving around David to strike his shield from behind. David flew forward off the catwalk, slammed into one of the jagged pieces of machinery, and hit the concrete floor with a *thud*. The crown bounced free, rolling across the floor to spin and rattle to a stop. All of a sudden, everything was quiet.

'You couldn't have done that earlier?' Saffron asked.

I walked forward and bent down next to David. His eyes were open and staring, and he wasn't breathing. I didn't think he'd hit hard enough to break his neck; more likely it had been the shock of the crown's connection being severed. I felt a little regret, but not much. Maybe David hadn't had much choice about his actions by the end, but those thralls he'd been commanding had had no choice at all. 'Little,' I said into my communicator. 'Civilians giving you any trouble?'

'Not since thirty seconds ago,' Little's voice said into my ear. 'The conscious ones were fighting like crazy, then all of a sudden they all spaced out. Now they're just staring.'

'Get them into the van,' I said. 'Then call the healer corps and tell them they've got some patients incoming.'

'Roger that.'

I broke the connection and looked at Saffron. 'Thralls have stopped fighting. Are they going to recover?'

'Probably,' Saffron said. She nudged the crown with her foot. 'We taking this?'

Ilmarin stepped up next to her, taking out and opening a small metal box that radiated time magic. A flow of air lifted the crown up off the floor to float down into the box, where it fitted snugly. Ilmarin closed the lid, I felt the spell around the box change, and all of a sudden the atmosphere in the room seemed to lighten somehow, as if something oppressive had been lifted. 'And that's that,' Ilmarin said.

I nodded. 'Search the place, then we're going home.'

With the crown and its bearer gone, the factory felt empty, a fortress without an owner. We found crude sleeping quarters, as well as a room that had presumably been David's. Unlike the dormitory for the thralls, it had an actual bed, but it still wasn't the kind of place any normal person would live in by choice. Apparently by the time he moved here, David had been sufficiently under the crown's control that it had no longer felt the need to waste time providing him with creature comforts.

'What are we looking for?' Chimaera said from behind me.

'Any other items he might have collected, and any other thralls who weren't caught up in the fighting,' I said without turning around. *And to give me a few minutes alone with you.* I didn't think Chimaera had noticed that I'd arranged things so that the two of us would be up here, out of earshot of Saffron and Ilmarin. He really was young.

'There's nothing here,' Chimaera muttered. He looked around at the rotten desk, the dirty bedsheets. 'Who'd *live* in a place like this?'

'Barrayar should have covered that at the briefing.'

I felt Chimaera shoot a glance at me, suddenly wary. 'What?'

'The crown's goals are to accumulate power and thralls. Comfort of its bearer is not a priority. Like I said, this was in the briefing materials.'

'Captain Rain gave us the briefing.'

'Oh?' I said inquiringly. 'I thought Mage Barrayar had been the one to recommend you for this assignment.'

I felt rather than saw Chimaera hesitate for an instant, the futures shifting as he decided what to say. 'No.'

'My mistake.' I nodded at the desk. 'You see the map there?'

'What map?'

I pointed. On the wall above the desk, several pieces of paper had been tacked to the plaster. 'The street map.'

'So?'

'You're not even looking at it.'

'Okay, I see it. So what?'

'You see the black circle marking the factory?'

Chimaera turned his head to look at the map, obviously annoyed. 'Yeah, I—'

The knife flashed past Chimaera's face to stick into the wall with a *tchunk*. Chimaera jumped back with a yell, tripping and sprawling.

I lowered my hand, looking down at Chimaera. 'Exactly how stupid do you think I am?'

Chimaera scrambled to his feet, a shield of flame flashing up around him. '*Now* you bring up a shield?' I asked him dryly. 'You're not very good at this. And don't bother with the fire bolt.'

'Yeah?' Chimaera asked. He was in a combat stance, eyes narrowed and set. 'Let's see how good that armour is against a real spell.'

'Ilmarin is listening to this entire conversation right now,' I told Chimaera calmly. 'If you want to be sentenced to death, then go right ahead and take your shot.'

Chimaera hesitated, and the futures of violence splintered. Direct threats wouldn't have deterred him, but the prospect of being caught attacking a Council member did. 'That was just to get your attention,' I told him. 'If I'd wanted you dead, I would have put it through your eye.' Actually, I would have just shot him – knife-throwing's a terribly inefficient way to kill someone – but I didn't see any need to get hung up on details. 'Now let's talk about what really went on between you and Barrayar.'

'What do you mean?'

'You think I don't know about the bounty?' I said. 'Whoever gets rid of me can go to Levistus and name his reward. I suppose Barrayar dangled a few.' I studied Chimaera, tilting my head. 'He could have offered something political, a junior aide position, but that wouldn't really have been appropriate for someone so young. He probably talked about promotion, didn't he? Making sure you only spent a year or two as a journeyman Keeper, instead of five to ten.'

I saw Chimaera's eyes flicker. He *really* wasn't good at this, but then that's what you get when you send kids to do this kind of work. 'You wouldn't have got it, by the way,' I added. 'A discreet assassination is one thing, but getting caught red-handed? Levistus isn't going to associate himself with something as clumsy as that. Of course, they wouldn't have let you be sentenced to death either – too much chance you'd turn on them. Some sort of suspended sentence or probation, I think. Enough to make sure that the next time they came asking for a favour, you didn't have a choice.'

Chimaera hesitated, but there was no violence in the futures now. Still, it was worth making sure that the lesson had sunk in. 'Ever heard of an adept called Talis?' I asked him.

Chimaera frowned.

I nodded. 'No reason you should have. Death magic adept, a life-drinker. Illegal under the Concord, of course, but he and certain Council members had an understanding, you might say. They'd turn a blind eye to his activities, and in return, every now and again, someone inconvenient to the Council would be removed. A few months ago, he had a conversation with Barrayar too. I suspect it went much the way yours did.'

'What's that got to do with me?'

'With you? Nothing at all.' I paused. 'Talis showed up at that party of Levistus's two months ago. Or at least part of him did.'

Chimaera didn't understand, at least not at first. It took a few seconds for him to get it, then his eyes widened and he went stiff. 'Wait, that was—?'

'Talis was quite experienced in his line of work,' I said. I didn't take my eyes off Chimaera. 'So the next time you're thinking about shooting me in the back, like you were on that rooftop, just remember what happened to the last person who tried.'

'I didn't do anything.'

I leaned in slightly and saw Chimaera flinch back. 'That,' I said softly and clearly, 'is why you're still alive.'

'Did the conversation go well?' Ilmarin asked.

I gave Ilmarin a glance. We were out in the street in front of the factory, with the security men loading up the thralls into the vans. Most of them looked dazed; a couple were crying. They hadn't removed the headpieces yet – that would be done under controlled conditions. 'Which one?'

Ilmarin nodded towards Chimaera. The younger Keeper wasn't looking at us. Actually, he'd been careful not to look anywhere in my direction since we'd met up with the others. 'With your young friend.'

'So you *were* listening.'

'It seemed prudent,' Ilmarin said. 'I hope you weren't actually intending to kill him.'

'No, but it won't do him any harm to believe otherwise.' I gave Ilmarin a sidelong look. 'What about you?'

'What about me?'

'Levistus's offer is an open one, as far as I'm aware,' I said. 'You haven't been tempted?'

'To commit murder in exchange for the favours of our esteemed Councilman?' Ilmarin said dryly. 'No, I have not been tempted. Somehow I doubt the reward would be worth the price. Besides, not all of us look favourably on the Council's attempts to use the Keepers as a way to remove their political opponents.' Ilmarin looked at me, tilting his head. 'Since we seem to be sharing confidences, were you telling the truth about that adept?'

'You mean Talis?'

'I was thinking more of what happened afterwards.' Ilmarin leaned against the van, eyes resting on me. 'Specifically, the incident at Levistus's party.'

'Oh, that party.'

'Levistus had invited over some visitors over from Washington. I understand he'd been hoping to make a good impression. I still don't know how that package came to be delivered to him right in the middle of appetisers. You'd have thought he'd know better than to open it, but I suppose they'd only scanned it for weapons, instead of for . . . other things.'

'I do remember hearing something, now that you mention it,' I said. 'Hope it didn't spoil their appetites.'

'I rather suspect that it did.' Ilmarin paused. 'So?'

'So?' I asked. 'Oh yes, Talis. Well, I didn't kill him, if that's what you're asking. And if I did, I certainly wouldn't have his severed head delivered to Levistus in the middle of their drinks and canapés. That would be wrong. Not to mention quite time-consuming to arrange.'

'I see,' Ilmarin said. He stood looking at me for a second. 'You know, you've changed somewhat from when we first met.'

'I suppose I have,' I said. From one of the other vans I saw Little signalling me. 'Excuse me a moment.'

'Trouble,' Little said quietly as I approached.

'The thralls?' I asked. The last of them were being loaded into the vans. 'Did we miss some?'

Little shook his head. 'Nothing to do with that. I just

got a call from the dispatcher. He had a call from head office. Was supposed to be a routine check-up, but the guy seemed really interested in whether you'd gone out. When he found you had, he hung up.'

I frowned. It's never a good sign when people take a sudden interest in your movements. It might be to check up on Chimaera, but I couldn't see how that made sense. As far as Barrayar was concerned, Chimaera would either kill me or he wouldn't. No reason to care about where I was.

But what if that had been the backup plan? If the goal had just been to keep me busy, then it didn't matter whether Chimaera succeeded or failed . . .

A nasty suspicion jumped fully formed into my mind. 'I have to go,' I told Little. 'Can you wrap this up?'

Little nodded. 'We'll handle it from here.'

Two minutes' work confirmed my suspicions. I made a quick side trip to pick up an item, then gated to the War Rooms.

The War Rooms are the seat of the Light Council, and the primary political power centre of British magical society. They're made up of a vast network of tunnels and caverns hidden away beneath central London, and they house not only the Light Council itself, but also the vast bureaucracy that carries out the Council's decisions. Up until a few years ago I'd never seen the War Rooms, and would have been turned away at the front door. Now I'm there more days than not.

I nodded to the guards on duty as I went in. I didn't quite run – I had enough time, and sprinting would send the wrong message – but I didn't hang around either. Even so, I couldn't help but pick up the mood as I walked through the tunnels. Once upon a time, the mages and adepts and functionaries I passed in the polished stone corridors would have stared as I went by; today, I barely got a second glance. Part of it was familiarity, but mostly it was that right now, the Council had bigger problems to worry about.

In October of last year, Morden had sent me and a team of Dark mages to raid the Vault, the Council's highest-security storage facility. The Council had been displeased, to put it mildly, which was the reason that I was currently occupying Morden's place on the Junior Council while Morden himself was sitting in a cell on a charge of high treason. But despite the personal consequences for Morden, the raid had been a success, and by the time the Council response team retook the facility, the Dark mages were gone, along with the Vault's entire stockpile of imbued items.

Magic items can be divided into three categories – one-shots, focuses and imbued items. Most people rank them by power – one-shots at the bottom, focuses in the middle and imbued items at the top – but while that's true, it misses the point. Imbued items aren't just objects, they're living things, and they have as much in common with a one-shot or a focus as you do with your mobile phone. From experience I've learned that it's very hard to make newcomers to the magical world understand just how dangerous imbued items are. They can grasp that imbued items are powerful, but they think that they're powerful in the way that a gun or computer is powerful – a tool that just needs you to push the right buttons. The truth is that wielding an imbued item is more like riding a large and not entirely domesticated animal. It might decide to do as it's told, and then again it might not, and if it comes down on the side of 'not', there's a good chance it'll decide that it should be the one calling the shots. Fast-forward a few months and you're living out of a warehouse in Deptford, kidnapping people off the street to turn into mind-controlled slaves, and believing the whole thing's your idea.

It would have been bad enough if the imbued items released into the wild had been a random collection, but they hadn't been. Despite their drawbacks, imbued items pack a hell of a punch, and while the Council might be bureaucratic, they're not in the habit of letting resources go to waste. If the best use they could come up with for an imbued item was to leave it gathering dust in the Vault . . . well, that should tell you something. According to the Council, Morden's team had taken away 127 imbued items from the Vault, and I suspected the real number might be slightly higher. That had been eight months ago. Since then, we'd recovered thirty-eight. The Splinter Crown would make it thirty-nine.

Having over a hundred of the most dangerous imbued items in the country go missing at once had caused complete chaos. Not all of them had resurfaced – in fact, most of them hadn't, probably because the Dark mages were keeping safe hold of them – but all too many had, and the ones that *had* resurfaced had tended to be the most destructive, controlling and just plain evil out of the whole set. It was coming to the point that I was starting to think that Richard or Morden had *deliberately* let the most dangerous items fall into the hands of the kinds of people who would misuse them. The Splinter Crown hadn't been the worst of them by a long shot, and since the start of the year the casualty rates for normals injured or killed from magical causes had tripled. For now, the police were managing to cover up the worst of it (mostly by calling injuries 'accidents' and deaths 'missing persons'), but I knew the Directors were afraid that if this went on for much longer, it was going to start leaking into the public eye. It wasn't just normals who were being hurt either – the casualty rate for Council security had gone through the roof, and they'd had to take in as many new recruits in the last six months as they usually did in three years. And that wasn't counting the activities of those Dark mages who *did* know what they were doing with their new items, nor the ongoing problems with the adept community.

All in all, the Council had been in more or less permanent crisis mode since autumn, with no sign of things calming down any time soon. Which was why, instead of eyeing me, the adepts and mages I passed in the corridors were caught up in their own worries. A few years ago, I might have appreciated it, but I'd learned enough since then to realise that at least in this case, the Council's problems were also everyone else's problems, and if not they were going to get that way.

Of course, none of that was stopping certain members on the Council from doing their best to get rid of me. I guess some things don't change.

I passed through the Belfry and into one of the anterooms leading to the Star Chamber. A little over half a dozen mages were scattered around the room, talking in booths, and unlike the mages I'd passed on the way in, they *did* turn to stare. These were the aides of the Council members meeting in the room beyond, and if I hadn't known already, their reactions would have been a big hint that I wasn't expected. You can make a good guess at the number of Council members in a meeting by the number of aides outside: in this case there were eight, suggesting that most of the Junior and Senior Councilmen were present, but not all.

The corridor behind was dominated by the two huge eight-foot, six-limbed golems flanking the door at the end. These were gythka, the personal guards of the Light Council, and their gold eyes watched me expressionlessly as I approached. There was a man between them, the sergeant-at-arms, and he didn't look happy to see me. 'Evening, James,' I said. 'I see you got the late shift.'

James looked uncomfortable. 'Uh, yes. Councillor Verus, I don't think—'

'That I'm welcome here? Let me guess, a certain someone hinted that they'd rather not be disturbed by any guests, me in particular.'

'That's not . . . I mean, could you . . . ?'

'No, I'm afraid I can't.' I came to a stop in front of James. 'This is a meeting of the Junior and Senior Councils, yes? Not Senior only?'

'Yes . . .'

'Then as a member of the Junior Council, I request and require entry.' I nodded at the mantis golems. 'You're noticing they're not moving to block me? Pretty sure you know what that means.'

James looked as if he'd rather be anywhere else, and I knew why. Whichever side he took, he knew he was about to get in the middle of a quarrel between Council mages. 'This isn't your call,' I told him. 'Now do the job that you're legally required to do, and open that door.'

James unlocked the wooden door and stepped out of my way. He didn't announce me, and I couldn't really blame him. I walked in, hearing the door swing shut behind me.

If the War Rooms are the centre of power of the Light Council, the Star Chamber is its heart. It's named after an old court of law from English history famous for its vast powers and lack of accountability. Maybe the Light mages who named it didn't know the associations of the name . . . on the other hand, maybe they did. From this room, generations of Light mages had sat and ruled, issuing the resolutions that spread to touch the lives of every mage in the British Isles and beyond. I'd never thought I'd be one of them.

For such an important room, the Star Chamber looks weirdly ordinary. Windows along one wall look out onto an illusory landscape of fields and sky, and a fresco of constellations is set into the ceiling. The room is dominated by a long mahogany table surrounded by comfortable chairs. Right now, eleven of those chairs were occupied: one by the secretary, four by members of the Junior Council and the remaining six by members of the Senior Council, the voting members of the Light Council and the most powerful mages in Britain.

'What's he doing here?' Sal Sarque snapped. He was dark-skinned and dark-eyed, and his grizzled white hair was cut short enough to reveal an old scar running the length of his scalp. His normal expression was a scowl, and he was wearing one now, his eyebrows lowered as he stared at me.

'Apologies for being late,' I said pleasantly as I crossed the room. 'It seems that, by some oversight, I wasn't informed of the meeting.' I pulled out a chair and sat next to one of the other Junior Council members, sensing her shift away slightly as I did. 'Don't let me interrupt.'

'You weren't informed because you weren't invited,' Sal Sarque said, biting off his words.

I sat back, meeting Sal Sarque's gaze. 'Seems to me what you were discussing is rather relevant to my interests.'

Sal Sarque and I had rubbed each other the wrong way pretty much on sight. He's the leader of the Crusaders, the most militant faction within the Council. They hate Dark mages in general and Morden in particular, so given that I was taught by a Dark mage and appointed by Morden, we were never going to get along. Events last autumn had only made things worse.

'I would tend to agree,' a second man said. With silver hair and a lined face, Bahamus is only missing a beard to look exactly like the popular image of a wizard. He has a measured way of speaking, and I've never seen him lose his temper. He's the closest thing I've got to an ally on the Senior Council, though I'm careful not to push it. 'Councillor Verus is clearly an interested party. I would be interested to learn the reasons for this . . . oversight as regards his notification.'

A couple of mages shot glances at the man sitting at the end of the table, but it was Sal Sarque who answered. 'I don't care who didn't inform him. He shouldn't be here.'

'I'm afraid I have to side with Sarque,' the woman sitting opposite from him said. Her name was Alma, and after Levistus, she's probably the member of the Council I'm most wary of. She has brown and grey hair that falls a little past her shoulders, and regular features that might be handsome but for a certain hardness to her eyes. 'Verus's suitability to sit upon the Council is precisely the issue in question. Until it is settled, I think it would be appropriate for him to remain outside.'

There was a snort of laughter from the man to Alma's right. He was big in every dimension with a thick beard, heavily muscled but running to fat, and his name was Druss the Red. 'Issue in question?' he said. 'You mean he,' he nodded at the man at the end of the table, 'is still trying to get rid of Verus, and you, for God only knows what reason, do what he tells you.'

'Given the security considerations—'

'Bullshit.'

'Regardless,' Bahamus said, 'Councillor Verus is still a member of this Council, and as such, has the right to be present. Unless anyone has an alternative interpretation of the law?'

There was silence. Futures flickered in which several Council members spoke up, but as I watched they faded. 'Fine,' Sal Sarque growled. 'Let's get on with it.' He nodded at Alma.

'As I was saying,' Alma said, turning to the rest of the Senior Council, 'I think, with hindsight, it is safe to say that elevating Morden to the Council was a mistake. It is now time to correct that mistake. Despite our usual reluctance to overturn an existing resolution, I believe that the decision to allocate a Junior Council seat to a Dark mage has proved unwise.'

'Morden has not yet been found guilty,' Bahamus said.

'Oh, come on,' Sal Sarque said angrily. 'Are you having a fucking joke?'

'You know perfectly well that I am no friend of Morden,' Bahamus said levelly. 'However, at present, he has been *accused* of a crime, rather than convicted. Until that changes, we cannot and should not reassign his office.'

'We've all seen the evidence against Morden,' Alma told Bahamus. 'His conviction is a formality.'

'Perhaps so,' Bahamus said. 'However, justice must not only be done, but be seen to be done. Taking this step before his conviction will clearly signal that we have no intention of abiding by the decision of the court.' Bahamus cocked his head. 'Besides. If the evidence is so overwhelming – which I do not dispute – then why the hurry? Morden has already been suspended from office.'

'Hmph,' Druss said. 'Not much of a mystery there. It's so that *he*,' he nodded at the end of the table, 'can get rid of *him*.' He nodded at me. 'This isn't about Morden.'

'So?' Sarque demanded. 'I call it cleaning up your mistakes. I told you Morden was a bad idea and you didn't listen. Now you want to keep his apprentice around to carry on where he left off?'

'Are you even paying attention to what's happening right now?' Druss demanded. 'We've got a hundred imbued items tearing this country apart, and you want to be doing a purge?'

'He's the *reason* we've got those items tearing the country apart!' Sarque snapped, pointing at me. 'He helped steal them!'

'Councillor Verus's presence at the Vault was authorised by us,' Bahamus said calmly. 'As you should remember, since you were there. You should *also* remember that Councillor Verus gave us multiple warnings that our defence of the War Rooms was a mispositioning of forces. Given that your reconnaissance team singularly failed to prevent the theft – a team that you took personal responsibility for – I don't think you are in a position to cast blame.'

Sal Sarque glared at me from across the table, and I met his gaze calmly. That 'reconnaissance team' had been led by a mage called Jarnaff, Sal Sarque's personal aide. Officially, they'd been there to secure the Vault from hostile attack and recover any stolen items. Unofficially, once we ran into each other, Jarnaff had decided to score some bonus points with his boss by getting rid of me, and he would have done exactly that if the same thing hadn't happened to him first.

The ironic thing was that I was being blamed for something I hadn't done. I hadn't killed Jarnaff. But it wasn't as though Sarque would believe me if I told him, and given the things I *had* done, coming clean wasn't exactly an option. The problem from Sal Sarque's point of view was that while he could expose me, he couldn't do so without revealing the fact that his 'reconnaissance team' had broken the law first, and he had more to lose than I did. So he just sat there and stared at me in silent rage.

'It seems to me,' Bahamus said, 'that we are discussing the issue without hearing from the one most directly affected by it.'

'Because it isn't his decision,' Alma said.

'Nevertheless, I feel that his input could be useful,' Bahamus said. 'Councillor Verus?'

All of the other faces in the room turned to me. I paused for a moment, looking back at them. Some looked hostile; most neutral. None were friendly. I knew that trying to argue was pointless. Debates in the Council rarely change the votes: those are bought and sold before the meeting takes place, and generally speaking, no one brings a proposal unless they know they can pass it. But it was a chance to make the rest of the Council listen, and that doesn't happen often. Besides, I still had one card to play. I just needed to lay some groundwork.

'Let me ask a question to all the members of the Council,' I said. 'Ever since the attack on the Vault, we've been tracking down imbued items and sending out teams to retrieve them. How many of those missions have you each led?'

'I don't see how that's relevant,' Alma said coldly.

'It's a simple question.'

'It doesn't matter who's leading the missions,' Sal Sarque said, a little too quickly. 'What matters—'

Druss laughed. 'He's got you there, Sarque.'

'As far as I know, the number is three,' I said. 'All of

which were led by Druss.' I looked at Sal Sarque. 'Though maybe you know better? I know that going after Dark mages is something of a special interest of yours.'

Sal Sarque flushed. 'I'm a Council member,' he snapped. 'Not some . . . adventurer.'

'I have to agree,' Alma said, cutting in. 'Verus, while your enthusiasm may be commendable, we on the Council are directors, not soldiers. Perhaps your lack of experience is showing. Our role is to give orders; that of the Keepers is to carry those orders out.'

'I think you misunderstand,' I said. 'I wasn't casting aspersions on your courage.' I didn't look at Sal Sarque, but I paused for just a second before going on. 'Instead, I would like to make the point that since the start of the year, I've led ten item retrieval missions. Nine were successful. That means that, counting tonight, I've been responsible for slightly over twenty-five per cent of the imbued items recovered.'

'You do not need to sit on the Council to go hunting around for lost items,' Alma said. 'Perhaps a position in the Keepers would suit your temperament better.'

'I'd argue that you don't really understand a situation until you've seen it on ground level,' I said. 'But again, that's not my point. My point is that out of all of the members of the Council to attempt to remove, you've selected the one who's doing the most to resolve this crisis. Now, as you say, I may be inexperienced, but to me this rather suggests that resolving the current crisis is not, in fact, your highest priority.'

'The proposal concerns Morden, not you,' Alma said smoothly. 'We don't mean to make any judgements about how qualified you may be for the position.'

Bitch, I thought. She was lying through her teeth, but I couldn't call her on it. 'For months, we've been hearing a constant stream of reports about how bad it is out there,' I said, looking around at the rest of the Council. 'Missing persons are at an all-time high, casualty rates with the Keepers and security personnel are enormous, and the Order of the Cloak are strained to breaking point trying to keep it hidden. At the risk of sounding naïve, this strikes me as the absolute *worst* time to get rid of the Council member most involved with the recovery efforts. Particularly for something that's going to happen anyway. To the best of my knowledge, none of you have the slightest doubt that Morden will be convicted. Why the rush?'

The table was silent, and looking around, I knew I hadn't changed anyone's mind. Morden once told me that Council meetings mostly consisted of sitting around listening to reports, and that all of the real decisions took place outside. Since taking his seat, I'd learned he was right.

But then, that was why I'd come prepared. I reached into my pocket and took something out.

'Enough wasting time,' Sal Sarque said. 'Let's vote on this.'

Alma nodded. 'I vote for the proposal.'

'So do I,' Sal Sarque said. 'Should have done this months ago.'

'What, get rid of anyone Levistus has a grudge against?' Druss said. 'I say no.'

'I agree, but for different reasons,' Bahamus said. 'Once again, this sends all the wrong messages. It will damage our political credibility, not to mention the war effort. I also vote no.'

There was a pause. The secretary had been tallying the

votes, and the scratch of his pen now stopped as he glanced towards the head of the table. One by one, everyone else did the same.

Vaal Levistus is one of the newer members of the Senior Council, but possibly also the most influential. He's a man in his fifties with European looks, thin white hair, a patrician cast of face and pale, almost colourless greyish eyes that fade into the background. Like Bahamus, he rarely shows expression and never raises his voice, but the two men give off very different impressions. There's a coldness about Levistus, something dispassionate that comes through in his manner and bearing.

From the moment I'd walked in, Levistus had watched the debate without saying a word. Quite possibly he hadn't been speaking before I came in either, and I knew why. Levistus might not have been the one to put forward this proposal, but it was his creation, and he didn't want to be associated with it any more than he had to. So he'd sat back, letting Alma and Sarque do the work for him. He'd already counted his votes and knew how this was going to play out. Or at least he thought he did.

'Councillor Bahamus makes valid points,' Levistus said. Levistus has a measured, almost atonal manner of speaking, smooth and precise. 'In ideal circumstances, we would prefer not to take actions that could be seen as pre-empting the trial's verdict. However, these are less than ideal times, and I believe that given the current crisis, security should be uppermost in our minds. We must remove not only Morden, but his appointees. Thus, while acknowledging Verus's service, I must agree with Alma. I also vote yes.'

Three to two, I thought. Everyone turned to look at the last Senior Council member sitting at the table.

Like Levistus, Undaaris had stayed quiet throughout the meeting, but for very different reasons. While Levistus is an empire-builder, climbing his way to power, Undaaris is a waverer who follows whatever current seems safest. I've wondered sometimes how the guy even got on the Senior Council. My best guess is that he was a compromise choice from long ago that the other Council members all agreed was no threat.

Undaaris shifted, visibly uncomfortable under everyone's gaze. 'Yes.' He cleared his throat. 'Well.'

Seconds ticked by. 'Well, what?' Druss demanded.

'Ah,' Undaaris said. 'It does seem a little . . .'

Levistus made a very small movement, so tiny that I'd never have seen it if I hadn't been watching. I knew that Levistus wouldn't have called this meeting if he hadn't bought Undaaris's vote already. How he'd done it I didn't know — promises or gifts or threats — and honestly, I didn't much care. I raised my hand above the table and into plain view.

'But I think we do need to . . .' My movement caught Undaaris's eye and he stared, his eyes fixed on what I held between thumb and finger.

'Need to what?' Druss said in annoyance. He glanced at me, saw nothing of interest and turned back to Undaaris. 'Get on with it.'

'What . . .?' Undaaris swallowed. 'What's that?'

I was looking into the distance over Undaaris's shoulder, pretending not to hear. After a moment I feigned surprise. 'What?' I said. I held up the item. It was a small green marble, about an inch in diameter. 'This? Just a storage focus.'

'Is there a reason you see it as an appropriate item to bring here?' Alma asked, her voice cool.

'Well, I did learn about this meeting at short notice,' I said. 'It caught me in the middle of something. Still, it might be useful. If the proposal goes through and I'm removed from the Council, I'll need to disseminate some information. Pass it on to my successor, that sort of thing.'

'Fascinating,' Alma said, in a tone of voice clearly indicating it was nothing of the kind. She turned to Undaaris. 'Councillor, your vote?'

Undaaris hadn't taken his eyes off the marble. 'Ah . . .' He took a breath, then tore his eyes away, staring down at the table. 'No.'

'I'm sorry?'

'I vote no.'

There was a pause. Sal Sarque stared at Undaaris, then shot a look at Levistus. 'Perhaps you need time to consider,' Levistus said, his voice cool. 'If you require—'

'I don't need any more time to consider,' Undaaris snapped. He didn't look up at Levistus. 'All right?'

'Something wrong with your ears?' Druss asked Levistus.

Levistus stared at Undaaris, not looking at Druss. Undaaris didn't lift his eyes off the table. 'Well then,' Bahamus said when no one spoke. 'Unless we hear from Spire, the resolution is rejected. Does anyone have any further comments?' He glanced around the table. 'In that case, the next order of business is the ongoing situation with the adepts. Our reports still indicate that there should be room for a negotiated settlement, but it's proving difficult to bring them to the table . . .'

The meeting was over, and the Council members were filing out into the anteroom. 'Ah, Verus,' Bahamus said, walking up to me. 'Can I have a word?'

'Of course,' I said. The two of us were standing off to the side by one of the booths, close enough to benefit from its privacy wards. Some of the other mages shot covert glances at us. 'Thank you for your support, by the way.'

Bahamus nodded. 'I must apologise for not giving you an earlier heads-up. We were notified as to the meeting, but for some reason Levistus felt it appropriate to leave his proposal off the agenda. I wasn't aware you hadn't been informed until the doors were closed.'

'Yes, that sounds like his usual way of doing things.'

'Perhaps, but it's still inappropriate,' Bahamus said. 'I'll have a word with Alma and Sarque and try to discourage them from supporting anything similar in future.' He paused. 'How exactly did you convince Undaaris to change his mind?'

Undaaris was just entering the room. He walked straight to where his aide was sitting, a mage named Lyle. The two of them spoke briefly: Lyle looked at me, then they headed for the door. 'I reminded him of a prior discussion,' I said, watching Undaaris go. 'Must have changed his mind.'

'Apparently it did,' Bahamus said, eyeing me. 'Do you think it'll stick?'

'That's always the question with Undaaris, isn't it?' I said. Levistus appeared in the doorway to the corridor. 'Oh, excuse me a moment. Thanks again.'

Levistus saw me coming and paused, waiting for me to approach. 'Councillor,' I said to him with a nod.

Levistus watched me without expression. 'Is there something you need?'

'Actually, I was hoping you could pass on a message to your aide Barrayar.' I kept my tone friendly, but the expression in my eyes was another matter. 'Tell him the next time he has an issue with me, come settle it himself instead of sending a boy to do a man's job.'

'I'm afraid I have no idea what you mean.' Levistus glanced down at my pocket. 'That data focus you were playing with looks similar to the one that was recovered in the White Rose case.'

'Does it?'

'The penalties for appropriating such a piece of evidence would be severe.'

'These focuses all look so similar.'

'Apparently they do.' Levistus stepped around me. 'Goodbye, Verus.'

'Goodbye, Councillor,' I said to Levistus's retreating back. He didn't turn to look at me, and as he disappeared through the doorway I gave an inward sigh. *And that's another day.*

3

'So how did that even work?' Variam asked.

We were sitting in the Hollow, a shadow realm linked to the Chilterns. It's a small forested island, floating in a multicoloured sky, and right now, it's our home. The stars were out, pinpoints of brilliant light shining down from above, and we were gathered around our camp-site, a circle of chairs in a clearing with dim sphere lights glowing in the darkness. The scents of grass and summer leaves were all around, and there was the occasional rustle of some creature moving in the undergrowth.

'Remember that business with White Rose?' I said. 'When Vihaela joined up with Richard, she brought along a whole lot of blackmail material from the White Rose vault. My guess is that's how she was able to partner up with Richard and Morden as equals.'

'I remember now,' Luna said. She was dressed more formally than she once would have, in a nice blouse and a skirt; she'd come straight from work. 'That was how Morden got his seat on the Council.'

I nodded. 'And I did some sniffing around and heard some rumours that Undaaris might just be one of those mages with some awkward little secrets in the White Rose vault. So I had a chat with him over the winter and dropped some hints. His reaction pretty much confirmed it.'

'But we *don't* have any of that stuff,' Variam said. Like Luna, he was in his business clothes. He'd been in Keeper

HQ all day, and had been the last to hear the news. 'What, they think Morden just shares that kind of thing around?'

'That's exactly what they think,' I said. 'Remember, they think Anne and I signed up with Morden willingly. The way they see it, I was Morden's aide, so I was on his side. So it's really not a big step for them to assume I'd have access to his files.' I shrugged. 'As long as they're going to assume the worst of us, we might as well take advantage.'

'You can't open that data focus.'

'Undaaris doesn't know that. But I guess it had been long enough since our last chat that he was starting to wonder if maybe I didn't really have anything after all. So when Levistus came to him, he probably figured that this might be a way to get rid of the problem.'

'Jesus.' Variam sat back in his chair. 'It was all a bluff?'

'I raised; he folded,' I said. 'It's not as bad as you think. There's really no way for Undaaris to be sure that I *don't* have access. I mean, what's he going to do, ask Morden himself?'

'It still doesn't seem that great a position though,' Luna said. 'I mean, from what you say, Levistus has three votes on the Council pretty much locked up. All he needs is for one more person to change their mind.'

'There are rules against resubmissions.' I shrugged. 'But basically, yeah, I'm hanging by a thread. What else is new?'

'So what's the plan?' Variam asked.

The four of us had been meeting like this for a long time. Somehow or other, Variam, Luna, Anne and I had become a team, and at some point, without ever actually saying it out loud, we'd just started taking for granted that if there was a problem, we'd get together to deal with it. Two years ago, we would have been meeting in my

Camden flat; one year ago, it would have been Arachne's cave. But my flat had been burned down, and while Arachne's cave was the closest thing I had left to a family home, it was less and less safe for me to visit. The Hollow was the first place we'd had for a long time that *was* safe. Shadow realms are hard to break into, and we'd done a lot of work to make this one even more so. It didn't have the amenities of a house in the city, but it was worth the trade-off. It's hard to explain just how big a relief it is to be able to go to sleep without worrying that someone will break in and kill you before you wake up.

'Actually, I was hoping to get some ideas from you guys,' I said. 'I've got some long-term stuff going with Arachne, but as far as dealing with the Council goes, I'm holding my own, but not much more. I'm open to suggestions.'

The three of them looked at each other, but this time, neither Variam nor Luna spoke up. 'What about Spire?' Anne asked.

Unlike the other two, Anne had already been in the Hollow when I arrived. She spends the most time in it out of any of the four of us, and I sometimes think she seems more comfortable here than she does in London. She hadn't said much until now, but then she usually doesn't. 'The seventh member of the Council,' Anne said. 'You said he's supposed to represent independents.'

'He's also a recluse,' I said. 'Doesn't show up most of the time, and usually abstains when he does.'

'But if you could get him on your side, you'd have the numbers in your favour,' Luna said.

'Well, it's worth a try. Though I've got the feeling that everyone else on the Council must have already tried the same thing.'

'I've got a question,' Variam said. 'How come you didn't know about this meeting until so late?'

'Because they were keeping it from me.'

'Yeah,' Variam said. 'But to call the meeting, they had to call every other member of the Council. And then all of them would have called their aides. And the guards, and the clerks, and everyone else.'

'What are you getting at?'

'You don't think maybe you should have someone to help you with this stuff?'

I sighed. We'd had this discussion before. 'It's not as simple as that.'

'Actually, it kind of is,' Variam said. 'If you'd had an aide the way all the other Council members do, you might have heard a bit earlier.'

'Yeah, well, for some funny reason, it isn't too easy for me to find an aide these days.'

All Council members – or almost all – have personal aides, who schedule their appointments, run messages and quite often carry out the actual negotiations while Council is in session. Aide positions are a major stepping stone in a political career, and they're hotly sought after by mages who have ambitions to sit on the Council themselves someday.

No one was looking to become my aide. For one thing, being associated with the first Dark mage ever to sit upon the Light Council of Britain is not the kind of thing most Light mages want on their CV. For another, word had got out that this particular job wasn't good for one's health. Morden's first couple of aides had died under mysterious circumstances, if being found burned to death with twenty broken bones counts as 'mysterious'. Since I'd taken over,

I'd had three aides myself. The first two had abruptly resigned their positions after receiving visits from the Crusaders – visits that had, presumably, spelled out what the consequences would be if they stuck around. The third had lasted a month. He'd quit when one of his family members had been kidnapped. Neither he nor the family member had been hurt, but ever since then, no one seemed particularly keen to take the position, and I couldn't really blame them.

'Maybe you aren't looking in the right place,' Variam said.

'Vari . . .'

'Look, you know Luna and I would have offered,' Variam said. 'But it's a full-time job and we don't have the time. I've got Keeper duties, and Luna's running the shop. I mean, I guess she could work evenings or something, but . . .'

'It wouldn't work,' Luna said. 'I can take the odd day off, but not every day of the week. Anyway, I'm not sure I'd want to. You know how I feel about those guys. I might have passed my journeyman tests, but I'm not a real mage as far as they're concerned.'

'And those are all valid reasons, but that's not why I haven't asked,' I said. 'The way things are right now, becoming my aide is painting a target on your back. My last three aides didn't quit out of hurt feelings. If they'd stuck around, odds are they'd have ended up dead.'

'Sounds like you need someone tougher,' Variam said.

I rolled my eyes. 'Just come out and say it, Vari.'

Variam didn't say it. He just looked pointedly at Anne.

It wasn't the first time Variam had made the suggestion. He'd floated it around the time of aide number two, and voiced it more forcefully after the departure of number three. I hadn't been comfortable with it then, and I wasn't comfortable with it now for a host of complicated reasons. Anne *could* do the job, and do it well: she's quiet, but she sees more than she lets on and she's very good at reading people. Equally important, she's probably more dangerous than any of us in a one-on-one fight. And while she runs a clinic in her spare time, she doesn't have much else to do, which was probably one of the reasons Variam was pushing this. I knew that both Vari and Luna were worried about how much time Anne was spending in the Hollow.

But I'd rather have Anne in the Hollow than dead. 'I don't see her jumping up and down asking for the job,' I said.

'I wouldn't mind,' Anne said.

The rest of us looked at her. 'Are you sure?' Luna asked.

'Would it help prevent something like this happening again?' Anne asked me.

'Yes, but there's a reason I haven't asked.' Actually there were three, but the first I didn't want to say in front of Luna and Vari, and the second I didn't want to say in front of anyone. 'The Crusaders went after you once already. If you're in the War Rooms every day, they're going to get a lot of opportunities to reach you again, and sooner or later, they *are* going to try.'

'You're in the War Rooms every day too,' Anne said.

'That's different. I'm a Council member now.'

'Isn't that bounty on you still open?' Luna asked.

'Yes, but they haven't actually tried to drag me off the streets.'

'They bribed a guy to kill you less than three hours ago,' Variam said.

'It wasn't a serious assassination attempt.'

Variam, Anne and Luna all looked at me.

'What?' I asked.

'Okay,' Variam said. 'I want you to stop a minute and think about what you just said.'

'Let's put it another way,' Anne said. 'If you did have an aide, would that make you safer?'

I hesitated. I wanted to say no. 'Probably.'

'Then I'll do it.'

I opened my mouth to argue, but then saw the way Anne was looking at me and stopped. I knew I wasn't going to win this argument.

'Good,' Variam said. 'So what have you heard about Richard?'

'Oh right.' I put the other issues out of my head. 'That. As far as the rest of the Council knows, he's got his hands full. The Dark mages following him still aren't happy with the division of loot from the Vault, and it doesn't seem like that last round of doling-out settled them. Council intelligence claim they're refusing to help any further until he shares the wealth.'

'Thank God Dark mages suck so badly when it comes to working together,' Variam said. 'If they'd attacked while we were busy with the adepts . . .'

I nodded. Our biggest advantage in dealing with Richard and Morden had always been that they were usually too busy with other problems to focus on us. By last year, Richard had manoeuvred himself to the top of the heap of the Dark mages of Britain, enough so that he'd been able to lead a significant number of them in a coordinated attack on the Vault. But Dark mages are Dark mages, and with the raid done, his alliance had immediately started squabbling over the loot. There hadn't been an outright revolt yet, but it was probably only a matter of time. 'From what I've heard, the one currently throwing a spanner in the works is Onyx. With Morden in custody, he's claiming he should be taking Morden's place on the triumvirate, and he wants the same kind of authority Morden had.'

'Is *that* going to work?' Luna asked.

'Hell no,' I said. Onyx is Morden's Chosen, and he's just as powerful as his master, but nowhere near as smart. 'And I seriously doubt he'll get any other mages to follow him. But he controls Morden's mansion, so as long as he's refusing to cooperate, he can hold Richard up.'

'Good news for us,' Variam said. 'They can keep on fighting each other.'

'It might not be as good as you think,' Luna said. 'Something I've been noticing for a while . . . you know how we get plenty of adepts in the shop? Well, I've been talking to them, and I've been hearing something about an association.'

'An association?'

'As in, mutual defence,' Luna said. 'You join up, and we'll protect you, that sort of thing. Except the last guy to come in was really definite that it had nothing to do with the Council. I pressed him, and he insisted. No Light mages involved, he said. I think he was hoping I'd join.'

'I'm pretty sure the Council isn't running anything like that,' I said with a frown.

'Which was what I thought,' Luna said. 'So if the Council isn't running it, and there are no Light mages involved, who does that leave?'

'You think it's Richard,' Anne said.

'It makes sense, doesn't it?' Luna said. 'One of the big

things adepts are scared of is mages preying on them. If Richard promises them they'll be safe from that . . .'

'Then that would be a pretty good motivator to join his team,' I said. 'So what do they have to do to join this "association"?'

'Nothing, according to him,' Luna said. 'But once you've got a bunch of people organised like that, it's not so hard to point them at a target, is it?'

Variam was frowning as well, and I didn't blame him. I didn't like the sound of this. 'The next time this person tries to talk you into joining, you think you can find out more?'

Luna nodded. 'I'll give it a try.'

We spoke for a while longer, then as the hour drew late, first Variam and then Luna said their goodbyes and gated back to Earth. Tomorrow was a work day, and they both had an early start. At last only Anne and I were left, sitting under the stars.

'I checked on Karyos,' Anne said. 'I was worried she was growing too slowly, but I think it's because she's in sync with the tree. She seems in good health.'

'That's good,' I said absently. 'Are you sure about this aide thing?'

'I think I can do it,' Anne said. 'Unless there's something you weren't saying with the others around.'

'It's not that.'

Anne looked at me.

I sighed inwardly. It's hard to hide things from Anne. 'Okay, I guess it is that. I'm worried about the jinn. And about you.'

'This again?' Anne said. 'You guys tested me for weeks.

Honestly, for a while back there I was feeling like a lab rat. And every single one of those tests came up negative. I'm not possessed by something.'

'None of the tests were able to find anything,' I said. 'But not finding anything doesn't mean there's nothing there. *Something* drove off a whole Crusader strike team and ate the ones that didn't run fast enough, and then on top of that it apparently managed to do a perfect disappearing act as well.'

'But it's been eight months! If whatever-it-was did that perfect a disappearing act, don't you think that sounds as though it really *has* disappeared? I broke it out of its prison, it went on a rampage, then it escaped.'

'But I don't think they can escape,' I said. 'Arachne was very clear about that. The jinn trapped in those items were trapped for ever. Their old bodies are gone. The only way they can affect the world is by bonding to a human.'

'Well, it doesn't feel like it's bonded to me,' Anne said with a shrug. 'And I don't really want to just sit around for ever in the Hollow on the off-chance that something might happen if I don't.'

I sat thinking for a moment. 'Let me talk to Dr Shirland,' I said at last.

Anne looked at me questioningly. 'You don't need my permission.'

'I do if I want to ask her about anything that concerns you,' I said. 'Otherwise she'll just tell me it's confidential. I want you to give her a call and clear me for it.'

'So you can do what? Vet me again?'

'I just want to be on the safe side.'

Anne didn't look happy. 'All right,' she said at last. 'But

if she doesn't give you a hard reason to rule me out then you'll take me on as your aide. Promise?'

I hesitated, then nodded. 'Okay.'

I'd built a small cottage on the Hollow's east side. Okay, 'built' is an exaggeration – it was more like the magical equivalent of a prefab – but it was comfortable, and it was nice to be able to leave my stuff out without locking everything up behind layers of security. The temperature of the Hollow was comfortably warm as I undressed for bed.

I used to have trouble sleeping. I had insomnia as a child, and learning to use my magic made it worse. Divination tends to encourage a state of hyper-vigilance – you're always watching and looking ahead, whether for opportunities or for danger. The more practised you become with it, the easier it gets to keep doing it in the back of your mind, but that same habit also makes it really hard to relax. Back when I lived in Camden, it was common for me to take an hour or two to fall asleep every night.

But I don't have trouble sleeping now, and the reason for that was lying next to my futon. It looked like a shard of amethyst, glinting deep purple in the light, and it was called a dreamstone.

Dreamstones are rare and obscure items, and most mages have never even heard of them. They allow the user to manipulate Elsewhere, that strange half-real place somewhere between thoughts and dreams. Exactly how they allow you to manipulate it is another question, and one whose answer I was still working out. I thought about taking hold of the dreamstone, then decided against it. Working magic through it without physical contact was slightly harder, but I was trying to push myself. I lay down on the futon and closed my eyes, channelling a thread of magic through the stone, and immediately I felt my mind starting to slip away, leaving my body behind. My last thought was that I'd forgotten to switch off the light.

I was floating in a sea of blacks and greys, currents of darkness flowing around me. There was no up or down, and nothing to see, but I formed a shape in my mind, a sense of someone's presence, and felt a sense of direction. I didn't *move* exactly – there wasn't anything to move through – but I could feel a shift, my environment rearranging itself. A door took shape ahead of me, and I stepped through.

I came down into brilliant sunlight. I was standing amid white stone columns, berry bushes growing around smooth flagstones. Beyond and below, green trees formed a canopy running down a hillside, stopping at a beach beyond which was a bright blue ocean. Above me, white clouds floated in a clear sky. There was a fenced platform on an overlook just ahead, with a view down to the bay. On it was a table with two chairs, one of which was occupied. 'Hey, you,' I said as I walked over.

'Hello, Alex,' Arachne said with a smile. In the real world Arachne is a spider the size of a minivan, but here she took the form of a woman, middle-aged with dark eyes, lines creasing her olive skin and black hair braided in an elaborate style. Clear gems hung on her forehead and she wore a simple white gown. The first few times that I'd met Arachne here she'd been in her spider form, but lately, I'd found her wearing this shape instead. I hadn't asked why, but I had my suspicions – I've always had the feeling that Arachne might share more with the myth than just her name. In any case, her appearance was entirely up to her: this was a dreamshard, something less than Elsewhere but more than a dream, and everything here was shaped by Arachne's mind.

'I was expecting you earlier,' Arachne said. 'Busy day?'

'You could say that,' I said, and told her the details.

Arachne listened to the story. Birds flew overhead, their cries carried on the wind. 'I imagine you didn't try to use the crown?' she asked once I was finished.

'Do you think I should have?'

'No,' Arachne said. 'I doubt it would have served you, and if it had, you would have come to regret it.'

With a sigh, I sat back in the chair. Absent-mindedly I reached out to the table and created a glass of iced water, lifting it to take a sip. It was the perfect temperature. 'It feels like I'm not making fast enough progress,' I said. 'The whole reason I got into this to begin with was in the hope of finding an item that was a good match. But most of them are the kind I want to throw as far as I can and run in the opposite direction.'

'We always knew that the odds were long ones,' Arachne said. 'As you said, any item that the Council could easily use wouldn't have been locked up.'

There had been more than one reason that I'd been out in Deptford this evening hunting down the Splinter Crown. Months ago, I'd volunteered to head the Vault recovery project, and ever since then, I'd been on raid after raid, tracking down the imbued items that I'd indirectly helped to steal. When the Council had questioned me as to why I was doing it, I'd told them that I wanted to protect the people caught in the crossfire. They probably thought I was just trying to prove something. Actually, both reasons were true, but there was a third one that I didn't think they'd guessed: I was also doing it in the hope of finding an item for myself.

Last year, I'd been forced to face something that had been nagging at me for a long time: as a diviner, I'm simply not a match for the heavyweights of the magical world. In the past I'd mostly stayed off the radar of the really scary people, and when that hadn't worked, my solution had been to run and hide. These days, that was becoming less of an option. 'Run and hide' doesn't work so well when you have people you care about, and over time I'd managed to accumulate a worryingly large number of enemies. It was Arachne who'd made me see the writing on the wall. If I didn't do something to push myself into a higher weight class, then sooner or later – and probably not very much later – I was going to end up dead.

The dreamstone had been floated as a way to solve that. Bonding with imbued items and manipulating Elsewhere have a fair bit of overlap, and the dreamstone gave me the ability to use Elsewhere more effectively; with practice, I ought to be able to use those same techniques to make use of the kinds of imbued item that other people couldn't. By going on these retrieval missions, I ought to be able to find an item that I could make use of myself. Or that had been the plan.

'It's not about easy or hard,' I said. 'I don't feel as though I'm getting anywhere at all.'

'Don't undersell yourself,' Arachne said. 'You can travel between Elsewhere, dreams and dreamshards at will now, and you can shape your environment in all three. Your defences against possession have grown to the point where I think even a mind mage would struggle to influence you.

If you'd picked up that crown, you'd have been in no real danger.'

'None of which gets me closer to what I need,' I said. 'Okay, so imbued items can't possess me. But I can't possess *them* either. I've tried twice now – first the sword, then the brooch in April. I can talk to them, more or less, but I can't change what they want. And if what they want is to go on a murdering spree, or set up a slave empire, then we just end up with a stalemate. I can't dominate them; they can't dominate me.' I looked gloomily down at the table. 'Maybe I should have taken the other dreamstone.'

'You shouldn't.'

'You said it was better for exercising control,' I said, taking a drink from the glass. 'Seems like right now that's what I need.'

'No, it isn't,' Arachne said firmly. The second dreamstone had been a twin to the one lying by my sleeping body right now. Anne and I had brought it together out of the deep shadow realm, but we'd had to give it up to Richard. I didn't know what use he'd put it to. 'I doubt you'd have even been able to make it accept you. It's a matter of personality, not what you feel you need, and you simply don't have enough of a desire to dominate and control.'

'Then what do *you* think I should be doing?'

Arachne studied me, and when she spoke, her voice was sober. 'For one thing, I wouldn't be in so much of a rush.'

I started to speak, but Arachne raised a hand to forestall me. 'Listen, Alex. Power always has a price. I warned you, at the beginning, that to choose this course of action was to pursue the most difficult path. For you to reach the point where you can personally challenge mages like Richard and Levistus will take more than hard work. You will have to make sacrifices. Significant ones. So do not be in too great a hurry to find an imbued item to bond with. It will happen, and when it does, you will find yourself wishing to go back to where you are now.'

'That sounds . . . foreboding,' I said slowly. 'Are you telling me this is a bad idea?'

'No,' Arachne said. 'But I also believe that from now, most of your choices are likely to be hard ones. I will help you while I can, but in the end the decisions will be your own.'

I sat thinking for a minute. 'Are you worried that something's going to happen?'

'Why do you ask?'

'That's the second time you've said something like that,' I said. 'About helping me as long as you can. It sounds as though you think there's a time coming up where that won't be true any longer.'

'I did say that, didn't I?' Arachne murmured. 'No one can see all things. But the world is not as friendly to my kind as it once was. Be prepared.'

I looked at Arachne with a frown. 'What can I do to help?'

'For now, practise with the dreamstone,' Arachne said. 'I think a time will come very soon where your skill with Elsewhere may be all that keeps you alive. Until then, stay close to your friends.'

Anne was already gone by the time I woke the next morning. I shaved, dressed, ate breakfast under the multi-coloured sky of the Hollow, then gated to London.

Dr Shirland lives in a small terraced house tucked away down a one-way street in Brondesbury. I rang the bell and was let in. She looked much the same as she had when I'd first met her – curly hair, round glasses, kindly expression – and her tomcat was sleeping on the same chair. I stroked the cat, accepted a cup of tea and sat, watching the woman over my teacup.

Ruth Shirland is a mind mage and a consulting psychologist, though she spends more time as the latter than the former. She has connections into magical society, but for the most part she seems quite content to live in her little house, seeing patients. To Council mages, it would seem a bizarre way to live. They'd ask her why she was working a psychologist's job for pocket change when she could make ten times as much in the magical world, and if she told them she didn't use her magic when working as a psychologist, they probably either wouldn't believe her or would decide that she was an idiot.

The truth is that independent mages like Dr Shirland are actually more common than Light mages and Dark mages put together. By becoming a Light or a Dark mage, you're taking sides in a war. It's true that the vast majority don't fight on the front lines, and most of the time there aren't any front lines to fight on in the first place, but the simple fact is, by signing up with either Light or Dark, you're cutting your own life expectancy. Most Dark mages die violently, often at the hands of other Dark mages, and it's not a lifestyle to choose if you're hoping to live long enough to have grandchildren. Becoming a Light mage is safer, but it comes with its own consequences – the Council offers privilege and power, but in exchange you have to spend a lot of time saying the right things to the right people, often the kind of people that you don't like very much.

Faced with those options, it's not that surprising that most mages choose neither of the above. They don't join the Council, but they don't follow the Dark way either. They obey the Concord, at least enough to stay out of trouble, but for the most part they don't bother the Council and the Council doesn't bother them. Sometimes they use their abilities to make their way in the world – enchanters charming people out of their money, chance mages scamming casinos – but just as often they don't, or at least not much. They just lead normal lives, staying off the radar of Light and Dark mages alike, going about their day-to-day business in peace. It was pretty much how I'd lived once, and sitting here and looking at Dr Shirland, I found myself – well, not *missing* it exactly, but feeling a little envious. Maybe sitting in cosy living rooms with cups of tea would get boring if I was doing nothing else. But being able to go back to it when you wanted, without having to absent-mindedly check the futures every five minutes to make sure that no one was going to take the opportunity to blow up the house with you inside it . . . that would be nice.

'So,' Dr Shirland said once we were both settled. 'I understand you're here about Anne?'

'That's right.'

'I have to admit, I'm not entirely clear what you're asking,' Dr Shirland said. 'Anne gave me the impression that it was some issue of her mental fitness.'

'Not exactly,' I said. 'When you were looking at Anne in October, did she tell you the whole story?'

'I didn't press her for details, but yes, much of it came out.' Dr Shirland pressed her lips together. 'Especially about those two "Light" mages, Zilean and Lightbringer.'

'It's what happened after that that I'm worried about.

When those two confronted Anne, she picked up an item that triggered something. That was the last I saw or heard. When I got there a few minutes later, they were gone and Anne was unconscious. She says she doesn't remember anything about what happened in between.'

'I'm still not clear on what you're asking,' Dr Shirland said. 'If you want to know whether she was telling the truth, then the answer is yes. Her memories go as far as taking the ring, but no further.'

'I want to know whether we can expect anything *else* to happen,' I said. It was a risk, telling all this to Dr Shirland – several of the events we were touching on would land us in serious trouble if she repeated them to the Council – but in the years since I'd met the mind mage, I'd never heard of her breaking her clients' confidentiality. 'The creature in that ring was a bound jinn. Now, I've had experience with exactly one creature like that before. It granted five wishes to anyone who picked it up, and when it was done it ate them. So what I'm asking is whether there's a risk of anything like that happening to Anne. Is that thing still around somewhere? Is it hiding in her head? And if it is, what can I do about it?'

Dr Shirland nodded. 'In that case, one of those questions I can answer definitely. There is no jinn, or any similar creature, hiding inside Anne's head. I've touched her mind on several occasions since October, and such entities leave an extremely obvious psychic footprint. There is absolutely no way that a jinn, especially a powerful one, could be concealing itself within her mind. It'd be like trying to hide an elephant in your living room.'

'Okay, so that's good news. Then if that thing didn't move into her head, what do you think *did* happen?'

'Here, unfortunately, I don't have any definite answers,' Dr Shirland said. 'While I'm familiar with possessing entities in general, I know very little about jinn. Very few mages do nowadays. The most I can do is make some educated guesses.' She set her teacup down on the table and looked at me. 'The memories that Anne does have are absolutely consistent with possession. When she took up that ring, she was desperate and emotionally vulnerable, and the jinn – if that's what it was – was able to take control. She might even have been willing to cooperate, at least at first: her situation was certainly bad enough. For those few minutes, the jinn would have had complete control of her body and actions. It might even have had access to her magic as well as its own.'

'But by the time I got there, Anne was unconscious on the floor,' I said. 'So what changed? I mean, that thing would have been trapped in there for God only knows how long. Why would it just pull back into its item and leave her alone?'

'I suspect it didn't have a choice,' Dr Shirland said. 'True possession is extremely difficult. To keep it up over the long term, the entity must confront and displace the host, and in that contest the host has a significant advantage. The entity is only likely to succeed if the disparity in mental strength is very great, such as an unusually strong entity pitted against a host who is unusually weak-willed. The longer the host allows the entity to remain, and the more use they make of its powers, the more vulnerable they become, but if they resist from the beginning, the odds are in their favour.'

'What if they *don't* resist from the beginning?'

'Taking permanent control of a host is not a subtle process,' Dr Shirland said. 'Once she let the creature in,

Anne would have quickly realised that it had no intention of leaving. I suspect there was a short, fierce struggle for control, which it lost. The psychic shock left Anne unconscious.'

'So that's it?' I said. So far, this wasn't anywhere near as bad as I'd feared. My guess had been that Anne had tried to make a wish to get rid of the Crusaders and backed out halfway through. 'This thing's gone?'

'It could be that after possessing Anne, the creature was forced back into its prison. In that case, once the item was removed from physical contact with Anne, it would lose any ability to affect her. In which case she's in no danger from it at all.' Dr Shirland paused. 'This is one possibility.'

Something about her tone of voice made me look up sharply. 'What's the other?'

'Anne is certainly not weak-willed,' Dr Shirland said. 'I do not think a jinn, no matter how powerful, would be able to take control of her if she resisted. But there is a part of Anne that might not *want* to resist.'

'I know,' I said flatly. 'I've met her. Do you think that was what happened?'

'It would certainly have had an effect,' Dr Shirland said. 'How much of one is harder to say. That part of Anne's mind is closed to me.'

'So if that other Anne wanted to let the jinn in, could it?'

'Now we're entering the realm of guesswork. In theory, it should be impossible for an entity to exercise that kind of control without some sort of direct or sympathetic link. I assume the ring is no longer in her possession.'

'Richard took it, as far as I know. So as long as she doesn't pick it up again, she's fine?'

'In theory.'

I paused. 'Could the other Anne make her do that?'

'You've put your finger on the problem,' Dr Shirland said. 'It's quite possible that Anne's shadow self might maintain a contract with the jinn, regardless of her conscious desires. As long as that internal conflict remains unresolved, Anne will be vulnerable.'

'Then how can we fix that?'

'Now you're starting to ask the really difficult questions,' Dr Shirland said. 'How much do you know about Anne's shadow?'

'It's an alternate personality from when she was captured by Sagash,' I said. I'd spoken to that other Anne just once, several years ago. Back then we'd been on the same side, but the experience had left me wary. 'More ruthless, less empathic. She couldn't do what she needed to survive, so she created someone who could.'

Dr Shirland looked at me, her head slightly tilted. 'Is that how you see it? Anne created an alternate personality?'

'Well . . .' I said. 'Yes.'

'Then what do you think she created that personality from?'

'What do you mean?'

'Imagine I ask you to create a personality that can do something you can't,' Dr Shirland said. 'Composing an orchestral symphony, say. How would you do it?'

'I'm not sure.'

'*Could* you do it?'

'Probably not.'

'Of course you can't,' Dr Shirland said. 'Because you don't have the skills or knowledge. Changing your own personality won't help.'

I looked at Dr Shirland. She looked back at me, her eyes mild and steady, and suddenly I felt uneasy. 'What are you getting at?'

'You can't *create* a personality. You can only use what's already there.'

'But I've met that other person,' I said. 'What you call her shadow. She's completely different from the real Anne.'

'In what ways?'

'Anne's a nice person,' I said. 'She's gentle and she's kind. That other Anne . . . I only met her once, but I got a pretty definite sense of her personality. I wouldn't say she was outright cruel, but she's more self-centred than the real Anne and a lot more aggressive. Plus her goals are different. Anne just wants a peaceful life. The other one wants power.'

'That's a fairly accurate summary of the differences,' Dr Shirland said. 'But you keep saying "the real Anne". They're both real.'

'Then if Anne didn't create that other self,' I said, 'where did it come from?'

'Anne had a difficult childhood,' Dr Shirland said. 'She was limited in the types of behaviour she could express. The traits she was free to develop are the ones you've identified as her natural personality. Soft-spoken, gentle, nurturing. Her more aggressive impulses were suppressed.'

'Does she even *have* that many aggressive impulses?'

'Everyone has aggressive impulses,' Dr Shirland said. 'They're a fundamental part of the human condition. If you meet someone who seems not to have any, they're either channelling them somewhere else or keeping them suppressed. Usually, in the latter case, it ends up turning inward and manifesting as depression. With Anne, things unfolded somewhat differently.'

'Because of what happened with Sagash.'

Dr Shirland nodded. 'Anne had always thought of herself as a healer, someone who used her magic to grow and nurture. When Sagash forced her to use her powers for death, it traumatised her, which was of course exactly what Sagash intended. His goal was to break her and reshape her to his desires. So Anne escaped to the only place she could find, to Elsewhere. In there, she created a place of safety, somewhere where there was no conflict or violence.'

'Well, what's wrong with that?' I said. 'I mean, it worked, didn't it?'

'It worked against Sagash because she could wall him out. What she could *not* do was wall *herself* out. Because when she excluded anything destructive or aggressive from her inner world, she also excluded part of herself.'

'Is that what that other Anne is, then?' I said. 'Anne's evil side?'

'She's the aspects of Anne's personality that Anne is unable or unwilling to accept,' Dr Shirland said. 'And those aspects aren't all negative by any means. She's more direct and willing to state her own desires, better capable of defending herself. Unfortunately, Anne hasn't made any progress towards coming to terms with that, and in fact she's continued to shunt off impulses and emotions to that personality in the ensuing years. In the long run, the state of affairs isn't sustainable. She'll have to resolve it or risk a complete breakdown.'

'Resolve it how?'

'Eventually?' Dr Shirland said. 'She has to integrate the two sides of her self. Become one person, not two.'

'How?'

'That's another very complex question to answer,' Dr

Shirland said. 'It's also not your problem. This is in Anne's hands, not yours, and it won't be any kind of quick or simple process. It'll take years.'

'Then if I can't do anything to help, why are you even telling me all this?'

'So you can better understand her, for one thing,' Dr Shirland said. 'But it also relates to your initial question. As long as she doesn't come into contact with that jinn again, I can't see any reason why the events of last autumn should disqualify her from a position as an aide. I'd also say that from a purely psychological standpoint, having some outside stimulus would be good for her. She's been a little too isolated lately and I don't think leaving her alone with the contents of her own head for company is a good thing.'

Walking back to the park I use for gating, I found myself replaying the conversation in my head, which in turn led me to thinking about Anne.

I'd told Dr Shirland that I'd come to see her because I was worried about the jinn. And that was true – I *had* been worried. Richard had as good as told me last year that manipulating Anne into picking that thing up had been his plan from the beginning, and I didn't think that he was done with her, not by a long shot. Quite frankly, I was surprised he'd left her alone. I'd been expecting him to show up at Anne's door with another of his offers, with a heavy degree of coercion thrown in. He hadn't, and I didn't know why – maybe Variam was right and he really was busy, maybe he was just biding his time – but until I had solid evidence to the contrary, I was staying on my guard. We had defences in place to give us some early warning, and if he or anyone else went after Anne, we'd know about it. So it wasn't as though this meeting had been a pretence.

But while I hadn't been lying, I also hadn't been telling the whole truth. The reason I'd been so reluctant to appoint Anne as my aide wasn't the jinn, and it wasn't the potential threat from anti-Dark elements on the Council either, though that was getting closer. It was about me.

I'd known Anne for around five years now. I'd been introduced to her via Luna, and to begin with, that was how I'd seen her – as Luna's classmate, just another apprentice, with a nicer-than-usual manner and a more-annoying-than-usual friend (Vari). Gradually, over the years, I'd stopped seeing her as an apprentice and started seeing her as a mage in her own right. But somewhere along the line, something else had changed too, and without quite noticing it, I'd found myself more and more attracted to her.

And my reaction to that had been to try as hard as I could to pretend it didn't exist.

If you're wondering why . . . well, that's an easy question to ask and a hard one to answer. To begin with, I suppose there was the age difference. When I first met Anne, I was twenty-eight and she was twenty – not the biggest of age gaps, but enough to put her in the 'child/student' box in my mind. But time had passed, and Anne was no longer twenty, or a student, or (by any possible definition) a child.

A bigger reason was my own past experience, or to be more honest, my lack of it. I spent my teens and my early twenties learning about magic and not very much else. I picked up a lot of skills in the process – combat, manipulation, mental discipline – but one thing I didn't get much practice with was romance, and spending so much of my formative time around Dark mages really didn't help. The simple truth is that I'm a lot more comfortable dealing with a woman who wants to kill me than one who wants to kiss me, and yes, I know how screwed-up that sounds. It's not that I *want* people to try to kill me, it's just that I grew up with the predator–prey game, and I know how it works. When it comes to stuff like this, I don't. What was I even supposed to be doing? Should I talk to Anne? For all I knew, approaching Anne was exactly the *worst* thing to do. I didn't really know how she felt about me, and having that conversation could destroy the relationship we had. I *liked* having Anne as a friend. Was it worth risking that, just in the hope of turning it into something more? I probably could have used my divination to figure out an answer, but I've always been uncomfortable with using my magic on my friends in that way. It feels like spying, and to be honest, it pretty much is.

And then there was the other reason.

The room was brown, the walls padded and soundproofed. A metal table rested in the centre, and on it was a mass of torn and bleeding flesh. Skin had been ripped and peeled away, hanging from hooks and wires, to leave skin and muscle bare to the harsh light. The body moved, twisting, and the eyes opened, looking out at me. Those were Anne's eyes in that ruined face, filled with agony, and they stared at me mutely. My stomach clenched and I wanted to vomit, wanted to look away, but all I could do was stare, hoping that if I kept looking I'd realise it wasn't true, that I wasn't seeing what was in front of me . . .

I pushed the memory away. That had happened last September. The Crusaders had managed to catch Anne, and when she didn't tell them what they wanted to hear, they'd tortured her. And since life mages are resistant to pain, they hadn't just tortured her, they'd tried to maim and flay her body so badly that even she wouldn't be able to withstand it.

Anne had lived, but it had been horribly close, and for weeks afterwards I'd woken up sweating thinking about *how* close. If we'd been even a couple of hours later, Anne would have died. If Luna and Variam hadn't reacted so fast, if Sonder hadn't helped, if Anne had been just a little bit less resilient, then she'd be gone, and our group would be three instead of four. Anne had been traumatised and it had probably been a big factor in her choice to pick up that item in the Vault the following month.

And the reason all of that happened had been to do with me. Oh, it hadn't been *directly* my fault. But the reason the Crusaders had gone after Anne had been to get information about Morden, and the reason they'd done that had been because they'd tried and failed to do the same to me, and because Anne had been seen with Morden and me on my first day as Morden's aide, she'd been marked down as an associate. I wasn't any less of a target nowadays – if anything, things were worse. The Crusaders wouldn't be likely to try kidnapping a Council member, but aides were another story.

So for Anne to become my aide – or for that matter, for her to be close to me in any way at all – would make it that much more likely that the same thing would happen again. I've never lived a safe life and I've always accepted that, but it's one thing to know that there's a good chance you're going to die a violent death, and it's something else to know that it might be someone else doing the dying in your place.

And that was the biggest reason I'd never had this

conversation with Anne. Because if I did, I could imagine it going two ways. In the first scenario, she'd tell me, 'Well, I kind of like you, but not in that way, and even if I did, you're just not worth it.' Which would be painful, to put it mildly. The second scenario was much worse. In that, she'd tell me that it was her choice, not mine, and that she was stronger than me, if anything, so *she* had more right to be worrying about *me*. And I wouldn't be able to argue about that, because it was true.

I suppose some of you might be rolling your eyes at this point. If you are . . . well, then it's a fair bet that you've never been in this position yourself. It's easy to say 'oh, it's their choice' when you don't have anything at stake. But if you know — not guess, *know* — that there's a good chance that doing something could cause someone you deeply care for to die a horrible death, would you still do it? If that doesn't make you hesitate, then either you don't care about them as much as you think you do, or (more likely) you're kidding yourself. The simple fact was that Anne would probably have a considerably higher life expectancy if she stayed away from me, and that was not a small thing to get past.

But then, if I *wasn't* around, that would open up new dangers. Because Richard was interested in Anne too. He'd been willing to go up against the Crusaders to protect her, and though I couldn't prove it, I was pretty sure that many of the events leading up to Anne coming into contact with that jinn were of his doing. I didn't know how central Anne was to his plans — maybe the Vault assault would have happened the same way anyway, and having this happen to Anne had just been an extra bonus — but I didn't think he was likely to leave her alone. Most of the protection that

Anne and Luna and Variam and I did have came from staying together. If we split up, we'd be in one kind of danger. But if I stayed around Anne, kept associating with her, then she'd just be in danger in a different way.

I sighed and shook my head. I was going around in circles and I wasn't getting anywhere. Maybe things would work themselves out, and in any case, I should be able to put it off a little longer. Shouldn't I?

4

It was a month later.

'Look, I get what you're saying,' Lucian said. 'But things are different now.'

'Different how?' I asked. We were sitting on a bench on Hampstead Heath. The full power of the July sun was beating down on us out of a bright blue sky, and even the grass seemed to radiate heat. Crickets buzzed from the undergrowth, and the sounds of chatter and laughter drifted up to us from the people scattered across the hillside below.

'You're part of the Council,' Lucian said. He was a curly-haired boy in his early twenties with a serious expression, and right now that expression was focused on me.

'I've always worked for the Council, ever since you've known me,' I said. Lucian had been a walk-in, one of the many adepts who entered my shop uninvited, hoping for help. Sometimes I was able to give them what they were looking for; sometimes I couldn't, and usually that would be the end of it. But every now and again one of those walk-ins would turn into a relationship that lasted, and over the years, I'd built up quite a network of contacts. Lucian had been one of the ones who had stayed, and over time he'd become one of my major sources of information about what was happening in the adept world. 'I've worked for other people too. That doesn't mean I've given them your name. Anything you tell me, I keep to myself.'

'I get that, but . . . Look, it was one thing when you

were just an aide. And you said that you weren't even doing that because you wanted to. I don't know whether you were forced into it, or something . . .'

'He *was* forced into it,' Anne said quietly from the other side of me. 'So was I.'

Anne had been officially appointed as my aide as of four weeks ago. Council aides are much more than personal assistants; if a Council member isn't present, their aide is expected to be able to negotiate on their behalf, and a lot of business gets done between aides without their bosses ever meeting at all. Navigating the various factions and agendas is difficult work and I'd kept an eye on Anne during the first fortnight to make sure she could handle it. There had been some hiccups, but all in all, she'd adapted pretty well. Like me, Anne wasn't brought up in the Light world, but her experiences with Dark mages had turned out to be quite applicable to the Council, and her habit of staying quiet and keeping her eyes and ears open had stood her in good stead.

One of the things that Anne had had to change had been her style of dress. Instead of her old jeans and jumpers, she'd switched to business suits, generally ones that showed off her figure. The one she was currently wearing was dark green, left her lower legs bare, and emphasised the narrowness of her waist, and Lucian had spent most of the first five minutes of our meeting sneaking glances while trying not to make it obvious. Between our work relationship and living at the Hollow, I was seeing Anne for hours at a time every day now. On one level it was nice, but at the back of my mind I couldn't help feeling that the longer I let things go on like this, the sooner I was going to have to make a decision.

I realised that Lucian was talking and pulled my attention

back to the present. '. . . on the Council,' Lucian was saying. 'You're one of them. I mean, when they're passing their laws to screw us over . . . you're one of the ones *doing* it.'

'I'm Junior Council, not Senior. I don't get a vote.'

Lucian looked sceptical and I could tell he wasn't convinced. To be fair, he had a point. Junior Council members might be non-voting, but I still had vastly more influence than Lucian did. 'Look, I'm not asking you to betray anyone. We just want to know more about this association of Richard's.'

'That *is* betraying them.'

'It might be made up of adepts, but it isn't owned by adepts,' I said. 'It doesn't matter who the figurehead is, it's Richard who calls the shots. And I'm worried about what he's using them for.'

'You mean the Council's worried,' Lucian said. 'They just don't want us getting organised.'

'They don't mind you getting organised,' I said. *Okay, skating around the truth there.* 'Taking orders from Richard Drakh is another story. I don't think you understand just how dangerous this guy is. Anyone who signs up with him is putting themselves on the front lines of a war.'

'Yeah, well, we're *already* on the front lines of a war.' Lucian said sourly.

'No. You're not.'

'Oh yeah? What about last October? The Keepers *murdered* twenty adepts who were just out there for a peaceful demonstration and what's the Council done? Nothing. They don't even care.'

I didn't have a good answer to that one. The demonstration that Lucian was talking about had started out as a protest but had quickly spiralled out of control. The

Keeper forces that had been on duty claimed they'd been attacked by Dark mages hidden in the crowd, and by the time the dust had settled there had been Council security personnel among the dead, which didn't exactly fit with the 'they were all peaceful protesters' narrative. But given how bad Council–adept relations were, none of the adepts had been in a mood to listen, and Lucian's version of the story wasn't even close to the worst one I'd heard. Plenty of adepts now believed that the Council was out to commit wholesale genocide.

The whole thing had made me realise exactly how awful lines of communication in British magical society were. Light mages can hate each other while still exchanging messages, even if the messages don't express much besides mutual loathing. But if there's a problem with Dark mages, or independents, or adepts, then there are no good ways to get people to sit down and talk to one another. Which made it all the more worrying that when it came to the adept community, Richard apparently *had* been sitting down and talking to them.

'You do realise that there's a good chance that Richard's the reason that protest turned violent in the first place?'

'Yeah, well, at least he's offering to protect us.'

'Richard's the kind of person that you need protection *from*,' I said. 'Have you forgotten how we met? You came into my shop asking for help because you were worried about Dark mages coming after you and your friends. Well, those same mages are the ones who are working for Richard right now. I know you think that you're getting some kind of safety if you sign up with these guys, but that's not how it works. Sure, they'll offer you protection – as long as you do as you're told. But as soon as you stop, they'll make a point of targeting you, just to send the message of what happens to other people who don't get in line. It's not getting into those sort of groups that's the problem, it's getting out.'

'Maybe that's better than the deal we've got now.'

I rolled my eyes. 'Lucian . . .'

'No, listen.' Lucian looked right at me, and I could tell he was serious. 'Do you know what it's like being an adept in this country? No matter what happens to you, the Council doesn't care. A Dark mage can pick you right off the street, or some monster can eat you in your bed, and they don't care. Maybe if you're *really* lucky some Keepers might come around afterwards to ask questions, but by then it's too late and most of the time they don't do anything anyway. Everything they do, it makes it obvious that they don't give a shit about us. But now, all of a sudden, we've got mages like you telling us "oh, it's really important you don't do this". It's pretty obvious why, isn't it? The only reason they've started paying attention is because they're afraid of this Richard guy and they don't want us on his side. It's like, we yell for help over and over and they don't listen. Well, they're listening now.'

'You join up with Richard, and they'll pay attention to you all right,' I said harshly. 'Just not the kind you want. You're signing up to be pawns.'

'Yeah, well, that's what they're going to say, isn't it?'

We stared at each other in the midday sun. On the path below us, a party of men and women went by, talking loudly, a dog bounding at their heels. From the baseball game on the far side of the hill came the *crack* of a hit, followed by shouts and cheers.

'I wasn't representing the Council when we first met, and I'm not speaking for them now,' I said at last. 'I'm telling you this because I don't want you hurt. Don't sign up with these guys. And if you care about your friends, don't let them join either.'

Lucian didn't look convinced. 'Was there anything else?'

I sighed inwardly. 'No.'

Lucian got up and left. I watched him walk away down the grassy slope, thinking over his words. If Lucian was willing to say those kinds of things to my face, how many adepts were thinking the same way?

'He's got a point,' Anne said in her soft voice.

I glanced at her. 'You too?'

'I know what you said was true,' Anne said. 'But think about how it looks to him. No one tells adepts anything about mage politics. I mean, nobody told *me* anything all the time I was in the apprentice programme. All I ever learned was second-hand from the younger apprentices. Now finally the Council's talking to them, and all they have to say is, "Don't join the other side." Adepts are going to think that the only reason the Council's paying them any attention at all is that they're worried they'll change sides.'

'Mm,' I said. 'The donkey and the shepherd.'

'What?'

'One of Aesop's fables,' I said. 'An old shepherd's watching his donkey grazing in the meadow when he hears an enemy army coming. He tells the donkey to run or they'll both be captured, and the donkey asks if the enemy army would make him carry a heavier load. When the shepherd says no, the donkey lies back down and says, "Then what difference does it make to me?"'

'Do you think that's what it is?' Anne asked quietly. 'An army?'

'It's what it sounds like to me,' I said. I didn't add what

I was thinking. You build an army because you're planning to fight someone. Who was Richard going to be turning that army against?

We gated from the heath to Wales, walking out of the trees into a secluded valley painted in green and gold, with a single small house sitting at the end over a river. A pair of buzzards circled on the thermals above, calling in their mewing voices: *kew, kew*.

'It's the front door, right?' Anne asked as we walked into the garden.

I nodded. 'We'll go around the back.'

The back door was locked, and I pulled out a loose stone from the wall to retrieve the key from its hiding place. 'Are you going to visit Morden?' Anne asked.

'Not planning to,' I said. 'Talisid was hinting about it, but I turned him down. I think he's still hoping I might shake out some information.'

'Is he still in that prison?'

'The bubble realm, yeah.' The key was sticking in the lock. Either it had rusted over the winter, or the last person to break in had managed to do some damage. I pulled it out and rubbed at it with a handkerchief. 'Why?'

Anne hesitated. 'This is going to sound weird, but I was dreaming about Morden.'

'You mean in Elsewhere?'

'No, just a regular dream. I was circling around his prison, looking for a way in.'

'Huh.' I inserted the key and tried again. It scraped, then turned, and the door promptly stuck. I banged it with my shoulder to force it open. 'You haven't been missing having him as your boss, have you?'

'Not even slightly.'

The inside of the house seemed very dark after the bright sunlight of the valley. We walked down the hall and turned into the kitchen. The room was dusty and felt abandoned, exactly the same as it had been since I'd last left it, except for the wires running across the edge of the front door and down to the open gym bag below.

'So who was it this time?' Anne asked as I walked over to inspect the device.

'I can see the future, not the past.' The bomb was a stack of plastique packed into the gym bag, the wires ending in contacts stuck into the blocks. It was crude but powerful, enough to blow apart the house, the victim and anyone else unlucky enough to be within thirty feet or so of the front door. 'I suppose I could get Sonder or someone to track down whoever it was, but honestly, I don't think it's worth it.'

'It feels a little bit strange that you don't even bother identifying the people trying to kill you any more.'

'Who has that kind of time?'

The house we were in was mine, a small farm cottage I'd bought a long time ago as a safe house. Unfortunately, the more you use a safe house, the less safe it gets, and after the third or fourth set of unwelcome visitors I'd reluctantly accepted that it was time to move on. There was no point in making that fact public though, so I'd moved out all my valuable possessions, left just enough stuff behind to make it seem as though I still lived there and arranged for electricity and water usage to add some credibility. Once that was done it was just a matter of checking back every few days or so to see whether anyone had left any unpleasant surprises.

'I know this probably makes me a bad person for suggesting it,' Anne said, 'but do you think we should stop disarming these traps?'

'The idea being that the next person to break in gets to be the target of whatever was left behind by the last one?'

'Pretty much.'

I'd checked the futures several times to confirm that cutting any of the wires would disable the thing, but I went ahead and looked at the longer-term futures just to make sure. It's never a good idea to be too sure you've outsmarted your enemy. 'Too much risk that someone innocent might get caught,' I said. 'Besides, leaving these things around just feels untidy.'

'Untidy?'

The fact that these traps were still showing up was actually good news, all things considered. Apparently word had spread that trying to kill me face-to-face was a bad idea, which was the reason that my would-be assassins were now restricting themselves to long-distance efforts. Obviously, having to deal with lethal booby traps wasn't ideal – so far this year there had been two bombs and one attempted poisoning, and that wasn't counting the magical ones – but I much preferred it to having my enemies come after me in person. For one thing, divination is very well suited to avoiding traps. For another, a long-range assassin is far less of a threat. The really scary killers are the ones who are willing to get close enough to make sure they don't miss.

I drew my knife and delicately sawed through first one wire, then the other. There was no visible effect, but the bomb was now an inert lump of chemicals. 'Clear,' I said, straightening up.

'Want me to pick up the post while I'm here?' Anne asked. She hadn't backed away. It's quite a vote of confidence when someone is willing to stand next to you while you defuse a bomb.

'Sure. I'll go put this one with the others.'

We gated to the War Rooms, and as we stepped out into the entrance hall, we stopped speaking out loud. The War Rooms have too many watchful ears, and while I've never found proof that the place is bugged, there are a lot of spells that can allow their caster to eavesdrop with little risk of detection. I ought to know since it's something I've done myself. Fortunately, these days I don't need to speak out loud to communicate.

So what happened in the dream? I asked Anne mentally.

It was strange, Anne replied. *I was circling the prison from the outside, trying to find a way in. And it was definitely Morden's prison, I knew that much. I think I was trying to get to him, and I couldn't break through the barriers, and I was really frustrated.*

We were talking via my dreamstone, the amethyst-coloured focus currently tucked away in my inner pocket. Arachne had told me that once I mastered its use, I wouldn't need to have it on my person at all, but I still found that doing so made this easier. It wasn't telepathy, not quite – mind magic telepathy works by broadcasting thoughts and picking them up in turn. This was more like opening a link. And it wasn't just thoughts either: I could pick up some of the emotions in Anne's mind, knew that she was watching the people around us as we spoke. I could even feel the echo of her memories of the dream, restless and circling, like a frustrated predator.

The dreamstone's linking ability was limited. While it worked very well on the people I knew best and was closest to — which meant Anne, Luna, Variam and Arachne — establishing a link with someone else was harder, and the less we knew and trusted each other, the more 'harder' shaded into 'impossible'. Then again, that wasn't too much of a sacrifice to make. The link was two-way, and just as I could pick up other people's thoughts and memories, they could pick up mine. I was fine with keeping people I didn't trust out of my head.

What did the prison look like? I asked curiously.

A castle of black stone rising up out of the haze, Anne said. *It reminded me of Sagash's shadow realm, but uglier and without the growing things. Why?*

Just curious, I said. I knew that the prison where Morden was being held was called San Vittore, but I'd never seen it. *You don't think he was trying to send you a message or something?*

Through a dream? It's possible, I suppose, but it seems like a funny sort of message. If he could do that, why not tell me directly?

Either way, if it happens again, let me know. I knew that Morden and Richard wanted something from Anne, and I didn't like anything linking them to her, even something as vague and nebulous as this.

I will.

With the morning errands done, it was time for the bulk of the day's work.

A lot of people get confused about how the Light Council works, so it's probably worth taking a minute to explain. The Light Council is split into two parts, the Senior Council and the Junior Council, and the biggest difference between the two is that the Senior Council members are voting while the Junior Council members are non-voting. This means that when a resolution is put before the Council, it's only the Senior Council members who get a say. The Junior Council have the right to speak on the topic, but not to vote on it.

If you're wondering why they have a Junior Council at all, the answer is that like a lot of political systems, it's a mix of circumstance and tradition. In the old days there was no Junior Council – there were seven Council members, and that was that. There was much less of a bureaucracy too – if you worked for the Council, chances were you knew at least one Council member directly. What changed all that was nothing to do with mages and everything to do with this country's regular inhabitants. In the eighteenth century, Britain was the home of the Industrial Revolution, which along with advances in agriculture led to the population increasing by a factor of ten. With more normals came more mages, and all of a sudden the Council rulership was too small to handle the job. So the bureaucracy grew and kept on growing, and somewhere along the line it got big enough that seven Council members weren't enough to oversee it all. But no one was willing to expand the number of voting members beyond seven (probably because none of them wanted their own votes diluted) and so the compromise reached was the creation of the Junior Council. To begin with there were only two or three of them, but that number had also gone up over the years until it reached the current status quo of six. Seven Senior Council and six Junior Council made up the full Light Council of thirteen.

Although Junior Councillors can't vote, in all other ways they have pretty much the same rights as the Senior

Council do. They can appoint aides (who gain the legal status of Light mages for the duration of their appointment) and they can't be sentenced or outlawed via Council resolution the way anyone else in the country can. This was why Levistus had been trying so hard to get me off the Council – as long as I held a seat, it severely restricted the ways in which he could go after me. Council members also can't be removed from office without a full formal trial, which takes for ever, as evidenced by the fact that Morden was still technically a Council member even though the Council had started proceedings against him nine months ago. Finally – and most importantly – to be raised to the Senior Council, you have to be on the Junior Council first. Which means that for the Senior Council, the question of who gets to be on the Junior Council is very important indeed.

When I'd replaced Morden in his Junior Council seat, despite my months of work as an aide, I had only a sketchy idea of what the Junior Council actually did. To be honest, I'd assumed that that wasn't likely to change. At the time I'd only recently become a member of the Keepers, who had responded to my promotion with all the warmth and enthusiasm of a housewife waking up to find a dead rat on her kitchen floor. They'd done the bare legal minimum to confirm my appointment, then had proceeded to freeze me out completely. Now that I was on the Council, I'd expected exactly the same thing to happen.

As it turned out, I was dead wrong. Turns out the Council works very differently from the Keepers – in the Keepers you're assigned jobs by your superiors, but members of the Junior Council are mostly free to select their own duties. There are provisions to force Junior Councillors who are slacking off to do more work, but there aren't any provisions to force them to do *less* work (possibly because it had never occurred to the guys writing the rules that someday they'd have a Council member who wasn't a Light mage). With hindsight, it made sense – if it had been possible for the other Council members to shut Morden out, they'd have done it already, and if they weren't going to do it for Morden, there was no reason to expect them to do it for me. But at the time, it had been quite a surprise to reach Morden's study in the War Rooms and find a desk full of work and a lot of impatient messages expecting me to pick up where he'd left off.

I could have avoided it. As I said, there are provisions to force slackers to do their share, but if I'd simply sat at home and refused to help, I don't think anyone would have forced the issue. But in the end, I hadn't. Partly it was self-interest: the more involved I was in the workings of the Council, the harder they'd find it to get rid of me. But probably a bigger reason was a sense of responsibility. This morning, it had been Lucian attacking the Council and me defending them, but up until a few years ago I would have been the one in Lucian's place. I'd hated the Council and everything it stood for, and I'd had nothing but bad things to say about how it treated everyone who wasn't a Light mage. Now that I was on the Council myself, I had a chance to do something to remedy that. It wasn't a huge amount of power, but it was more than 99.9 per cent of people in magical society would ever have, and it felt wrong to waste the opportunity.

'So what have we got for today?' I asked Anne.

The study I'd inherited from Morden was a small, comfortable room in dark-panelled wood tucked away behind one of the administration blocks. Like all of the War Rooms, it was deep underground, but an illusion feature covering the back wall helped improve the aesthetics. I had it set to a view of a forested hillside, with an audio of birdcalls and the sounds of a distant river, giving the room a pleasant, airy feel. The desk dominating the centre of the room was covered in papers. Mages are slow to adapt to new technology, and the Council still hadn't fully shifted over to computers. A proposal to digitise the War Rooms was currently working its way through the bureaucracy, which probably meant that the Council would start bringing in desktop PCs somewhere around the invention of quantum computing.

'First, some bad news,' Anne said. 'The Order of the Cloak are very definite that they don't have any records on those adepts you saw with Richard. Nothing from the pictures; nothing from the descriptions. I asked them to get in touch if they did hear anything, but I don't think we can expect much.'

'Damn it,' I said. Last year I'd managed to briefly eavesdrop on a meeting between Richard and a set of adepts that, with hindsight, had probably been important. Unfortunately, at the time I hadn't known that it *was* Richard, and by the time I'd started chasing it, the trail had gone cold. The Order of the Star had already sent me away empty-handed, and the Order of the Cloak had been my last hope. 'I can't shake the feeling that they've got something to do with his new adept association. If we could track them it might be a way in.'

'And on that topic, we're still not hearing back from those other adepts from the association,' Anne said. 'The messages have gone through, but they're not answering.'

'Because we haven't managed to get hold of the right people, or because they don't want to talk to us?'

'I think it's probably the second.'

I wondered what these adepts were going to do once they *were* ready to start talking. 'What else?'

'Julia's trying to get your help on reviving the ID resolution again.'

'Oh, come on.' I rolled my eyes. 'Tell her whatever it takes to make her go away. Next?'

'The Keepers want a meeting about the Splinter Crown. They say some new details have come up from interrogating those thralls. And Druss's aide wants an update on the item recovery leads.'

I've had to learn a lot of things since joining the Council, and one of the more useful concepts I'd picked up was the Eisenhower Matrix, a method of ordering tasks by importance and urgency. The idea is that you file every task into one of four quadrants: important and urgent; not important but urgent; important but not urgent; and neither important nor urgent. Depending on which of those four a task is in, you do it, delegate it, schedule it or ignore it.

The ID resolution was an example of a task that was neither important nor urgent. The Directors wanted a registry of all the magic-users and magic-involved people in the country, and they kept bringing the idea back no matter how many times it was vetoed by everyone else. For some reason Julia had decided that my support would help (or more likely, she was just pestering everyone on the Council no matter their status). I didn't want to help with the resolution, and given that Julia was Alma's aide, I didn't want to get involved with her either. In this situation the best way that Anne could help me was by keeping them at arm's length and waiting for them to give up and go away.

The Keeper meeting was urgent but not important. After all this time, it was unlikely that the information they'd turned up would be anything useful – it was far more likely that they were just using it as another opportunity to dig for evidence that I was a security risk. The Keepers had never got over the episode a year and a half ago where they'd done their best to arrest me at Canary Wharf. I'd escaped and made them look stupid into the bargain, and they weren't going to forgive me for either of those things any time soon. On the other hand, I couldn't openly ignore the request either. 'Can you handle the Keepers? If you go in my place, they can quiz you, but you should be able to get out of anything compromising by telling them you weren't there. Just let me know if they try to pull anything.'

Anne nodded. 'And Druss?'

'I'll have to go,' I said. Giving reports to Druss did nothing to aid the recovery effort, but it was politically important. Druss the Red was one of the few (if marginal) allies I had on the Council, and if he asked for something, I did it. That's how patronage works. 'Get back to his aide and schedule a time. Anything else for the day?'

'Just the usual. There's the security briefing, but . . .' Anne frowned. 'That's odd.'

'What?'

'A new notification.' Anne touched the message focus. 'It wasn't there when I checked just a minute ago. It must have just come in as soon as I started reading.'

I looked up, alert. 'What does it say?'

'It's asking for you at one of the secure conference rooms

at your earliest convenience. But it doesn't say who you're supposed to be meeting or who sent it.'

'Doesn't need to,' I said. A tingle had gone through me at Anne's words. I knew exactly who'd sent that message. Important *and* urgent tasks you do right away.

The secure conference rooms in the War Rooms are far below the Belfry. We took the stairs down, winding our way deep into the earth. The deeper we got, the fewer people we saw. More than a thousand people use the War Rooms every day, but even so, that number doesn't even come close to filling the place. There are lower levels that are all but deserted: some holding living or training quarters that are currently mothballed; others marked as 'storage', though exactly what they're storing isn't specified.

We came to a halt at the end of an empty corridor. A blank metal door stood before us, with an outdated speaker system by its side. I pressed the button by the microphone. 'This is Verus.'

There was a pause, then a voice sounded through the speaker. 'I see you've brought your aide.'

'Yes.'

There was silence. By my side, I felt Anne shift. I had the feeling that the person on the other end was involved in a discussion as to whether to ask me to send Anne away. If they did, I was going to tell them no. I'd already looked through the futures of us coming down this corridor, and I was pretty sure that I was going to win an argument if they chose to start one . . . but the silence stretched out longer than I was expecting, to nearly a minute.

At last the voice came through the speaker again. 'Please come in.'

I pushed the door and it swung freely. Anne and I walked inside.

The room within was more spartan than the rooms I was used to meeting in, walled and furnished in concrete and metal. The secure conference rooms are older than the blocks in which the Council usually conduct their business, and they're not designed for comfort: the temperature was a few degrees colder than the upper levels of the War Rooms, which are kept at a steady twenty-two degrees centigrade all year round. The only reason people use the rooms down here is if they don't want attention.

Two of the three mages occupying the conference room were ones I'd been expecting. White-haired Bahamus, sitting at the table, looked calm and comfortable, and Talisid, balding and unobtrusive, stood a little way off to the side. It was the third mage who made me stop and stare. I'd had time to check the futures, but the thing about divination is that you never have the time to check *everything*. So you take shortcuts. In this case I'd confirmed that it really was Talisid who'd sent the message, and I'd checked the futures for any sign of danger. But while I'd confirmed that Talisid would be there, I hadn't checked to see who *else* would be there, and the mage sitting at the end of the table watching us enter was one of the last I'd expected.

Maradok is a mage with straw-coloured hair and a long, mournful-looking face. He could be an English civil servant, if you don't look too closely at his eyes. I'd seen him off and on in briefings over the past few months, and our relationship had been cool, for good reason. I looked at Talisid. 'What is he doing here?'

'I was about to ask the same with regard to the healer,'

Maradok said. 'I was under the impression this was a secure briefing.'

'Anne is here because she's my aide and because I trust her,' I said coldly. 'Neither of which applies to you.'

Talisid coughed. 'Perhaps some introductions are in order.'

'No, no, I think we all know exactly who everyone else is,' I said. 'What I'd like to know is why you called me here using what was *supposed* to be our secure contact method to meet someone who's tried to have me assassinated.'

'And I would like to know why an ex-Dark apprentice with no security clearance is accompanying him,' Maradok replied.

Bahamus lifted a hand. 'Enough.'

Maradok is from Council intelligence, and this was the second time we'd crossed paths. The first time had been a year and a half ago, when he'd sent a team of Light mages to kill me in my sleep. That attack was the reason that I was living in the Hollow now, as well as the reason that Luna was currently running the Arcana Emporium instead of me. When I'd called him on his actions, Maradok had told me that he'd done it because long-range divinations had predicted that I was going to be instrumental in aiding Richard's rise to power. It hadn't convinced me, to put it mildly, and nothing in the intervening months had made me like him any more.

'Perhaps we should start at the beginning,' Bahamus said. 'Verus, Anne, would you care to take a seat?'

With misgivings I pulled out a chair, picking the leftmost place at the table so that I could watch Bahamus and Maradok at the same time. 'I believe all of you have met in person with the exception of Mage Anne Walker,'

Bahamus said. 'Mage Walker, these are Mages Talisid and Maradok. Both work for the Council in an advisory capacity.'

He means they're both Council intelligence, I voiced silently to Anne. *They work for the Guardians, which means they report to him but also to Sal Sarque.*

Isn't that the same guy who sent that fire mage who burned me nearly to death? Anne asked.

Yes.

Great.

'It's a pleasure to meet you at last,' Talisid said courteously. 'Verus has spoken very well of you.'

'Thank you,' Anne said in her soft voice. 'That's very kind. Mage Maradok, it's a pleasure to meet you too.'

Maradok inclined his head. 'Likewise.'

He's looking at me like he's a snake and I'm a bird he's deciding whether he wants to eat, Anne voiced silently.

Oh, don't worry. I'm pretty sure that's how he sees everyone.

'Now that that's out of the way,' Bahamus said, 'we have a matter of some importance to discuss. From the fact that your aide is here, I assume you are willing to take responsibility for bringing her in on this.'

'That would be correct.'

'I would like it noted for the record that I consider her a security risk,' Maradok said. There was no heat in his voice; he could have been talking about the weather.

'Your reservations are noted,' Bahamus said. 'Is there anything else?'

Maradok nodded. 'The decision is of course yours.'

Does this guy have something specific against me? Anne asked.

I think if he really had a problem with you, he'd be making more noise. This sounds more like him covering himself in case things go wrong.

'To business then,' Bahamus said. 'Have you been following the progress of the case against Morden?'

The change of subject caught me slightly by surprise, but only slightly. I'd had a feeling this would come up. 'I'm familiar with it.'

'You're aware of the current state of proceedings?'

'To the best of my knowledge, there hasn't *been* very much proceeding,' I said. 'The indictment was issued last year, and Morden pleaded not guilty. He made his first appearance in court at the end of the winter.' That had been a big deal, publicity-wise – having a member of the Light Council in court had drawn quite a crowd. 'But since then, as far as I'm aware, very little has happened. The prosecution asked for more time for their inquiry, which was granted, and that's been about it. There's some talk about choice of representatives, but everything seems to have stalled.'

'Have you spoken with Morden about this?' Talisid asked.

'No.'

'Why not?' Bahamus asked.

'Because I don't have any particular interest in helping him,' I said. 'As I'm sure you're aware, I didn't become Morden's aide voluntarily. Anne and I were coerced into our positions, and once Morden was arrested, we were able to distance ourselves. I don't see any particular reason to reopen our relationship.'

I could feel the eyes of all three men upon me, and I schooled my face to stillness. I was fairly sure that they'd been listening very closely to my choice of words there, trying to decide whether they could trust me. Oddly enough, while I've had to conceal things from the Council before, this was one time where I was being completely honest. *Why are they asking about Morden all of a sudden?* Anne asked silently.

Test of loyalties, I suspect. I wondered whether the men in the room with me actually believed that I'd been an unwilling servant to Morden, or whether they just saw me as a rat jumping off a sinking ship. Talisid probably believed the former; Maradok the latter. I wasn't sure about Bahamus.

'And has Morden contacted you?' Bahamus asked.

'No,' I said. 'Forgive me, Councillor, but I believe these are all statements I've made already. Is there something you're working towards?'

'As you say, the case against Morden has not proceeded quickly,' Bahamus said. 'While there are procedural issues to work through, the greater reason for the delay is a question of strategy. To put it simply, the Council has to decide what to do.'

'I was under the impression that there was no strategy to decide upon,' I said, keeping my voice carefully neutral. 'Every time it's come up in the Council, official policy has been unanimous.'

'When I say the Council has yet to decide,' Bahamus said, 'I mean the Senior Council. The circle of people brought in on it has been very small.'

I didn't ask why, if it was so secret, Talisid and Maradok knew about it when I didn't. I already knew the answer: I might be on the Junior Council, but I was still an outsider. 'Then if the Senior Council has been discussing this in closed session, what decision have they reached?'

'That has been a matter of some debate,' Bahamus said. 'At present, we are considering two possible courses of action. The first possibility is simply to proceed with the trial and press for the strictest possible penalty. Morden has committed treason and is an accessory to murder. He will be tried, found guilty and sentenced to death.'

I nodded. It was what I – and pretty much everyone else – had been expecting.

'This course of action, however, comes with drawbacks,' Bahamus said. 'For one thing, killing Morden, no matter how personally satisfying it might be, will do very little to improve our strategic position. Right now, the core of the effective opposition to the Light Council among the Dark mages of Britain is Mage Drakh and his cabal. While Morden may have functioned as a front for Drakh, he has done very little to contribute to those actions of Drakh which concern us most seriously. If Morden is removed, Drakh's organisation will survive, and if anything may actually be strengthened in the process. Morden has been clear that he intends to plead his innocence at the trial. Regardless of what evidence we bring before the judge, many Dark and independent mages will discount it. As a result, we risk making Morden a martyr, and in doing so, eliminate any hope of a negotiated settlement. The militants among the Dark mages will use Morden's rise and fall as proof that attempting to work with the Council, and work within the system, is hopeless.'

I raised my eyebrows. That was something that hadn't occurred to me – and something I wouldn't have thought a Senior Councillor would have thought of either. Usually they're so committed to the Light-mage point of view that they're quite unable to see how their actions come across to anyone else. *I guess you don't get onto the Senior Council by being stupid.* 'That does seem like a valid concern,' I said. 'Of course, you could argue that given the general attitude and beliefs of Dark mages, hoping for a negotiated settlement via peaceful means is naïve.'

'Possibly,' Bahamus said. 'But we have to take the long view. Ultimately, this period of tension *will* settle down into some kind of arrangement, whether explicit or implicit, and at present, Morden is effectively the figurehead of all Dark mages in Britain. It will be much harder to negotiate any kind of agreement if he is dead.'

I remembered my conversation with Lucian this morning, and how I'd been thinking about the problems of having no lines of communication. Apparently I wasn't the only one aware of the issue. 'Am I right in thinking that the Council might also be reluctant to set the precedent of executing one of its own members at all?'

'There is some truth to that, yes.'

I nodded. Rulers don't like turning on their own if they can avoid it. It gives the common folk ideas. 'I'm assuming you wouldn't be telling me this unless you were considering an alternative.'

'Which brings us to the second possible course of action,' Bahamus said. 'It is clear that the primary motivating force behind the attack on the Vault was Mage Drakh. Under this plan, we would instead focus on him.'

'What would you do, raid his mansion?' I asked. 'I was under the impression that the Keepers had looked into that already.'

'Indeed,' Bahamus said. 'Their conclusion was that to have any realistic chance of capturing Drakh, the attempt would require an inside man.'

Alarm bells went off in my head, and I lifted both my hands. 'Oh no,' I said. 'Not this again. I have done that particular trick *far* too many times by now. Everyone on Richard's side of the fence has had more than enough time to figure out that I was working for you guys during the attack on the Vault, and I'm pretty sure that if I even got *near* them, they'd—'

Bahamus raised one hand. 'Calm down, Verus. As you say, your allegiance is known. You were never considered as a possibility.'

'Okay.' I let out a breath in relief. 'Then if it's not me you're considering . . . ?'

Bahamus simply looked at me.

'Wait. *Morden?*'

'He is the most natural choice, wouldn't you say?'

'You're hoping to get *Morden* to betray *Richard?*'

'From what you've told us, and from all we've been able to discover, Mage Drakh is the undisputed ruler of his cabal,' Talisid said. 'The only two with the influence to make requests of him are Morden and Vihaela. Of the two, Morden seems the best choice for several reasons.'

'I'm not arguing with that, but . . . what possible motivation would Morden have to help?'

'For one, the fact that we have him under arrest,' Talisid said. 'For another, the fact that if he chooses not to cooperate, we will regretfully have to revert to our initial plan. Namely, his execution.'

'And if he says yes, then what?' I said. 'He gets to retake his seat on the Council as though nothing happened?'

'No,' Bahamus said. 'Regardless of any mitigating factors, Morden is clearly guilty of his crimes. He will be removed from the Council, one way or another. However, if he cooperates, he will keep his life and his freedom. And the ruling that keeps one seat of the Junior Council open to Dark mages will be allowed to stand. His legacy – if you can call it that – will live on.'

Something about Bahamus's last words made me look up. The older mage was looking at me steadily. 'The seat will still be for Dark mages,' I repeated.

'Under the circumstances, I would prefer it should the seat remain in the hands of someone whose loyalty had been established. I am certain I could persuade a majority of the Senior Council to share this view.'

I sat quite still. *Was he saying . . . ?*

Is he bribing you? Anne asked.

It sounds like it, doesn't it? 'I . . . see.'

'Can we count on your cooperation in this matter?' Bahamus asked.

'I don't have any objection in principle,' I said slowly. 'However, I have to wonder what it is that you're hoping for me to contribute.'

'To start with, you would be the one conducting the negotiations with Morden,' Bahamus said. 'Given your extensive history with him, you would seem to be the most qualified.'

'So I'm the one who gets to tell him to turn Richard in or we chop his head off?'

'Essentially.'

'Okay,' I said. 'Assuming he agrees to the terms, what's the next step? I mean, he can't exactly hand you Richard while sitting in a cell. Are you going to let him out on bail?'

'No,' Talisid said. 'He would, to put it mildly, be considered a flight risk. And I seriously doubt any of our usual security measures could keep him in the country should he be set free. However, he still has followers. We expect him to work through them or similar intermediaries.'

And no prizes for guessing who's going to be the go-between. Still, it's not as though I was expecting to get this for nothing . . .

'I realise that this is short notice,' Bahamus said, 'but I'm afraid that we will need an answer from you now.'

I looked back at the three men in front of me. All three were watching me closely, though with subtly different shades of expression. I already knew that this was not a do-it-or-else offer — if I said no, Anne and I would be walking out. But with deals like this, you don't get take-backs. I was going to have to pick a side immediately.

I thought quickly and made my decision.

5

Why did you say yes? Anne asked.

We were walking back up through the tunnels of the War Rooms, the temperature slowly rising as we drew closer to the surface. *Do you think I shouldn't have?* I asked.

Not exactly, Anne said slowly. *But isn't it going to be dangerous?*

Probably, I said. *But if I said no, they'd just find someone else. This way at least I get to stay in the loop. And honestly, I think I've got a better chance of dealing with Morden than some random Council functionary.*

We passed out of a storage wing and took a spiral staircase upwards, our footsteps echoing off the stone. *Besides*, I said, *I think what Bahamus was saying is basically right. Executing Morden isn't going to solve any of their problems unless they get Richard as well. And Morden might be able to do that.*

Might?

Richard's pretty good at seeing things coming, I admitted. *Honestly, even if they do turn Morden, I wouldn't give the plan more than a fifty-fifty chance at best. Most likely result is that they recover a few more imbued items and do his organisation a bit of damage, but nothing fatal.*

We walked a little way further in silence. *That isn't what's really bothering you though, is it?* Anne asked.

I nodded. *The way Morden was arrested.*

What about it?

You remember how that happened? I said. *The Keepers sent a*

strike team to Morden's mansion. And Morden gave himself up.
No resistance, no escape attempts. He just let them arrest him.

Okay . . .

Why? I asked. *If he'd wanted to run, he could have. And if*
he'd wanted to fight, he could have given the Keepers a pretty
hard time of it. He didn't do either.

You think he wanted to be arrested?

Maybe, but that doesn't make much sense either. It's not as
though he's accomplishing anything sitting in that cell. Anyway,
I don't think we can make much of a guess at his motives. What's
really bothering me is something different. This offer is designed
to appeal to Morden's self-interest. Do what the Council says, or
they'll kill you. Right?

Right.

But by letting himself be arrested, he's put himself in danger
already. I mean, if the Council had wanted his trial done, they
could have finished it and had him executed already. Or he could
have been killed 'resisting arrest'. Not like it's the first time that
has happened. So letting them arrest him points to one of two
things. Either he's got some kind of trump card that he's very
confident is going to get him out of jail . . . or he believes enough
in what he's doing that he's willing to put his life on the line to
do it.

Anne frowned, thinking. *I've never really thought about*
what Morden believes in. Do you really think he could be that
dedicated?

I don't know, I said. *Doesn't exactly seem to fit with the Dark*
mind-set. But if it is, then this whole 'offer you can't refuse' is
going to be a lot less convincing than Bahamus and Maradok
are hoping it'll be.

Are you going to go see him?

Not much point putting it off. Sort out those meetings with the

Keepers and with Druss, then it'll be time to look up visiting hours.

One of the differences between magical and mundane society: there are a lot fewer prisons.

The habit of dealing with lawbreakers by sticking them in a confined space for a long time is pretty new, historically speaking – it only really caught on in a big way a couple of centuries ago, and so far the Light Councils of the world haven't chosen to follow suit. For one thing, it's a lot trickier to imprison a mage than a normal. While there are ways to make it harder for a mage to use their magic, it's time-consuming, takes a lot of resources and isn't guaranteed to work. Doing it on a large scale for a significant fraction of the magical population would be prohibitively expensive . . . or at least that's what the Council says. My personal suspicion is that it also has a lot to do with the Council lacking the religious and moral beliefs that brought the mundane world's prison reform movement about in the first place. Either way, if you commit a crime against the Council, you won't generally be thrown in prison. Minor offences are punishable by fines or service; major ones usually get the death penalty, and there isn't much in between.

Every now and again, though, the Council does need to confine someone, either because neither a fine nor execution is an option, or (more often) because they simply haven't decided what to do with them yet. And that's why they have San Vittore.

'Are you carrying on your person any one-shot items, focus items, imbued items or magical items of any sort?' the stone-faced guard asked me.

'No.'

'Do you have on your person any kind of blade or edged weapon, any kind of firearm or projectile weapon, any kind of explosive device or anything that could be assembled into an explosive device?'

'No.'

'Are you carrying any drugs or drug-related items or paraphernalia, any flammable or corrosive liquids, any alcohol in any form, any poisonous or infectious materials such as pesticides, insecticides, cyanides, laboratory specimens or bacterial cultures, and are you carrying any gas or pressure containers including but not limited to aerosols, carbon dioxide cartridges, oxygen tanks, Mace, pepper spray or liquid nitrogen?'

I looked at the guard with raised eyebrows. 'Oxygen tanks?'

'Are you carrying any of the listed items?'

'No, I keep those in my other coat.'

'Are you carrying any cameras or other photographic devices, mobile telephones or other communication devices, laptop computers, tablet computers, personal computers, tape recorders, digital recorders, digital music players, CD players, DVD players or anything that can record, project or store digital information in any way?'

'You know that nobody actually uses CD players any more, right?'

'Are—'

'—you carrying any of the listed items, I know,' I said with a sigh. 'The answer is still no. I already had all these questions asked by the guy who scanned me.'

'Are you aware that bringing any of the items listed, or any other item that can facilitate an escape in any way, whether knowingly or unknowingly, will be considered a breach of the First Clause of the Concord and punishable to the fullest extent of the law?'

'Yes,' I said. 'Can we go now?'

The guard pushed a set of forms across the table. 'Read and sign, then follow me. You are not to travel anywhere unaccompanied in this facility under any circumstances. Attempting to do so will result in immediate termination of your visit and prosecution to the fullest extent of the law.'

For someone who uses long words, this guy has a really limited vocabulary. I scanned the forms, scribbled my signature in two places and dated it. 'Let's get on with it.'

The guard examined the signature, put the forms away in a drawer, then got to his feet and headed towards the door at the back of the room. I followed.

We came out into a corridor of grey stone, the floor worn smooth from years of use. San Vittore is divided into wings, stretching out from a single central node, and through the narrow windows to the left and right I could see other corridors receding into the distance. The corridors were walled in grey, with red tiles on the roof. Beyond the corridors, both above and below, was nothingness, a black void with barely visible lines of purple and red spidering through the darkness in a strange, disturbing way that made your eyes ache if you stared at them for too long. I didn't know what would happen if you stepped off the edge into that darkness, and I didn't really want to find out.

All in all, while San Vittore did look like a fortress, it didn't look like the old Middle Ages kind — instead the design made me think more of the big low-slung polygon-shaped fortifications that had evolved in Europe during the age of gunpowder. It definitely didn't look like a castle rising out of the haze, which suggested that Anne's dream had been just that.

We passed through a guard post, followed by another checkpoint, this one staffed by mantis golems, their silver and gold eyes swivelling to watch us as we passed. The more we walked, the more I was struck just by how over the top the security here was. Even getting in and out of the bubble realm was fantastically difficult – maybe a dedicated gate magic specialist might have been able to figure out a method of entry other than the Council facility that held the linking portal, but I couldn't – and once you were inside, your problems would only multiply. Even with all Morden's power, I couldn't see him escaping.

Which, again, raised the question of why he'd allowed himself to be taken here. Well, I would be meeting him face to face soon enough. But I still would have felt a lot more comfortable knowing what he was really up to.

The guard stopped in front of a solid metal door. 'You have forty-five minutes,' he told me. 'Inner and outer doors won't open if there are any unauthorised presences in the airlock. Understand?'

I nodded. I didn't bother to ask if we'd be watched while I was inside: I already knew the answer would be yes. The door swung open with a hiss of hydraulics and I stepped inside into an airlock-style room, empty stone with metal doors ahead and behind. The outer door closed behind me.

As I stood in the airlock, I was uncomfortably aware of just how easy it would be for the guards to forgo letting me out. Yes, this prison was supposed to be for Morden, but now that I was inside, it would stop me just as easily. I'd scanned the futures extensively before coming (and taken precautions just in case) and everything I'd done or seen had indicated that there was no risk, but all the same, I couldn't help but feel uneasy. Like all diviners, my first line of defence against any threat is manoeuvre, and being unable to withdraw from a position makes me uncomfortable. With hindsight, that might have been one of the reasons I'd never visited Morden until now.

But let's be honest, a much bigger reason is the little fact that you were one of the people who got him sent here. Sure, he might not take it personally. But if it were me, I'm pretty sure I would.

My thoughts were cut off by the hiss of the inner door. I straightened and walked through.

For a cell in solitary confinement in a maximum security prison in a bubble realm floating in the void, Morden's quarters weren't bad. Okay, so there were no windows or phones or computers, and as far as I could see the only source of entertainment was a half-stocked bookcase, but the floor had a carpet and the bed looked fairly comfortable. I'd been half-expecting a dungeon with bars and chains, but apparently Morden's rank still earned him a decent living space.

Morden was sitting behind a table, and he'd obviously been expecting me. The Dark mage looked a little thinner than when I'd seen him last, the angles of his face more defined. The attitude of confidence didn't change though – as I entered, he nodded to me in a companionable way that gave no hint that he was a prisoner. I'd never been quite sure whether that ever-present confidence of Morden's was fake, a performance to impress people, or whether he really was just that sure of himself.

'Verus,' Morden said. 'I was wondering when you'd stop by. Why don't you take a seat?'

I hid a smile. Even here, he was still acting as though he were in command. 'Thank you.' As I walked over, I noticed a gold chain hanging from the bookcase behind Morden. It was placed in such a way that anyone entering the room would see it.

Morden cocked his head at me. 'Wondering when that will be yours?'

'I know exactly when that will be mine,' I said dryly. 'When I'm an actual member of the Council instead of your representative, which seems unlikely ever to happen.'

'Really?'

I looked back at Morden, eyebrows slightly raised. I didn't see any need to disclose the details of Talisid's offer. *And I know why you have that thing hanging there too. It's a reminder that until sentence is pronounced, you're still a member of the Council, with all that implies. But right now you're the one in the weaker position, not me.*

'So,' Morden said. 'To what do I owe the pleasure?'

'Well,' I said. 'Odd as it may sound, I was wondering if you had any advice.'

'Advice?'

'I've been filling in for you in your position for more than half a year now,' I said. 'And honestly? I'm wondering how you lasted as long as you did. Not a week goes by where there isn't some plot to kill me or unseat me. How did you manage to survive when so many of the Light mages hated you so much?'

'Ah.' Morden settled back in his chair more comfortably. 'That's really no great mystery. The fact is, the majority of the Council mages don't hate me. Or you, for that matter.'

'Could have fooled me.'

'Oh, I'm not saying they wouldn't happily unseat you,'

Morden said. 'But they'd do that to anyone if they thought it was to their advantage. You're right that they have some personal animosity, but it's not you they have a problem with, it's the disruption you represent.' Morden steepled his fingers, looking rather like a professor explaining a point to a student. 'The key to understanding the Council is to realise that the majority of its mages don't believe in anything greater than themselves. They might pay lip service to the Council's official purpose, but they don't have any deep-seated loyalty. So while they might protest the presence of a Dark mage, it's not out of any particular moral indignation. It's simply because you're pushing your way into their private club.'

'Seems as though you got a little more hostility than would be explained by just that.'

'Only because I was the first. If there's one thing the Council can agree on, it's that their power and privileges shouldn't go to anyone else.' Morden shrugged. 'But that kind of resistance is temporary. Given a few years, it should fade.'

I noticed that he said *should fade* instead of *would have faded*. Apparently he wasn't ready to put it in the past tense. 'I don't think the Guardians and the Crusaders are just temporary resistance.'

'The Guardian ideology was always going to be the major stumbling block in Dark–Light integration.'

'And Levistus?' I said. I'd started this conversation as an icebreaker, but I was curious now. 'You think that's what's driving him?'

'Levistus is an interesting case,' Morden said. 'He's the type of person who can only exist once a structure has grown old enough and influential enough that people genuinely cannot conceive of a world beyond it. It's no surprise that he rose to the Council: his entire world *is* the Council. That's not to say he's stupid or parochial, but it would simply never occur to him that the centre of Britain could ever be anything other than the Light Council and the mages who control it. Most organisations end up run by people like him, once the creators and the zealots have died off.'

'Hmm,' I said. I looked at Morden speculatively. 'If that's what they believe in, what about you?'

Morden smiled. 'Personal questions, now? I'm flattered by your interest. But in any case, I think that should explain how I was able to gain this position.'

'To be honest, I'm a little surprised,' I said. 'I was expecting an answer that was more . . . tactical.'

'You were expecting something to do with White Rose?' Morden asked. 'Oh, that made things easier, but all it really did was accelerate things. Do you think any amount of secrets could have enabled me to buy my way onto the Council if they'd *really* been determined to stop me? If they'd simply stood together and declared that they were not admitting a Dark mage, no matter what, then that would have been the end of it. But they were more concerned with their own individual self-interest.'

'Hmm,' I said. Something about what Morden was saying seemed backwards. I'm used to thinking of *Dark* mages as the self-interested ones. Could that have been the real reason that Morden had been able to succeed? Because the Council had reached the point where they weren't different enough from their enemies? 'So you're saying the Council isn't so averse to dealing with Dark mages after all.'

'They never have been,' Morden said. 'It's the disorgan-isation of the Dark mages that the Council dislike, not their ethics. They can't negotiate with them as a group, because there's no binding representative. Once I explained to them that by including me on the Council they would *have* that representative . . .' Morden shrugged. 'Well.'

'Funny you should mention the subject of the Council negotiating.'

'Yes, I rather suspected that might be why you were here.' Morden rested his chin on his hands. 'So what message does the Council have for me today?'

'You know what the sentence is for your charge,' I said, watching Morden carefully. His eyes didn't flicker. 'It probably won't surprise you that a good number of the Council would be delighted to see you dead.'

'But?'

'But as you say, some of them do see that having a single Dark representative to negotiate with is more beneficial than having a corpse.'

Morden nodded. 'I assume that this generosity does not come without a price.'

'The problem from their point of view is that in everyone's eyes you clearly committed the crimes you're charged with,' I said. 'So they can't exactly just pardon you.'

'What did they have in mind instead?'

I'd been looking into the futures in which I broached the subject, probing for how Morden would respond. It wasn't working. Divination isn't much help against someone like Morden – he's too self-controlled. 'They want to use you to catch a bigger fish,' I said, and stopped. We both knew there was only one 'bigger fish' that I could mean.

Morden nodded. 'I see.'

'You don't seem very surprised.'

'It was always one of the logical paths for them to take,'

Morden said. 'I assume the quid pro quo is that I'm allowed to live?'

'That's the long and the short of it.'

'Let me guess,' Morden said. 'Proceedings are to be halted?'

I nodded.

'Have you thought through the implications?'

'Yes,' I said. 'Halting proceedings isn't the same as finding you not guilty. A not guilty verdict ends the case. Halting proceedings just suspends it. Which means they can hold it over your head in the future. It's a way of keeping you on a leash.'

'You aren't selling it very hard.'

I shrugged. 'It's nothing you couldn't figure out yourself.'

'There is a second implication you may not have considered,' Morden said. 'If I do indeed help the Council to catch this "bigger fish", everyone will know about it, especially once I'm released without charges. Which will severely affect my credibility among Britain's Dark mages. I'll still be their representative, but they will no longer trust me, which will leave me with no one to turn to but the Council itself.'

I nodded. The Council wanted a Dark representative, but they wanted him defanged. 'That seems accurate.'

'So what would you advise?'

'In your position?' I said. 'It doesn't seem to me as though you have very much choice but to accept, given the alternative. It'll cause problems, but you can solve problems. You can't solve being dead.'

'And what if I decide I might be willing to die for my cause?' Morden asked. 'What's the Council's plan then?'

I paused. Morden was looking at me, and there was no

visible expression on his face. 'Is that really true?' I asked. 'Do you want to become a martyr for this?'

Morden looked back at me for a long moment, then suddenly smiled. 'No.'

I let out a breath I hadn't realised I was holding, then wondered, only then, why I'd been so scared. *It's not as though he can do anything. Is it?* 'So you're going for the stay-alive option.'

'I'm in no particular hurry to die,' Morden said. 'So, do the Council have any ideas on how I'm supposed to catch Drakh for them? Somehow I doubt they're planning to let me out on bail.'

'They aren't terribly keen on that idea, no.'

'Then what exactly am I supposed to be doing from inside here?'

'They suggested that you could contact Richard.'

'Hand-delivered via a Council agent, no doubt,' Morden said dryly. 'Are they really that stupid?'

'Not quite,' I said. Actually, that *had* been their first suggestion. I'd had to explain to them that Richard might be just a tiny bit suspicious of a message that the Council had finally 'allowed' Morden to send after nine months of solitary confinement. 'Do you have any direct way of getting in touch with him?'

'If I had, do you think I'd be here?'

'A more realistic plan is working through an intermediary,' I said. 'Someone who'd follow your orders and is sufficiently close to Richard. I was wondering if you had any suggestions.'

'Suggestions?' Morden raised an eyebrow. 'There's really only one person who falls into both of those groups.'

I sighed. 'I was afraid you'd say that.'

'But you were hoping I might point you to someone else?' Morden shook his head. 'It's Onyx or no one.'

I grimaced. It was what I'd been expecting to hear, but I still wasn't happy about it.

We talked for a little while longer, discussing approaches. I was surprised by how easy it was. By the summer of last year, Morden and I had become . . . well, we hadn't been even remotely close to *friends*, but we'd had an efficient working relationship. That had been based on my acceptance of his authority, so I hadn't expected it to last, but oddly enough, it had. We just fell back into the old patterns, except this time with me taking the lead. And instead of arguing or trying to assert dominance, Morden went along with it.

'I'm a little surprised with how you're taking all of this,' I said once we'd finished our arrangements.

'How do you mean?'

'Last year, you were on the Light Council and one of the most powerful Dark mages in Britain,' I said. 'Now you're imprisoned and awaiting trial. I was expecting you to be a little more . . . resentful.'

'Resentment is an unproductive emotion,' Morden said. 'Our relationship was built on realities of power.'

I gave Morden a sceptical look. 'You really don't hold a grudge?'

'Not particularly.'

I met Morden's eyes. He didn't look angry, but I couldn't help wonder what his true feelings were. Would I be so calm in his position? 'Somehow I don't think Onyx is going to be so accepting.'

'Ah yes,' Morden said. 'I'll admit that Onyx has not developed as I had hoped.'

'You really thought he was ever going to go any other way?'

'I have known him significantly longer than you,' Morden said. 'When I first took Onyx on, I judged him to have potential. Unfortunately power can be a discouragement to growth, and he's had difficulty adapting. I'd rather hoped that his association with you might have inspired him to look beyond his current set of problem-solving tools, but he seems to have decided that he's learned all he needs to know.'

'Which is a nice way of saying that he deals with anything in his way by smashing it,' I said sourly. 'And this is the guy you want me to liaise with.'

'The Council are hardly going to do you favours for free.'

I glanced up sharply. Morden was looking at me inquiringly. *Does he know what Bahamus offered? Or was that just a guess?* 'Well.' I rose to my feet. 'I suppose I've got a job to do.'

'You do indeed,' Morden said with a nod. 'Oh, and watch your back.'

'Watch it for what?'

'I'm sure that not everyone on the Council is happy with the thought of my trial being cancelled,' Morden said. 'Some of them might find it . . . convenient, shall we say, if any negotiations were disrupted? And if that disruption happened to negatively affect a certain Junior Council member whom they also had little love for, that would be a case of two birds with one stone.' He smiled slightly. 'As I said. Watch your back.'

I looked back at Morden, then left. I felt the Dark mage watching me go.

6

It was two days later.

The communicator nestled in my ear chimed. 'Hi, Alex,' Luna's voice said. 'You free?'

'For a little bit,' I told her. 'What's the news?'

It was 10.30 p.m., and I was in Shepherd's Bush, perched on the roof of a block of flats in an apartment complex. The roof was bare of shelter, and a wind was blasting across it from east to west, blowing my hair into my eyes and doing its best to send my coat flying up into the night sky. Even on a summer night like this, it wasn't a comfortable place; in winter it would be horrible. But what the roof lacked in comfort, it made up for in elevation, and I had an excellent view down over the fence to the industrial park next door . . . and to the shapes hiding in the shadows within.

'I've heard back from Stephen,' Luna said. 'You remember that adept I was telling you about? Well, he finally got me an invite. We're going out for drinks tomorrow night.'

'That sounds more like a date than a recruitment.'

'Give me some credit,' Luna said. 'Yeah, he tried to make it sound like that, but it's definitely a sounding-out. For one thing, there are going to be other people there, and from the sound of it they know more than Stephen does.'

'If they know more, isn't there a chance they're going to recognise you?'

'I don't advertise that I'm a journeyman, you know,'

Luna said. 'What, did you think I'd hung up a sign behind the counter? It's like you said, there isn't much communication between adepts and the Council. They're not going to know every mage by name, much less some mage's apprentice. As far as they know, I'm just another adept.'

'Mm,' I said dubiously. It sounded sketchy to me. Yes, it wasn't likely that a random group of adepts would be particularly up to date on Luna's status regarding the Council. But Luna was my apprentice, and I wasn't exactly a nobody any more. If these guys really did see themselves as members of a resistance group, then they'd probably be going to at least some effort to check out potential recruits, and if they did that, it wouldn't take much digging for them to find out who Luna really was. In which case, Luna might find herself a much less welcome guest than she'd been expecting.

On the other hand, Luna's pretty capable of taking care of herself these days, and she's comfortable with – and able to take advantage of – a higher level of risk than would be the case for me. 'Make sure you have some backup, okay?'

'Yes, Mum,' Luna said. 'So how's your stakeout going?'

'Well, there's good news and bad news,' I said. 'Good news is that I'm pretty sure I've found Cinder. Bad news is that apparently I'm not the only interested party.'

'I know this is a crazy thought,' Luna said, 'but maybe if you want to talk to Cinder, you could just call him?'

'Believe it or not, that did occur to me,' I said. 'I've got an emergency contact that I was using last year. When I tried it, I got "the number you have dialled has not been recognised". And when I tried to trace him, I ended up at a place in Bethnal Green that by a funny coincidence just happened to have burned down last month.'

'Think that might be something to do with the guys you're looking at right now?'

'Let's just say I'm getting the feeling that I'm not the only one having trouble with uninvited guests these days.'

'In which case he's probably not going to react that well to you turning up at his front door.'

'Probably, but I'm kind of on a clock here,' I said. 'Talisid's authorised me to contact Onyx, but he and Bahamus aren't going to wait around for ever. And if I'm going to walk into Onyx's mansion, I need an in.'

'Doesn't sound to me like where you're going is any safer, but your call,' Luna said. 'Your beacon on?'

'Yup, and Anne's standing by,' I said. I'd been tempted to bring her along, but there are diplomatic advantages to being alone. 'Feel free to hang out with her if you feel like giving me some backup.'

'You're lucky I don't have much of a social life,' Luna said. 'Just make sure to call before you get shot this time.'

'What do you mean, "this time"?'

'You heard.' The connection closed with a click. I shook my head, turned my attention back to the industrial park ahead of me, studied it for a moment longer, then jumped down to the fire escape.

Divination is handy for getting into places you're not supposed to be. I made my way across the street, up onto a low rooftop, through the razor wire and down into the industrial park without really thinking about it. Most of my attention was on the shadowy forms I'd glimpsed moving into position earlier. Without my vantage point I couldn't see them any more, but I could track them through the futures in which I encountered them. From looking at what would happen in those futures, I'd already established that they weren't friendly.

The interesting thing was that four of the presences had the solid, reactive future lines of constructs . . . and pretty simple constructs too. They were also even *more* hostile than the human members. Having constructs in the area under kill-on-sight programming strongly indicated that whoever these people were, they weren't interested in a peaceful resolution.

The bad news was that while I hadn't been detected so far, I couldn't see any realistic way to make it into the warehouse without changing that. The building had only a limited number of entrances, and all of them were within clear view of at least one observer. I'm pretty good at avoiding notice, but I can't turn invisible in the way that illusionists or radiation mages can. If I wanted to get inside, someone was going to see me.

But they don't know that I've seen them first. Let's take advantage of that.

I turned right and began working my way around the warehouse, aiming for the east side. Twice I had to stop and freeze, letting the shadows hide me as a watcher got a little too close. The night was warm and breezy, and the rushing traffic from the nearby A road hid the sounds of my footsteps. I turned a corner and down an alley. To my right was a line of garages; up ahead was a single, unmarked door.

The figure hiding in the shadows saw me instantly, and I felt violence flicker in the futures. The orange glow of the lights silhouetted me but left him hidden, and I kept to a steady pace. I passed his hiding place without slowing and came to a halt in front of the door.

I put a hand to my pocket and searched through it, taking out something and studying it with unseeing eyes. Beneath my jacket, my shoulders were tense. If this guy decided to just shoot me, I was going to have to move very fast. I was wearing my armour, but at this kind of range . . .

The futures spun, then settled. There was a very quiet whisper of movement, just barely audible over the wind, as he slipped out of the shadows and moved up. I didn't react as he stepped in behind me and lifted an arm to bring the butt of his gun down on the base of my skull.

The best way to take someone out in a fight is to catch them by surprise. The second best way is to make them think *they've* surprised *you*. As the blow fell, I spun right. The gun whistled past my ear as I kicked the man's leg out from under him. He staggered, going down to one knee, and before he could recover, my stun focus discharged into his neck. Energy flashed through him and he jerked and went limp. The gun clattered to the ground.

I picked up the pistol – it was an automatic of some kind – and engaged the safety as I studied my attacker. As I got a better look at him in the orange light, I downgraded him in my mind from 'man' to 'boy'. He couldn't have been much more than twenty, but he was wearing body armour and that gun hadn't been loaded with blanks. I didn't recognise him, but I hadn't really been expecting to.

Better not hang around. I stepped to the door and knocked, the sound echoing through the metal. My stun focus is a simple life effect: it'll put someone down, but for no more than a few minutes, five or six if you're lucky. Charging it takes a while and I didn't want to be around when this guy woke up.

Twenty seconds passed, then thirty. I knocked again, louder. I knew that the people inside could hear me, but . . .

The futures shifted and I looked ahead. *Shit.* Someone had heard something. Two people were approaching from behind the garages; worse, they were bringing one of the constructs with them. I hammered on the door more loudly. Still nothing.

No time to be subtle. I leaned in close to the door, pitching my voice to carry. 'Kyle! It's Alex Verus. I'm not with these guys. Open the door!'

I heard someone call out a question from behind. 'I know you can hear me,' I snapped at the door. 'What, you want proof it's me? Last time we met was outside Richard's mansion. Anne spotted you by your missing leg. She didn't realise it was you at first, because she wasn't around when you lost it and when Deleo and Cinder killed every single one of—'

The door jerked open and I found myself staring down the barrel of a very large revolver. The person behind the gun was in his early twenties, lean and dangerous-looking with close-cropped hair, and we stared into each other's eyes for about two seconds. Then he lowered the gun, and I darted inside and helped him slam the door.

The inside of the warehouse was dark and smelled of oil and metal. Distant shouts drifted through from outside, but Kyle ignored them as he slammed bolts across the top and bottom of the door and turned up the corridor. 'What the hell are you doing here?' he said curtly.

'I would have been just as happy to talk over the phone,' I said to Kyle's retreating back. 'Except someone doesn't answer their voicemail.'

'Sure, we'll just have a public number for our personal

phones,' Kyle shot back. 'And while we're at it, we can add a note saying "PS, please don't trace us". You been paying any attention to what's going on?'

Kyle is an adept, an ex-member of a vigilante group called the Nightstalkers who went after Deleo and me a few years back. It worked out badly and Kyle was one of only two survivors. Somehow or other, by the time I saw him next, Cinder had recruited him. I had no idea what the two of them had been up to since.

We passed through another metal door, which Kyle again bolted behind us, and out into a wider room. Fluorescent lights shone down from above, metal tables held papers and weapons and a wooden stairway led up into what looked like an attic. A heavily built man in body armour glanced up from where he was working on a gun and scowled at me. 'What the fuck are you doing here?'

Where Kyle is lean and tough, Cinder is big and tough. He's a Dark fire mage and an old enemy, now sometime ally. We don't exactly drop around for tea, but the fact that neither Cinder nor Kyle had attacked me indicated that they were still willing to treat me as more or less on their side. 'Looking for you,' I said. 'What's with the goons?'

'Pyre,' Cinder said briefly and looked at Kyle. 'How long?'

'Maybe five minutes,' Kyle said.

Cinder gave me a scowl. 'Long as you're going to stick your head in, you might as well make yourself useful. What's the count?'

'At least six humans,' I said. 'Seven counting the one I knocked out at your back door; he'll be up by now. And four constructs. They looked like the same anthroform ones that Deleo makes.'

Cinder grunted. 'In-built spells?'

'Didn't get close enough to check,' I said. 'Is there a reason you're not going out there to fry them?'

'This isn't the first time Pyre's come calling,' Kyle said. 'His new constructs are fire-resistant.'

'Ah,' I said. That was not such good news. Constructs are dumb as rocks, but hard to kill. The only really reliable way to get rid of them is with massive firepower, and I don't carry that sort of thing around. Cinder does, but if his spells weren't going to affect the things . . .

The sound of shattering glass echoed faintly through the warehouse. 'Here they come,' Kyle said.

Cinder nodded and moved to the room's main doors. Kyle turned and walked back to the one we'd entered by. Their movements looked practised, as though they didn't need to talk to know where the other was. 'Hey,' I called to Cinder.

'We're busy,' Cinder said without looking.

I sighed. *Screw it.* 'You want some help?'

'Kyle,' Cinder ordered.

I turned to see Kyle pull a gun out of thin air with a flicker of light. Kyle is a space magic adept and his particular trick is dimensional storage, pulling items into or out of a small spatial pocket that only he can reach. From what I've seen, the main thing he uses it for is weapons. 'That dinky little pistol isn't going to do shit,' Kyle told me as he set the gun down on the table.

'It's not mine,' I said, walking over. The weapon on the table looked . . . strange. The curving magazine and stubby shape made me think of a sub-machine-gun, but the magazine was huge – thicker than the gun itself – and the barrel was short and wide. A folding stock completed the weird design. 'What is it?'

'Saiga-12,' Kyle said. 'Ever used a shotgun?'

'The double-barrelled kind.'

'This is semi-auto. Safety is here, lever is here. Ten-round magazine, double-ought buckshot.' Kyle pulled out two more magazines and set them down next to the gun. 'You keep pulling the trigger, it'll keep firing, but the recoil is a bitch so aim after each shot.'

'The guy out there was wearing body armour.'

'Doesn't matter. You hit someone centre mass with this, he's not getting up any time soon.'

'And the constructs?'

'Yeah, that's the tricky bit, isn't it?' Kyle said. 'Try not to let them grab you.'

I felt a flash of fire magic from somewhere off to the left, and a fraction of a second later a hollow boom echoed through the building. 'Front door's gone,' Kyle called.

Cinder gave me an irritated look. 'Stop standing in the open.'

That sounded like good advice, so I grabbed my stolen pistol and my borrowed shotgun and moved into the cover of the stairway. As I did, I looked into the futures where I ran past Cinder. Through the double doors, into another wide open room, around a corner and— *ouch*. 'Three of them coming in,' I told Cinder quietly. 'Construct in the lead, two guys behind. They're shooting on sight.'

'So are we,' Cinder said.

The warehouse fell silent. I crouched behind the stairs, listening. Kyle was somewhere behind watching the back door, but I was focused on the futures of the people ahead of us. They were coming closer, moving more cautiously now as they spread out into the warehouse interior.

There was the quiet scuffle of a footstep from one room

over. I glanced at Cinder to see that the big man wasn't moving. He was standing just behind the wall, out of sight of anyone looking in, and he was staring at the wall as though he could see through it. From looking through the futures I could tell that more were coming.

It struck me suddenly that both of the men in this room were ones I'd met while they were in the process of either threatening to kill me or actually trying to kill me. Now I was crouched down behind them holding a semi-auto shotgun, and both of them seemed okay with that. My life is weird.

I suppose the fact that I can make deals with enemies is a big reason why I'm still alive in the first place. Still, you have to wonder why these two trust me. What are those guys waiting for, anyway? They have to know we're—

There was a shout from the direction of the other room, and Cinder's hand made a quick snapping motion. Something small and glowing shot through the door and disappeared, and there was a dull red flash and a *whoom*. Warm air rolled over me, and I heard a scream.

Shouts and gunfire sounded from the next room over. A bullet ricocheted off metal with a *clang* and went whickering somewhere over my head. I heard the *bang bang bang* of pistol fire, then it stopped.

The room was still once more. 'Give us the fucking gauntlet!' someone yelled from around the corner.

Cinder didn't move.

Heavy footsteps sounded from the next room. Cinder leaned around the corner again; I felt another spell go off, and there was a *whuff* sound. Smoke started to seep in through the doors, and I heard coughing and choking.

There was the echoing *crump* of an explosive from the

other side of the room, and I looked around to see Kyle drop something and pull out a gun that looked like a king-size version of my shotgun with a drum magazine. He slid open a hidden gun port in the door and started firing through it with a *chunk-chunk-chunk*.

I couldn't see anything to shoot at, and I was less than confident of accomplishing much if I could, so I looked ahead. It's hard to see far in combat, but I did my best, skipping over the details of the fighting to the pale, threadlike futures beyond. Cinder and Kyle looked all right – probably – but I caught a ghostly image of someone attacking me. *How? If they're not getting past . . . oh shit.* 'Cinder!' I called. 'They're coming in from upstairs!'

'You've got a gun, haven't you?' Cinder said without turning.

'I knew you'd say that,' I muttered, and ran up the stairs.

The sounds of battle echoed from behind me, the booms of Cinder's fire spells overlaid by the heavy report of Kyle's shotgun. The stairs came up into a narrow corridor; there were doors on either side, but my divination told me that the one on the end was the one I wanted and I darted through.

The room looked like someone had tried to convert an old office into a bedroom but hadn't done much other than throw a mattress on the floor and call it a day. Faded carpet lined the floor, and clothes were piled half in and half out of a suitcase. The only furniture was a tiny table with a handgun and a small framed picture, but all my attention was on the window at the far end. It was open, and a figure was just in the process of climbing through. It was man-shaped, wearing ill-fitting clothes, and its head came up to stare at me with blank eyes as I lifted my newly acquired weapon and fired.

Kyle had been right about the recoil. The shotgun kicked back into my shoulder; I hadn't taken a proper stance and the flicker of pain told me I was going to have a bruise. I *had* taken time to aim, and the shotgun blast caught the construct right in the chest. It staggered, and I put a second shot into its torso that sent it falling out the window.

It would have been nice if that fall had been all the way to ground level, but I already knew that the window led straight out onto a roof. Worse, the construct wasn't alone. I advanced cautiously, picking my way around the mattress; I didn't make it even halfway there when I heard gunshots and shards of glass pattered to the floor. I changed direction, crossing the mattress and coming to a stop before I showed myself. Whoever was controlling that construct, they hadn't changed its orders, which meant that it was going to be trying to get in again right about . . . *now*.

The construct reappeared in the window. Now that I was close I could see the ways in which its disguise wasn't quite perfect: the features were slightly off, as though made by a sculptor who didn't know his trade, and the movements stiff and clumsy. A bloodless hole in the neck marked where one of the pellets had gone high, and as the eyes locked onto me it reached out for my head.

I'd had time to brace properly this time, and I fired three times into the construct's face from less than two feet away. The shotgun made a roaring *phoom-phoom-phoom*, and the thing's face disintegrated, sending it sprawling back onto the roof.

More gunfire came from out in the darkness, and I ducked as the window shattered, glass raining around me. From looking into the futures where I poked my head out, I could see that the construct was lying on the rooftop, and this time I'd managed to do some real damage. Its face was a ruined mess: one eye had been mangled completely and the other was staring blankly up at the sky. I wasn't naïve enough to think I'd destroyed it, but I had to give Kyle credit. This was going *much* better than the last time I'd tried shooting a construct.

There was a moment's pause. I could hear shouting from below, but all my attention was on my battle up here. The construct wasn't getting up, at least not yet. I looked ahead to see what would happen if I moved out on the roof and to the right. The gunshots had come from straight ahead, so there might be a chance to . . .

Dammit. There were two people out there, not one. The second guy was hiding to my right, around the corner of the building, ready to fire. I didn't fancy my chances of advancing against both of them.

But then, I didn't need to. These guys didn't seem to have anything heavier than the constructs, which meant that Cinder ought to wipe them out if they got close. I only needed to hold my position.

The futures shifted. I looked ahead and . . . *oh.* I was about to be blown apart in fifteen seconds. I tapped the wall to check . . . *good, bricks. That should be strong enough.* I placed the shotgun on the floor, stood up, waited, then stuck my hand out.

The grenade came sailing through the broken window and I caught it one-handed, tossed it back out next to where the construct was lying, then dropped.

The explosion made my ears ring. Shrapnel pockmarked the ceiling, but the grenade fragments that would have hit me were stopped by the wall at my back.

I kept still and waited, looking ahead to see what would

happen next. The interesting question was whether the other guy understood what had just happened. I suspected he probably hadn't. When throwing a grenade, there's something of an instinctive reflex to duck, so I doubted my would-be killer had kept his head sticking up long enough to watch me catch the thing and throw it back. More likely he'd decide that he must have missed, in which case he might try again.

He did.

I threw that one back too.

The second explosion seemed louder if anything, and a sharp pain went through my eardrum. I heard someone shout something; my ears were ringing too much to make out the words but he didn't sound happy. I didn't bother answering; instead I just picked up my shotgun and waited. *Your move, guys.*

There was another pause. There's a lot of waiting in battles: when one wrong move can get you maimed or killed, people are understandably reluctant to make hasty decisions. From down below I heard another explosion, followed by more gunfire. I didn't like the idea of someone coming up behind me, but I couldn't take my attention off the window long enough to check.

The futures moved as the guys out there made a decision. There was a scraping sound and I knew the construct was getting back up. From a glance through the futures I saw that they were sending it through the window again, and they were following up behind it to cover it this time. Probably they were planning on using it as a shield against my fire, with the intention of shooting me if I exposed myself.

It was a tricky situation. I could keep blasting the construct, but that wouldn't really accomplish anything. I

had a dispel focus in my right pocket that could take the
thing out, but it was a touch range weapon and I didn't
like the idea of grappling with a construct while I took
fire from the guys behind. With darkness and the element
of surprise I could *probably* destroy the construct before
they could land a shot . . . but *probably* isn't *definitely*, and
I don't like taking chances I don't need to.

I still had some space to work with. I ran back through
the room, jumping the mattress. I heard a shout from
outside and knew they'd seen me, but I kept going out of
the door. Once I was out in the corridor I stopped, flattened
myself against the wall and held still.

Glass crunched from inside the room as the construct
clambered its way through the window once again. It was
slower now, the battle damage taking its toll. *Crunch, crunch,
crunch* as shards of glass broke under its feet, then there
was a pause and I knew it was turning, scanning the room.

Silence. I knew that if I poked my head out I'd see the
construct but nothing else. They knew I was outside the
room, but they didn't know where. The last they'd seen,
I was running, so there was a decent chance they'd assume
I'd still be running. In which case their next move would
be to send the construct further in while they moved up
to the window . . .

There was the *crunch* of footsteps as the construct started
moving again. *Got you.* I waited for two seconds, then came
around the corner, gun raised.

The construct was less than five feet away, and now that
I got a good look at it I could see just how badly mangled
it was. The shotgun and grenades had shredded its face, and
holes pockmarked its clothes where shrapnel had been driven
into the body. But it was still moving, and while one eye

was gone, the remaining one locked onto me as I came into view. Shooting a construct doesn't work very well: they don't have organs, and they can't bleed out or suffer from shock. In theory if you maul the body badly enough it'll break the animating spell, but you'll usually run out of bullets before happens. The construct's hands came up as it stepped towards me, ignoring the threat of the gun.

I wasn't aiming at the construct. I sighted over its shoulder just as a figure appeared in the window behind, and for the first time I got a look at the guy who'd been trying to kill me. He was wearing a bulletproof vest and a ski mask, and his eyes had just enough time to go wide before I pulled the trigger.

The shotgun blast went past the construct's left ear and took the man behind him in the chest. He dropped out of sight.

The construct advanced towards me, but I wasn't in a hurry any more. I backed down the corridor at a leisurely pace, letting the construct follow, and switched the shotgun to my left hand as I searched in my pocket for my dispel focus. Once I'd found it I let the construct catch up. The construct reached for my neck and I ducked under its arms and drove the focus into its body. My dispel focus is a long sliver of silvery metal, rather like a screwdriver without a handle. It's a close-range weapon, but it's good at what it does. The construct spasmed, its hands clutching at empty air, then the life seemed to go out of it and it crumpled to the floor. The futures in which I had to deal with being strangled vanished.

And there we go. I looked ahead to see that the man I'd shot was being dragged away from the window by his buddy. I could have finished them off, but I was pretty sure they weren't coming back, which meant they weren't a threat any more. Besides, I didn't really want to kill anyone if I could avoid it, even if the little bastard *had* tried to drop a grenade on me. I headed downstairs.

By the time I made it back to the ground floor the battle was winding up. The door Kyle had been guarding was open, and another construct was lying on the ground; this one had apparently taken enough of a mauling that it had been put out of action. Kyle was nowhere to be seen, but I could sense fire magic nearby and I followed it through the main doors.

Cinder was in the next room over. Crates were scattered around, some of them burning, but all of his human adversaries looked to be either dead or fleeing. The only enemy still on its feet was one of the constructs, and it was missing an arm. It came lumbering towards Cinder, reaching out with its remaining hand.

A blade of searing red light formed at Cinder's fist. He stepped in close to meet the construct and rammed the blade through its body and out the other side. The construct jerked as Cinder dragged the blade up through the thing's torso, cutting it almost in two. An acrid scent of burned hair filled the room and the construct collapsed to the floor, the huge split in its body glowing red, clothes smouldering and igniting from the heat. Cinder turned to shoot me a look.

I nodded down at the construct. 'Thought they were fireproof.'

'Fire-resistant,' Cinder said curtly. 'What happened up top?'

'One dead construct.'

'You kill the handlers?'

'No.'

Cinder grunted and turned away. I thought about asking what had happened to the ones down here, but there was a putrid-sweet whiff of burned flesh in the air and I had a feeling I already knew the answer.

Footsteps sounded behind and I turned to see Kyle jog in through the back door. 'Lost them,' he said briefly. 'Winged one, but I didn't want to push too close.'

'More coming?' Cinder asked me.

I concentrated. It was hard, because Kyle and Cinder kept moving around – unlike my friends, they haven't learned the drill for when I'm path-walking. 'Nothing immediate,' I said after a minute. 'You should be clear for ten to fifteen minutes, but I can't give you any promises past that.'

'Long enough,' Cinder said. 'Kyle.'

'I got it, I'm on vacuum duty,' Kyle said. 'Hey, Verus, give me my gun back.'

I handed over the shotgun. 'I kind of want one of my own now.'

'Chat later,' Cinder said curtly. 'We leave in ten.'

After seven minutes, Kyle had finished packing. By nine minutes and thirty seconds, we were stepping through a gateway. Staging points took up another five minutes, gating to a place where we could sit and talk took three, getting seated in the restaurant took another two and it took six minutes more for our food to arrive.

'I can't believe you still have an appetite,' I told Cinder.

We were sitting in a McDonald's somewhere in western England. Through the windows I could see dark skies, the shadows broken up by the white and red lights of cars zooming by on the A road. It wasn't the first time I'd met Cinder at the restaurant here. Maybe it was his preferred meeting place for business negotiations. Then again, maybe he just liked the food.

Cinder shoved another handful of fries into his mouth. 'Why wouldn't I?'

'That frigging smell,' I said. I was the only one without a tray in front of me; just the thought of eating turned my stomach. I don't know whether burned human flesh really does have a different scent from burned animal flesh or whether I'm just imagining it, but one thing I know for sure is that it lingers. I could *still* smell the stuff if I let myself think about it. 'It doesn't bother you?'

Cinder shrugged.

'I mean, I'm not exactly squeamish,' I said. 'But that particular putrid smell—'

'Do you mind?' Kyle said. He was holding a Quarter Pounder and giving me a look. 'I'd like to keep this down.'

'How can *you* eat?'

Kyle grimaced. 'You get used to it.'

Kyle had cleaned out everything valuable or useful from the warehouse, scooping it all into his dimensional storage like a gigantic vacuum cleaner. Watching him was like watching one of those stage magicians who pulls out a never-ending stream of flower bouquets and coloured handkerchiefs, except in reverse. I'd never really considered the applications of that kind of space magic, but now that I thought about it, I could see how big an advantage it was. One of the big problems with being hunted is logistics: running away is fine in the short term, but you still need a place to store your stuff and sleep, and that makes you vulnerable. But if you can carry everything with you, then moving your base becomes a ten-minute operation. That explained why I hadn't seen any wards on the warehouse: why bother to ward a place when you're just going to abandon it as soon as you're found?

What it *didn't* explain was why Cinder was being hunted in the first place. It's true that being a Dark mage isn't exactly a safe way of life – if you aren't willing to deal with the occasional assassination squad trying to kill you in your sleep, you've got no business being on the Dark side of the fence in the first place – but this seemed excessive even for him.

'So who were the goons?' I said. I wasn't worried about being overheard; no one was close enough, and the hum and clatter of the kitchen behind the counter would have drowned it out anyway. A fast-food restaurant is a pretty good place if you want to discuss something private. 'You sounded like this wasn't your first run-in.'

'Third,' Kyle said.

I looked at Cinder to see that the Dark mage had a mouth full of fries. He made a vague waving motion at Kyle, apparently happy to let the adept do the talking, so I turned back to him. 'You said a name I thought I recognised back there,' I said. 'Pyre. Are we talking about the same guy? Dark fire mage based out of London, used to hang out around Dagenham . . . ?'

'That'd be him.'

'Great,' I said sourly.

'Not a fan?'

'He's a piece of shit,' I said bluntly. I'm normally a bit more circumspect when it comes to expressing my opinions of other mages, but one nice thing about Cinder is that I don't have to guard my words much. 'Why's he got his sights on you guys? I'm pretty sure you aren't his type.'

'What's that supposed to mean?'

'Nothing.'

'Well,' Kyle said, 'if we're sharing stories, I want to know how you met the guy. He another acquaintance from your old days?'

'Not that old.' I sighed: Cinder was looking at me inquiringly and I knew I was going to have to share. 'I ran across him about three years ago. There was a girl I knew, an adept, new to the country. She'd let Pyre take her out a couple of times, and was just starting to figure out that that had been a mistake. I did some looking into it, found out that other girls who did that and then tried to break things off afterwards tended to disappear. Enough of them that it was a pattern. Tried to get the Council interested, but it was the usual story. No breach of the Concord.'

'So what did you do?'

'Managed to help her,' I said. 'Couldn't help the others.'

'Others?'

'A lot of others,' I said shortly. It had been one of my more bittersweet memories. The girl had been called Xiaofan, and I'd managed to save her, and that had been something I could be proud of. But I hadn't been able to save Pyre's other victims, and even at the time I'd known he was just going to keep on doing the exact same thing. I still wonder sometimes whether I was right to walk away. The thing was, if I *hadn't* walked away, if I'd tried to stop him, then realistically speaking, there were only two ways it could have gone. One of us would have finished up in the ground, and I hadn't been at all sure that I would have been the one left standing. So I took my winnings and went home, and left Pyre to carry on doing what he did.

It hadn't been my fight . . . but then, that's how people like Pyre always keep getting away with it, isn't it? The ones who can stop them won't, and the ones who want to stop them can't.

'Mm,' Kyle said. 'Well, I guess it's comforting to know that he's a complete arsehole to *everyone*.'

'Which brings me back to my question of why you,' I pointed out. 'I mean, no offence, but I'm pretty sure neither of you are *that* attractive.'

'Shows how much you know.'

Cinder gave Kyle a look.

'Fine, fine,' Kyle said. 'The reason Pyre's been chasing us all around London like some demented British version of Wile E. Coyote is because he wants something we've got.'

'What's the something?'

Cinder put down what was left of his burger and shifted position, adjusting himself so that his back was to the other people in the restaurant. Then he peeled the glove off his left hand.

I raised my eyebrows. The glove had looked bulky, but as Cinder took it off I saw that it was actually thin: the bulk had come from what it had been covering. Under the glove was a gauntlet. It looked to be made out of some kind of blue scale armour, with articulated plates covering the fingers and wrist. Dark stones were set in a line behind the first finger, and the flexible parts of the gauntlet underneath the plating seemed to be made out of black mail. That glove of Cinder's must have carried some sort of shielding spell, because now that it was removed I could sense magic radiating. The sheer power of the aura told me what sort of item this was, even if I hadn't recognised it. 'Okay then,' I said.

'You recognise it?' Kyle said.

'Yeah,' I said. The description of that gauntlet was in the file currently sitting in the drawer in my office in the War Rooms, the one that listed the imbued items stolen in the raid last year. It was called the Dragon's Claw, and it was a powerful defensive item designed for magical combat. The Council had wanted it back quite badly, judging by the number of words that they'd underlined in its description.

'This isn't going in your report,' Cinder told me.

'Yeah, I don't think the Council needs to know about this little detail.' If they did, the first thing they'd do would be demand that I go after Cinder and get it back.

Cinder nodded and pulled on the glove again. I felt the magical aura wink out as the leather covered the scales. 'So that's why Pyre wants you guys so badly,' I said. 'What's the deal, all the other Dark mages on Richard's team got a big hefty imbued item and he's feeling left out?'

'He wasn't even on the team in the first place,' Kyle said. 'Did some bullshit minor stuff, and now he's claiming he was cheated. As though anyone would have taken a nut like him on any kind of serious job.'

'Yeah,' I said, frowning. Something wasn't quite adding up. 'Though I'm kind of surprised he's got the balls to pull something like this without backup. I mean, don't get me wrong, the guy's dangerous, but he's a predator through and through. He goes after easy targets.'

Kyle and Cinder looked at me.

'Oh,' I said, catching on. 'He *does* have backup. Who's his friend?'

Cinder swallowed the last bite of his burger. 'Onyx.'

'Oh,' I said. *Well, that changes things.*

'You up to date on that whole situation?' Kyle asked.

'I know Onyx and Richard aren't getting on,' I said. 'Heard it was something to do with Onyx wanting to take Morden's place.'

Kyle snorted. 'Yeah, like that's going to happen. The whole thing started right after the raid. You know how Onyx was there? Well, he was ordered specifically *not* to do that, because it'd implicate Morden. Drakh was pissed and when the items got parcelled out, Onyx didn't get one. Onyx didn't like that one bit.'

'Mm,' I said slowly. 'And he made friends with Pyre since then?'

'Yeah.'

'Sounds like he's trying to gather his own cabal to rival Richard's,' I said. Two mages isn't much of a cabal, but I suppose Onyx figured he had to start somewhere.

'That's about the size of it.'

'Um,' I said. That implied a few things. Cinder is connected to Rachel, and Rachel is Richard's Chosen, so by having Pyre go after Cinder, Onyx was attacking Richard in an indirect sort of way. These sorts of proxy battles are common when mages fight – a personal confrontation is risky, so they work through agents instead. It was more subtle than I'd have expected from someone like Onyx, but maybe he was testing Richard, seeing how far he could push him. If Pyre managed to hurt or kill Cinder, and Richard did nothing, maybe Onyx would take that as a sign that he could keep going.

Of course, subtle or not, it was still stupid. Onyx is not remotely in Richard's league, and the fact that Richard hadn't responded to the younger mage's provocations just meant that he had bigger fish to fry. If Onyx ever made it to the top of Richard's priority list, he'd be splattered like a bug on a windshield.

Cinder finished off his last few fries and looked at me. 'You haven't said what you want.'

'I need to go set up a meeting with Onyx,' I said. 'Was hoping you guys could give me an in.'

Cinder raised an eyebrow. 'You want to talk to him?' Kyle said. 'Why?'

'Can't really go into the details, sorry.'

To those of you not familiar with Dark mages, it might seem a bit odd that I was asking Cinder were for something like this. After all, if what Kyle and Cinder were saying was true, Pyre and/or Onyx had just tried to kill them. A Light mage would look at what had just happened and conclude that the whole thing was a bust and that they should go find someone else, or approach Onyx directly.

It sounds logical, and it's also completely wrong. The fact that Kyle and Cinder were in a state of open war with Onyx and Pyre didn't make any difference at all. It goes back to the whole thing about lines of communication. Dark mages don't respect Light mages, and if they get a message from one, the most likely thing they'll do is ignore it. If they get a message from another Dark mage, particularly from one whose strength they respect, they'll listen. If anything, the fact that Cinder had survived several attempted assassinations would make Onyx *more* inclined to listen.

Kyle frowned. 'Maybe I'm a bit out of date, but doesn't Onyx hate you? Like, really hate you? To the point where he was trying to kill you in the Vault just because you stayed in range?'

'Yes, he does, and yes, he did,' I said shortly. The Council was *really* going to owe me for this. 'Could you put me in touch? I really don't want to just walk up to Morden's mansion and knock on the front door.'

Kyle looked at Cinder. 'I guess we could try . . .'

'Sure you want to?' Cinder said.

'Don't really have a choice.' It was tempting to just stay the hell away, but that wouldn't really accomplish anything except running out the clock. 'I know you aren't exactly on speaking terms, but what's the guy's mental state like at the moment? I mean, aside from the "being a psychopathic killer" part.'

'Aside from that, right.' Kyle snorted. 'What, you're wondering whether he's sane enough to talk to?'

'Pretty much.'

'Hasn't gone crazy yet,' Cinder said.

'He's a psycho, but he's a rational psycho,' Kyle said. 'If you can give him a good reason not to attack you, he won't. It's just that there has to *be* a reason, because this guy's spent a long time using excessive amounts of violence on anything that annoys him or gets in his way, and it usually works. So if he thinks it'll work on you . . .' Kyle shrugged. 'You get the idea.'

'So how do you deal with him?' I said. 'That space magic trick of yours is handy, but I don't think it'd slow down someone like Onyx.'

'It wouldn't, and that's why I stay the hell out of his way,' Kyle said. 'Especially after . . .'

'After?'

Kyle shut up, and I looked at him curiously. 'Especially after what?'

'You going to tell him?' Cinder said. There wasn't any expression on his face, but all of a sudden, I had the odd feeling that he was amused.

'It doesn't matter,' Kyle snapped.

'I could tell him.'

'You don't need to tell him!'

'Okay,' I said, looking between the two. 'I think I'm missing something here.'

Kyle shot Cinder a dirty look and turned back to me reluctantly. 'So, Onyx might have a kill-on-sight order out on me if I go back to his mansion.'

'Because you hang out with Cinder?'

'Besides that.'

I raised my eyebrows. '*Besides* that?'

'Yes,' Kyle said. 'Can we drop it?'

'No, no, this I have to hear. What did you do, steal his silverware?'

'Something like that.'

I cocked my head. 'Except that if you'd stolen something he wouldn't be waiting for you to show up, he'd be hunting you down to get it back. Sounds more like you *tried* to steal his silverware.'

Kyle glowered. 'I was trying to get someone out of the mansion and it didn't work. Drop it, okay?'

'*Someone*', *huh?* Just out of curiosity, I sorted through the futures in which I mentioned all the names of people I knew who might have been connected to Onyx. To my surprise, I got a hit after less than a dozen tries. 'Selene? Really?'

'Told you he'd guess it,' Cinder said.

'Jesus.' Kyle rolled his eyes. 'This? This is why people hate diviners.'

'So you were trying to do a rescue,' I said, and looked at Cinder. 'Didn't realise he was the hero sort.'

'Still playing white knight,' Cinder said.

'Oh, screw you both,' Kyle said.

'Sure you don't want to tell me the story?' I asked.

'No,' Kyle said shortly.

I looked at Kyle thoughtfully. Selene had been one of the slaves at Morden's mansion that I'd met back when I'd been an involuntary guest there. I'd hardly spoken to her and I didn't remember much except an impression of dark hair and wary eyes. I hadn't even known she was still alive – being a slave to a Dark mage is a hazardous job. Apparently Kyle had decided to stage a rescue and it hadn't worked out.

The parallels were a little too close for comfort. Back when I'd been dealing with the adept leading Kyle's group, Will, I'd been aware of the similarities between him and me. Now it was looking like he hadn't been the only one. I hoped Kyle's path wouldn't land him in the same place mine had.

I was also glad Kyle hadn't asked me for help, and vaguely ashamed that I was glad. I *really* didn't need any more problems right now. 'So,' I said, turning back to Cinder. 'How long will it take for a connect?'

'Few days,' Cinder said. 'Week at most.'

And if Onyx said no, I'd have to figure out a way to get the guy to listen to me without getting killed on sight. Well, one problem at a time. 'Anything else?'

Cinder shook his head. 'He gets in touch, he's interested. He doesn't . . .' He shrugged. 'Good luck.'

7

As things turned out, I didn't have to wait long – Cinder got back to me within forty-eight hours. The message he relayed from Onyx was short, specifying only a time and a place. Once he'd said his piece, Cinder broke contact. He'd done his part; now I was on my own.

I reported back to Talisid, who passed my information on to Bahamus. They were happy enough to authorise the meeting. They were *not* happy about the level of authority I wanted.

'I'm sorry, Verus,' Talisid said, 'but we really can't authorise anything like that.' We were talking through an audio-only link, so I couldn't see Talisid's face, but I could imagine his expression.

'You can, and you'd better,' I said shortly.

'We'll need to see any provisional agreement before we can authorise it.'

'How are you expecting this to work?' I said. 'You think I'm going to go meet Onyx, he tells me his requests, I tell him yours, then I go back to you and you suggest changes to the deal, then I go back and meet him again, and we repeat that cycle three or four times until we've got an agreement everyone is happy with? Is that your plan?'

'Is there something wrong with that?'

'Is there—? Are you serious?'

'What exactly is the problem?' Talisid asked. He had an

annoyingly patient tone of voice that I'd become familiar with.

I took a breath. Losing my temper wasn't going to accomplish anything, no matter how frustrating the Council can be. To be fair, Talisid's idea *was* reasonable . . . if you were dealing with a Light mage. *Anne would have understood without me having to explain.* 'The number one rule when you're dealing with Dark mages is that you have to negotiate from a position of strength,' I said. 'The worst thing you can do is make them think you're weak. If I don't have the authority to settle terms, then in their eyes, that automatically makes me weak. And by implication, that makes *you* weak.'

'I don't follow.'

'A Dark mage who's serious about negotiating a deal goes there in person. If he does send a proxy, he'll send one with the authority to close. If he doesn't, other Dark mages are going to see that as timid at best and a deliberate waste of their time at worst. If they decide to express their displeasure about that, guess who's the most obvious target for them to vent their feelings on?'

'Perhaps if you present it more diplomatically . . .'

'Onyx is a thug,' I said flatly. 'He's powerful, brutal and short-tempered. When you're dealing with people like that, you present your offer and you do it fast.'

'Well, I'll discuss it with Bahamus,' Talisid said. 'But I don't think he'll be able to commit to anything that permanent. Remember, you're negotiating in the entire Council's name.'

'Then tell Bahamus he can bloody well go do it himself.'

'Verus . . .'

'I'm not kidding,' I said. 'This is already really dicey. I'm trying to negotiate something between Morden, the entire Council and Onyx. That is *way* too many people who don't trust each other. The best result that I can realistically hope for is to come back from Morden's mansion with a take-it-or-leave-it offer from Onyx that you probably won't like very much. A prolonged negotiation is not an option. Even if Onyx is willing to be that patient – which he won't be – it's a guarantee that news is going to leak. At which point you can say bye-bye to any chance of catching Richard.'

Talisid was silent, and I knew I'd got through. 'All right,' he said at last. 'I'll tell him, but I can already tell you, he isn't going to like it.'

Talisid was right – Bahamus didn't like it – but I didn't back down, and in the end he had to give in. By the time the date of the meeting with Onyx rolled around, I had his agreement that I had full authority to negotiate with the Dark mage. Or so he said, anyway.

In reality, I knew there was nothing stopping Bahamus from backing out, and I figured that there was at least a fifty-fifty chance that he'd try to argue with any terms I came back with. If that happened, the deal was doomed, but oh well. At least by then, I'd be out of range. Now I just needed to make sure I survived the meeting.

'You look pretty well armed,' Anne said.

'Yeah, well,' I said. We were in the Hollow, and I was finishing my preparations. I was wearing my armour, the plate-and-mesh following the lines of my body, and I could feel the imbued item's presence, watchful and protective. A webbing belt held a short-sword on my left side and a gun on my right, along with a host of pouches. Normally

I go to an effort to hide my gear, but I wasn't bothering this time, and that let me bring a larger arsenal than usual. The dreamstone was there, along with condensers, force-walls, glitterdust, life rings, flares, explosive, antitoxin, a revivify, salves and generally more tools than I was ever likely to use. That wasn't counting the coat I was wearing over my armour, or the vest beneath it. 'This is one of those situations where the time for subtlety has been and gone.'

'I thought you liked to keep your weapons hidden,' Anne said. She was sitting on my bed with her arms curled around her legs, and she'd been watching me gear up with apparent interest.

'That's because I like to avoid escalating things,' I said. I checked my gun, made sure that it was loaded and that the safety was on, then tucked a spare magazine into a pouch. I thought about adding a second, then decided it was over-kill, even for this. If you're ever in a situation where you need more than one reload, you're in more trouble than a handgun can help with. 'The idea is, if you don't look like you're armed, then someone is more likely to shout at you to stop rather than just trying to kill you on sight. Onyx is *already* at the point where he's trying to kill me on sight.'

'Do you think all that stuff is really going to help?'

'Probably not,' I admitted. 'If things go bad, odds are I'm going to be dead inside thirty seconds. Probably more like ten.'

'Then why bother?'

'For the cases where we don't get into an all-out fight with Onyx but we do run into some other kind of trouble. Besides, it sends the message that I'm taking him seriously. There's a chance that might help.'

I finished checking my gear and headed out. 'You know,

you could stand to be wearing a little more yourself,' I told Anne as I started channelling through my gate stone.

'This is what I'm used to,' Anne said. For this meeting she'd gone back to her old outfit of jeans, running shoes and a light jacket. They had some magical reinforcement, enough to be better than nothing, but not by much.

'You really need to get some proper armour,' I told her. 'I know those things you're wearing have been treated, but there's only so much you can do with fabric. Even a knife thrust would probably go through.'

'If someone's close enough to do that, I'm not really worried.'

'And if they just shoot you?' I said. 'That hasn't worked out too well in the past.'

'I'm quite a lot tougher now than I was then,' Anne said. 'Armour's a good idea for you because you can't afford to take any serious hits. I can.'

'If someone gets a head shot, it won't matter how tough you are.'

'Same for you,' Anne pointed out. 'Besides, armour slows you down.'

'I think you just undervalue armour because your own abilities ignore it.'

'I've also seen it be more of a hindrance than a help. Whenever I see someone wearing a big clunky suit, I know that if I get in close, they're not going to be able to move fast enough to get away.'

'That's exactly what I'm saying. You see the cases where armour doesn't save someone, but you don't see the ones where it *would* . . .'

We kept going as I opened the gate to our first staging point and from there to another. It was an old argument that we'd had several times. Ever since Anne had been targeted last year, I'd been trying to convince her to wear something more protective, and she'd been refusing. To be fair, she did have a point. Like most life mages, Anne is incredibly resilient, and any injury that doesn't kill her instantly is basically nothing more than an inconvenience. Unfortunately, battle mages have *lots* of ways of killing you instantly, and while a set of armour probably isn't going to do much if they manage to land a direct hit, it can make the difference. I think Anne just likes being able to move as freely as possible, which, to be honest, is how I used to do things as well. If I was being *really* honest I might have considered that my pressuring her on this subject might be an indication of an increased tendency to worry about her, but that was a topic I was trying to avoid thinking about. In any case, it was brought to an end as we gated from the second staging point to where we were meeting Variam and Luna.

All mages use staging points – empty, out-of-the-way places that you use in order to avoid gating directly from one destination to another. It's possible, if difficult, to trace one gate, but tracing a series of them is usually impractical. I have a dozen gate stones linked to staging points these days, and I rotate them on a daily basis and replace them on a monthly one.

Unfortunately, gate stones are useless for going anywhere you haven't been already. Morden's mansion was a place I'd visited before, but it wasn't exactly practical for me to set up a gate stone for there, and given how secret this meeting was supposed to be, I sure as hell wasn't going to ask around to see if someone else had one. Luckily, while I can't use gate magic myself, I have friends who can.

'Took you long enough,' Variam said as we walked in and let the gate close behind us.

'Oh hush,' Luna said. 'You guys ready?'

'As we'll ever be,' I said. The staging point was a clearing in a forestry area, pine needles covering the ground. The occasional bird chirped from above, but only rarely; coniferous woods are sparsely inhabited, which makes them ideal for my purposes. 'You good to go?'

'Yeah, except for one thing,' Variam said, looking at Anne. 'Why are *you* here?'

'Vari . . .' Anne said.

'I'm serious. Alex was saying there's a good chance Onyx is going to try to kill him on sight.'

'I said he *might*,' I said. 'I don't think it's likely. I've taken what precautions I can, and I've spent a long time path-walking. Everything I can see indicates that we're not walking into a trap.'

'Except you've also said that path-walking isn't reliable at long range or against psychopaths,' Variam pointed out.

'If he was intending to just kill me, I don't think—'

'*Vari*,' Anne interrupted. 'Are you going to open a gate, or am I going to have to ask someone else?'

'I don't like it,' Variam said.

'You don't have to. Now could you please help?'

Variam scowled but turned away and started work on a gate. 'He's not happy,' Luna murmured just loud enough for me to hear.

'Yeah, well, I don't blame him,' I said. Variam has always been protective of Anne. He's eased off over the years as she's become clearly more capable of taking care of herself, but he still gets jumpy about watching her go into danger. It's not just concern for her safety – Variam has his own worries about Anne, ones that he's shared with me but not (as far as I know) with Anne or Luna. 'This is a long way off safe.'

'I thought you said you had a trump card.'

'I have, but we're walking into a Dark mage's mansion. If Onyx decides "screw it" and cuts loose, this is going to get ugly.'

'Yeah, I can guess. Why did you agree to do this again?'

I was spared having to come up with an answer to that by Variam's gate spell completing. An orange-red halo of fire faded into an oval portal, linking our woodland with another. I followed Anne and Vari through.

The gate closed behind us and I turned to Variam. 'Thanks for the lift,' I said. 'I'll call you when—'

'We're staying,' Variam said flatly. 'You get into trouble, you call us for backup. Okay?'

Luna and Vari were both looking at me, and it was clear they'd agreed on this beforehand. 'All right,' I said. 'Thanks.'

Anne and I walked away down the hillside. 'You know, if things go wrong,' Anne said once we were out of earshot, 'I really doubt they'll be able to get to us in time.'

'I doubt they will either,' I said. Both Anne and I were carrying beacons that Variam could use to home in on us and open a gate to our location. Variam's pretty good with gate magic, and he could probably get the portal open in maybe two minutes. Unfortunately, if you have someone like Onyx trying to kill you, two minutes is about one minute and fifty-nine seconds longer than you can afford to wait.

'You didn't explain to Vari exactly what your "trump card" was, did you?' Anne asked. 'Because I don't think he'd have let it go without mentioning it if you had.'

'I didn't think either of them would react too well,' I
admitted. I could feel the weight of the vest between my
armour and coat.

'You think?' Anne asked dryly.

We walked a little further in silence. It was a clear summer
day, and the woods were beautiful in the morning light.
Sunbeams slanted down between the leaves, painting dappled
patterns on the grass and undergrowth, and birds sang from
above. The wind rustled through the trees above us, but
beneath the shelter of the branches, the air was warm and
still. The Welsh countryside is one of the few good memories I have from my time with Richard. I'd been a city boy
growing up, and my stay in Richard's mansion had been
the first time I'd ever been able to just wander off into the
woods alone any time I'd wanted, and I'd liked it. It hadn't
been a coincidence that my old safe house had been in Wales.

'Any more weird dreams?' I asked after a while.

'No,' Anne said. 'You?'

'No. Last chance to back out and let me do this solo.'

'That's not going to happen.'

'I knew you'd say that. Okay, we're getting close. Mental
only from now on.'

Anne nodded.

As far as the mansions of Dark mages go, Morden's is
one of the nicer ones. It's set amid trees and rolling hills,
the landscape hiding the full spread of the buildings.
There's even an access road and a gravel area set aside for
parking. The previous times I'd seen the place it had been
empty, but this time I saw that outside the front entrance
were several flashy-looking sports cars. Apparently Onyx
had been making some changes. Anne and I walked straight
up the front drive: I rang the bell and waited.

A minute passed, then two. *Did they even hear us?* Anne asked.

Oh, they heard.

Footsteps approached from behind the door. I saw Anne shift her gaze slightly, staring at the walls, and I knew that she was counting the people beyond them. To her senses the living creatures within the mansion would appear as patterns of glowing green light, visible through the bricks and stone.

The handle turned and the door scraped open to reveal a boy of maybe twenty, his hair close-shaven, dressed in combats with a leather jerkin and an oversized gun in a holster at his waist. His stance was arrogant and he stared down his nose at us from the top of the porch. 'Well?'

'You know who we are and what we want,' I said shortly. I could already tell that this kid was going to try to play games and I wasn't in the mood. 'Take us inside.'

The kid looked me up and down. 'You armed?'

I took a breath. I was wearing combat armour with a gun on one side and a sword on the other, and this guy asked if I was armed. 'What do you think?'

The kid nodded at the front porch. 'Drop your weapons.'

'What?'

'Something wrong with your ears?' the kid said. 'You want to get in, that's the deal.'

I turned to look at Anne. She looked back at me. I turned back to the kid, drawing my 1911 in one smooth motion. He'd just started to jerk backwards when I fired.

The bullet kicked up a splinter from the floor at his feet. The kid began to reach for his own gun and froze as he realised that I'd already sighted on his head. 'Listen closely,' I told the boy. 'You may work for Onyx, but that doesn't mean you can get away with the same shit. Now run back to whoever you report to and tell him we're on our way.'

The boy hesitated, stared down the gun's barrel, then backed off and disappeared. *Was that necessary?* Anne asked telepathically.

I holstered my gun. *If we let someone like* that *push us around, Onyx would probably kill us on general principle. You watch. He'll be back.*

The kid reappeared in less than two minutes, glowering. 'This way,' he told us. 'Follow me and don't run off.'

What does he think he's going to do if we try? Anne asked in amusement.

I let the kid lead us into the mansion, and as I did I directed a message back in the direction from which we'd come. *Vari. We're in.*

There was a moment's resistance – I always find it harder to contact Variam than Anne – then I heard Variam's voice in my head. It was a little blurry, with underechoes – Vari seems to have trouble focusing his thoughts into a single message. *Got it. Tell us if things go wrong.*

The kid – I'd learned from looking ahead that his name was Trey – led us through the mansion's corridors. *What do you see?* I asked Anne.

Well, we're not alone, Anne said. Despite everything, I had to admit that having Anne by my side made me feel a lot better. There aren't many people I'd rather have with me if trouble starts. *I've picked up fifteen others so far.*

Any you recognise?

Just Onyx, Anne said. *I don't think I've met any of the others. But they seem young.*

Spread out?

Right ahead in a group.

Guess they're waiting for us, I said. *Well, game time.* We came to a door; Trey opened it without knocking and led us into the room beyond.

It had been a long time since I'd visited Morden's mansion, but when I had I'd done a pretty thorough mapping and the layout hadn't changed. The room we were walking into had originally been Morden's ballroom, a wide room along the mansion's west side with parquet flooring and chandeliers above. Onyx, though, had done some redecorating.

Chairs and side tables had been pushed up against the walls, leaving most of the floor clear. Many were knocked over or broken: the ones that were whole were cluttered with rubbish and half-eaten meals. The parquet floor itself was cracked and burned, and there was a splintered crater in one corner that looked like it had been made by a hand grenade. One of the chandeliers had been shredded, and the lights from the remaining ones mixed with the daylight through the windows.

The people that Anne had sensed were scattered around the edges of the room, and they were not the most attractive-looking crowd. Lots of visible weapons, not much attention to personal hygiene. One had what looked like an AK-47 propped up against his chair; another was cleaning his nails with a flick knife. Ages ranged from teens to thirties, but as Anne had said, they skewed young. Taken as a whole, they had an undisciplined, wolfish look; all were watching us as we walked in, and I didn't like the looks in their eyes.

Out of all the people in the room, only two didn't turn to face us. One was the only girl in the room, a thin dark-haired figure near the back wall. She was sweeping up some debris with a dustpan and brush and kept her head down. Something about her body language told me she was trying not to attract attention.

The second was one I recognised instantly: Pyre. He looked younger than his age, with short, tousled blond hair. There was a long dining table at the centre of the room, and he was sitting near our end of it, leaning back in his chair and playing with a lighter, apparently absorbed in the flame as he clicked it on and off with long white fingers. He was good-looking, in a boyish, almost feminine way; he might have looked delicate if I hadn't known more about him. I didn't know if he recognised me; we'd never come face to face, and it was possible that he'd never figured out that I'd been involved in that business a few years ago. I hoped not.

And then there was Onyx, sprawled in a high-backed chair at the end of the table so that he was facing the door. He hadn't changed much since I'd last seen him; he never does, really. Same whip-like, slender build; same dangerous stillness. The only difference I could see was a bit of gold jewellery to offset the black of his clothes. He watched us from beneath lowered brows as we drew closer, and his eyes were opaque.

Trey peeled off as we entered, withdrawing to one side. I kept going, stopping in front of Onyx's table. Half my attention was on Onyx and Pyre, the other half on the futures, and I could sense the possibilities of violence, not close, but not far away either.

Onyx didn't speak, watching us with his flat, deadly eyes. The silence dragged out. 'Well,' I said at last. 'You seem to be doing well for yourself.'

'You wanted to talk,' Onyx said.

'Great, let's skip the pleasantries,' I said. I nodded at the people around us. 'I've got an offer to make. It's confidential.'

'So?' Onyx said.

'As in, you might not want an audience.'

'What's the matter, Verus?' Onyx said. 'Feeling shy?'

Several of the guys leaning against the walls laughed. They weren't nice laughs. 'I don't think you're going to want this spread around,' I said.

Onyx withdrew his feet from the table and placed them on the floor, leaning forward slightly. The laughs from the audience cut off abruptly. 'I don't care what you think,' he said softly into the silence.

I stood still for a moment. Every one of my instincts was telling me that discussing something like this in front of this kind of a crowd was a *really* bad idea, but arguing seemed worse. 'The Council want to make a deal,' I said.

'Of course they want to make a deal,' Onyx said. 'That's all they ever want to do, talk and make deals. Just like you.' He tilted his head. 'So what are you offering?'

'Help,' I said. 'Items. There's a lot on the table. Question is if you're willing to work with them.'

'Yeah?' Onyx said. 'That's funny. Because I think the question is why I shouldn't just kill you right now and have what's left thrown out of my mansion to show the Council *exactly* what I think of cowardly little shits like you.'

There was a rustle of movement around the room. I didn't turn to look. 'Because if you try,' I said, 'you won't have a mansion, or any followers. And maybe not a life either.' Without taking my eyes off Onyx, I undid the button on my coat and opened it.

I felt the people against the walls stop moving. Beneath

my coat and over my armour I was wearing a vest with a series of long rectangular blocks hanging off it that were connected with electrical wire. I don't know how many of them could identify plastic explosives, but they recognised what the set-up meant, and all of a sudden no one seemed very keen on getting close. Pyre looked up from his lighter and paused.

'You think a bomb's going to scare me?' Onyx said.

'I think it might make you think twice.'

Onyx gave a single contemptuous glance at my vest. 'You didn't bring enough.'

'To get through your shields?' I said. 'No, but enough to kill everyone else in this room. Oh, and by the way? This isn't a conventional explosive. You might survive it. Maybe. But I guarantee you, once it's done, you'll need a new place to live, because neither you nor anyone else is going to be using this mansion ever again.'

'That's your plan?' Onyx said.

'That's about half of it,' I said. 'But honestly? It's also just meant as a kind of general "fuck you". If you're going to pull the same shit you tried back in the Vault, then this time you're going to pay for it.'

Onyx rose to his feet in a smooth, graceful motion. He walked around the table, holding my gaze. 'Know what, Verus?' he said. 'I don't think you've got the balls.'

I unfolded my left hand and saw Onyx's eyes flick down to the detonator that had been concealed within my fingers. I'd taken it out before we'd even stepped through the front door. 'Come try me, you little shit,' I said calmly and clearly.

I'd known from the beginning that the big danger of this plan was the possibility of Onyx calling my bluff. There are a lot of people like Onyx in the Dark world, and it's a very bad idea to assume that they're stupid. They might not be book-smart, but they have an instinctive understanding of brinkmanship and how to use the threat of force to get what they want. Trying to bluff someone like that is dangerous – they can sense immediately when someone is too scared to go through with their threat. Besides, in terms of simple destructive power, Onyx was right: I wasn't carrying enough explosives to get through his shields.

Which was why I wasn't bluffing at all. I hadn't loaded this vest with high explosive. If I had, with Anne next to me, I would have been too reluctant to pull the trigger, and Onyx would have smelled that fear like a wolf sniffing out prey. So instead, I'd loaded the vest with the most lethal chemical weapon I could find. Anne would survive it just fine, and I probably would as well, providing Anne could treat me fast enough. The other people in the room . . . not so much. Even Onyx might not make it if he didn't see the danger and adjust his shields before the stuff touched his skin. I still didn't give us good odds of both making it out, but we could do it, and if he tried what he was thinking of doing right now, then I was going to push this button and take my chances.

Maybe that came through in my expression. I think it did; I wasn't trying to hide my intentions and Onyx sensed it. 'Get out,' Onyx said. He kept his eyes on me, but the message wasn't for us.

The crowd obeyed. They didn't quite break into a run – they moved just slowly enough that they could pretend that they weren't being chased – but they didn't dawdle either. Only Pyre and Onyx didn't move. The door slammed and the four of us were alone in the room.

Onyx lowered one hand and leaned back on the table. 'Okay, Verus. Talk fast.'

Okay, so far so good. 'You and the Council have a mutual enemy,' I said. 'They want to make a deal.'

'Yeah?' Onyx said. 'Who?'

'Richard Drakh.'

The half-sneer vanished from Onyx's face and he stared at me blankly. Seconds ticked away.

'Well?' I said when Onyx didn't answer.

'This some trick?' Onyx asked at last.

'No.'

'You trying to push something?' Onyx took a threatening step forward. 'If you're lying again—'

'No!' I snapped. 'If I didn't mean it, you think I'd come *here*?'

'So why?'

'Because while the Council might hate you, they hate Richard a lot more,' I said. 'That raid on the Vault was a step too far and now he's at the top of the Council's hit list. Enough that they're even willing to make a deal with you.'

Onyx gave me that blank stare again.

'It's a trick,' Pyre said, speaking for the first time. His voice was quite at odds with his appearance; deep and masculine.

'How would it be a trick?' I said.

'You want us to do your dirty work,' Pyre said.

'You mean, get rid of Richard yourself?' I said, and shrugged. 'That would be nice, but realistically speaking, I think we both know that's not going to happen. If you could do that, you'd have done it already.'

'Then what do you want?' Onyx demanded.

'They want a time and a place,' I said. 'Find Richard. They'll do the rest.'

'They,' Onyx said. 'You won't be anywhere near, huh?' The sneer seemed half-hearted; I had the feeling he was thinking.

'He's lying,' Pyre said.

'Shut up,' Onyx said absently. He walked across the room, began to wander back, turned on me abruptly. 'How much?'

'An imbued item,' I said. 'Or amnesty for something, if you want, so long as it's not too heinous.'

Onyx laughed. 'Gonna have to do better than that.' He walked back to his chair, dropped into it, then looked at me with an unpleasant smile. 'I want all of them.'

'All of what?'

'The imbued items from the Vault,' Onyx said. 'The ones you've got back, and the ones Drakh still has.'

I stared at Onyx for five seconds — just long enough to check the futures — then shook my head. 'You're delusional,' I said. I glanced at Anne. 'Time to go.' I turned and started towards the exit.

Anne followed instantly, the picture of obedience . . . at least on the surface. In my head, she sounded less certain. *Is this a good idea?*

Trust me.

Pyre's watching us. He's thinking about it.

I know.

I reached out and took hold of the door handle, and Onyx's voice sounded from behind me. 'Okay, okay. I'm just fucking with you.'

I turned to see that Onyx was grinning. Pyre wasn't. 'You ready to be serious?' I asked.

'Let's say ten,' Onyx said. 'Five from Drakh's, five from your stores.'

'The entire contents of this mansion and the people in it aren't worth ten imbued items,' I said. 'Two.'

'From your vaults?'

'Onyx, I'm *only* talking about the ones in our vaults,' I said. 'Because you and I both know that you'll steal anything you can get your hands on from Richard's stores, no matter what we agree on.'

Onyx didn't bother to deny it. 'Seven, then.'

I relaxed very slightly. There was no violence in the futures any more. Maybe Onyx would keep his word and maybe he wouldn't — actually, I was fairly sure he wouldn't — but you don't bargain with someone you're planning to kill. We argued back and forth, Onyx alternating between haggling and threatening. Pyre said nothing, watching us with his blue eyes.

Being a diviner is all about preparation. Whenever I go to a meeting like this, I gear up first — for every one hour I spend talking to mages I don't trust, I spend five to ten hours planning for contingencies and getting hold of the right gear. Admittedly, this meeting had been more extreme than usual, but the basic situation was the same. When you're a diviner, pretty much every mage you meet has the potential to kill you in a straight fight, which is why you don't give them one.

But the thing about preparation is that you usually don't end up using it. Every now and again, when I go to one of these meetings, all hell breaks loose, and when that happens, my preparation and skill are the only things keeping me alive. But for every one meeting that goes like that, there are ten more where nothing in particular happens. It probably doesn't seem that way if you listen to me tell you about it, but that's because if everything goes to plan, there's nothing to tell. And most of the time, meetings do go like that. It's just that the ones that *don't* are the ones that get you killed.

In the end, the meeting with Onyx turned out to be one of the uneventful ones. Despite our past history and despite his threats, we finished up our negotiations, said our goodbyes and left on as good terms as could realistically be expected. And half an hour after arriving, Anne and I were walking back out through the front door.

I can't believe that worked, Anne said.

Please don't jinx it, I said. *Anyone following?*

Just that boy, but he didn't get too close. Onyx and Pyre stayed in the ballroom. I think we're clear.

Yeah, well, keep scanning just in case. I switched mental frequencies. *Vari? We're out. Be ready to gate.*

There was a moment's pause, then I heard Variam's voice in my head. *Got it. Ready to go as soon as you are.*

There's always a rush of relief after a successful operation. We didn't completely relax until we were past the second staging point, but once we did, you could feel the tension go out like flowing water. By the time we arrived back at the Hollow, the others were laughing and cracking jokes.

'So what's the plan?' Vari asked me.

'I go back to somewhere where there's a phone signal and give Talisid the news,' I said. 'And probably hear him complain about what I had to promise Onyx.'

'He'd better not after all this,' Luna said.

'You can come along and tell him that if you want,' I said with a grin.

Luna shook his head. 'Nah. Vari's got his Keeper thing and I said I'd come along.'

'Keeper thing?' I asked Variam.

'Drinks and stuff,' Variam said. 'They said I could bring a guest.'

'Oh, don't be so modest,' Luna said. She looked at Anne and me. 'It's the Carpenter Club. It's only supposed to be for Keepers with at least three years' service. It's Vari's first invite.'

I looked at Variam with interest. 'Sounds like they're impressed with you.'

Variam shrugged uncomfortably.

'I'm afraid I'm going to have to go too,' Anne said. She gave me a slight smile. 'Fun though it sounds to hear Talisid second-guess everything we did in the mansion, I've probably got about fifty patients waiting. I couldn't really get the message out that I'd be away.'

I nodded, fighting off a twinge of disappointment. 'I'll let you know how it goes.'

I waited until everyone was gone before taking off the vest. It had definitely been the right choice, but I still didn't want to have to explain it to Variam, and especially not to Luna. After divesting myself of my heavier items, I returned to London to call Talisid.

Talisid, as predicted, was not happy. 'The amnesty is one thing,' he told me. 'That's to be expected. But handing over so many imbued items is really not acceptable.'

'It's not "so many": it's four. As of yesterday, there are eighty-five imbued items from the Vault lists still missing. I don't really think that pushing it up to eighty-seven is going to make that much difference.'

Talisid paused. 'Why not eighty-nine?'

'Half in advance, half on completion,' I said. 'Onyx is fully expecting you to stiff him on the deal, by the way. And he's also demanding proof that Morden's actually on board with this.'

'Why would he even care?'

'Why, were you hoping you could cut Morden out of the deal completely?' I asked. 'For whatever reason, Onyx won't move without hearing from him. You'll have to figure out how.'

'I suppose that's possible,' Talisid said. 'Do you think it's some kind of trick?'

'Honestly, I think keeping Morden in the loop is probably a good thing,' I said. 'He's probably smart enough to catch Richard, assuming he wants to. Onyx isn't.'

'All he needs to do is feed us a time and a place.'

'I doubt it'll be that easy, and even it if is, Onyx would find some way to screw it up.'

'The Keepers are confident that they can handle Richard if they can reliably locate him.'

'I suppose.' I frowned. 'Have you brought them in on this?'

'We're approaching the stage where we're going to need them.'

'I thought the idea was to keep this need-to-know.'

'They *do* need to know. We can't exactly expect them to cooperate in a major assault without some advance warning.'

'So how much "advance warning" did you give them?'

'It's mostly in terms of hypotheticals at the moment,' Talisid said. 'But we've briefed the mission leader and told him to start assembling his squad.'

'Mm.'

'Well, I'd better report to Bahamus,' Talisid said. 'Good job, by the way.'

'Yeah,' I said. 'See you.'

The communicator cut off and I sat down, frowning as I stared at the focus. All of a sudden I was feeling uneasy. How many people had Talisid told?

According to him, it was just the mission leader. But the mission leader would probably have told his assistant. And it wasn't just Talisid. There was Bahamus, and Maradok. Figure that each of them had probably told one other person too. And those were just the bits of the operation I knew about. Talisid hadn't brought up the Keepers until I'd pressed him, which meant there could be others. Actually, it meant there probably *were* others.

There's a saying that the chances of a secret leaking is proportional not to the number of people who know, but to the *square* of the number of people who know. By my count that number was now way too high. And the Keepers are filled with people who hate Dark mages, which by their reckoning includes me. There was a very good chance that word had already leaked to Sal Sarque and the Crusaders.

What would the Crusaders do if they heard rumours of me having secret negotiations with Morden's cabal? They'd want to know more, and judging by their past behaviour, they'd probably go about it violently. In fact, the last time something like this had happened, their approach had been 'kidnap/torture it out of them'.

I checked the futures. No immediate threat. It's pretty hard to catch a diviner unless you have some way of getting around their precognition. The Crusaders nearly managed it last year, but since then I'd been more careful.

But then, the last time, they hadn't gone after me, had

they? They'd gone after Anne. And now that Anne was my aide, that gave them a double reason to think that she might know something. I checked to see if Anne was answering her phone . . . she wasn't, which didn't necessarily mean anything, but it was worrying enough for me to investigate further. What if I gated to her flat . . . ?

It's scary how life can go from zero to a hundred so fast. I sat looking at that future for exactly two seconds before jumping to my feet so quickly I knocked over my chair. I fumbled out my gate stone and started channelling while also pulling out my phone and typing the alarm code, trying to juggle both tasks at once. I saw the sending bar fill and light up, the 'delivered' notification appearing below. That code would bring Variam and Luna running at full speed, no questions asked, but I didn't know how long it would take them to notice, and right now every second could mean the difference between life and death. I poured power into the gate stone, gambling that it would still function. The air shimmered, then flickered as the gate began to materialise faster than was safe, the spell hanging on a knife edge between completion and catastrophic failure; I snatched half-glimpsed threads out of the futures, changing the frequency of the channelled spell without checking to see what would happen, and it wavered and settled. A portal appeared in mid-air and I jumped through.

I came down into the living room of a small flat in Ealing, decorated in blues and greens. There were plants on the window-sill, a sofa along the wall and three men all in the same room with me. Two had already turned towards the gate; one raised a gun.

Like I said, being a diviner is all about preparation. The

three men around me were alert and ready, but I'd known that I was about to arrive in the middle of them and they hadn't. The gunman hadn't been ready to fire, and as I lunged he hesitated an instant before pulling the trigger. Too long. The bang was loud in the small room; the bullet went high and I hit him below the breastbone, then used my stun focus as he doubled over.

Air magic surged behind me and something slammed into my side, sending me spinning. I came up with my knife in one hand as the second man swung some kind of weapon; I blocked and slashed the wrist to send it bouncing to the floor. Another spell nearly hit me and I slid sideways to use my attacker as a shield. A fourth man had appeared from somewhere or other and for a few seconds it was a whirl of steel and magic, my blade against clubs and spells. It was three against one but the living room was cramped and they had to worry about hitting each other while I could go all out. Fleeting images: the mage at the back, face drawn and eyes set as he tried to line up a spell on me; sweat dripping down the brow of the nearest man as he swung a baton; the couch overturned, the cushions a trip hazard. Seconds stretched into an endless moment.

The third man tried to grab for the gun on the floor and I stabbed him in the back. He staggered and went to his knees; in the second that I was distracted a baton came down on my shoulder. My armour took the blow but I stumbled, the knife twisting out of my hand. A second blow cracked across my arm and I turned the motion into a roll, pulling out a pouch and dumping the contents into my hands in a single practised motion, and as the baton-wielder stepped in to aim the blow that would crack my skull, I threw glitterdust in his face. He yelled, dropping his weapon as he grabbed at his eyes, the sparkling motes clinging to the cornea, blinding him. I hit him low, and he dropped.

All of a sudden the only ones still up were me and the mage. He had a shield active, a bubble of hardened air. I know all about fighting air mages. I tried to rush him, pulling out my dispel focus, but a blast of wind drove me back against the couch. I tripped and rolled to my feet, scooping up the gun as I did and levelling it.

For a moment there was a pause, the two of us facing each other across the overturned couch. The air mage was slim and dark-skinned, hands up in a defensive stance; he wasn't wearing armour but I could sense the auras of defensive magic beneath the shield. I had the gun aimed but I knew a shot wouldn't get through; it was tempting to drop it and go for something else but the air mage was focusing on it in a way that suggested he saw it as a threat. The other three men weren't getting up: the one I'd stunned was still out of it, the guy I'd stabbed was crawling for the door and the third guy was groaning and clawing at his eyes. Seconds ticked by. I ran through attack patterns in the futures, trying to see a way through for a killing strike. *Dangerous.* I could get through – maybe – but not without exposing myself as well. I needed an edge—

Magic pulsed from elsewhere in the flat, something powerful. Not air magic. All of a sudden I remembered why I was here. *Anne!*

'John!' the air mage yelled. 'Caliburn! Get in here!'

I tried to dart for the door, but a wind wall drove me back. *Anne!* I called. *Where are you?*

There was an instant's pause before the answer. *In the bedroom and doing just fine, thanks for asking.*

I hesitated an instant, my concentration split. *What's going on?*

Just do me a favour and stay out of range. Oh, you might want to hold on to something. The connection cut off abruptly. I took one look at the futures and dived behind the sofa.

There was a pulse of magic from the next room over, like the first but ten times as powerful. It was a type I didn't recognise – similar to Anne's life magic but with strands of something else woven in, something dark and hungry, and it hit my senses like a hammer. The room went black as a light-eating wave of darkness swept outwards and then in again, there and gone in a flash.

I staggered to my feet. I felt disorientated; like most diviners my magesight is sensitive, and a spell this powerful is like a fire alarm going off in your ear. Luckily the air mage didn't look any better. I tried to rush him, but apparently he'd had enough. A whirlwind drove me back and the air mage reached the window in two bounding leaps, then jumped through it in a crash of splintering glass. Shards glanced off his shield as he soared up into the street and out of view.

I didn't try to chase the mage – he was long gone and in any case, I didn't care. I darted out into the small hallway and into Anne's bedroom.

And there was Anne, alone. She was wearing the same clothes that she'd worn to Morden's mansion, and they showed no signs of wounds or damage. She whirled to face me as I came through the door, her hands coming up. 'Alex? What are you doing here?'

'Rescuing you, or at least I thought I was.' I was scanning for threats. There was movement at the edge of my range but I couldn't sense anyone coming closer. Maybe they were hanging back until they figured out what was going on . . . *worth a try*. I pulled out a gate stone and started casting.

'Where are they?' Anne asked.

'The guys in the living room?' The gate was forming fast, but I wasn't sure if it'd be fast enough. 'They should be out of it.'

'The ones in here.'

I paused, looked at Anne. She was looking around as if confused. 'What do you mean, the ones in here?'

'There were three,' Anne said. She looked puzzled. 'I was going to trigger the barrier and send a signal to you and Luna and Vari, but—'

Air magic flared from somewhere out in the street. I heard a crack of thunder and the house shivered. 'Talk later,' I said. 'Running now. Where's that air mage?'

'Flying out at the front,' Anne said. She was recovering, her focus coming back. She glanced up at the ceiling. 'Now he's circling over. I think he's aiming for the window.'

'How long?'

'Maybe fifteen seconds . . .'

'Got it,' I said with satisfaction. The air shimmered and formed into a portal. 'Go!'

Anne darted through. There was another clap of thunder and the window fractured, cracks running through the glass. *Too slow.* I gave a mental middle finger to the air mage and was just about to jump through when something caught my eye.

There were fewer signs of struggle here in the bedroom: whatever had happened, it had apparently been too fast to leave much of a mess. The laundry basket near the door had been kicked over, the clothes left in a pile, but the bed itself was still neat and untouched. There was no sign that anyone else had been here at all . . . except for one thing.

As with the living room, Anne had decorated her bedroom with potted plants. I'd noticed them the last time I'd been here: there had been a cluster of violets, and a white flower of some kind I didn't recognise, all growing and healthy. The pots were still there, but they were empty of anything except earth.

A cold feeling went through my stomach. I didn't know what I was looking at, and I didn't have time to stop and think. I jumped through the gate and let it close behind me.

8

It was two hours later.

'So when are you going to tell us what *happened*?' Variam demanded.

'I already told you,' Anne said. 'I don't know.'

We were in the Hollow, gathered in one of the clearings under the afternoon sun. It was a lot like the last time we'd come here to meet, with one difference: Anne was on one side, and the rest of us on the other.

'What do you mean, you don't know?' Variam said. He was still wearing his red and gold dress robes; he and Luna had come running straight from the Carpenter Club as soon as they'd seen my alarm. 'You had a Crusader hit team attack your house! How do you just forget something like that? "Oh, I'm sorry, I know there was a bunch of assassins in my bedroom, but I really wasn't paying attention."?'

'It's nothing to do with attention,' Anne said. 'I told you how the attack went right up to the point where I fell back. I was going to try to catch one as he came through the door. Then the next thing I remember, Alex was bursting in.'

'So what happened to the guys chasing you?'

'I guess they were the ones Alex took care of.'

Variam threw up his hands. 'That is such *bullshit*!'

'I'm sorry, were you there?' Anne said pointedly.

'You said there were two guys chasing you when you

ran into your bedroom,' Variam said. 'The one who was in the lead was using force magic, and he was white. Right?'

'Yes . . .'

'Well, *Alex* already told us that the mage he was fighting was an air mage, and he was black,' Variam said. 'So what, you're saying that the guy chasing you not only changed his magic type from force to air, but spontaneously managed to change his race as well?'

'Then maybe he left? There were plenty more outside. Why is this so important anyway?'

Variam looked about to explode when Luna touched him lightly on the shoulder. 'Vari.'

Variam switched his glare. 'What?'

'This is pointless,' Luna said. As she withdrew her hand the silver mist of her curse flowed back down her arm to cover the fingers once again. 'We *know* what happened.'

'Oh yeah?' Variam spread his arms. 'Then how about you fill us all in.'

'Remember last year at the Vault?' Luna said. She was wearing a white blouse that left her arms and shoulders bare, with a long pleated turquoise skirt. The fit and design made me pretty sure it was Arachne's work; she would have drawn plenty of attention at that party. 'When Alex caught up with Anne, she was out cold, but whatever had happened, it had driven those Crusaders off. And she didn't remember anything about that either.' Luna turned to look at Anne. 'It's exactly the same.'

'I didn't fall unconscious,' Anne said.

'Not this time,' I said. 'But Luna's right. It has to be the jinn.'

'It might not be . . .'

'*Anne*,' I said. 'Wake up. There is *no way* this is anything else.'

'But how?' Anne said. She was looking defensive now, hunted. 'Back then, it was because I picked up that ring. And I know it was a bad idea, but . . . I haven't touched it again. I haven't even seen it.'

The four of us looked at each other. 'Okay, hear me out here,' Luna said. 'Is this necessarily such a bad thing?'

'Are you kidding me?' Variam asked.

'I just think it's worth pointing out that so far, the *only* times this jinn has done its possession thing has been when Anne's been cornered by a bunch of Crusader arseholes trying to torture and kill her.' Luna shrugged. 'Don't know about you, but I'm fairly okay with this.'

Anne shot Luna a grateful look. Variam didn't. 'You're *okay* with her having a freaking eldritch abomination hanging out in her head?'

'As long as it's only eating people like that? Yeah, I don't really see the problem.'

'It's not inside her head,' I said. 'I asked Dr Shirland about that specifically.'

'Then where the hell *is* it coming from?' Variam asked.

'I don't know.'

'I haven't touched the ring that jinn was bound in,' Anne said. 'I know, I picked it up the first time, and I know, it was a mistake. But I haven't done it again. I haven't even gone close.'

'I know.'

'Then how is this happening?'

'I don't know.'

'I still don't think you should be beating yourself up

over it,' Luna said. 'So far, every time this thing's come out, it's been pretty helpful.'

'If it can possess Anne whenever it wants to,' I said, 'then I can promise you, it won't take long for it to *stop* being helpful.'

'So what, you'd rather have her be defenceless the next time these guys show up?'

'That's how these things *work*,' I said. 'Of course they're helpful. At first. Then as you start depending on them, the price goes up. Did you forget *how* Anne got trapped in the Vault with those Crusaders? Richard and Vihaela very specifically engineered that situation to force her into doing it.'

'Why does that make a difference?' Luna asked. 'It's not like the Crusaders were going to leave her alone if she didn't.'

'Think,' I said. 'What does Richard gain from protecting Anne? You think he's doing this out of the kindness of his heart? Or because he's suddenly so interested in her welfare? There is *always* a price for this kind of help. And the fact that we don't know what that price is – *that's* what scares me.'

'So what are we going to do?' Variam asked.

I didn't have an answer to that. Neither did Anne or Luna. We stood in silence around the clearing.

We stayed together for another hour, but Variam's last question hung over the conversation like a cloud. At last Variam was called away on his Keeper duties. Luna stayed; Anne didn't.

'I'd better go,' Anne said, rising to her feet. 'I haven't checked on Karyos.'

'I could come with you,' Luna suggested.

'I'd . . . rather be alone,' Anne said. 'Sorry.' She walked away.

Luna frowned after her. 'That's not good.'

'She's feeling as though we don't trust her,' I said.

Luna raised her eyebrows at me. 'Yeah, I wonder why.'

'Not now.'

'I'm just saying, you and Vari could have been a little nicer.'

'Not *now*.'

'Fine,' Luna said. 'So what's the plan?'

'Why do you all keep asking me that?'

'Because you're the first person we think of when this sort of crap happens, and you're usually pretty good at it,' Luna said. 'Sorry.'

Which was a tacit way for Luna to admit that she couldn't think of any solution, and she wasn't expecting Variam to come up with one either. *Great.* 'You made it sound like you were okay with Anne having a superpowered evil side.'

'Well, I kind of am in the short term,' Luna said. 'But I learned my lesson from the monkey's paw. You don't get something for nothing.' She paused. 'You think there's any way to use that? One jinn to counter another?'

'Runs into exactly the same problem,' I said. 'The thing's not on our side. No, I think that right now, we don't know enough. The first step is to find out what we're dealing with.'

'Arachne?' Luna asked.

I shook my head. 'If she knew anything, she'd have told us already. I'm thinking of something a bit more direct.'

'Need any help?'

'Thanks, but no. This is going to be a one-man trip.'

*　*　*

I stayed in the Hollow after Luna had left, waiting for evening. The sun set beneath the miniature world's tiny horizon, the sky fading through shades of purple and gold as the stars came out, first in ones and twos and then in clusters, shining down in a million pinpoints. I've never been able to work out exactly what the sky is that you can see from the Hollow. They aren't real stars – they can't be – but at the same time they seem *too* real to be just an illusion. Sometimes I wonder if they're a reflection of another world, just as the Hollow is a reflection of ours.

I waited for an hour after night had fallen. Anne didn't come back. She knows the Hollow better than any of the rest of us, and with her magic she's quite capable of sleeping in a tree or curled up in a bush. I could probably have found her if I'd gone looking, but I didn't. I don't like using my divination to spy on friends, though I was pretty sure that what I was about to do would be just as likely to upset her, and for exactly the same reasons. But I needed to know more.

Once I knew it was the right time, I stripped to my underwear and lay down on my futon. The night was warm enough that I only pulled the duvet up to my waist. The dreamstone glinted off to my right, and I took a last glance at it before closing my eyes. I didn't feel the need to touch it any more – I'd been practising enough that it was easy. Sleep came.

I stepped through the door and the world solidified into verdant woodland. Birds sang in the treetops, and shafts of sunlight slanted down between the leaves to fall upon the undergrowth of the forest floor. The temperature was pleasantly warm, that of a summer afternoon, and the air smelled of grass and seeds. This was Elsewhere . . . or Anne's part of it.

Arachne had been teaching me about differing levels of dreams. True dreams are constructs of the unconscious mind, and while with training one can learn to become partly conscious of them, there isn't much you can do with them. A dreamshard – such as the one in which I'd visited Arachne – is created more deliberately. It's shaped by the whim of its creator, and it makes for a comfortable place in which to meet, or be alone.

Elsewhere is a very different story. It's less of a dream and more of a world, one that doesn't work the same as ours. What happens here may not touch our reality, at least not physically, but the dangers are real, and not everyone who goes there comes back. When you visit Elsewhere, you don't see its 'pure' form – you see an interpretation, shaped either by yourself or by another. In this case, the version of Elsewhere that I was seeing was shaped by Anne. Anne spent a long time here when she was younger – maybe too long – and her Elsewhere feels more real than mine, more detailed and vivid.

I couldn't see through the forest cover, but I knew where I was. Over to my left were the great trees, spiralling behemoths the size of small mountains, with houses and platforms built around their branches. The times I've visited Anne, that's where I've met her, and I've always found it beautiful. This time, though, I had a different destination in mind. I turned right and started walking.

Normally when you visit another person's Elsewhere you always find them, or a doorway to their dreams. It doesn't matter what direction you go in, the place reshapes itself around you. With the dreamstone and my newfound skill, though, I could shape my own path, finding the destination that I wanted. The trees ended at a wall of black glass, mirror-smooth and darkly reflective. I jumped up to the top.

The inside of the wall was as different from the outside as night and day. Outside was forest, the green canopy stretching on and on for ever; inside was black glass, perfect and lifeless, straight lines and smooth curves. The wall had a parapet, but despite its neatness, there was something wrong with the design. There were no stairs, no gates or towers, nothing that would make the wall useful to living people, as though it had been sketched in abstract and left unfinished.

The wall formed a circle, and at the centre was a tower, rising up into the grey sky. Looking up, I could see a balcony. Once upon a time I would have gone looking for a staircase or a door, or some other way inside. This time I fixed my eyes on the tower, focused and walked forward. There was a moment's resistance, then my foot came down on black stone.

I was standing on the balcony. The view was amazing, seeming to stretch out for ever, but I didn't pause to look; I'd seen it before. High arches led into a sitting room of dark wood and green glass. It was empty.

I frowned. *Where is she?*

I walked across the room and opened the door at the end to reveal a corridor with white sphere lights glowing from the walls. I kept going deeper, my footsteps echoing inside the tower. They were the only sound; the stillness was absolute. I climbed a flight of stairs, picked out a door and opened it.

Inside was a bedroom. The far wall was open, a line of arched windows following the curve of the tower and giving a view out onto the landscape beyond. A storm was raging in the distance, sparks of lightning flashing at the base of a vast anvil-shaped cloud.

To the left was a double bed, the sheets and duvet rumpled, and it was occupied. Lying on it was Anne . . . or someone who looked just like her. She had her hands behind her head and one knee up, long hair spread over the pillow, and was wearing a red chemise with black lace, cut long with slits in the side to leave her legs bare. 'Long time no see,' she said with a smile.

'Last time you met me downstairs.'

'Last time *I* was the one who needed to talk to *you*,' the girl who looked like Anne said. She patted the bed next to her. 'Come on, don't be shy.'

I looked around for a chair; there wasn't one. I crossed the room and sat on the bed, a little distance away. The girl raised her eyebrows but made no move to close the distance. 'I've wondered,' I said. 'What should I call you?'

'Just "Anne" is fine.'

'That feels a little misleading.'

'But I *am* Anne,' the girl said. 'Just not a part she likes to think about.' She tilted her head. 'You can keep thinking of me as "not-Anne" if it makes you feel better.'

How did she know that? I'd never used that name to Anne, not once. 'Should I give you time to dress?'

She laughed. 'I never know whether you're serious when you do that. It's funny either way.'

I paused, looking at not-Anne. She looked back at me.

'So,' I said.

'So?'

'Last time you came to the point a lot faster.'

'Last time we were in a little more of a rush.' She smiled

at me. 'Sure you're in such a hurry to talk? We can always do that after.'

'I . . . think I'd like to settle this first.'

Not-Anne rolled her eyes. 'God, you're slow. How many invitations do you need?'

I raised my eyebrows. 'I'm slow?'

'What do you think?'

'I think . . .' I looked at Anne, or this reflection of her. The more I looked at her, the harder it was to remember that she *wasn't* Anne. And she had all of Anne's slender beauty, posed in a way that made it hard not to look. I knew exactly what she was implying, and it was more tempting than it should have been. 'I think you're trying to distract me.'

Not-Anne laughed again. Her mood seemed to shift more quickly than Anne's, amusement to annoyance and back again in an instant. 'Okay, *sometimes* you're quick. Though you'd be more fun if you were a little easier to manipulate.' She sighed, stretching in a way that made her body shift under the chemise. 'Go on, ask it.'

'Today, in Anne's flat, when I spoke mind-to-mind,' I said. 'It was you I was talking to, wasn't it?'

'Ding ding, advance to round two.'

'Except it wasn't just you. You were sharing space with the jinn.'

'Ding ding, round three.'

'So where is it?' I said. I looked around the tower. 'Here?'

'Bzzt. Sorry, you are not a winner. Weren't you listening to Dr Shirland? This tower is single occupancy. I like my privacy, thank you very much.'

'It sure as hell wasn't single occupancy today,' I said.

'Okay, so the jinn's not a permanent resident. But somehow,

it's getting in. And if it's getting in, then it's also getting out. So how exactly is that happening?'

'Answers on a postcard?'

I took an angry step towards her. 'Stop playing around and answer the question!'

'Or what?' Not-Anne stretched, crossing her wrists above her head with a smile. 'You'll punish me?'

I glared at not-Anne, took a breath. *She's playing like this is a game.* I tried not to think about the fact that if it *was* a game, then I was pretty sure I was losing.

The problem was that it was Anne. This kind of thing is usually something I'm good at, but it was too easy for her to put me off-balance. 'That jinn is getting in. And you know what? I'm pretty sure you've got something to do with it.'

Not-Anne shrugged.

'Are you going to say anything?'

'Why?' Not-Anne sat up and hopped off the bed, then walked past me. I turned to watch as she opened the wardrobe, talking over her shoulder. 'It's not my job to find things out for you.'

'I'd say it concerns you in a fairly major way.'

'Oh, not disagreeing.' Not-Anne took out a blue velvet dressing gown and slipped it on, then turned to face me, tying the belt around her waist. 'I just don't see the problem.'

'You don't have a problem with some incredibly powerful disembodied entity possessing you?'

'Who says we're being possessed?'

'That seems to be what's happening.'

'No, that's what's happening to *that* Anne.' Not-Anne pointed through the windows into the distance. 'I, on the other hand, am doing just fine.'

I stared at not-Anne for a second. 'You're not getting possessed at all, are you? When Anne has these blackouts and the jinn takes over . . . you can think and remember. *She's* the one who can't.'

Not-Anne looked at me.

'What happened in Anne's flat today?'

'I told you. Do your own legwork.'

'Damn it!'

'You really need to relax more,' not-Anne said, walking over to the windows. She turned and sat on one of the sills, crossing one leg over the other. The distant clouds formed a backdrop to her head and shoulders. 'Look, Alex, it's not like we're on different sides here. You want Anne healthy and happy and alive. So do I. Haven't you noticed that the only time I've pulled the trigger on this has been when we really, really need it? Would you rather those Crusaders had managed to get us today? Because I'm pretty sure you don't.'

'No,' I said. 'This was the better option. But I've got the feeling that this isn't going to stop.'

'Who *wants* it to stop?' not-Anne said. 'I don't know about you, but the way I see it, having a jinn in your back pocket is a pretty handy last resort. Besides, stop acting so high and mighty. It's not as though you've never got your hands dirty.'

'That's not the part that worries me,' I said. 'Remember the first time we talked? You told me that one thing you and Anne agreed on was that you're not going to be a slave again. What's going to happen when you call on that jinn one time too often and it decides it doesn't want to leave?'

'I don't know, Alex, what do *you* think's going to happen?' Not-Anne tilted her head. 'What terrible thing do you think that jinn's going to do to that other Anne, the one you care about so much? You think maybe it's going to take control? Lock her away in her own mind, in some prison where she could never see anyone else again? But hey, who'd do something like *that*?'

I was silent.

'You know what it's like to be a prisoner?' not-Anne said, and her voice was hard. 'Shut away in the dark, only let out when she needs you to hurt something, like an attack dog on a leash? So yeah, when that jinn first showed up with his offer, you'd better believe I said yes. Because I am *done* with being chained up in the basement.'

I didn't have a good answer to that. From her perspective, this arrangement really *did* suck. And I could see how she could grow to resent it. Anne relied upon her other self to survive, but she wasn't willing to let it out.

But while I did feel sympathy, I wasn't totally naïve. When you spend time in Elsewhere you learn to trust your instincts, and my intuition told me that if not-Anne ever got fully loose, it could be really bad news for everyone around her. 'What do you think about Dr Shirland's solution?' I said. 'The two of you becoming integrated?'

Not-Anne gave a short laugh. 'Yeah, right.'

'You don't agree?'

'Alex, don't take this personally,' not-Anne said. 'But you really don't understand me or Anne as well as you think you do.'

I paused. 'When that jinn came to you, what was its offer?'

'Is that all you care about?' Not-Anne walked to the bed, grabbed a pillow off it and threw it at me. 'Figure it out yourself.'

I caught the pillow and lowered it. Not-Anne was sitting on the bed, her face turned away from me, and there was something different about her pose. I didn't think she was trying to produce an effect this time. 'It's not the only thing I care about,' I said quietly.

'Do you know what it feels like to have your skin pulled off in strips, layer by layer?' Not-Anne didn't turn to look at me; her voice was cold and distant. 'Having your body violated with hooks and scalpels? Knowing that it won't end until you're nothing but a torn and bleeding pile of flesh?'

'No,' I said. 'Though I'm not sure you'd want to trade your experiences for mine.'

'Like it matters.'

I looked at not-Anne for a long moment. 'I'm sorry,' I said at last. 'I should have come earlier.'

'Just—' Her voice wavered, steadied. 'Just go away.'

I paused. 'Is that really what you want?'

'Yes, I—' Not-Anne took a deep breath. 'Not now.'

I stood looking at not-Anne a little longer, then turned and let myself out. I took a last glance as the door closed behind me; she was still facing away, looking out at the distant sky.

It was the next day.

The bell above the door went *ding-ding* to announce another customer. The sounds of the Camden street outside swelled, then became muffled as the door swung closed once more. It was another bright sunny day, and the shop was bustling.

'I'm worried,' I told Luna.

'I got that part.'

'What do you think I should do?'

'Why are you asking *me*?'

We were in the Arcana Emporium, or maybe I should call it the Arcana Emporium Mark 2. It looked cleaner than it had been when I'd owned it, but then that's what you expect from a building that's just been renovated. The walls were bright white, the tables and shelves covered with pale green cloth, with the same old merchandise lined up neatly upon them: crystal balls, wands, daggers, statuettes of stone and glass. There was even a herb rack, placed in more or less the same position as the old one. You really couldn't tell that the place had been burned down.

The clientele hadn't changed at all. Teenagers in jeans and T-shirts, men with beards and women with big handbags, a pair of Americans in baseball caps. Most would be tourists or window-shoppers; some would be there because they thought they knew about the magical world; a much smaller fraction would be there because they actually did. And rarest of all, you'd have the ones who genuinely needed something: an adept, perhaps, or a novice. But those sorts of customers usually arrived very late or very early. The middle of the day was tourist time.

Luna was standing behind the counter, waiting at the till. The number of customers in the shop waxed and waned, but relatively few spent any time buying anything. Mostly they were there to look and point, and there was plenty of room for me to talk, as long as I did it quietly.

'I'm starting to realise how big a problem this is,' I said. 'Up until this year I figured it was something we could solve with magic. Like, figure out the connection to the jinn, shut it down, fix things that way. Talking to her, though, it made me realise that it's not that at all. That other part of Anne's still going to be there, and she's still going to be watching and waiting. And the thing is, I can see her point. She *has* been treated pretty badly. If I were in a position like that, I'd probably grab on to the first chance I got too.'

'I guess.'

'But it's not like we can just give her what she wants and make her happy. Because from what I've seen, I'm pretty sure that the kinds of things that make *her* happy are really unlikely to make anyone *else* happy. She's got all of the parts of Anne that Anne doesn't want to face. What happens when all the stuff that's been sealed up like that for so many years gets to have—'

'Oh, I'm sorry,' a voice broke in. 'How much are the crystal sphere things?'

Luna and I looked up to see a smiling and round-shaped woman in a hat. 'The crystal balls?' Luna asked. 'Ten pounds.'

'Oh, I didn't mean the large ones. I meant the ones one size smaller.'

'Those are nine pounds.'

'And the very small ones?'

'Seven-fifty. The prices are just underneath, on the shelf.'

'Oh, they are? I didn't see them.'

Once the woman was gone, I turned back to Luna. 'What do you think?'

'About what?'

I looked at her.

'Oh right. Look, Alex, I don't know. Do we have to have this conversation *now*?'

'I've got to spend this evening prepping for the Council meeting tomorrow,' I said. 'Besides, *you* spent more than enough time bugging *me* back when I was the one running this place.'

'And now you're getting your own back,' Luna muttered. 'Great. Okay, look, I'm going to ask again. Why are you asking *me?*'

'Because it's a choice between you or Vari, and when it comes to talking about these kinds of things, Vari's got even less patience.'

'Isn't there a much more obvious candidate here?' Luna asked. 'As in, you know, the person you're talking about? How about instead of having this conversation with me, you have it with *her?*'

'And how am I going to bring that up?' I said. '"Hi, Anne, so I went into your mind without telling you and had a chat with the part of yourself that you're ashamed of and keep cut off from everyone else, and we had a talk about the thing that you've already made really clear you don't want to talk about with anybody. Now would you like to talk about it some more?"'

'I'm not saying it's going to be a good conversation, but it seems like a better solution than moping around my counter.'

'Have you got any advice?'

'Like what?'

'You're Anne's best friend,' I said. 'If anyone would know, it ought to be you.'

Luna sighed. 'I suppose I am. But that doesn't mean I know everything about her. Actually, in a lot of ways, the more time I've spent with Anne, the more I realise I don't know much about her at all. I mean, she trusts me and I trust her. And I've opened up to her a lot. There were times, when things were really bad, and I was lying on my bed crying, and having her there to talk to . . . it really helped. And I knew she'd never tell anyone else. But she's never really done the same. I think you might actually know more of her secrets than any of the rest of us. Ever since you went to find her in Sagash's castle, I've noticed that she acts differently around you than she does around everyone else. Even Vari.'

'But I don't know what to say,' I said. 'I mean, if I'm dealing with someone like Onyx threatening me, or someone like Levistus trying to get me killed, I know exactly what to do. With something like this, I don't. I'm not a psychologist.'

'So go to an actual psychologist, then. What's that woman's name, the mind mage? Dr Shirland?'

I sighed. 'I asked her. She says she's happy to see Anne, but she won't call her up and nag her to come, because the patient's supposed to be the one making the decision to participate and pressuring her would be unethical.'

'Then it sounds to me like you're back to asking Anne.'

Another customer came to the counter and again we broke off. This one wanted suggestions for a present for his girlfriend, and while Luna was busy with him two more joined the queue behind. I was left alone with my thoughts for a good ten minutes. I didn't come up with any answers I liked.

'Okay,' Luna said once she was finished, turning back to me. 'Maybe you should focus on the part you can do something about. Like the question of how that jinn's getting access.'

'Yeah,' I said. 'Well, as far as that goes, I've got a guess. Back when I spoke to Dr Shirland, she thought that the jinn wouldn't be able to possess Anne without some sort of connection. I was mostly worried about Anne finding that jinn's item and picking it up again, but now that I think about it, that wasn't exactly what Dr Shirland said. What she said it needed was a sympathetic link. And that got me thinking. Linking minds is exactly what my dream-stone does. And I'm not the only mage who has one.'

'Who else— *Oh*,' Luna said. 'Last year . . .'

'We got another dreamstone for Richard,' I said. 'Yeah. Arachne told me at the time that it was different from mine, less for talking, more for dominating. What if *that's* how the jinn is getting in? He's sitting off in his mansion somewhere and giving it access to Anne's mind?'

'And you think that dark-side Anne is letting it in.'

I nodded. 'Dr Shirland was pretty sure that it wouldn't be able to just brute-force its way into Anne's mind. But if you've got someone letting you in through the back door . . .'

Luna thought about it. 'How would he know when to set up the link? I mean, he's got other things to do, right? I can't really see him just sitting around all day waiting.'

'I don't know,' I admitted. 'But out of all the ways it could be getting access, this is the best answer I can come up with.'

Luna frowned. 'I don't like it, but it fits.' A customer made to approach the counter, but Luna glanced at them with a *wait please* gesture and they withdrew. 'Explains why he wanted that dreamstone. He's been planning this a long time, hasn't he?'

'We already knew that.'

'So what's he doing all this for?' Luna asked. 'What's his endgame?'

'My best guess is that he wants Anne,' I said. 'It's not like he'd be the first one. Sagash and Morden already tried.

With Anne's power and the jinn's power, all concentrated in one person . . . that would be pretty scary.'

'Don't know if either of them would be keen on following his orders,' Luna said. 'Okay. So if that's true, how do we stop it?'

'Shut off his access to Anne,' I said. 'Which means getting that other Anne to stop opening the back door. Which brings us round in a circle.'

'Yeah, well,' Luna said, 'then I'm going to go round in a circle too. You should be having this conversation with *her*.'

I made a face but didn't answer. The customer approached Luna again and this time she turned to talk to him, leaving me alone with my thoughts in the busy shop.

9

'And that brings us up to date,' Bahamus finished. 'We have not heard further from Onyx, and all signs indicate that negotiations have come to a close.'

'They aren't closed until we agree,' Sal Sarque said. 'And by "we" I mean the whole Council, Bahamus, not just you.'

'I agree,' Alma said. 'Why were we not consulted?'

Bahamus inclined his head. 'You are being consulted now.'

'This seems very ill-advised,' Undaaris said sharply. 'I think a matter like this should have been brought before the entire Council from the beginning.'

'There were security considerations,' Bahamus said. 'In any case, the final decision is of course subject to a full Council vote.' He nodded in my direction. 'If you have any further queries about the details, Verus is better informed to answer.'

Several pairs of eyes turned in my direction; none were friendly. *Thanks, Bahamus*, I thought. Well, it wasn't like I hadn't seen this coming.

'Very well, Verus,' Alma said coolly. 'Perhaps you would like to inform us as to how you plan to carry out this . . . escapade.'

'I'm afraid I can't take credit for the plan or its execution,' I said. *You're not hanging this one on me.* 'But the basic idea is that Onyx will supply us with a time and a place where Mage Drakh is due to make a scheduled appearance.

The Keepers will prepare the area in advance, then move in once his presence is confirmed.'

'What kind of appearance?' Druss asked.

'Onyx hasn't given details,' I said. 'However, from some hints he's let slip, and from some additional information gathered by Council intelligence, it seems probable that it involves the adept defence association we've been hearing about. Mage Drakh apparently has been due to speak at one of their gatherings for some time. It seems likely that this is how Onyx is planning to track Drakh down.'

'You think he's going to be there?' Druss asked.

'I think it's plausible,' I said. 'Exactly when he'll be there, and whether Onyx will be informed enough to know, is another question.'

Bahamus cleared his throat. 'Onyx's information, in this regard at least, seems accurate. We've cross-checked the other details he's supplied, and all have been corroborated.'

'How do we know he's not setting us up?' Sal Sarque demanded.

'We don't,' I said. 'Council intelligence is reasonably sure that Onyx and Drakh are not working together. How-ever, Onyx could still be planning something of his own.'

'You think he is?' Druss asked.

'Personally?' I said. 'No. I think Onyx intends to set two of his enemies against one another. He doesn't need to betray us. From his perspective, no matter whether we beat Drakh or Drakh beats us, he comes out ahead.'

Druss gave a slow nod, and from out of the corner of my eye, I could see that even Alma and Sarque looked grudgingly convinced. I'd noticed over the past months that the fastest way to sell the Council something was to tell them that people were acting out of self-interest.

'How many of these adepts are there?' Sal Sarque asked. 'We going to have enough to deal with them?'

'The Keepers are planning to deploy additional security forces,' Bahamus said. 'The adepts should not be a concern.'

'The majority of the adepts are not aligned with— Drakh.' I said. I caught myself from saying 'Richard' just in time. 'I don't believe an aggressive approach is necessary.'

'Yes, Verus, your feelings on the subject of adepts are well known,' Alma said dryly. 'The Council will decide how to deal with the issue in due course.'

I set my teeth but didn't answer. Alma glanced to one side. 'Levistus?'

'The plan seems . . . potentially workable,' Levistus said. His eyes rested upon me, considering. 'Depending on whether this associate of Verus can deliver on his promises.'

'Onyx is not my associate,' I said sharply. 'And I most certainly would not count on him to deliver on anything.'

'Regardless,' Levistus said, looking at Bahamus, 'I must still question the price.'

An argument started over the terms, and how many imbued items they should be paying. I hid my irritation as they second-guessed my performance in the negotiations.

'Any amount of imbued items is too many,' Sal Sarque said for at least the third time. 'It sets a bad precedent—'

'And you think having Drakh running around with more than fifty is better?' Druss asked.

'I don't see why—'

'If I may,' a new voice said, 'I have a question for Verus.'

The other members of the Senior Council turned to look at the man who had just spoken. He was tall and thin, and wore a suit with a red silk scarf knotted loosely around his neck. This was Spire, one of the swing votes of the

Council. I'd only seen him in the Star Chamber four or five times.

'Well?' Alma said when Spire didn't go on.

Spire turned to me. 'What do you think of this plan?'

'I'm . . . not quite sure what you mean.'

'It's quite simple,' Spire said. 'You've answered many questions as to the technical details of this operation. However, you have been silent as to whether, in your personal opinion, this plan is likely to work.'

'That would be a decision for the Senior Council,' I said.

'Indeed,' Spire said. 'And as a member of the Junior Council, you have the right to advise.'

'Come on, Verus,' Druss said impatiently. 'Stop dancing.'

I hesitated. 'I don't have full access to the operational intelligence involved.'

'We understand this,' Spire said. 'Go on.'

I could feel everyone's eyes on me. Bahamus's gaze was especially sharp and I chose my words carefully. 'As I said, my access is limited. However, based only on the information available to me, then my best guess would be no.'

Several of the Council frowned. 'Excuse me?' Alma said.

'You just said Onyx was going to hold up his end,' Sal Sarque said.

'No, I said I didn't think he was intending to sell us out,' I said. 'But it's not Onyx's intentions I'd be worried about.'

'Then what should we be worrying about?' Druss asked.

'About Onyx screwing things up,' I said. 'I really don't trust him to carry out this kind of plot without botching it somehow. That's problem number one. Problem number two is that within an hour of returning from our meeting with Onyx, my aide and I were attacked by a group of mages and adepts.'

'And this is relevant because . . . ?' Alma asked.

'I think we can safely assume the timing was not a coincidence.'

'I fail to grasp your reasoning,' Levistus said. 'Are you implying that you were attacked by Drakh?'

'No,' I said. 'I don't think those men were sent by Drakh.' I carefully didn't look at Sal Sarque; I knew damn well where those men had come from. 'However, they knew about our negotiations. And if they could find out, so can others.'

Alma frowned. 'This seems speculative—'

I cut her off. 'It's well established that Richard Drakh has an effective intelligence network. The Keepers have been trying to get him for years and he's always managed to evade them. If one group has caught wind of this, then I think it's likely that Richard Drakh has too, and if he hasn't he will soon. He may not know the details, but he'd only need to hear a rumour of me meeting with Onyx to become suspicious, and once he starts investigating it won't take him long to find out more.'

I was about to keep going, but Alma raised a hand. 'Thank you, Verus. Your opinion is noted.' She glanced around. 'Regardless of whether we accept the specific terms, I think it would be appropriate to vote on whether to move forward with the plan.'

I sat back; my part was over. 'I agree,' Bahamus said. 'I vote in favour.'

'I vote in favour as well,' Sal Sarque said. 'Though I'm noting my reservations about the way in which we were notified and the people we're going to be working with.' It was obvious from the glance he shot me that he wasn't only talking about Onyx.

'Well, I vote against,' Druss said. 'Sorry, Bahamus, but

this whole thing smells dodgy. Relying on someone like Onyx? Bad idea.'

There was a silence. Heads turned to look at Undaaris, who hunched slightly under the gazes. 'Well,' he said. 'There are many issues to consider . . .'

'Today, please,' Alma said.

'I . . . I'll abstain.'

I saw Levistus shoot a glance at Undaaris. Levistus sensed my gaze and flicked his eyes to me, and for an instant it felt as though we shared the same thought. *I may hate you, and you may hate me, but I'll at least give you credit for deserving more respect than Undaaris.*

'I also abstain,' Spire said.

Two to one, I thought. Everyone turned to look at Alma and Levistus.

Alma tapped her fingers on the table. 'A risk, but worth the attempt,' she said at last. 'I vote in favour.'

I felt rather than heard several of the mages around the table let out a breath. The secretary's pen scratched. *And that's it*, I thought with a sense of foreboding. The decision was made.

The mages of the Council came filing out of the Star Chamber in ones and twos, their aides splitting off to join them. Bahamus was towards the middle of the crowd, and gave me a cool look as he passed.

Anne glanced after him. *Did something happen?*

I didn't do a very good job of backing his proposal, I admitted. Maybe I should have kept my reservations to myself.

Movement in the futures caught my attention, and I turned to see Spire walking towards us. 'Verus,' he greeted me. 'If you're not too busy, perhaps you'd like to have a word.'

'Alone?'

Spire inclined his head to Anne. 'Mage Walker is welcome to join us should you so wish.'

'In that case, I'd be happy to.'

We started walking together, Anne falling in a little behind us. I caught the glances from other aides as we left the anteroom; everyone would know about this meeting soon. 'You aren't worried about being seen with me?' I asked.

'Should I be?'

'No, but that doesn't seem to stop plenty of others.'

We walked down the corridor and into one of the conservatories. The War Rooms might have been designed as a fortress, but people have been living here for a very long time and they've added quite a few amenities over the years. The conservatories are my favourites. There are two of them, and they look like very nice ceremonial gardens that somehow happen to have been transplanted deep underground. There are flowers, shrubs, small trees and even a fish pond fed by a bubbling fountain. I'm not sure how they keep the plants growing, but it's certainly a pleasant place to walk. As a side benefit, the open paths and the noise of the fountain make it very hard for anyone to eavesdrop.

'What would be your estimate of the chances of this plan's success?' Spire asked.

'Maybe ten or twenty per cent.'

'So low?'

'If anything, that's being generous,' I said. Privately I'd have put it in single figures. 'To be successful, an operation like this needs to be kept secret. Too many people know.'

'Then what do you think the most likely outcome will be?'

I shrugged. 'Based on Richard Drakh's previous behaviour, I'd expect him to let the Keepers spring their trap and be nowhere near when it closes. The Keepers rough up or kill a bunch of adepts and have nothing to show for it. Relations between the Council and the adept community break down further, and Drakh gets away and makes the Council look foolish.'

'That does seem plausible,' Spire said. 'But why do you base that on his past behaviour?'

'Drakh has always been . . . well, the best word would be pragmatic,' I said. 'Maximum return for minimum risk. He's fine with retreating if it serves his purposes.'

Spire nodded. 'But in that case, why attack the Vault?'

I was silent for a moment. 'Presumably because he felt that what was in there *was* worth the risk of fighting.'

We stopped by the fountain. Water foamed and bubbled from the ornamental feature at the far side; below the surface, koi hung lazily, keeping position with an occasional twitch of their fins. They were each more than a foot long, their scales a mixture of gold and white and red. 'Do you know why Morden was raised to the Senior Council?' Spire asked.

'I assume his acquisitions from White Rose had something to do with it.'

'Vihaela's dowry, yes. Do you know how many previous Dark mages have attempted something similar?'

I shook my head.

'You can look it up in the histories if you're curious. But he wasn't the first, or the twentieth.'

I looked at Spire. He was tall enough that the two of us were on a level. 'So why do you think he succeeded where all the others failed?'

'Morden no doubt believes it is due to his special acumen,'

Spire said. 'Personally, I think the answer is simpler. The Council is experiencing one of its periodic transitions. Morden was in the right place at the right time.'

I shrugged. 'I suppose that's possible.'

'You think Drakh might overthrow the Council, don't you?'

I glanced at Spire sharply; he tilted his head. 'You've clearly considered the possibility,' Spire said. 'That if you hold out long enough, Drakh might take care of your enemies for you.'

'I would of course never consider siding with Richard Drakh against the Council.'

'It won't happen, you know. The Council will simply adapt.'

'Don't people always think that *every* long-lived institution is immortal right up until the point where it falls apart?'

Spire smiled fleetingly. 'Perhaps. Here's another question for you. If you were on the Senior Council, what would you do with that position?'

I looked at Spire, considering. *What the hell.* I might as well tell the truth. 'First, I'd put an end to Levistus's constant attempts to get me killed,' I said. 'Once I was done with that, I'd use my position to try to speak for the people who don't have any kind of a voice. Right now, the only ones who have any real representation on the Light Council are Light mages. The remaining 99.9 per cent of British magical society are left out in the cold. Independents, adepts, sensitives, magical creatures and yes, even Dark mages. They're all real, and they're all out there, but if you listen to the discussions in that chamber, then half the time it's as though they don't even exist, and the other half they're treated as potential enemies.'

'And you think all of those groups have similar interests?'

'No,' I said. 'I'm not completely naïve. I'm aware that any political system will disproportionately favour those with influence and power. But there has to be some sort of balance. Right now, the Council *only* represents those with influence and power. That's not sustainable. Perhaps it's as you say, and Morden took advantage of that situation to get his seat. But in that case, it raises an obvious question, doesn't it? If Morden was the counterbalancing element, and now he's in prison, who's going to take his place?'

'A very good question,' Spire said, and nodded to me. 'Thank you for the discussion, Verus. We'll talk again. Mage Walker.' He turned and left.

Anne and I watched him go. *Well*, I said once he was gone. *That was interesting.*

Do you think that went well or badly?

I'm not really sure, I admitted. *But one thing's for certain: I don't think we can count on him to bail us out when we're in trouble.* I glanced at Anne. *I'm going to visit Arachne. Want to come?*

I'd . . . rather not. Sorry.

Okay. See you tomorrow.

'. . . and that's when we split up,' I finished.

'I see,' Arachne said. She was hunched over me, her two front legs almost brushing mine. It's how she prefers to talk. Her eight eyes watched me opaquely, but I could hear the thoughtful tone in her voice. Around us, the clothes and threads of Arachne's lair shone in the light.

'So?' I said. 'What do you think?'

'Based on your meeting with Anne's other self,' Arachne said, 'then I would agree. Your dreamstone theory does seem like the best explanation. And, as Luna said, it fits with Richard's previous actions.'

'Then how do you think we should stop it?'

'I'm afraid I don't have any advice better than hers,' Arachne said. 'Talk to Anne.'

'But you're *you*,' I said. 'Haven't you got anything that could help? Some sort of item, or a spell?'

'Only to a very limited extent,' Arachne said. 'I could weave a shield, some sort of cocoon to screen Anne from the jinn's influence. But it would require her to remain here, and she'd be unable to leave without losing her protection. I doubt very much she'd be willing to live like that for ever. Besides, I'm not at all sure it would work. Shields function best when they protect against something from outside. The jinn's access comes from within.'

'Have you got anything that would work from within?'

'No, and even if I did, I wouldn't use it. Any kind of effect powerful enough to prevent Anne's other self from acting would have the potential to cause lasting mental damage to both sides of her personality. I can't get you out of this one.'

'I know,' I said, raising a hand. 'You're going to say I should talk to her.'

'There's a reason everyone keeps giving you the same advice.'

'And I'm going to. But I'm starting to think it's not going to work.'

'Why?'

'We know all of this was set up by Richard,' I said. 'The Vault, the jinn, everything. It wasn't the only thing he was aiming for with that raid, but it was definitely up there on his priority list, and he's been planning it for a long time. Now, *maybe* if I talk to Anne, I can persuade her, and *maybe* she can figure out some way to fix this. But even if I do, my gut tells me that it won't be that easy. Richard wouldn't have staked that much on this plan if I could undo the whole thing with a pep talk. There'll be some other way for the jinn to gain access. One way or another, this is not going away.'

'Unfortunately, that does seem quite possible.'

'And that's not the only problem,' I said. 'There's Rachel. That prophecy of Shireen's said that if I wanted to live, I'd have to turn her against Richard, and I still haven't found any way to do that. I've tried to get in touch with her, and it hasn't worked. Even if it did, she'd probably just try to kill me on sight. And then if *that* isn't enough, I still need to find some way to get an edge against Levistus or Sal Sarque or whoever else tries to get rid of me next. None of the imbued items we've found have worked and we're running out of time.'

'So what course of action are you considering?'

'I've tried all my personal sources of information,' I said. 'And I've asked you, and all my other friends. I think I need to go further.' I looked at Arachne. 'With your permission, I'd like to speak with your . . . acquaintance in the tunnels below.'

Arachne was silent.

'Is that okay?' I asked.

Arachne withdrew her legs from either side of me and walked away. The movements of her eight legs were slow, almost sluggish. 'Arachne?' I asked. 'Are you okay?'

'Yes,' Arachne answered. She turned back to me, legs moving in intricate steps. 'Perfectly.'

I looked at her doubtfully. 'You seem a little . . .'

'Something long foreseen,' Arachne said. She waved one leg towards the tunnels beyond. 'Go ahead.'

'Right now?'

'One time is exactly as good as another.'

I rose to my feet and started across the room, then paused in the tunnel entrance. Something about Arachne's manner felt off. 'Are you sure you're all right?'

'I'll be fine, Alex,' Arachne said. 'I'll be waiting here.' She lifted a leg. 'Go.'

In the caverns beneath Arachne's lair lives a dragon.

I've only met the dragon twice, and both visits are hard to remember. There was something disorientating about the experience, like looking through an unfocused lens or trying to retrace a path you followed in a dream. Dragons don't fit in our world, or maybe it's more accurate to say that we don't fit in theirs. According to Arachne, dragons exist outside time as we perceive it, only touching our timeline at points of their choosing. To them, our world is like a story in a book: they can flip between pages as they choose, and if they decide to leave, we have exactly as much ability to stop them as a fictional character has to stop you from closing the book and putting it on a shelf. So Arachne says, at least, and nothing I've seen has given me reason to doubt her. But while Arachne will tell me about dragons in general, she shuts up when I probe for specifics as to this dragon in particular. Some of the things she's said have implied a special relationship, but what that relationship is, I don't know.

The tunnels beyond the lair went down and kept on going. To begin with they looked to be carved out of rock, but the further I went the more jagged and bumpy they became; something about them made me sure that they had existed for a very, very long time. Occasional forks and turnings appeared in the light of my torch, but I walked by without paying attention. Normally I'd use my divination to navigate under these kinds of conditions, but somehow I knew that in this place, that didn't matter. If the dragon wanted me to find it, I'd find it.

I can't say exactly how long I walked. It felt like maybe an hour, but it could have been more. Gradually I realised that I wasn't walking through a tunnel any more. My divination was still showing me a narrow path, but the light of my torch wasn't revealing any walls. I clicked off the torch and let my eyes adjust to the darkness.

As my night vision set in, pinpoints appeared in the blackness around me, coalescing into stars. Not the sky of the Hollow, but the constellations of Earth: the Great Square of Pegasus, Orion, the bright Summer Triangle of Vega, Deneb and Altair. The stars were below me as well as above; peering down and to the left and right, I could see others, ones that would never appear in the sky of England. I was walking on a thick pathway, twisting and winding, hanging suspended in a bottomless void. The starlight was enough to see by; I put away the torch and kept walking.

My footsteps were the only sound in the silence. Stars twinkled, bright against the darkness, the ribbon of the Milky Way a curving shape above my head. As I walked I began to make out other paths to the right and to the left, visible as black bands against the starry backdrop. Connecting paths linked my route to theirs, and the distance between them grew shorter the further I went, converging to a point.

At the centre of the web, the paths linked to form a small island. Through some trick of the starlight, the middle of the island was illuminated, revealing a heavy stone chair. Sitting straight-backed upon it was a human shape. I approached and stood in front of her, studying her.

At first glance she looked like a woman of indeterminate age, maybe thirty and maybe fifty. She wore a white garment that left her arms bare and looked something like a cross between a pleated dress and a toga. Her features were plain and ordinary, yet at the same time there was something regal about them, as though she was accustomed to being obeyed. She looked human, but even if I hadn't known what to expect, I think I would have guessed that she wasn't. It was the eyes: even from a distance they didn't look quite right.

Mages usually steer clear of dragons. Received wisdom is that they're dangerous and hostile, and the mages in stories who go to dragons usually come to bad ends. I don't think the stories are completely true – dragons aren't hostile to humans, any more than you're hostile to an ant. Dangerous, on the other hand . . . that's hard to argue with.

There was a reason I hadn't come here before. Dragons can tell you your future, after a fashion. But I've never known whether they tell you what's going to happen, or whether hearing it from them is what *causes* it to happen. The one thing I was absolutely sure of was that this wasn't going to be comfortable.

I bowed slightly. 'Thank you for seeing me.'

The dragon looked at me without answering.

'Is there something I should call you?' I asked. 'Because we were never exactly introduced.'

The dragon spoke, its voice clear and musical. 'You have three questions.'

Right, I thought. *Not one for small talk.* I chose my words carefully. 'How can I break Anne free of the jinn's influence?'

'You cannot.'

I waited for the dragon to continue. It didn't. 'Is—?' I began, then stopped myself. I'd been about to ask, '*Is that it?*' 'That is . . . not as helpful an answer as I was expecting.'

The dragon watched me.

Okay, let's try adding more context. 'I've been told that to live, I have to turn Rachel against Richard,' I said. 'How can I accomplish that?'

'You must convince her of the truth of her fears.'

What fears? About the only emotions I ever saw from Rachel these days were anger and contempt. If she was afraid of anything, I didn't know what it was. 'Fine,' I said. 'Then please answer me this, as well as you can. How can I become powerful enough to protect the people I care about and stay alive?'

'You cannot.'

'What?'

The dragon looked at me.

'What am I supposed to do about *any* of those answers?'

'That is your decision to make.'

'No,' I said. Frustration pushed out my lingering fear and I walked forward, coming to a stop in front of the dragon. 'This is useless. You said you'd answer three questions. Answer them in a way I can understand!'

'You are a child looking through a keyhole.' Grey eyes looked steadily into mine. 'I may show you the other side, but I can neither bring you the key nor turn it. In the past you have rendered service to Arachne, and it is for this reason that you are here. Should you wish it, I will answer more fully. But be warned: in looking at your paths, you will change them. There is no turning back.'

'Then let's hear it.'

'The jinn's influence on your companion is due to the link between them. It was established at their first contact and is a function of the jinn's own power, which is far beyond yours. If you attempt to sever the link, it will destroy you. Rachel does not fear you as you are now, but she fears what you might become. Yet mad and broken as she is, she sees you more clearly than you see yourself. The next time you meet, do not talk; listen. Until you understand the ways in which the two of you are alike, any attempt you make to alter Rachel's path will fail. Finally, you do not possess the capacity to amass sufficient power to protect your friends and to stay alive; only one of the two.'

A chill went through me. 'What do you mean?' But even as I said it, I knew the answer.

'There are many paths for you to increase your abilities, but only one that will enable them to reach their fullest potential: that which you already wielded and abandoned. Yet even should you win the battle of minds, the power within is too great for your body to long sustain. You will burn like a candle, bright but short-lived.'

I stared back at the dragon. 'Or I could run away,' I said. 'That's what you're saying, isn't it? I could gain enough power to stay alive, but not if I want to protect everyone else.'

'Yes.'

I looked away. 'If I take that path,' I said after a moment, 'then who?'

'Do you really want to know?'

'No.' I paused, looked back at the dragon. 'Yes. I mean, I already know. It's Anne, isn't it?'

'Anne and Variam,' the dragon said. 'Luna's fate lies along another path.'

I looked away again, out over the island. Stars in a void formed bright pinpoints above the rugged stone. 'So that's the choice I'm going to get,' I said quietly.

'No,' the dragon said. 'It is the choice you would have had.' It nodded to me. 'Go.'

I looked back at the dragon. Now that I was close, I could see its eyes; they were cloudy and opaque. Something tugged at me, urging me to look into them; with an effort of will I averted my gaze, then turned and walked away. The dragon said nothing, and when I turned back to look after fifty paces, the woman and the chair were gone.

10

It was a week later.

The communicator went *ping*, signalling an incoming call. It was windy up on the hillside, and the sound was lost in the background noise, but I'd already seen the message coming and stopped what I was doing, walking over to my pack. Anne watched as I towelled my neck and arms before pulling out the focus. 'Verus.'

'This is Talisid.' Talisid's voice was hard to hear over the sound of the wind in the leaves, and I had to hold the communicator close to my ear. 'We've had the signal from Onyx. We're on.'

'When and where?'

'Friday evening. At the Tiger's Palace.'

Wonderful. 'When do you need me in?'

'The Senior Council is meeting this afternoon, and the Keepers are finalising plans. They're closed meetings, but make sure you're available in case you're needed.'

'. . . Okay.'

'I'll be in touch.' The light on the communicator winked out.

Anne walked over. '"In case you're needed"?'

I sighed and tossed the communicator back into my bag. 'It means that now they've made the deal, they don't need me any more. Knowing the Council, they won't tell us anything about what the plan's going to be or what we'll need, but they'll still expect us to make ourselves available.'

'So not much point rushing.'

'Nope. Back to work.'

We were in Wales, in a little valley hidden by the curve of two hills. It was a quiet and deserted spot, which was why I'd picked it for hand-to-hand practice. Anne had asked me to teach her a year or so back, and I'd agreed, even though it had struck me as a weird request. Like all life mages, Anne is basically unbeatable in hand-to-hand – her touch can inflict anything from healing to paralysis to death, and unless you're a life or a death mage, there's no way to stop it. But when I'd made that argument to Anne, she'd pointed out that she'd more than once ended up in close quarters with things that her magic *didn't* work against, due to them not being alive. In any case, she'd spent more than enough of her own time helping me out with my own physical training, so I'd gone along with it.

I went back and picked up the pads, slipping them onto my hands. The earth and grass were soft enough that we had no need for a mat. 'Left, then right,' I told Anne.

Anne sighed but obeyed. The combination was a basic one: left jab, right straight. Anne steadied herself, then hit. One-two, one-two.

'Don't drop your guard,' I said after the fortieth hit.

'I know,' Anne said. She kept her hands up for the next ten combinations, then started to let them droop. When she went in for number sixty-three, I reached out and tapped her on the forehead. Anne flinched and stepped back.

'I shouldn't be able to do that,' I told her.

Anne dropped her hands and stepped back. 'I'm getting tired.'

'I thought life mages didn't get tired.'

'Just because I can mute those receptors doesn't mean

it's a good idea,' Anne said. 'How many of these do you want me to do?'

'A few thousand.'

'Seriously?'

'That's how many repetitions it takes for something to sink into muscle memory.'

'Aren't we ever going to do more than just punches?'

'What were you expecting, high kicks?'

'Well . . . kind of.'

'Are you flexible enough for those?'

In answer, Anne lifted up her right knee, then wrapped her right hand behind the calf and pulled it up until her foot was above her head. She held her balance on one leg, looking at me with raised eyebrows and a 'what you think of that?' expression.

I nodded, bent forward to inspect her standing leg, then poked her hard in the thigh. Anne yelped and lost her balance, tumbling to the grass.

'That's why you don't do high kicks,' I told her.

'You are such a jerk!' Anne bounced up and swiped at me. I leaned back and let it breeze by, then stepped back. Anne took a step forward, realised I was already out of range and settled for glaring at me. 'You could have just told me.'

'This way's faster.'

'You're not the one getting jabbed in the leg!'

'Take that same pose again,' I said. 'I promise I won't touch you this time.'

Anne gave me a suspicious look but obeyed, folding her leg upwards, wobbling slightly. 'I'll reach in slowly,' I said. 'Try to dodge.'

I bent forward, reaching for the same spot. Anne hopped

away, started to fall and brought her other leg down fast. 'Any time you take a foot off the ground, you lose balance,' I said. 'Keeping both feet low with good balance lets you move, and movement is what keeps you alive.'

'So what do you do then?' Anne said. 'Just simple punches?'

'Have you ever seen me do a complicated move in a fight?'

'I haven't exactly sat around to watch.'

'One of my first self-defence teachers told me that I shouldn't bother with any technique that I couldn't learn in five minutes,' I said. 'Idea is, if you can make it work in five minutes, then practising will make it better. If you *can't* make it work in five minutes, then you probably won't be able to make it work in a high-stress situation. When your life's at stake you want something that works every time. Simple is good.'

We worked for another half-hour before I called it a day. Anne wasn't sweating (another one of those unfair life mage things) but her reactions were getting slow and it was obvious she was running out of energy. As soon as I let the pads drop, she did too.

'So are we going back to the War Rooms?' Anne asked once we'd both had the chance to catch our breath.

'I don't think it's worth the effort,' I said. 'They'll call if they really need us.'

Anne yawned. 'They usually do, don't they?'

I looked at Anne. She was lying on the grass with her hands behind her head, and didn't seem in a hurry to leave. 'Want to go somewhere?'

'Where?'

I shrugged. 'You've done your shift at the clinic, and I've cleaned out my in-tray. I'm sure the rest of the Council will want us available, but it won't be for anything useful. So why don't we have some fun for a change?'

Anne tilted her head to look up at me. 'Okay.'

So we did.

It was a relief to spend some time doing something that didn't involve political manoeuvring. I'd been on the Council for nine months now, and I'd become reasonably adept at playing the game, but one thing that I hadn't anticipated back when I'd started was the degree to which it would wear me down. When I was in the War Rooms, there was no such thing as a casual conversation. Every sentence was studied for hidden meanings, every action taken as a message, and wherever you went, people were always watching. Even with the mages whom I considered allies, like Belthas and Druss, I had to be on guard, making sure that I stayed useful enough for them to keep me around. I had no friends in the War Rooms; there were allies of circumstance, and that was about it.

When you're spending your days in that kind of environment, you need a safety valve, and for me, that had been my circle of friends: Anne and Variam, Luna and Arachne. No matter how bad things got, I knew that I could always find them and relax in their company, even if it was only for a little while. It probably isn't a surprise that out of all of them, the one I'd come to rely on the most was Anne. We'd been spending a lot of time together recently, though in most cases it was dominated by work – there was always some new political problem or threat to talk about. But now, for a change, we had some time to ourselves. It was a strange feeling.

We went for lunch in La Rochelle, then visited Nara in

Japan. I'd picked the countries semi-randomly for reasons of safety (if I didn't know where I was going next, no one else would either) but as the day wore on and no signs of danger appeared, I began to relax. It's not something I get to do very often these days.

'They're so cute,' Anne said. We were under one of the trees in Nara Park, and Anne was stroking one of the deer. It was light brown and rather fat, and it was chewing its cud with a self-satisfied expression.

'It doesn't seem to care about us very much, does it?' I asked. Nara's a big tourist attraction, and the deer here get a lot of free food, which probably explained this one's weight.

'He's got a full stomach and he's feeling lazy,' Anne said. She scratched the deer between the ears; it blinked at her. 'I saw pictures of this place when I was younger and I really wanted to come here.' She paused and looked at me. 'Is that why you picked it?'

'You might have mentioned it,' I said. It had been a couple of months ago in Arachne's cave; Anne had been talking to Luna and I'd been within earshot. 'I wonder if the Hollow's ecosystem would support deer.'

'Not a whole herd of them,' Anne said. 'But a few would be fine.' She looked at me. 'Could we?'

'It's your home as well.'

Anne smiled. It's not something she does often, and seeing it always gives me a warm feeling. 'Then let's.'

Evening found us back in London, on Hampstead Heath, in Pryors Field, one of the less well known parts of the park. It doesn't have the views of Parliament Hill, but for that same reason it's less crowded, and you can still look out south and west past the Royal Free Hospital and over London. In fairground season the place is crowded with tents and marquees, but right now that area was empty and the only other people sharing the field with us were dog walkers and a collection of students playing Frisbee. It had been a hot afternoon, and even with the coming dusk, the earth still held the warmth of the day's sun. We lay back on the grass and watched the sky darken from blue to violet.

'What do you think you'd have done if we'd never met?' Anne asked.

'That's a funny question,' I said. 'You mean just you?'

'All of us,' Anne said. 'Me, Luna and Vari. All your problems with Levistus started because you got drawn into that hunt for the fateweaver because of Luna, right? And then it was because of Vari and me that you had to deal with what happened at Fountain Reach and with Sagash. If you'd never met any of us, you'd never have got into any of that.'

'I guess that's true.'

'So what would you have done instead?' Anne asked. 'Where would you be?'

I thought about it for a moment. 'Probably running my shop.'

'Do you think you'd still be on the Council?'

'I think if Luna hadn't pulled me into things, I'd have kept on running the Arcana Emporium and minding my own business.'

'Do you wish things had stayed that way?'

I considered briefly. 'No.'

'Why not?'

'Well, for one thing, I probably wouldn't be alive,' I

said. 'Remember the Nightstalkers? They wanted me dead for something that had happened *way* before I met you guys. And if you hadn't been there, they probably would have managed it.'

'I'd forgotten about that.'

'But . . . even leaving that out, the answer's still no.'

'Wouldn't your life be a lot easier?'

'It'd be easier,' I said slowly, 'but it'd *mean* less. That was something I only realised last year. The reason I ran the Arcana Emporium so long wasn't so that I could sell stuff. It was because every now and again it actually made a difference. I guess it's something you think about more when you're a diviner. You can always get away from conflicts. But if you take that far enough, staying away from conflicts also means staying away from *life*. I can stay safe if I keep my distance, but it's a pretty empty sort of existence.'

'Do you think what we do at the Council *does* make a difference?' Anne asked. 'A lot of the time it feels as though no one listens.'

'I think it does,' I said. 'One of the things I keep noticing with the Council is that I'll say things that no one else seems to have thought of. Most of the people in that room never talk to anyone outside the inner circle. I think that'll have an effect, over time.'

'Assuming no one kills us first.'

'Well, there's that.'

We lay there for a little while in silence. Below us, the Frisbee floated into the air, thrown on a long pass; four people raced after it. A woman was walking across the path, a Golden Retriever running back and forth at her feet, sniffing at the grass. One of the students jumped for the Frisbee; the other players dashed forward, trying to score.

'So what about you?' I asked Anne.

'What do you mean?'

'You said that all my problems started because I got drawn in,' I said. 'But you didn't get drawn in so much as dragged. What do you think your life would have been like without all this?'

'I have trouble even imagining it any more,' Anne admitted. 'It's been so long.'

'What if you got to choose?' I asked. 'Say you got to rewrite your life, change how things have gone. Any way you liked. What would you pick?'

Anne was silent for a while. 'Peace,' she said at last. 'A normal life.'

'You mean without your magic, or . . . ?'

Anne shook her head. 'Everyone in the magical world always acts as though those are opposites. Either you're a mage, or you're a normal. I don't want to give up being a mage. I want to be a mage and live *like* a normal. A house, a garden, a family. Not having to look over my shoulder.'

'Is that it? You wouldn't want more?'

'Like what?'

'I don't know. If you ask most people what they dream about, it's stuff like winning the lottery or becoming famous.'

'Winning the lottery wouldn't fix any of my problems,' Anne said. 'And every bit of fame I've had has made my life *worse*. If I could make every mage in the world except for you and Luna and Vari forget about me, I would.'

'No ambitions?'

'Back when I was young, I used to dream about having adventures,' Anne said. 'Then I actually had some, and half of them were me being hunted or tortured and the other half were trying to save other people and knowing that I was the only one who could do it and if I made a mistake they were going to die. I don't want any more adventures. I want a peaceful life with the people I care about.'

I hesitated, but only for an instant. 'Is that what the other side of you wants too?'

Anne was silent for a moment, and when she spoke, her voice had changed. 'You spoke to her again, didn't you?'

'Can you tell?'

'I can tell when things are different.'

We sat for a little while. 'Are you angry?' I asked.

'Yes,' Anne said. 'No. I don't know.' She shook her head as if trying to brush away an insect. 'It's . . . hard. Any feelings I have about her are mixed up.'

'Can you talk to her?'

'I did last year. Dr Shirland took me into Elsewhere and we went to the tower. She was different from how I remembered.'

'Yeah,' I said. 'I don't think she's happy about being locked up. How'd the conversation go?'

'Not well,' Anne said. 'At least I didn't think so. Dr Shirland said that the more we talked, the easier it'd get.'

'You know she's the reason the jinn can reach you.'

I heard Anne sigh in the twilight. 'I know. I was always afraid of it. I just hoped that if I stayed away . . .'

'Did you keep talking to her?'

Anne was silent.

'You stopped in the autumn,' I said. It wasn't a question. 'After what happened on your birthday.'

'I suppose.'

I looked over. 'Have you been back since?'

Anne didn't look back at me.

'Anne.'

'No,' Anne said. 'And yes, you're right. Do we have to talk about this?'

'We don't have to,' I said. 'But it'd probably help.'

Anne didn't answer. 'Why did you stop?' I said. 'Dr Shirland seemed to think it was helping, and I could tell the difference too. You seemed less on edge.'

'You know why,' Anne said.

'I know what caused it,' I said. 'I don't know *why*.'

'Because I don't have to go to the tower to know what she's feeling.'

I looked at Anne, questioning.

'She was with me when we were being tortured,' Anne said. Her voice was distant, and she didn't meet my eyes. 'She always is, when something like that happens. The worse the danger, the closer she gets, until we blend together. Then afterwards, when everything's quiet again, she fades. Except this time she didn't, not completely.'

The sun had dipped below the horizon and the light was fading from the sky. Down below, the Frisbee game went on, white T-shirts and bare arms and legs standing out in the gloom. 'What did you feel?' I asked quietly.

'Rage. Hate.' Anne's voice was low. 'She wants to be safe, just like me. Except she wants to do it by killing everyone who's ever hurt us and anyone who might do it again. And the closer I get to her, the more *I* want that too. It's like a wave, pulling me under. The only thing I can do is wall her off.'

'Dr Shirland thinks that the answer is to merge,' I said. 'Become one person, not two.'

Anne gave a short laugh. 'Yeah, right.'

I looked at Anne, disturbed. That had been not-Anne's reaction exactly. She'd even sounded the same. 'It seemed like she knew what she was talking about.'

'You don't understand,' Anne said. 'You think there's some way for us to compromise, don't you?'

'It would be good if there was . . .'

'Imagine you bring someone to a party,' Anne said. 'You walk in the door and it's filled with people. You decide you want to get a drink. The other person decides she wants to kill everyone in the room. How do you compromise about something like that, Alex? Do you kill *half* the people in the room?'

'Is she really that bad?'

'Yes,' Anne said flatly. 'She is. You don't know what she's like. I do. She wants you to feel sorry for her so you'll give her an opening.'

I opened my mouth, then hesitated. Because Anne was right — I did feel sorry for that other Anne, locked up and kept away from the outside world. And there was a pretty good chance that Anne was right and she *had* produced that effect deliberately. I'm not immune to being manipulated and Anne knows me well enough to have a good chance of succeeding at it.

But I could also see not-Anne's side of the story. From her point of view, she'd done what she'd had to do and what she'd been made to do, and in return she'd been shunned. And she hadn't struck me as the kind to accept an unjust punishment for ever. I didn't think that keeping her locked up was going to work, and I had the nasty feeling that the longer Anne kept doing that, the more trouble she'd be storing up.

Dr Shirland had made it clear that in the end, the only

one who could solve this problem was Anne. If I kept pushing her, would it help? Or would it just make her resentful?

In the end what swung my decision was remembering what Luna had said. Anne was under enough pressure. Right now, what she needed more than anything was people on her side. 'All right.'

'You agree with me?'

'I'm not sure how comfortable I am with it,' I admitted. 'But you know yourself better than I do. Just remember that if you ever want to talk about it, you can.'

It was dark enough that I couldn't make out Anne's face any more, but I could feel her relax. 'Thank you.'

We lay there for a little while longer, watching the stars come out one by one in the dusky sky. Below us, the Frisbee match ended. The players gathered up their bags and clothes, laughing and calling to one another, and headed away eastwards towards Parliament Hill. 'It's easier like this,' Anne said.

'What is?'

'Everything.' Anne gazed up at the stars. 'I wish all my days could be this way.'

The dog walkers and the rest of the people in the park had vanished. We stayed as the summer evening turned into night.

'. . . and so that's the current state of play,' Talisid said.

I was sitting in a coffee shop, people all around me. It was evening in the West End and the place was bustling, the whirr of the coffee machines blending with the noise of the crowd. Talisid and I were talking through a communicator focus, audio only, and I was keeping my voice down just to be on the safe side, but honestly, I probably could have been as loud as I liked and it wouldn't have made a difference. Most of the crowd wouldn't have paid attention and the few that did would have just assumed I was using a hands-free. The air smelled pleasant, a mix of coffee beans and food from the bakery.

'So let me get this straight,' I said to Talisid. 'They're going ahead with the assault, but they don't want me there. But they also want me to be on call during the operation. So I'm supposed to be close enough that I can come if I'm called, but not close enough that I'll be there if I'm not.'

'Yes,' Talisid admitted.

'Am I the only one noticing the problem with this?'

'The two directives may have come from different people.'

I sighed. 'Of course they did.'

'I'm sorry about the way that this has unfolded,' Talisid said. 'I imagine you feel as though you're being shut out. This operation was largely yours from the beginning.'

'Oh, it's what I expected,' I said. 'The Keepers were never going to want me on board.' While I had some friends in the Order of the Shield, the biggest and most influential of the Keeper orders is the Order of the Star, and they'd hated me ever since their attempt to arrest me for treason. It had always struck me as backwards – shouldn't *I* be the one holding a grudge against *them*? – but I guess they really don't like being made to look foolish. 'Just out of curiosity, if everything *does* go pear-shaped and they decide they need my help after all, how exactly do they expect me to get there in time?'

'Presumably via gate.'

'Firstly the Tiger's Palace has wards; secondly the Keepers

are going to set up an interdiction field; and thirdly there's the little detail that I'm a diviner and can't use gate magic.'

'Gate stone?'

'Sure, I'd really have a gate stone keyed to *there*. Look, just forget about it. I'll figure something out.'

'I could ask the Keepers in charge . . . Are you close enough to reach the area on foot?'

I glanced out the window. I was in the middle of Soho; the Tiger's Palace was two blocks away. 'Not really, no.'

'I see . . . Hopefully things will go to plan.'

'Which they won't, because it's the Tiger's Palace,' I said. The Tiger's Palace is run by a rakshasa named Jagadev. He hates mages and humans in general, and it's a good rule that anything associated with the place is going to be bad news. 'Have they confirmed that Richard's going to be there?'

'Divinations have been unreliable,' Talisid said. 'But what human intelligence we've been able to gather has provided some support for Onyx's claim.'

In other words, this whole thing was happening because of the deal I'd negotiated. Depending on how things went tonight, that could be anything from quite good to very bad. 'Assuming Richard's going to be there, how carefully are you hiding your preparations? Because I'm not sure how you're expecting to go undetected moving in . . . how many men was it? A hundred?'

'The Keepers are not willing to go in undermanned,' Talisid said. 'And I agree with them. We've yet to have a direct confrontation with Drakh's cabal, and their full capabilities are still unknown. But yes, there's a very high chance that we will be detected on approach, at which point we expect Drakh to attempt an escape.'

I was pretty sure that the Council had had a direct confrontation with Drakh's cabal already, just last year at the Vault, and that it had gone decidedly in Richard's favour, but I didn't bring that up. 'Keep me updated, please. If this is going to get messy, it'd be nice to have some warning.'

'I'll do what I can. Talisid out.' The communicator clicked off.

I lowered the communicator and looked at the two girls on the other side of the table. 'Did you catch all that?'

'I got the gist,' Luna said. '"Not close enough"?'

'I don't see the need to keep Talisid updated with every little detail,' I said. 'Besides, it's not like he tells me everything.'

'I think that was going a little further than not telling him everything,' Anne said.

'Oh, he'll be fine,' Luna said. 'We ready to go?'

'I think we'll move about half an hour from now,' I said. 'We want to go in when the crowd's busiest.'

'You'd be a lot safer if I was with you,' Anne said.

'Not this again,' Luna said.

'I don't like the idea of you two in there alone,' Anne said. 'Remember, I lived there.'

'And that's exactly why you can't go in,' I said. 'Jagadev kicked you out under sentence of death.'

'That didn't stop you going back.'

'We need someone on the outside as backup,' Luna said.

'If I'm outside and things go wrong fast enough I won't be *able* to give you any backup,' Anne said. 'You know I can't do anything at range. If someone shoots you and I'm not close . . .'

Luna started to argue, but I raised my hand and she stopped. 'Richard may be there,' I said.

'He might not be,' Anne said.

'I don't care,' I said. 'We know that Richard wants you, and we know he still has some kind of influence over that jinn. I don't want you in the same room as him. End of discussion.'

Anne didn't look happy, but she didn't argue. We settled down to wait.

It was half an hour later when we paid our tab and headed out. We turned down two side streets before coming to a stop. 'You ready?' I asked Anne.

'I suppose,' Anne said. 'You'll tell me when anything goes wrong?'

I smiled slightly. 'Don't you mean *if* anything goes wrong?'

'No.'

I glanced around. We were at the corner of two of the Soho back streets. Music and laughter spilled out of a bar with a flashing neon sign above, and on the other side was a pair of shops with tinted windows and ribbon curtains over the doors. There was enough light to make out the groups of people on the street, but not enough to see their faces. The air smelled of sweat and spilled alcohol. 'You going to be okay?'

'I used to live here,' Anne said. 'I can find a place to watch.'

I nodded. 'I'm not going to tell you to stay outside no matter what. I'd prefer that you did, but you're right that this might be dangerous, and if it is, we might need you. But promise me that if you do come in, you'll tell us first, okay?'

Anne seemed to relax a little bit. 'Okay.'

'See you soon.'

We split up, Anne going down one street and Luna and I going down another. 'You're good at that, aren't you?' Luna asked once we were out of earshot.

'What do you mean?'

'If you'd told her to stay outside, she wouldn't,' Luna said. 'But she wouldn't break a promise like that.'

'I'm not trying to manipulate her,' I said sharply. 'Having her anywhere near Richard is a bad idea.'

'I know,' Luna said with a sigh. 'I'm just worried.'

We turned down another street and halted. Up ahead was the entrance to the Tiger's Palace, hidden away at the bottom of a set of steps. At least, that was how I remembered it. Right now, the enormous queue of people trailing up the steps, past three buildings and down the alleyway was making it a lot less hidden.

'You weren't kidding about it being busy,' Luna said.

'Mm,' I said. I was doing mental arithmetic. Adepts are maybe a tenth of a per cent of the population. London's population is nine million or so. Call it ten thousand adepts. I'd expected that maybe one or two per cent of that number would be showing up tonight. Eyeballing the crowd, I was pretty sure I'd underestimated.

'So I'm assuming you have a plan for the whole "banished from the Tiger's Palace on pain of death" thing?' Luna asked.

In answer I took a handful of woven threads from my pocket, tied them around my wrist, then pulled loose one of the knots. I felt a pulse of magical energy, very brief, and quickly damped down. Illusion magic is very difficult to detect. Focusing on my arm with my magesight, I could just barely see the weave, and only if I concentrated. I was pretty sure that most other mages wouldn't be able to see it unless they knew exactly what to look for.

'Very nice,' Luna said approvingly. 'Arachne?'

'Good guess.'

'Wasn't a guess,' Luna said. 'You're actually dressed well now.'

'Shouldn't you also be worrying about being recognised, Miss Fashion Critic?'

'I was invited,' Luna pointed out. 'It won't exactly work if I pretend to be someone else.'

'You like living dangerously, don't you?' I said. 'Fine.'

The queue was enormous, and it wasn't moving fast. We joined the back, and had to wait less than sixty seconds before another couple joined the queue right behind. 'Well, this brings back memories,' I said quietly to Luna. The line was noisy, with a group of girls just in front having a loud conversation, so I wasn't worried about being overheard.

'Of what?'

'Going out clubbing.'

'You went out clubbing?'

'Not very often. You?'

'Queuing up to get onto a packed dance floor, brushing up against everyone?' Luna said. 'What do you think?'

'Okay, silly question.'

'I really wished I could,' Luna said. 'Though it's a funny thing: once I'd been training with Chalice and I was confident enough, I went out one night with Vari, and it was crap. The music is awful, everything is overpriced and it's so loud you can't talk.'

'That's pretty much the club experience.'

'At least I didn't miss much.'

The line shuffled forward, approaching the corner of the Tiger's Palace. 'So what's Jagadev's angle?' Luna asked.

'Tiger's Palace has always been an adept hangout,' I said. 'Jagadev hosts it as a venue for mages too. Probably he's going to claim he's just a disinterested service provider.'

'You think the Council'll buy that?'

'Hell no,' I said. 'Richard is radioactive right now. Which is what worries me. Jagadev's not dumb, and he's been doing this stuff a long time. If he's willing to associate himself with Richard, it must be because he's getting something out of it, and the most likely reason I can see is that he thinks it'll be really bad for us.'

'Whoever loses, he wins?'

'I think he's inviting a bunch of powder kegs and then withdrawing to a safe distance. Wouldn't be surprised if he isn't even here.' A thought struck me. 'Wait a sec.' I reached out to Anne through the dreamstone. *Hey. You there?*

Anne's answer came instantly; she must have been waiting. *Of course.*

Picking up anything on your lifesight?

There's a big crowd inside the Palace.

Jagadev?

No Jagadev.

Figures. Richard?

No sign of him either. But there are people on the rooftops.

Civilians?

Not with the gear they're carrying, Anne said. *Either the Council is getting started early, or Richard is really serious with his security. Or both.*

The queue crawled slowly forward. As we approached the entrance I grew close enough to see to the front of the line. There was a cluster of security men, a lot more than you'd need just to check IDs, and they were questioning each person in turn. As we watched, a pair of guys were turned away. They started to argue; one of the bouncers stepped up, looming over them, and they backed off in a hurry. The third guy who'd been with them hesitated, looked after them, then turned and was let in.

Try to stick to mental only from now on, I said to Luna. *You ready?*

Let's do this.

We reached the front of the line. 'Name?' one of the bouncers asked. Like his companions, he was big and nasty-looking. They were wearing suits, but they didn't look at home in them.

'Alice Trent,' Luna said.

'Contact.'

Luna blinked. 'I'm sorry?'

'Your contact,' the bouncer repeated, unsmiling.

'My— oh, right, right. I was invited by Stephen.' Luna blinked up at the bulky man, her eyes innocent. 'I don't know his last name, but that's okay, right? He said I should use his name. I've got his number if you want me to call him.'

A second man was flipping through a list. The bouncer glanced across; the man looked up and nodded. The bouncer looked back at Luna. 'ID.'

'Right, here you go.' Luna fumbled in her purse. 'A driver's licence is okay, right?'

The bouncer studied the card, handed it back, then looked at me. 'You with her?'

'Yeah.' I let a little bit of anxiety show in my voice. 'That's right.'

'List says plus one,' the other man said.

The bouncer nodded, already dismissing us. 'Full search before you go inside.'

The second line of bouncers searched us. I submitted without complaint. Illusions can be given away if someone gets close enough to touch, but Arachne had been careful – the braid around my wrist wasn't making me look taller or shorter, it only made fine changes to my features and the colours of my clothes. I'd been more worried about the guy picking up on the items I was carrying, but my coat was lined with damping fabric and I'd made sure not to carry any obvious weapons. It was just as well I hadn't – the guy was thorough. Once the bouncer was done he jerked his head to indicate that I should go. The other bouncer gave a last glance at the item he'd taken from Luna's bag – a long-handled hairbrush – then shoved it back in and handed it over. Luna rejoined me and we passed through the doors and into a corridor lined with concrete and metal.

I suppose you couldn't have got away with wearing your armour, Luna thought.

Would have liked to, but no. It was a small but definite effort to keep the connection open. The downside of not being a mind mage – Luna couldn't just think loudly and expect me to hear. *I don't think there's any way they could have missed that.*

Are you going to be okay with no weapons?

Oh, I'll figure something out.

The hum of conversation sounded from behind the doors ahead of us, swelling to a roar as we pushed them open. We walked out onto the club floor of the Tiger's Palace.

11

The main floor of the Tiger's Palace is the only part of the building that most guests see, a huge room with a high ceiling and walls of unpainted concrete that give it an industrial look. A scaffolding high above holds lights and sound equipment, and a mezzanine level with a balcony runs around the room about fifteen feet up, leading into a VIP lounge with tinted windows. Surrounding the main room on three sides is a warren of smaller rooms and corridors, the entrances guarded by locked doors and stone-faced security.

Usually on Friday evenings the club floor is blanketed with clashing lights and pounding music, but there was none of that tonight. The room was well lit, and the only sound was the noise of the crowd. And it was a big crowd, people packed in tightly enough to fill the room from one wall to the other. At the far end, next to the balcony stairs, a stage had been erected, currently empty but for a couple of microphone stands.

Holy crap, there's a lot of them, Luna said. *How many do you think?*

Must be close on a thousand, I said. The entrance we'd come through was slightly raised, and from our position at the top of the steps we were looking out over a sea of heads and shoulders. Everyone was talking, their voices raised, and the noise was a steady low roar. I could see a variety of people, everything from teenagers to people who looked like they'd come straight from work, but taken as a whole, I guessed the average age to be somewhere in the twenties.

Come on, Luna said. *We're visible up here and I don't want to have to make up some story about who you are unless I have to.*

We descended into the crowd. I'd been thinking of getting a drink, but changed my mind when I saw the line at the bar. As I moved, I scanned the crowd with my magesight. I picked up magic, and a lot of it.

Do you think they're all adepts? Luna said, echoing my thoughts.

Even if only half of them are, this is the biggest gathering I've ever seen, I replied. *And it feels like more than half.* There were pinpoints of magic *everywhere*, a kaleidoscope of earth and force and life and space and everything in between. The good news was that I was pretty sure no one was going to be able to spot us by our auras. On the flip side, I really did not want to be in the middle of this crowd if it turned ugly.

Do you think we can get up to the balcony? Luna asked.

Maybe once the show's started and they're distracted. Incoming call. My earpiece chimed and I turned away towards the wall and murmured under my breath. 'Receiving.'

'Hey, Alex,' Variam said into my ear. 'Got that dream-stone?'

'One sec.' I reached out to Variam. There was the usual brief struggle, then a mental *click* as the connection took. *Got you. Let's hear it.*

Everyone's gearing up. I could feel Variam's emotions mixed in with his thoughts, nervousness and excitement and anticipation all blended together. *We just had the last briefing ten minutes ago. They weren't exactly heavy on the restraint angle.*

I frowned. *The restraint angle?*

As in, first priority is getting Richard, second priority is getting his associates, third priority is arresting anyone from the adept crowd who's involved in this defence association thing. Avoiding collateral damage didn't get mentioned. I think it's probably down around seventh or eighth.

'Damn it,' I muttered. *Are you serious? The whole reason we're in this mess is because the Keepers got trigger-happy last year, and now they're planning a repeat performance?*

Hey, I'm not the one giving the orders. Anyway, they've got a point. If they can get Richard, it'll end this whole war before it starts.

It worries me that you're using the word 'war'.

Just calling it like I see it. How are things looking on the ground?

Crowded, I said. *Lots of room for collateral damage. When are the Keepers going to move?*

Orders are not to move until someone gets eyes on Drakh. Then we go all in. Anne's not there, right?

She's watching outside.

Make sure she stays there. I could feel tension and worry in Variam's thoughts. *Gotta go.*

I broke the connection to Variam and reached out to Luna. *That was Vari. As soon as Richard shows, things are going to get violent.*

Yeah, that's not exactly news, Luna said. *Take a look up on the balcony.*

I scanned the balcony. Shapes moved in the shadows, but I couldn't pick out faces. *Anyone I should recognise?*

Well, I'm not a hundred per cent sure, Luna said, *but I saw someone that really looked like Vihaela.*

My heart sank. *Well, that pretty much kills any chances that this night was going to end peacefully.*

I think that ship sailed a long time ago. How are the Council going to know when Richard shows up?

They'll have watchers in the crowd. No point looking; they'll be well hidden.

I think I saw Stephen a second ago, Luna said. *Who's that?*

A man had climbed onto the stage. He tapped the microphone and the *thud-thud-thud* echoed through the speakers out over the club floor. Conversations slowly died away as people turned to face him. 'Hello,' he said, his voice reverberating through the room. 'Good evening.'

I frowned. Something about the man's face was familiar. He was thin, with glasses, a receding hairline and a hooked nose. *I've seen that guy before.*

Mage? Luna asked.

No, not exactly . . . My eyes narrowed. *Wait. That meeting in Manchester.*

The what now?

Richard took me there back when he was posing as Archon, I said. *He was talking to a bunch of adept leaders, and this guy was one of them. I've been trying to get the Keepers to trace him, but they haven't been making much effort.*

Pretty sure they'll be interested now.

'Thank you all for coming tonight,' the man said. 'And there's a reason I say that, because it's not an easy thing to do. Once upon a time adepts could walk the streets in Britain safely, without having to be afraid. But it's become clear over the past year that that's no longer the case. I think the events of last autumn made that even more clear. Make no mistake, right now, we are living in the eye of the hurricane. Just by being here, you – all of you! – you're taking a step to assert yourselves. You're saying to the Council, we will not be your sheep. We won't sit here and be exploited. You deserve the same rights and privileges as anyone else. By being here, you're taking your first step towards taking those back.'

Is this supposed to be a recruiting speech? Luna asked.

I think it's the warm-up act, I said. I was busy scanning the futures, looking for signs of Richard. It wasn't easy – crowds are the absolute worst places for divination, and the possibilities kept flickering.

Not doing a great job of it.

You're not the intended audience.

'. . . ever since the beginning,' the man was saying. 'This is the way they keep you under control. Weak, and vulnerable. But you have the power to take your future into your own hands. All you have to do . . .'

I switched my attention away from the man, scanning the room. The crowd was paying attention, but the murmurs of background conversation hadn't died away and I didn't get the sense that this guy had them in the palm of his hand. I reached out through the dreamstone. *Anne?*

I'm here, Anne replied instantly. *Are you okay?*

What can you see?

A whole lot of people, Anne said. *Some are familiar, but there's one up on the balcony that's hidden behind a web. I think it might be—*

Vihaela.

Did she see you?

Not yet, and I hope it'll stay that way. You safe out there?

Someone on the roof was patrolling. Council, I think. It wasn't a problem.

Mm. Call me as soon as anything happens, all right?

I think you should be worrying more about yourself.

'Alex,' Luna said quietly. 'I think something's happening.'

I took a glance into the futures and my heart skipped a beat. *It's go time. Follow me.*

I started pushing my way through the crowd, clearing a way for Luna. I got some angry looks, but no one seemed willing to make an issue of it. *I thought I felt a gate*, Luna said.

So did I, I said. *We need to find a way to the upper level. What's changed?*

'. . . but we can't do this alone,' the man was saying. 'I know that's a difficult thing to accept. I didn't want to believe it either. But no matter how strong and powerful we are, we need allies. That's why we're here today.'

The crowd has, I said. *Listen.*

Luna did, and it took her only a second to notice. The crowd had gone quiet. They'd been distracted before, listening with half an ear while talking and drinking; now all of a sudden they were focused on the speaker. Looking around, I could see dozens of eyes staring silently at the stage. *What the hell?* Luna said. *Was it something he said?*

It's not him, I said. *Close your eyes. Can you feel it?*

Luna frowned but obeyed. *I don't . . .* she began, then paused. *That's weird.*

What do you feel?

I'm not sure. Luna sounded confused. *It just sort of feels right. But when I stop and think about what he's saying . . .*

Charm magic, I told her. *It's telling you to trust him, to go with the flow. But it's not actually convincing you. That's why you're confused. Your emotions and your thoughts are telling you two different things.*

How come it's not affecting you?

I've had a lot of experience dealing with mind-affecting spells.

'. . . been working on this for a long time,' the man was

saying. 'Many of you have asked me what's been going on, and we haven't been able to tell you, but now at last . . .'

What about Richard? Luna asked. *Is he here?*

He's here.

Luna twisted her head. *Where?*

Up there, I said, nodding up at the balcony. *I don't know what happened, but a few minutes ago something changed. Up until then the futures were blurred, then all of a sudden they snapped into place. We don't want to be in the middle of the crowd when he shows up.*

Yeah, not arguing with that. Bit of a problem, though. Luna tilted her head towards the stairs. *Don't think those guys are keen on letting us through.*

The stairs up to the balcony were just ahead. We'd made it close enough that I could see over the heads of the crowd, and it didn't look good. I'd expected the stairs to be guarded, but I'd been figuring on maybe one man. Instead there were three, and looking into the futures in which I shoved my way through, I saw that more were above.

Don't suppose you have some spell in your box of tricks that'll get us through that many? I asked Luna.

I could fight my way through, if that's what you're asking.

Not so much, no. I scanned the crowd. *There, on your two o'clock. You see?*

Luna went up on tiptoes, craning her neck. A little to our right, almost hidden by a set of speakers, was a small unmarked door. *I see it. Guards?*

Doesn't look like it. It'll be locked, but I can probably get it open if you cover me.

'. . . and now he's here,' the adept finished. 'I present to you Mage Richard Drakh.'

There was a rustle and a murmur as everyone in the

crowd looked up at once. A figure appeared on the balcony, looking down over the people below.

Richard looked subtly different from how I remembered. In the past, I'd always been struck by how ordinary he seemed. He just looked average in almost every way: not tall, not short, not handsome or ugly, not thin or fat. *I* knew how dangerous he was, but I also knew that to a stranger's eyes, there was nothing about him to catch the attention at all . . . at least, not until you'd seen him in action. He had the perfect everyman appearance, the kind of look that fades into a crowd.

Richard didn't look like an everyman any more. It was hard to say what had changed; his clothes were perhaps a little more impressive, his stance a little different, but there was no doubt about the impact. The crowd were receptive and primed, but even without the enchantment effect, I had the feeling he would have caught their attention. He looked like a king addressing his subjects.

I wanted to keep looking up at him – the impulse tugged at me to stand and watch and listen – but I pulled my eyes away to see Luna staring up at him. *Luna. Luna!*

Oh. Right. Luna blinked. *I didn't realise he was so—*

Door.

Right.

We pushed our way through the crowd. I don't think anyone even noticed; they were too busy staring. Making it to the door, I felt Luna take up a position at my back.

'Adepts of Britain,' Richard said. His voice was deep and powerful; it echoed around the room, and unlike the previous speaker, he wasn't using a microphone. 'You are at a crossroads. For all your lives you have been ruled by the Light Council. Now, for the first time, you have a choice.'

I listened with half an ear, taking out my lock-picks. I pulled one from its case – and fumbled it, dropping it to the concrete, as I seemed to hear something in the distance, a far-off cry. *Anne?*

Richard was still speaking. 'The decisions of the Light Council determine every aspect of your lives. Where you can go; what is permitted; even whether you live or die. They have decreed that you should follow the Concord, yet the Concord grants you no protection . . .'

There was no answer. I reached out, suddenly afraid, groping for Anne's presence and finding nothing. *Anne!* I called into the void. *Where are you?*

Then suddenly Anne was there. *Right here. Quit panicking.*

Jesus. I felt my insides unknot. *Don't scare me like that.*

Like what? I'm fine.

I knelt down and grabbed my pick from where it had fallen, inserting it into the lock. *What happened?*

Guard got too close, Anne said. *But then he turned around and started hurrying back. Something happen in there?*

Yeah, you might say that. My communicator chimed. *Hold on.* 'Vari?' I said under my breath.

'We're moving,' Variam said without preamble. 'Gate's hot. Don't get in the middle when the shooting starts.'

'No, wait! There's a—' I realised I was talking to a dead line and swore.

'Alex?' Luna murmured under her breath. 'You're not invisible.'

Looking around, I realised that people were giving us distracted glances. Most of them looked as though they'd rather be listening to Richard, but one guy in particular was staring and frowning.

'Over the past year, I have met with you and listened

to your stories,' Richard said. 'Over and over again I have heard talk about taking action. But when your leaders finally took action last year, it was to launch a protest. You gathered using only words, and brought signs and placards as though you were dissatisfied students. You know full well how that ended.'

My pick slipped and I hissed under my breath. The lock on the door wasn't an especially good one, but lock-picking is a tricky business and I was short on time. *Luna? Could use some help.*

Luna lifted a finger and a wisp of her curse drifted out, twining itself around the lock and my picks. In my mage-sight, I saw the silver mist turn to gold. I tried again and this time, the futures opened up, the actions leading to success multiplying. The lock clicked and the door opened.

I pulled the door open and Luna and I disappeared through before anyone could stop us. Richard was still talking. '. . . violence not because of what you were doing, but because of your potential. They feared what you might—' The door shut, cutting off his voice.

We were in an unlit room that smelled of metal. I pulled out a tiny pocket torch and switched it on, the bright beam picking out machinery. There was no visible exit except for where we'd come in, but I knew there would be a door hidden in the back. I started walking, and as I did I felt something in the distance. It was far away and hard to pin down, but I had the feeling that it was gate magic. *Anne*, I said. *Any news?*

Nothing much, Anne said instantly. *Oh. Except for all the Council people gating in. Did you mean them?*

Yes, yes, I did. The door at the back was locked too. I bent down and got to work on it. *Can you stay out of their way?*

Kind of working on that at the moment.

I switched out my hook pick for a half diamond and carried on working. *Back off and keep your distance*, I told Anne. *They're looking for people trying to break out, not people coming in. If you stay away they aren't going to chase you.*

You really don't need to worry about me.

Anne! Don't come in. Okay?

Fine, whatever. Staying outside. Happy?

Good. We'll see you soon.

'Were you talking to Anne?' Luna asked.

'Yeah. Can you tell?'

'No. Can anyone else?'

'Hope not,' I said. It was one of the reasons I'd been trying to shift over to using the dreamstone where possible. Council communicators were supposed to be secure, but they were also supposed to always work, and they'd failed at that too many times for me to be comfortable with the things. As far as I could tell, the dreamstone worked no matter the range and it was impossible for anyone else to detect. 'Sounds like the Keepers are coming in numbers.'

'What are they going to do?'

'Standard Order of the Star doctrine is to surround the building and establish a perimeter. They'll put up an interdiction field to stop anyone escaping, then they'll move in.'

The lock clicked and we stepped out into a corridor. I could still hear Richard's voice, muffled through the bricks and concrete, and I could still feel the faint tug of the enchantment trying to make me stop and listen. 'What's the plan?' Luna whispered.

I turned left, heading for the stairs. The interior of the Tiger's Palace was a maze, but I had my divination to guide me and we traced a route through the corridors that would take us up to the mezzanine level without meeting any more guards. A set of fire stairs led us up to a balcony and back to the club floor, almost exactly above where I'd picked the lock.

Richard was still talking. It was hard not to stop and listen but I forced myself to shut the words out. Odd phrases filtered through – he was talking about the history of adepts in Britain, and at other times, I'd have wanted to know more – but I made myself concentrate on finding the source of the magic. Unfortunately, this was one time my magesight was failing me. There were hundreds of magical auras, and I couldn't tell which was the right one.

Which way? Luna asked.

Working on it, I said. Richard was saying something about the Hermetic Accords . . . *no. Focus.*

What?

Look for some kind of magic source, I said. *Wide-area effect. Something this powerful should be easy to see.*

I thought enchantment magic was impossible to spot? Luna said. *Anyway, with this much noise I'd have more luck trying to find a dropped contact lens.*

Well, it's not like we have another way to spot them.

Who says we have to spot them?

I felt a shift in the magic around Luna and looked at her to see the mists of her curse swirl, forming spiralling patterns. Luna gazed into the distance for a moment, as though she were watching something fascinating but very far away, then seemed to snap back to the immediate present. She took a step back and pointed. 'This way.'

I frowned. 'That's the way we came.'

'No, I've got a good feeling about this way.'

Luna started walking and I followed. She turned right, then up a small staircase that I hadn't noticed. We went up, left and left again. I had no idea where we were going and I could hear movement around us, but somehow we didn't bump into anyone. Luna led us into a narrow, dark corridor. Light and the sound of Richard's voice spilled from an open doorway.

I took one look at what I'd see if I went forward and everything fell into place. *Of course. It* would *be her, wouldn't it?* The doorway led into a smaller balcony on the second floor, looking down over the main room. Strange equipment lined the balcony, opaque crystals resting on metal stands. I didn't understand how they worked, but I was pretty sure I could guess what they did. They were psychic amplifiers, and I was willing to bet they were linked to broadcast devices hidden across the club floor. Jagadev had installed magical foci throughout the club designed to manipulate the thoughts and feelings of anyone who stayed here long enough, and from this room, he – or anyone skilled enough in mind or charm magic – could play the crowd like a violin. *Sneaky bastard.* I guess I shouldn't have been surprised. I remembered the time I'd come to the Tiger's Palace to a meeting of Dark mages, searching for Anne, and wondered how many supposedly 'neutral' meetings Jagadev had manipulated over the years.

Can you see if there's anyone there? Luna asked.

Oh yeah, I said. The woman standing on the balcony was small and delicately beautiful, with long black hair and a diamond-shaped face. She had one hand resting on the spheres, and was concentrating. *Our old friend.*

Got a plan for what to do next?

You know what? I said. *I think this is one of those times where subtlety is overrated.*

I walked quickly and quietly to the doorway, Luna in tow. The woman had her back to the door and was entirely focused on her spell. I reached her in three quick strides, grabbed her by the hair, and yanked her head back. She started to struggle and froze as she felt the knife blade at her throat. 'Hello, Meredith,' I said into her ear. 'We just keep running into each other in this place, don't we?'

'Wait! Don't hurt me!'

'Who said anything about hurting?' I said.

'I—' Meredith paused. 'Alex?'

'Good memory,' I said. 'Now how about you explain what you were doing with that focus?'

'What?'

I dug the knife in slightly. It's one of my better-hidden weapons, an innocuous-looking piece of metal that reshapes itself when supplied with the right magical charge. The mass limitation means the blade has to be thin, more of a stiletto than a fighting knife, but it's long enough.

'Wait! I'm telling the truth!'

'I am *really* not in the mood for games.'

'I'll tell you, I'll tell you! Just—'

I dug the knife in further, on the edge of drawing blood, and Meredith gasped. 'Drakh! It was Drakh! He and his Chosen, they made me! I didn't have a choice!'

'Made you do *what?*'

'A sway the crowd effect, the equipment was already—'

'I know what spell you were using,' I told her. 'I want to know exactly what effect Drakh and Deleo wanted you to produce. What were their instructions?'

From our position, we could look out over the crowd below, and I could see a sea of faces, though Richard himself was obscured by the balcony rail. None of them seemed to have noticed us; the lights on the ceiling were arranged so as to cast the patch of wall with the balcony in shadow. 'He— They wanted the crowd malleable.' Meredith spoke fast, the words spilling out. 'He said to start while Andrei was doing his speech. Just make everyone feel good, have them go with the flow. So they'd agree to everything. There wasn't going to be any fighting.'

'Oh?' I said. 'And when the Keepers showed up, what were you meant to do then?'

Meredith hesitated.

'You were going to whip them into a frenzy, weren't you? Instant lynch mob.'

'I didn't have a choice! They were going to kill me if I didn't!'

I made a disgusted noise. Meredith took it as a sign of violence and tensed; futures of her trying a desperate attack flashed into view. 'Oh, relax,' I said. 'I'm not going to kill you unless you give me a reason. Though given what you were just doing, it wouldn't take much. Did you think for even a second about how many people in that crowd were going to die if you followed through with your plan?'

'What are you going to do?' Fear laced Meredith's voice.

'Nothing,' I said. 'We're going to sit right here and listen to how much the crowd likes Richard *without* you tipping the scales.'

Meredith subsided. From a glance at the futures I could tell that she wasn't going to try anything. Meredith can fight if she has to, but she won't if she has any other choice.

Meredith had had me distracted enough that I'd let the

connection with Luna lapse. I linked with her thoughts again to find that she was already talking. *So not that this isn't fun to watch*, Luna was saying, *but do we have a plan for when Richard notices his audience have stopped making puppy eyes?*

Down below, Richard was still talking, but the effect of Meredith's spell was wearing off. I could hear murmurs as people started to shake off the enchantment, ripples of movement going through the crowd. *Still working on that part*, I admitted.

Then maybe we should move before they come looking to see what the problem is.

Not a bad idea. I looked ahead into the futures where we did just that. *Uh-oh.*

Uh-oh?

Company. I switched connections. I was getting more practised with using the dreamstone, able to shift more quickly between links. *Vari? How long until you guys make an entrance?*

They're busy with the interdiction field, Variam said. *Call it ten minutes.*

Great.

Why? What's going on?

No, no, we're fine. See you soon. I switched back to Luna. *We've got Deleo thirty seconds out. Vari and the Keepers are ten minutes away. We're going to have to stall until then.*

You don't ask for much, do you? Luna said with a mental sigh. *Got one of those life rings?*

That's the backup plan. Hex the equipment in case we have to make an exit.

Got it. Luna concentrated, tendrils of silver mist reaching out to soak into the focuses nearby.

'Can I—?' Meredith began.

'Shut up,' I told her.

Running footsteps sounded from the corridor. I pulled Meredith around to put her between me and the door, and Luna stepped to the side to open up space. A moment later, Rachel appeared in the balcony doorway with two men behind.

It had been a while since I'd seen Rachel, and judging from her expression, the time we'd spent apart hadn't improved her opinion of me. She was wearing her black domino mask on top of what looked like combat gear. As soon as she saw me, her hand came up, green light glowing at her palm.

If she fires, run, I told Luna. I kept Meredith between me and Rachel. There was a moment's pause.

'Alex,' Rachel said coldly. The disintegration spell hovered about her hand, ready to strike, but she didn't fire. 'I should have guessed.'

'Nice to see you too,' I said. My disguise was still up, but it's always been really hard for me to fool Rachel. 'How's life?'

Rachel stared at me for a second. Futures flickered, and I knew she was calculating the odds of hitting me with a spell without killing Meredith in the process. Apparently she didn't like her chances, because she took a step forward.

'Ah, ah.' I stepped backwards, forcing Meredith at knife-point. 'I wouldn't.'

'You've got nowhere to go,' Rachel told me.

'I'll survive the drop off this balcony,' I told Rachel. 'She won't.'

'I should just kill you.'

'If you could kill me without hitting Meredith, you'd have done it already.'

'Who says I need her alive?'

I felt Meredith stiffen and smiled slightly. 'Richard does, which is the reason he sent you here in the first place. I doubt he'll be too pleased if you come back with the news that everyone's dead. That's the thing about your disintegration magic, isn't it? Not so great if you *don't* want to kill everyone in the room.'

Rachel stared at me but didn't speak. The two guys behind her exchanged glances. They looked like hired muscle: dark glasses and cheap suits. 'Maybe he—' one of them began, stepping forward and reaching into his jacket.

Rachel spoke without turning. 'Shut up and stay out of my way.' The man glared angrily at Rachel's back, which suggested that he was even dumber than he looked, but did as he was told.

From behind, I could still hear Richard speaking, but the crowd was getting restless. '. . . association was formed for your protection,' he was saying. 'However, as things stand, it is not strong enough.'

'Why do you care?' someone called out from the club floor.

'You do,' Richard answered.

'Why should we listen to you?' someone else called. 'You're one of them.'

'Looks like the honeymoon's over,' I told Rachel. 'What do you think? You reckon if Meredith got back on that gear, she could regain control of the crowd?'

Rachel's eyes narrowed. Again the futures flickered, possibilities of her firing on me blinking in and out. 'Let her go right now, and I won't kill you.'

'Nice offer. Did you say that to all the guys you caught at Richard's mansion too?'

'You are correct,' Richard said to the crowd below. 'I am a mage. I am not, however, part of the Council. I have no investment in controlling or subjugating you, and I have no interest in forcing you to obey mage laws or in keeping you away from the levers of power. What I can offer you is the chance to be masters of your own fate.'

'So while we've got the chance to chat,' I said to Rachel, 'there's something I've been meaning to ask you.'

'Of course there is.'

'Yeah,' I said. 'Though it's a little different this time.' Ever since my trip to the tunnels, I'd been turning over in the back of my mind how I ought to play this. The last few times that I'd met Rachel I'd tried to plant seeds of doubt, chip away at her relationship with Richard. But the more I'd pushed, the more resistance I'd encountered, and my last attempt in the Vault had been a total failure. Maybe it was time for a different approach. 'I'd like to know why you hate me so much.'

'What's that supposed to mean?'

'Of course I have an agenda,' Richard said behind me in response to some question from the crowd. 'I have never pretended otherwise. I am not helping you out of altruism. What I offer is an alliance.'

'We've run into each other a lot of times now,' I told Rachel. 'Sometimes we're allies, sometimes we're enemies, but one thing that's never changed is how much you hate me. What I want to know is why. I mean, you *won*. You always wanted to be powerful and feared; well, you got it. You're Richard's Chosen, and everyone gets out of the way when they see you coming. Yeah, there are bigger dogs

out there, but I'm not one of them. So what's your problem
with me that makes you want to kill me so badly?'

'You know what you did,' Rachel said.

'You mean when I peeked into your head?' I said. 'That
was four years ago. Get over it.'

Rachel stared at me. The possibilities of her trying to
kill me hadn't stopped; she was still trying to line up a
shot. I could feel Meredith's breathing as I held her close;
she was keeping very still, maybe hoping that everyone
would forget about her. To my right, Luna was still pouring
her curse into Meredith's equipment. I could feel the
volume of the spell building; the focus was probably already
beyond repair.

Then the possibilities of violence winked out. 'All right,
Alex, I'll play,' Rachel said. 'You want to know why I hate
you? It's because you're such a fucking hypocrite.'

I raised my eyebrows. 'And this is because . . . ?'

'You act like you're better than all the rest of us,' Rachel
said. Her voice became high and mocking. 'Oh, look at
me, I'm Alex Verus! All those other mages are so mean
and nasty, but I'm different, I'd never do anything like
that!' She looked at me in disgust. 'You're in it for yourself,
just like everyone else. That's why you left Richard.'

'I left Richard because of what he did.'

'Bullshit,' Rachel said. 'If you'd cared so much, you never
would have signed up. You knew what Richard was, we
all did. You knew *exactly* what being his apprentice was
going to mean.'

'Yeah, well, maybe I was slow on the uptake,' I said.
'Or maybe I just decided I didn't like what I was turning
into.'

'Right, because you *changed*,' Rachel said. 'You used to

be one of those evil Dark mages, but now you've seen the light and turned over a new leaf. That's the story you tell everyone, isn't it?'

'And what if it is?' I said, nettled. I'd meant to just keep Rachel talking, but she was getting to me. 'Just because you can't change, doesn't mean no one else can.'

'You never changed,' Rachel said. 'You left Richard because you couldn't handle taking orders.'

'I left because of what happened to those two kids.'

'Oh please. You've killed more people than most Dark mages do in their whole lives. What, you think it's different when you do it? You do the same things they do, you're just more self-righteous about it. You really wanted to be so good and pure, you would have got out a long time ago. You didn't because you wanted the same things. You wanted to be powerful and feared. And that's why you're on the fucking Council right now.'

'I got this job because your boss forced me into being Morden's aide at gunpoint,' I snapped. 'You have a problem with that, take it up with him.'

'Yeah?' Rachel said. 'So if you hated it so much, why haven't you quit?'

'I . . .' I trailed off.

'Go on, Alex, tell me.' Rachel took a step forward, glaring at me. 'Why haven't you? Not like it's hard! Then you could go back to that stupid shop you won't shut up about. Except you won't, because that's not enough for you, is it? You want to be the boss, you just don't have the balls to admit it.'

'And you don't?' I said angrily. 'You gave up everything to be where you are now. You killed everyone who got in your way. The only reason you didn't kill me as well was that I didn't give you the chance!'

'I paid my dues,' Rachel said coldly. 'Richard taught us that. Take what you want, and pay for it. But you never listened, did you? You thought you could get it all for free. Richard held up his end of the deal. *You* were the one who betrayed *him*. And you've been doing the same thing ever since. You trick people into listening to you, they give you an inch, then you fuck them over and leave them holding the bag. You think I haven't seen what you've been doing, trying to use me to get to Richard? How stupid do you think I am?'

Okay, time to give up on that plan. 'You'd still be better off without him.'

'You don't care whether I'd be better off without him,' Rachel said. 'You want us apart because it makes us weak, and you want Richard weak because you're scared of him, because he's the one person you've never been able to con or trick. You want Richard's power, but you're too scared to earn it.' Rachel stared at me. 'And you wonder why I hate you.'

I didn't say anything.

'You know what else I think?' Rachel said. 'I think if she isn't doing her job, it doesn't matter that much if she's alive.'

My divination gave me just enough warning. As the green ray stabbed out from Rachel's hand, I shoved Meredith left while using the momentum to push myself right. The ray passed between us as I grabbed Luna's hand and the two of us went over the balcony railing.

Air rushed past and my stomach dropped. Shouts and

screams sounded from below. I broke my life ring just in time and air magic caught us, slowing our rate of fall. For one heart-stopping moment I thought that we were too heavy, that the ring didn't have enough power for two, then we slowed just in time and hit the floor in the centre of a circle of scattering people.

Luna and I scrambled to our feet. Looking upwards, I saw Rachel's white face glaring down at us from the balcony. Meredith was nowhere to be seen. 'Okay, interesting conversational strategy,' Luna said, pulling stray strands of mist off me from our fall. 'Did it work?'

'We're alive, aren't we?' I muttered. Rachel wasn't firing on us yet; maybe even she wasn't willing to shoot into a crowd.

'I guess,' Luna said. 'But Alex? Wasn't the plan *not* to be in the middle of the crowd when it turned nasty?'

I looked around to see that the entire crowd of adepts was staring at us. We'd even attracted enough attention to distract them from Richard. And as I thought about Richard, I looked up to see him staring down right at us.

Variam's voice spoke into my ear. 'Fire in the hole.'

Richard met my gaze, and even at a distance, I saw him smile.

The main doors burst open with a thundering boom. Turning, I saw Council security and mages in combat gear come pouring through the doorway. Shouts and screams came from the crowd of adepts, people trying to push away from the Council security and finding nowhere to go. We had the Keeper force on one side, Richard's cabal on the other, and a crowd of panicking adepts all around us.

'You know,' I told Luna, 'this is turning into a really crappy night out.'

The Council security formed a line, a long semicircle of grim-faced men holding sub-machine-guns levelled at the crowd, and behind them came the Keepers, surrounded by glowing shields of red and white and blue. Yells rang out as the adepts backed away. The Keeper ranks parted and a man stepped forward.

12

The man leading the Keepers had thinning hair and a
steady stride, and a translucent shield of air magic shimmered around him. I'd seen him before in the War Rooms:
this was Nimbus, the Director of Operations for the Order
of the Star. 'Mage Drakh,' he called out. He didn't raise
his voice, but his words echoed like thunder across the
room. 'You are under arrest on suspicion of violation of
the first and second clauses of the Concord. You will order
your followers to stand down and come with us.'

Richard stood in plain view on the balcony, looking
down at the Council force. If he was worried, he wasn't
showing any sign of it. 'You would start a battle in the
middle of an innocent crowd?' Like Nimbus, Richard's
voice rang out across the club floor. 'Is this Council policy
nowadays?'

'The only one intending to start a battle is you,' Nimbus
said. 'Cooperate, and no one will be harmed.'

A barely perceptible ripple went through the crowd. I
looked around for a way out. We weren't that far from the
doors, but there were a *lot* of people in the way.

'Thank you for the invitation,' Richard said. 'I respect-
fully decline.'

'Don't play games, Drakh.' Nimbus's voice was hard.
'This building is surrounded and your cabal is outnum-
bered. You are not fighting your way out of here.'

Alex! It was Anne's voice. *We've got trouble.*

Thanks, Anne, I noticed. At least Rachel wasn't eyeballing us from the balcony any more.

'Fighting our way out?' Richard's voice was calm. 'You should worry about yourself.'

Figures stepped up behind Richard on the balcony. Rachel was there on Richard's left side, with Cinder flanking her. There were other mages too, most of them masked, destructive spells crackling around them. On Richard's right, though, was a shape I didn't recognise. It looked like a woman, taller than Richard, but shaped out of living darkness.

Vihaela's aura just changed, Anne said. *Got a lot less human and a LOT more powerful.*

Yeah, I think I'm looking at her, I said. That black shape didn't have a face, but with Richard standing right next to it I could judge its size, and it was Vihaela's height. *What's she doing?*

I don't know, but whatever it is, it's dangerous. Don't get close!

'Last chance, Drakh,' Nimbus said. 'Are we doing this the easy way, or the hard way?'

The flow of reinforcements through the door hadn't stopped, and more and more Keepers were lining up on either side of Nimbus. I saw Caldera, standing close to Nimbus's right side, along with Rain. Slate and Trask were there too, and I caught a glimpse of Variam's turban, meaning that Landis was there as well. There had to be at least thirty Keepers there, and those were just the ones that I could see. The crowd around us was shifting, worried. There was the occasional angry shout or call, but for the most part the adepts packed onto the club floor felt scared. That double line of Council security with levelled guns looked menacing as hell, and the Keepers behind them were even worse. If a fight started the crowd would want to run . . .

. . . but run *where*? The Keepers were blocking the exit. I looked around, craning my neck, and felt a chill. At the far end of the room, I could just see the stairs leading up to the balcony, the ones that had been guarded when Luna and I had been looking for a way up. They weren't guarded now; instead they were blocked off by heavy metal grates. 'Verus to Nimbus.'

'The easy way would be for you to take your men and leave,' Richard said calmly. 'But we already know you're not going to do that.'

'Hard way it is,' Nimbus said.

'Verus to Nimbus,' I said again. There was no answering chime and I swore. They must be on a different circuit. I could figure out how to get through, with enough time—

Magic glowed around Nimbus and he soared up into the air. 'This gathering is at an end.' His voice boomed out around the room. 'All of you will lie down on the floor and—'

The shape next to Richard raised an arm. Black lightning flashed, tearing through Nimbus's shield and slamming him against the wall. Nimbus's head hit the concrete with an audible *crack* and he dropped from sight.

He hadn't even hit the ground before everyone opened fire.

Spells flashed out from both sides, fireballs and force blades and bolts of lightning crossing in mid-air. They impacted on shields with a crash, energy flaring in all directions. Screams and shouts came from the adepts, and the second line of security men threw a volley of grenades into the crowd. I had just enough time to push Luna down and shut my eyes before they went off with a sound like the end of the world, blotting out my hearing and knocking me flat.

I struggled back to my feet. Spots flashed before my eyes, and all I could hear was a high-pitched ringing. All around, the crowd was in chaos, people's mouths opening and closing silently. A warning from my precognition made me twist aside just as a group of adepts charged past.

Luna was still on her hands and knees, shaking her head; she hadn't had the instant's warning that I had. Another adept came barrelling towards me; I deflected him out of Luna's way, caught Luna by one hand and pulled her to her feet. *Luna, it's me. Follow me.*

Alex? What's going on?

Flashbangs. We need to get to cover.

The crowd was panicking, adepts pushing and shoving. I saw a girl go down under a pack and be trampled. Up above I could catch glimpses of the battle, magical attacks soaring overhead in eerie silence. One of the Keepers crossed the room in a single enormous leap, wings of fire trailing behind him. Another bolt of darkness leaped out from that shape next to Richard, knocking him down into the crowd and out of sight.

Alex, are you there? It was Anne's voice. *Don't get close to Vihaela!*

Not my priority right now! An adept cannoned into me and I bounced off, still trying to shield Luna. Another swung a fist, maybe deliberately, maybe in panic. I hit him in the neck and he went down gagging, then I pulled Luna into the shelter of one of the speakers near the wall.

My hearing was starting to come back; I could hear distant shouts and screams. The crowd was a whirl of motion and faces and I couldn't see what was going on. *Vari!* I called, reaching for him.

Little busy! Variam shouted back.

Can you patch me through to whoever's in charge?

No! Nimbus was the only one with the permissions to do that and he's down. Stop distracting me!

I swore, then pushed myself up on the speaker, craning my neck for a view. The crowd of adepts was a panicking mob. On the near side of the room, the line of Council security was holding, but on the far side they were engaged in a mêlée, batons and fists rising and falling. I couldn't hear gunfire yet but I knew it wouldn't take long. Spells still flew back and forth between the Keepers and the Dark mages on the balcony, but the layers of overlapping shields on both sides were holding off the attacks.

Right now it was hard to see who was winning, but I'd spent a lot of time working with Council forces over the past year and I could tell that they were leaderless. Their two wings were disjointed, uncoordinated. I looked to the right and saw the door Luna and I had used earlier, still unguarded. I could get it open, try to fight my way up to Richard and Vihaela . . .

I hesitated for a long moment, then dropped down. *Luna. You're okay for me to leave you?*

I . . . yeah. Go do your thing.

I turned and walked towards the line of Council security, tearing Arachne's bracelet off my wrist and dropping it to the floor. The spell fizzled away and I was myself again. The crowd around me didn't notice: they were far too busy pushing and shoving to get away from the men with guns. I twisted, letting them bounce off me, as I pulled out my wallet and took out a sheet of paper, unfolding it just as the crowd parted to leave me face to face with the Council security line.

Three or four sub-machine-guns shifted to point at me. I kept walking forward at a steady pace, holding up the sheet of paper in plain view. 'I'm Mage Verus of the Junior Council.' I had to shout to be heard over the yells and roars. I pointed at one of the security men. 'Who's your commanding officer?'

The security men hesitated, their eyes flickering from me to the paper. 'Uh . . .' the guy I'd addressed began.

'Take me to him.' I folded up the paper, sticking it back into my pocket, giving the men just enough time to see the letterhead, but no more. It was a memo on parking regulations outside the War Rooms. 'Rest of you, hold the line.' I walked straight through the guns, which wavered, then went back to pointing back in the direction of the crowd.

Somehow no one questioned me. The line closed up behind me as the security man led me through the ranks, ducking as bolts of fire screamed overhead. I was searching with my eyes and my divination, looking for order in the chaos, and I spotted it before the security man did, changing direction towards the steps leading up to the exit.

There was a small knot of figures there, and at the centre was Rain. He's a captain in the Order of the Star, and my old boss, tall and dark-skinned and intense. Right now he was holding a blue-tinged shield in a bubble over the Keeper ranks, while arguing with a mage behind him. Other Keepers stood around him, their attention on the long-range battle with the Dark mages on the balcony. 'I don't care!' Rain was saying. 'He's not around and we need those men!'

'Rain!' I shouted.

Rain's head snapped around. 'Verus? What the hell are you doing here?'

'Your left flank's overextended,' I told him. 'If they keep pushing forward it's going to turn into a bloodbath. I need command of this force, now.'

'What?' Caldera appeared from behind Rain. 'You can't—'

'I'm a Council member and with Nimbus down, I'm taking tactical command,' I said. I didn't take my eyes off Rain. 'Rain. Please?'

Rain hesitated for a long moment, then nodded. 'All right. What do you need?'

I pointed out towards the adepts. 'That crowd is panicking. They're trying to run, but there's nowhere for them to run *to*. If your line of men keeps pushing they're going to start trampling each other and they'll end up fighting like rats in a trap. We need to move this whole force to the right. Stand aside and let the crowd funnel out through these doors.'

'We're here to detain them, not let them get away,' Caldera said angrily.

'That crowd outnumbers you ten to one,' I told her. 'Right now they're in too much of a panic to remember that. If you try arresting them one at a time, that's going to change. Either way, this is not a request. I'm giving you an order as a member of the Junior Council. If you can't follow it, get out of the way and leave it to someone who can!'

Caldera glared at me and I turned to Rain. 'You take the left flank. Pull them back. I'll take charge of the right.'

Rain nodded and turned away, pushing his way through

towards the left. *Okay.* I took a breath and turned back the way I came. Movement at the corner of my eye caught my attention and I pointed. 'Slate. Trask. You two, with me.'

Slate gave me a narrow look. A stocky and tough-looking death mage, he'd never liked me even back when I was with the Order of the Star, but he was one of the few of the Keepers I was sure wasn't corrupt. 'Doing what?'

'You going to follow orders or not?'

Slate scowled but didn't argue. I kept moving and felt the two of them move in behind me. Up ahead, I could see that the right flank of the Council lines was stable. The battle mages were still taking shots at each other, but everyone had had enough time to get shields up. A couple of security men had gone down to something I hadn't seen; ahead, a scattering of adepts were on the floor as well. There was a no-man's-land between the two groups maybe fifty feet wide.

I strode out into the open, turning to face the line of Council security. 'All right, boys!' I had to shout at the top of my voice. 'Everyone move to the right in an orderly fashion! Yes, I said right!' I swept my arms to get the message across, pointing. 'You! Stop staring and move your arse!'

Some of the security men hesitated, and I caught mutterings.

'. . . is he?'

'. . . no, that's Verus, I saw . . .'

'. . . why? I thought—'

'Hey!' I yelled. 'This isn't a fucking committee!'

I had my back to the crowd of adepts, some of whom were definitely turning hostile. A projectile of some sort went whistling over my shoulder. I ignored it and kept shepherding the security men as they started to move. 'That's it. Steady pace.'

A future of my death flashed up on my precognition. I sidestepped and a bullet went whining through the space my head had been occupying, ricochetting off the floor. One of the security men grunted and stumbled. I pointed. 'You, get him on his feet, pull him back. Slate, get rid of that sniper.'

'What sniper?' Slate shouted back. 'I can't see shit!'

I turned and walked towards the adepts, my arms spread wide, making myself as obvious a target as possible. The adepts on the ground fell back, but my eyes were scanning the walls. *There.* I saw a twitch of movement in a small balcony high on the left wall, a mirror image to the one Meredith had been using. I turned and walked back towards Slate, absent-mindedly twisting my head aside to avoid a second bullet, and pointed over my shoulder. 'Top balcony, ten o'clock. Kill him, please, he's getting on my nerves.'

Slate lifted his hand and energy gathered for a spell. I was already turning away, scanning the club floor. The mêlée on the left flank was still going on, but I could see Rain in the middle of the crowd, pulling people aside and restoring order. The Keeper force with the line of security men wheeled to the right under my direction, shifting anticlockwise around the wall.

With the adepts separated, the Keepers were free to focus on Richard's group. Concentrated fire hammered the balcony, but the black shape at Richard's side had some kind of dome up that deflected the attacks with ease. Richard didn't even seem to be fighting; he was focused on something he was holding in one hand.

Alex, what are you doing? It was Anne's voice. *You're right out in the middle!*

That lifesight of yours is pretty precise, isn't it? I picked out a strand from the futures and turned to shout at a couple of the security men. 'You two! Down!'

One of the men didn't hear, but his partner dragged him down just as a volley of metal spheres flew overhead, striking chips from the wall behind. I saw the adept who'd taken the shot, a skinny kid trying to hide in the crowd. There was an unused flashbang lying on the floor, and I pulled the pin and lobbed it. The flashbang flew through a neat arc and exploded right in the kid's face just as he popped up for another shot. He disappeared under the feet of his companions.

Anne sounded more frustrated than worried. *You're going to get killed!*

I appreciate the thought, but you're kind of distracting me.

I was starting to attract serious attention. Another bullet whined past my head, followed by two more. I didn't have time to track their location; a blast of flame scorched the floor where I was standing and I had to jump aside, heat rolling over my skin and clothes. I dodged two more projectiles and a force blade, then felt a surge of magic from the balcony, life magic mixed with something darker. I turned back just in time to see the black shape next to Richard pointing at me. Bolts of darkness arrowed down.

The world went black as the spells struck, blotting out everything around me with a crash. It was over in an instant and I was left unharmed. The spells had struck precisely on either side of where I'd been standing. I looked up at the black shape and gave it a half-bow, half-salute. *Guess I should be glad Vihaela and Richard don't want me dead just yet.*

Turning around, I saw that several of the Council security had stopped to stare at me. 'Come on, people!' I yelled at them. 'This isn't a spectator sport!' I ducked another bullet then strode towards them. 'You're nearly there, just—'

The force mage up on the balcony made more of an effort this time. A storm of blades converged on me.

A shield of fire flared up, orange-red and roaring. The force blades struck the barrier and disintegrated, and Landis leaned out from the battle line, lanky and relaxed. 'Verus,' he called over. 'Not that I don't appreciate you encouraging the troops, but perhaps you might see your way back to the lines?'

Looking back, I saw that the Council force had done as I'd ordered. The security men had moved around to the side, leaving the main exit clear. The crowd of adepts had an open path to the doorway, but they were hesitating. To get to the exit, they'd have to run across the Council security's line of fire.

'The way out clear?' I called to Landis.

'It's been taken care of.'

'You have a mind mage with you?'

'Gladius should fit your bill.'

'Good.' I pointed at the line of adepts. 'Tell him to make a few of them run for that exit. Shouldn't take more than two or three.'

'The sheep and the flock, eh?' Landis put one hand to his ear and began talking. I turned towards the adepts, watching, tense. Spells were still flying overhead.

Twenty seconds passed, then suddenly one of the adepts broke away from the crowd, followed an instant later by a second, then a third. They kept running, crossing the floor. Hundreds of adepts watched with bated breath as they reached the exit and disappeared through it, one, two, three.

There was an instant's pause, then one other guy took a step forward and, as though it had been a signal, the whole crowd followed. They moved faster and faster until they were running, charging for the open doors.

'Stand down!' I yelled at the top of my voice. 'Let them pass!' But the noise was tremendous and I knew that most of them couldn't hear. The crowd charged forward, wild-eyed and stampeding. They were trying to steer clear of the security line, but sheer numbers were causing the swarm to bulge outwards.

A future jumped out at me: gunfire, adepts falling to be trampled under the mob. I caught a glimpse of one of the security men raising his gun. There wasn't time to pass an order; without thinking I reached out through the dreamstone and hammered at him, screaming fear and nameless threat across the distance between us. I saw him flinch and step back; an instant later Rain was there, shouting at him and pushing down his gun.

The crowd of adepts reached the exit and poured through. Off to one side I could see Caldera, watching the stream of people with a sour look on her face, but my heart lifted as I saw they weren't going to stop. I turned to Landis. 'Landis. You and five other Keepers, with me. We're going to go hit these bastards from behind.'

'Lovely!' Landis rubbed his hands together. 'Just show us where to go, Verus, there's a good chap.'

Luna was waiting at the door we'd used earlier. She still had her wand out, but the security men nearby had their guns pointed away from her; apparently she'd managed to convince them she was on their side. 'Alex!' she called as I drew closer. 'Door's locked.'

'Slate?' I called over my shoulder.

I could feel Slate's annoyance, but he didn't hesitate. A kinetic bolt punched the lock out of the door and I kicked it open without breaking stride. 'You and your squad, with us,' I called, pointing at a sergeant. 'Stay behind and cover our flanks.' I walked through into the machine room, Landis and the other Keepers right behind.

I didn't waste time on subtlety this time around. With my divination I could see a path that would take us straight to Richard's balcony, and I led my group straight down the main corridor. One of Jagadev's men waited in ambush down a side passage; I saw him before we were anywhere near and gestured with one hand, pointing through the wall. Landis sent a fireball curving over my shoulder and around the corner to explode in a flash and a sharp *whoompf*. There was a scream, abruptly cut off.

'Alex, Landis!' Variam called through the communicator. 'They're moving!'

'Moving where?' I said, then called back over my shoulder. 'Trask! Fire traps just after that second door up ahead, thirty foot spread.'

From behind, Trask wove a spell. Water magic flowed past, sweeping down the corridor. Red energy met blue with a flash and a hiss, the heat extinguishing.

'Richard and Vihaela just vanished,' Variam said. 'The others are doing a fighting retreat.'

'Shit.' I turned and yelled, 'Double time!' then broke into a jog. Steam rolled away from the heated concrete as I ran through the disabled trap.

'What's going on?' Luna yelled from behind.

'They're running!' I called back. 'Need to cut them off!'

We sprinted through the Tiger's Palace. I listened with one ear to the reports from Variam and with another to Landis, trying to locate us in my mental map of the place. Richard was abandoning the adepts, pulling his team back. 'He's heading for the west wing,' I called back to Landis. 'Pull teams from the east and reinforce that perimeter!'

'Our perimeter squad won't last long against that lot,' Landis warned.

'I know, we're going to have to catch— ah shit. Everyone back!'

The mages behind me slowed to a trot. We'd lost most of the Council security; Slate had been marking them off in ones and twos behind us, guarding the intersections. The corridor we'd been following ended in a stairway going up. I walked to the foot of the stairs.

Green and black death struck like a thunderbolt. I was already jumping back, the bolt crashing into the concrete where I'd been standing. The follow-up was instant, a black mote flying down the stairs to bloom into a sphere, and I only barely made it out of the spell's radius. Death energy washed over me, stinging and numbing my skin. 'Goddamn it, Vihaela!' I yelled up at her. Those ones had *not* been aimed to miss. 'Make up your mind!'

Vihaela's laugh floated down the stairs. 'Sorry, Verus. No more freebies.'

'Not this bitch again,' Slate growled. 'Flank her?'

I shook my head. 'It'd take too long.'

Landis cocked his head for a moment, listening. 'Help's on the way.'

'We can only attack one at a time up these stairs.' I looked at Landis. 'Can you take her one-on-one?'

'Thought you'd never ask.'

'Come on, boys,' Vihaela called down. 'I'm getting lonely up here.'

Landis was moving along the wall, getting into position. 'So how come you aren't powered up any more?' I shouted at Vihaela. I'd had a glimpse of her through the futures and she looked human again. 'Did you run out of rings and have to turn back into regular Sonic?'

'I can't really follow the reference,' Vihaela called back, 'but if you're asking why I'm not pulling out anything special, I'm not feeling pressured enough. Why don't you do something about that?'

'Funny you should ask.'

Landis stepped out around the corner. Vihaela struck instantly, but a barrier of flame roared into existence in front of Landis, intercepting her attack. Landis started climbing the stairs, moving slowly and steadily, one hand up maintaining the shield. Green and black flashes showed through the barrier as Vihaela's spells struck it, but they weren't getting through.

'Come on!' Slate shouted, running forward.

'No, wait!' I said, frowning. Something was wrong. I'd seen Landis go up against Vihaela before and they were closely matched. He shouldn't be able to push her off the high ground this quickly. *What's she planning?*

'We can back him up!' Slate said. But he didn't move forward, and neither did Trask.

'Wait,' I said again, looking through the futures. It was hard seeing past the chaos of combat, but there were commonalities. Landis took another step up; he was almost out of sight.

Then suddenly I saw what Vihaela was planning. There

was no time to talk; instead I reached out through the dreamstone, hammering a connection through. *Landis, it's a trap, get back NOW!*

Landis moved instantly, jumping back down the stairs. As he did there was a flash and a hollow *boom* as the stairwell exploded, chunks of concrete flying out to be melted by his shield. Landis touched down and with a rumbling shudder, the stairway collapsed. A cloud of dust and smoke rolled over us.

'What the fuck?' Slate said, coughing and waving his hand in front of his face.

'Demolition charge,' I said curtly. Vihaela had been holding off on pulling the trigger, probably waiting until Landis was standing right on top of it. 'Landis, you okay?'

'Quite all right, thank you.' Landis slapped at his shoulders, sending concrete dust puffing into the air. 'That mine was quite deep-buried, wasn't it? Would almost think they knew we were coming.'

'Yeah, no shit. Slate, can you smash a way through?'

Slate and one of the other mages were inspecting where the foot of the stairs had been. The smoke was clearing to reveal a massive pile of rubble. 'It'll take all day to get through this shit,' Slate said sourly. 'We need Caldera.'

One of the other mages started talking into his communicator and I cursed. *Too slow!* 'Come on,' I called and started running in a different direction. If I got back far enough we could use the first floor corridor . . .

I'd made it up the stairs and had just started to double back when I felt the gate magic pulse. I'd been talking to Variam through the dreamstone, getting him to help organise the perimeter defence, but as soon as I sensed the spell, I stopped. *Wait*, I told Variam. *Never mind.*

What was that that just went off?

Gate spell. I slowed to a walk. There was no point hurrying any more.

I thought we had a ward up against that?

Yeah, so did I. I kept going, though I doubted there was much point. It was technically possible that some of the Dark mages might have stuck around, but I really doubted it. *It's over. Tell the others I'll be down once I've had the chance to find out the details of exactly how this got screwed up so hard. I doubt I'll be long.*

'So what's the butcher's bill?' I asked Landis.

It was half an hour later. The club floor had been converted into an improvised headquarters, prison and field hospital, with mages standing around talking and directing security personnel. Over at the far side, Anne and a couple of other life mages were healing the wounded. The adepts from the crowd who'd been too slow or injured to escape were in a huddle against the wall, guarded by a security detail. Rain was out on a perimeter sweep, and Variam and Luna were deeper inside the building. The air was filled with the buzz of talk and orders.

'Seventeen,' Landis said. 'Three of ours, six of theirs and eight from the crowd.'

'Is that dead or wounded?'

'Dead,' Landis said. 'Total casualties are far higher, of course. Still, the healer corps is doing good work, including your friend Miss Walker. I don't expect we'll lose any more.'

'Who were the three of ours?'

'Security men. Reynolds, White and Kowalski. All killed by sniper fire from those balconies. They were targeting the Keepers by preference, else it would have been worse.

The shields kept the bullets away from the Keepers, but unfortunately most of the security detail were outside the defensive radius.'

I grimaced. I was pretty sure those snipers had been Jagadev's work. It was the kind of thing he'd have done. 'I should have figured out quicker where those shots were coming from.'

'Well, they paid for it in any case. One of the shooters got away, but we took care of the other two. The rest of the casualties were all inflicted while you were pursuing Richard and Vihaela.'

'Any prisoners?'

'Several.'

'Richard's cabal?'

Landis shook his head. 'No such luck, I'm afraid. They'll be interrogated, but none seem particularly knowledgeable. I suspect we'll find that all were hired muscle.'

'And meanwhile,' I said sourly, 'Richard and Vihaela, along with all their important supporters, have vanished into thin air.'

'It does appear that way.'

'The eight from the crowd,' I said. 'What happened to them?'

'Trampled or shot.'

'I suppose it's too much to hope that none of them were killed by our own side?'

'I rather expect so,' Landis said. 'I wouldn't be too hard on the security men. They were being fired upon, and some of those adepts were using quite dangerous attacks.'

'That's not how the adepts are going to see it,' I said, then raised a hand to forestall Landis's reply. 'I know, I know. It's not their fault.'

My earpiece pinged. 'Boss, Alex,' Variam said. 'You there?'

'Just finishing up,' Landis said. 'How goes things up above?'

'Well, this thing's definitely a gate focus,' Variam said. 'But it's locked down tight. I don't know if they sabotaged it, but I can't get it working and it doesn't look like anyone else can either. Could use Alex if he's around.'

'I'll take a look,' I said. 'We one hundred per cent sure that Richard and his gang used that to get out?'

'Abeyance says so,' Variam said. 'Not like there were many other options.'

'Yeah,' I said. The item Variam was studying — a free-standing arch in one of the first-floor rooms — was what we'd found when we'd pursued Richard and Vihaela to their last known location. The interdiction field the Keepers had thrown over the Tiger's Palace had prevented gate spells, but if you're willing to spend enough time and effort it's possible to shield a gate focus against outside interference, rather like laying down a landline to prevent your signal from being jammed. 'And you know what that means.'

'Means they not only knew we were coming, they had enough warning to set up stuff like this,' Variam said. 'Council's not going to be happy.'

'The Council had enough bloody warnings,' I said shortly.

'Bet you they still blame it on us.'

'No bet. Hang around, I'll be up there in five.'

'Got it.'

Near the door, I could see Nimbus sitting up with one of the healer corps tending to him. He was looking bad-tempered but didn't shoo the mage away, possibly because he wasn't yet able to stand. 'You think I ought to talk to him?' I asked Landis, nodding in Nimbus's direction.

'I rather suspect it'd be a bad idea,' Landis said. 'Our dear friend Nimbus is not the most humble of mages, and I doubt it'll sit well if you remind him of how he was taken out of the fight in one move. If you're not interested in making enemies, I'd suggest a discreet withdrawal.'

'Wonderful,' I said with a sigh. 'Then I think I'll check in with Variam and get the hell out of here.'

'Oh, Verus?'

I paused, looking back.

'Good work back there.'

'Mm,' I said. 'There are seventeen bodies that say I could have done a lot better.'

'It really could have been so much worse,' Landis said. He patted me on the shoulder. 'For your first field command, I'd say you did extremely well.'

'That's . . . good to hear.' Landis might be eccentric, but he's perceptive. If he gives you a compliment, he means it. 'So you think this *wasn't* a failure?'

'Tonight was the first skirmish in what I suspect will be quite a long war,' Landis said. 'I'd get some rest if I were you. I'm sure you'll have a busy day explaining all this to the Senior Council tomorrow.'

13

'What I want to know,' Sal Sarque said, 'is how the *fuck* this was allowed to happen.'

'We have just spent an hour and a half on a detailed review of precisely that,' Bahamus said.

Sal Sarque jabbed a finger at Bahamus. 'Don't play games. I didn't say how this happened, I said how this was *allowed* to happen. This was your plan.'

'One that you voted for.'

There were thirteen people besides me in the Star Chamber: the secretary, plus the seven senior and remaining five junior members of the Light Council. Everyone had shown up this time. The Junior Council, including me, were gathered at the lower half of the table, or as I thought of it, the kiddy table. For obvious reasons, I didn't say that (or anything else) out loud. The Senior Council were in an extremely bad mood and no one wanted to draw attention.

The meeting had started as a debrief of last night's events and had quickly devolved into Sal Sarque blaming Bahamus and Bahamus defending himself. No one had tried to blame me just yet, but I knew that was just a matter of time. Bahamus was getting priority because he was more important and because he'd been the one to first propose the plan. I was next.

'Let's all calm down, shall we?' Druss said. 'End of the day, we lost three security and no mages. Could have been a lot higher.'

'I'm sorry, Druss, but the numbers are irrelevant,' Alma said. 'We could have lost every security man we sent and it would have been an acceptable trade. Our objective was Drakh, and now not only has he escaped, everyone *knows* he's escaped. He's made the Council into a laughing stock.'

'Better to have them laughing than our people dead,' Druss said.

'No,' Alma said. 'Drakh has just demonstrated that it is possible to flout Council law without consequence. If we don't make an example of him, and soon, we'll lose far more than that.'

'Oh?' Sal Sarque said, turning on Alma. 'And how exactly are you going to do that? You couldn't even find him before!'

'While that is an important question,' Levistus cut in, 'before we move on to the question of what steps to take, I think there are still some unanswered questions about last night. In particular, I'd be interested in hearing Verus's explanation for his presence.'

Seven pairs of eyes fixed on me as the whole Senior Council turned to face me at once. 'I wanted to keep an eye on things,' I said.

'You weren't authorised to be there!' Sal Sarque snapped. 'You were specifically ordered to stay away!'

'You mean that second-hand message I got passed? Yes, I was, and I was *also* told to be close enough that I'd be available to reach the site on short notice. I don't know how you were expecting me to do both.'

Sal Sarque looked about to explode, but before he could speak, Druss raised a hand. 'I think we're getting off topic. Why *were* you there?'

'You might remember at our last meeting that Spire

asked me whether I thought the operation would work.' I nodded at Spire, who was watching quietly with his fingers steepled. 'I told him that I thought the odds were against it, because there was too great a chance of the plans being leaked. I think events have borne me out on that front.'

'A leak?' Sal Sarque was turning a purplish colour. 'You *were* the leak! How else did they know?'

'How about from one of the literally *hundreds* of people that you and your staff decided to inform? Between your personal staff and the aides and clerks of everyone else on the Senior Council, the Keeper team, the security contingent supporting the Keeper team and every other bureaucrat and administrator that's been involved in this operation by now, it'd have been a bloody miracle if Drakh *didn't* find out.'

'Your presence could have contributed to their preparations,' Alma began.

'Yes, I'm sure they had time to bury a demolition charge in solid concrete *and* set up a free-standing gate focus in the ten minutes I was in the building,' I said. I was getting pissed off now. 'Oh, and you might want to bear in mind that while I was there I also shut off the enchantment effect that they were using to manipulate the crowd. If I hadn't, that Keeper team would have been rushed by a mob.'

'You want credit for that?' Sal Sarque said contemptuously. 'You think those adepts of yours would have stood a chance against our forces?'

'Have you seriously not figured out what was going on last night?' I said. 'Richard *wanted* you to mow down those adepts. The more you killed, the better! If it had turned out into a full-scale combat, you'd have killed hundreds, and you'd have turned every single adept in Britain against you. Why do you think Richard stuck around? He stayed because he was trying to bait you into orchestrating a civilian massacre right in the middle of London, and he came pretty close to succeeding.'

Sal Sarque stood up, his fists clenched. 'We are not going to go soft on those Dark mages just because they use human shields!'

'They don't *need* to use human shields. From what I've seen, you seem more than happy to commit atrocities without any help on his part.'

'All right!' Druss raised his hands. 'Let's all calm down, shall we?'

Sal Sarque sat down, but from his expression I could see he was still furious. 'What's done is done,' Druss said. 'As far as Drakh goes, we might have lost face, but we're not really any worse off than we were yesterday. He was out there then and he's out there now.'

'As far as *Drakh* goes?' Sal Sarque said. 'What about the *other* thing that happened last night?'

'Sarque,' Alma said warningly.

Sal Sarque opened his mouth, shot a glance down the table at me and the rest of the Junior Council and closed it again. There was a moment's silence.

'Is there something we should know?' I asked. The pause was stretching out and no one else seemed keen to speak.

'No,' Sal Sarque said curtly.

'Oh come on,' Druss said wearily. 'Not like we can exactly keep this one a secret.'

'The information is still sensitive,' Alma said.

'I think it's a matter of closing the stable door after the horse is gone,' Bahamus said.

'Long gone,' Druss said, then turned to address me and the others. 'There was a raid on our Southampton facility last night. Was timed to coincide with the Tiger's Palace attack.'

The Southampton facility is one of the Council's secondary storage depots. It's not as well defended as the War Rooms or the Vault, but it still has some fairly important stuff. 'So that there wouldn't be a quick response force,' I said.

Druss nodded. 'Didn't go as well for them as the raid on the Vault. They managed to break into the areas near the loading dock, but they couldn't breach the bubble and they had to withdraw. Was bloody, though. They killed all the staff in the areas they got control of.'

'Was it Onyx?' I asked.

'What makes you think that?' Bahamus asked.

'A violent operation with a high body count that isn't all that successful at getting to the objective,' I said. 'Plus he'd have known when to time it.'

'Well, you're right,' Druss said. 'They used shrouds and shot out all the visible cameras, but they missed the hidden ones. We've got footage of Onyx from three angles, along with that fire mage he's taken up with.'

'This is a matter for the Senior Council,' Levistus said.

'I agree,' Alma said with a nod. 'We'll determine how much to release later. Until then, all details are considered sealed to the Star Chamber until further notice.'

There was a rustle of movement as several people sat back. 'Now,' Alma said. 'It's clear that Drakh's cabal had advance warning of our operation. The question is how.'

'I'm afraid it's as Verus said,' Druss said. 'With all the eyes we brought in on it, it could have been any of a hundred people or more.'

'Regardless, we should conduct an investigation,' Bahamus said.

Undaaris nodded. 'I agree. This sort of a leak is concerning.'

'You considered maybe the leak's coming from that guy right there?' Sal Sarque asked.

'Oh, give it a rest, Sarque,' Druss said wearily. 'You hate Verus, we get it. Do it on your own time.'

'I agree,' Bahamus said with a frown. 'This is growing unseemly. Regardless of your personal disagreements with Councillor Verus, it is clear from the reports of last night that without his actions, the outcome of the raid would have been considerably worse.'

'Didn't sound like it to me,' Sal Sarque said, then as Druss started to respond, threw up his hands. 'Fine! If that's how you want to play it. How about the important question? What are we going to do now?'

There was a silence. I kept my mouth shut, and so did the rest of the Junior Council, but it didn't seem as though any of the Senior Council seemed eager to talk either. Looking around, I realised why. The last plan had gone badly. No one wanted to be responsible for the next one.

Then Levistus spoke. 'We need to make a public response.'

'I agree,' Alma said. 'A swift one.'

'Onyx,' Bahamus said.

'You really think he was the one behind this?' Druss said.

'Who cares?' Sal Sarque said.

'On this matter, Sal Sarque has the right of it,' Bahamus said. 'It doesn't matter whether Onyx was the leak. What does matter is that he double-crossed us, and if every Dark mage in Britain doesn't know that already, they soon will. He should be taught a lesson.'

'No,' Druss said.

Bahamus looked at Druss. 'Excuse me?'

'We're not going off half-cocked after Onyx,' Druss said. 'Did you read the reports this morning? We had thirty-six Keepers at the Tiger's Palace last night. Out of those, twenty-four were on the club floor and actively engaged against Drakh's cabal. Yes, some of them were busy dealing with the adepts and the small fry, but for the most part, they were trading punches with Drakh and his crew.'

'We're aware,' Alma said. 'What's your point?'

'The *point* is that according to the Keepers on the scene, Drakh had maybe ten to twelve mages up on that balcony. Two to one in our favour. We had three Keepers seriously injured last night. You know how many Drakh lost?'

'The reports didn't say,' Bahamus said.

'Zero. Twice their numbers, and we took three casualties to their none.' Druss looked at Sal Sarque. 'Nimbus made a big noise about how those adepts shouldn't have been allowed to escape, but it sounds to me like our boys were losing. If Drakh hadn't pulled out, it would have been a total fucking disaster.'

'How were that number of Dark mages able to defeat a full Keeper force?' Alma asked.

'Was it Drakh?' Undaaris asked.

Druss shook his head. 'From all accounts, Drakh just played to the crowd.'

'Then how?' Alma asked. 'For two years we've been pouring resources into the Keepers as a whole and your Order of the Shield in particular. The idea was to be able to *defeat* Dark mages in open conflict, not hold them to a stalemate. And from what you're saying, it sounds as though you barely managed even that.'

'Because they were punching above their weight,' Druss said. 'I'd lay bets that every one of those Dark mages was weighed down with imbued items. I've been warning you for months that most of the really combat-effective imbued items from the raid on the Vault haven't been showing up. I think we just learned what Drakh was saving them for.'

'It wasn't most of those Dark mages that were the problem,' Sal Sarque said. 'Just one.'

'Yes, I was just coming to that,' Alma said. 'A mage cloaked in a black shroud strongly suspected to be Vihaela. According to these reports she not only singlehandedly disabled Nimbus and Ares and held off all attempts at a counterattack, but *also* managed to intercept the flanking team intended to prevent Drakh's escape.' Alma laid down the reports and looked from Druss to Bahamus. 'You describe this as Drakh's cabal "punching above their weight", but frankly, it seems as though you barely engaged the cabal. You couldn't even get past this one mage.'

'We were already aware that Vihaela was one of the most dangerous members of Drakh's cabal,' Bahamus said. 'It seems that whatever she's acquired from the Vault, it's given her a significant power boost.'

'She wasn't using it when Verus's team ran into her later,' Druss said. 'Could be it's got limitations on how long it can be used.'

Alma shook her head. 'I'm not interested in tactics, Druss. I want to know why you're unwilling to move against Onyx.'

'This *is* about tactics,' Druss said. 'Because if we go charging off against Onyx the way we did last night, and Drakh and Vihaela do a repeat performance, there's a really good chance we're going to *lose*.'

'We'll be ready for them next time,' Sal Sarque said.

'How?' Druss said. 'We don't even know what they were using.'

The argument went on for some minutes. Bahamus and Sal Sarque wanted to go after Onyx; Druss and Undaaris were against. I was pretty sure that for Bahamus, it was personal: Onyx had double-crossed him and he wanted to teach him a lesson. Sal Sarque just seemed to want to take revenge and Onyx was an obvious target. Undaaris didn't care about the principles of the thing but was obviously nervous about another confrontation. With neither side willing to compromise, the debate dragged on.

'Enough,' Levistus said at last. 'This is pointless.'

'*You* were the one arguing for a response,' Bahamus said.

'Which is why this is pointless,' Levistus said. 'Disposing of Onyx will accomplish nothing.'

'He attacked the Council,' Bahamus said.

'And in due course, he will be dealt with,' Levistus said. 'But as regards our larger position, it will accomplish nothing at all. Onyx is not even part of Drakh's cabal. Focusing our strength against him would send the message that we are afraid to move against Drakh directly.'

'He's got a point,' Druss said. 'If we go after Onyx and Drakh steps in, we're in trouble. If he doesn't, it'll just look like we're chasing the easy target.'

'Then what do you suggest?' Alma asked Levistus.

'If we are going to make an example of someone in Drakh's cabal, it should be someone significant,' Levistus said. 'Ideally, we should move against Drakh or Vihaela. Given the circumstances, neither appears to be a practical target. This leaves one obvious candidate.'

Oh, I thought. *Right.* I'd been expecting Levistus to try to pin the blame on me. He'd considered it – I'd seen futures in which he'd tried exactly that – but in the end he'd held back. Probably because he'd decided that this was a more inviting target.

'You're talking about Morden?' Undaaris said questioningly.

'Who pointed us towards Onyx?' Levistus asked.

'You're suggesting he planned this from the start,' Alma said.

'I doubt we'll be able to prove it,' Levistus said. 'Morden will have covered his tracks. But I don't see how anyone could look at the facts and seriously consider any alternative.'

'Morden hasn't gained anything from this,' Druss said. 'In fact, he's worse off than he was at the start.'

'I disagree,' Levistus said. 'Morden is a member of Drakh's cabal. What helps Drakh, helps him.'

'And you seriously think he's done all this as part of some elaborate plan to sacrifice himself?'

'Who can predict the actions of a Dark mage?' Levistus said. 'I doubt we'll ever know one way or the other. However, one fact is clear. Morden was to deliver Drakh to us. He has failed quite comprehensively. I see no reason to prolong his stay of execution.'

Druss started to argue, but I only listened with half an ear. I'd been scanning the faces of the other Senior Council members, and I could see which way the wind was blowing. Alma's expression was neutral, but Bahamus's face was hard and he was nodding at Levistus's words. Druss might still vote against the proposal that Levistus was building up to, but if he did, he'd be the only one. Morden's membership on the Light Council was about to be removed, and mine with it.

* * *

'So what happens now?' Luna asked.

It was later that day, and Luna and I were on the second floor of the Arcana Emporium. The room we were in had been my bedroom once, though it was arguable whether you could really call it the same room: the fire had gutted it so thoroughly that it had been rebuilt pretty much from the ground up. Luna had chosen to restore it to something fairly similar to its original design, though she had left out the dividing wall, turning the room into something more like a studio flat. A bed sat by the window, a sofa in the middle of the floor, and there were French windows leading out onto a small balcony. It had been painted white and green and was quite clean and pleasant-looking, but an observant viewer might have noticed that the place had a slightly unused feeling, more like a spare room. The truth was that while there was a bed here, Luna never used it. By the time the Arcana Emporium passed into her hands, Luna had been given several sharp lessons in the things that can happen when you have enemies who know where you sleep, and her solution had been to set up a dummy bedroom above the shop. So far it hadn't proved necessary, but as I've had occasion to learn, the time to set up these kinds of things is *before* you need them.

'Well, they didn't pass an execution order,' I said. 'But they came pretty close. The resolution they finally hashed out is basically an emergency powers bill. It lets the Council suspend a bunch of legal restrictions "for the duration of the current crisis". And since I doubt Richard's going away any time soon, that's going to be a pretty long time.'

'Does that mean they can just pass another death sentence for you?'

'No,' I said. 'I think that was what Levistus was angling

for, but Bahamus wouldn't go along with it so he backed down. I still have the protections from being on the Council.'

'Um,' Luna said. 'If they kill Morden, doesn't that mean you *stop* being on the Council?'

'Yeah, you've kind of put your finger on the problem.'

I was sitting on the sofa while Luna was cross-legged in an armchair. Normally a Saturday afternoon like this one would be prime season for the shop, but after yesterday's excitement Luna had decided to take the day off. 'So what are they going to do?' Luna asked. 'Just go over to that prison and cut his head off?'

'From what I could gather, they're going to try to see what they can squeeze out of him first,' I said. 'I know Undaaris and Levistus still want to get their hands on all those files Morden inherited from White Rose. But once he doesn't turn them over, or even if he does, then yeah. Head-choppy time.'

'So then what?'

'Then I'll stay on as interim Junior Council member while new ones get nominated and the Senior Council decides who's getting the seat.'

'Hm,' Luna said. 'Could they just have you stay?'

'It's possible.'

'How possible?'

'A few months ago, I would have said no chance,' I said. 'But a few things have changed since then. For one thing, I've got more influence than I used to. For another, the Council are right about to get into a war. Some of them have realised that, even if not all of them have. There's a chance that they won't want to deal with the internal disruption of throwing me out on top of everything else.'

'Or Levistus could take the opportunity to get rid of you while everyone's scared enough to listen to him,' Luna pointed out.

'That too,' I admitted. 'Still, I don't think he'd be able to get a death sentence passed any more.'

A large-to-medium-sized fox trotted in through the door and approached the sofa. 'Hi, Hermes,' I said, and offered a hand for him to sniff. 'There's more. So when Onyx did that raid last night? Turns out one of the things he stole from the Southampton facility was a certain statue that used to be on display at the British Museum.'

'At the— Wait. *That* one? The one we used to reach the fateweaver?'

'Yup.'

'You think that was what he was after?'

'I doubt it,' I said. 'It was originally in the Vault; they only moved it there a month or so ago as part of the Vault upgrade. More likely he saw the thing after smashing his way in, recognised it, and decided to grab it while he had the chance.'

'You don't think he's figured out some way to get inside, do you?' Luna said. 'I mean, Onyx is pretty dangerous already. If he got hold of that fateweaver . . .'

'The Council spent a ton of effort trying to get into that thing and failed,' I said. 'Onyx doesn't have anywhere near the resources that they do. If it had been Richard who'd stolen it, I'd be worrying. I'm not so concerned about Onyx.'

'But they *did* figure out a way in,' Luna said. 'The cube.'

'Which is why I'm bringing it up,' I said. 'I figure that Onyx is going to spend a while trying and failing to brute-force a way in, then when that doesn't work he'll go looking for the thing that worked last time. Let's make sure that we have that cube really well hidden by then.'

'Okay.'

'I figure that somewhere overseas should work. A stasis field would probably be best — that'd mess up any kind of sympathetic tracking spells he might try using the gate focus as a link.'

'Okay.'

'Anyway, it's not something we have to do right this minute. The Hollow's wards ought to hold against any basic spell. But there's no point taking chances.'

'Okay.'

I cocked my head. 'What's wrong?'

Hermes padded over to Luna's chair, looking up at her expectantly. Luna reached down to scratch the fox's head, the silver mist of her curse pulling back from her fingers as she did. 'What were you doing with Deleo?'

'You mean last night?'

'Yeah. I know you were buying time. But that wasn't all of it.'

'No,' I admitted.

'Because whatever it was, I don't think it worked,' Luna said. 'Usually when I see you get into these kinds of sparring matches, you give as good as you get. This time you were weirdly . . . defensive, I guess?'

'Remember how I told you that I went to see the dragon beneath Arachne's lair? It told me that if I wanted to get results with Rachel, I should listen to her.'

'It didn't *sound* as though you were listening,' Luna said. 'More like you were arguing and losing.'

'Thanks.'

'So what did you learn?'

I grimaced. 'Nothing good. I suppose now I've got a better idea of why Rachel hates me so much. I've just got no freaking idea how it's supposed to help.'

'Why would you expect it to?' Luna said. 'Okay, so there's a reason I'm bringing this up. Vari and I were having an argument a couple of weeks ago. Landis and Vari were on a job and ran into someone, there was trouble, the other guy attacked them and they fought back. I was saying it might not have been the other guy's fault, he could have had reasons to be suspicious of a couple of Keepers. Vari's answer was that *everyone* has a reason. And when I thought about it, he was right. It's not like anyone just wakes up one morning and thinks, "Hey, you know what, I feel like being a bad guy today." Everyone's got some way to justify what they do. They'll say that the other guy's an arsehole, or they don't have any choice, or it's not like it matters, or it's just the way the world works, whatever. The point is, knowing *why* someone's after you doesn't really help. I mean, look at Deleo. She wears a freaking domino mask and acts like two different people depending on whether it's on or off and she's got a disembodied piece of the best friend she murdered riding around in her head carrying on conversations with her. She is *literally* insane. What are you expecting to get out of talking to her?'

'Shireen told me that I needed to help Rachel and redeem her,' I said. 'That was years ago and I'm getting the feeling I'm running out of time. I'm at the point where I'm willing to try most things.'

'Is *giving up* one of those things?' Luna said. 'Look, I haven't said anything until now, because I know you still feel bad about what happened to Shireen and you want to help her. But maybe it's time to admit that it's not going to happen. I mean, you remember what *else* happened around then, right? First Deleo tried to kill you, then you found out her secret and she tried to kill you even harder, then you found out that she'd been spending the last decade tracking down everyone who showed up at Richard's mansion and killing *them*. How big a murder spree does she have to rack up before you start considering that this "redemption" thing isn't all that likely?'

'I don't exactly have a choice,' I said. 'If I don't turn Rachel, I've had it.'

'How do you know?'

'It's a dragon prophecy. They don't get things wrong.'

'Did Arachne's dragon tell you the same thing?' Luna said. 'As in, did you ask what would happen if redeeming Rachel didn't work?'

'Not exactly, no.'

'Then how do you know it is a dragon prophecy?'

'Because Shireen told me,' I said. I could see where Luna was going with this.

'And how do you know she's telling the truth?'

'I suppose I don't,' I said reluctantly. 'But she's been honest with me in the past.'

'From how I understand it, she's been trapped inside Rachel's head for years,' Luna said. 'If I were stuck in a position like that then I'd probably be willing to stretch the truth a bit too.'

'There's no proof of that,' I said. 'Besides, is this really about you not trusting her, or is it that you just think Rachel's a lost cause?'

'A bit of both. And don't you think it's time to stop calling her that?'

'What?'

'Rachel,' Luna said. 'When you're talking to other mages, you call her Deleo. When you're talking to her, you call her Deleo. But when you're talking to us, you call her Rachel. It's because that's how you still think of her, isn't it?'

'It was what I called her when we were apprentices.'

'Yeah, well, she's not an apprentice now,' Luna said. 'I thought about this when I picked my mage name. I decided that I'd use my mage name for formal stuff, but not for anything personal. So if I'm entering a duelling competition or doing something with the Council, then I'm Vesta, but to you and Anne and Vari and to anyone else I'm friends with, I'm just Luna. A lot of mages don't do that – once they pass their tests, they switch over to using their mage name for everything. But Deleo *kills* people for calling her her old name. What message do you think that sends?'

'What are you getting at?'

'You and Shireen still call her Rachel,' Luna said. 'It's like you think she's still the same person. What if she's not? What if Rachel's dead and Deleo's what's left?'

'Then I'll just have to work with what I've got,' I said. 'Look, I see what you're getting at, but when I asked the dragon how I could split Rachel away from Richard, it gave me an answer. It wasn't a very comprehensible answer, but it made it clear that it was possible.'

'How?'

'It told me that Rachel saw me more clearly than I saw myself,' I said. 'And that until I recognised the ways in which we were alike, I wasn't going to get anywhere.'

Luna frowned. 'What ways?'

'I don't know,' I said. 'But thinking about it, there was

one thing I *did* learn from that conversation last night. Up until now, I've been trying to get Rachel to turn against Richard by . . . well, manipulating her, I guess. But it's really obvious now that that's not going to work, because Rachel knew exactly what I was doing. She always seems to be able to do that. I can't trick her the way I can other people.'

Luna frowned. 'You think she knows you that well?'

'The dragon said so, didn't it?'

'Then what about everything else Deleo said?' Luna asked. 'Do you think *that* was true?'

'I don't know,' I said with a sigh. 'Some of it hit a bit close to home. You remember back during your journeyman test, when I had that split-up with Caldera? Well, we were talking as well as fighting, and a lot of what she was saying was *really* close to what I heard last night from Rachel. About how I'm so arrogant, don't think the rules apply to me. It was different rules she was talking about, but apart from that they used practically the same words. If people as far apart as those two tell you the same thing . . .' I trailed off, thinking. 'It never really occurred to me, but I guess they're alike in a way. Because in their different ways, they both *did* follow the rules. Rachel as a Dark apprentice, Caldera as a Light Keeper. They did as they were told, changed themselves to fit in. Then after spending years and years working without any kind of reward, I show up, break all the rules, don't do as I'm told and get promoted over their heads. I guess it's not surprising that they're pissed.'

'That sounds like their problem.'

'But that wasn't really the part that bothered me,' I said. 'I'm okay with being bad at following other people's rules.

What bothered me was her telling me that I wanted the same things as her.'

'That's not really true.'

'It kind of is,' I said. 'I didn't join up with Richard for no reason. Yes, he's really good at being persuasive, but he didn't have to try very hard. The truth was, I *loved* the idea of being powerful and feared. If I hadn't, I never would have agreed to go with him in the first place.'

'Okay, so maybe you did want that back then,' Luna said. 'But that was then. You're different now.'

'Am I?' I said. 'The feared part, maybe. The powerful part? I don't think so. I wouldn't have spent so long studying and training otherwise.'

'None of that makes the other things she was saying true,' Luna said. 'You're not selfish. You worked really hard to help me, and Vari and Anne as well. All three of us know that. That's why we trust you.'

I smiled at Luna. 'Have I ever told you I really appreciate how loyal you are?'

Luna shrugged. 'Most people don't have to think about this kind of stuff. They pick friends based on whether they're fun to hang out with. When you've dealt with the kinds of things we have, it teaches you to pay a lot of attention to whether someone's going to be there when things go wrong.'

'I know the feeling. But maybe you and Rachel are *both* right.'

'How?'

'You've seen me help you and your friends, so you see me as unselfish and trustworthy,' I said. 'Rachel's seen me turn against Richard and build up my own strength, so she sees me as power-hungry and manipulative. Maybe you're both seeing me clearly, just from different sides.'

'If you say so. How's this supposed to help?'

'The dragon told me I needed to understand the ways in which Rachel and I are the same.'

'You both talk a lot?'

'We both want to be powerful,' I said. 'Anne doesn't. She's got more power than she needs and more than she's really comfortable with. She'd be a lot happier if she could just live quietly. You and Vari are both in a good place. You're both okay with the level of power you can wield. I'm the only one out of our group of four who has *less* power than he wants. Or needs.'

'Again, how's this supposed to help?'

I sighed. 'No idea. Let me know if you have any sudden revelations.'

A few days passed.

'I'm still not seeing why you need me along,' I said into the focus.

'We already went through this,' Lyle said.

'I'm not the one negotiating.'

'The legal formalities require that a Council member be present.'

'So get your boss to go,' I said. 'Or someone from the Junior Council. It's not like I'm the only choice.'

'But you *are* Morden's aide.'

'Make up your frigging mind,' I said in annoyance. 'Either I'm there in my capacity as Junior Council, which means I'm a Council member, or I'm there in my capacity as Morden's aide, which means I'm *not* a Council member. You can't have both.'

It was afternoon on the following Wednesday, and I was in my office in the War Rooms. Anne was sitting curled up in her usual spot on the sofa, reading a letter and listening with half an ear. I was arguing with Lyle and currently losing.

I'd known for a couple of days that I was going to be forced to be involved in the (supposedly) final negotiations with Morden. I hadn't been keen, since I had a nasty feeling Levistus had yet another trick up his sleeve to screw me over. I'd become even less keen once I found out that both Levistus *and* Sal Sarque's aides were going to be there too.

'Look, Alex, you know how this is going to go,' Lyle said. 'Why are you giving me a hard time about this?'

'*I'm* giving *you* a hard time?' I said. 'You're trying to get me to spend the afternoon with two people who've repeatedly tried to kill me. If you were in my position, you'd be putting up much more of a fuss.'

'Barrayar is tasked with the actual negotiation,' Lyle said. 'You'll be there in a purely ceremonial capacity. You won't even have to enter Morden's cell.'

'Oh, that sounds great. I can hang out with that lovely girl that Sal Sarque's taken up with instead. How do you think that conversation's going to go? "Hi there, lovely weather we're having, planted any bombs in my house recently?"'

Lyle sighed. 'Do you really want me to go to the Council on this?'

I was silent. Lyle had already brought this request to me via Anne twice, and both times I'd dodged it. This time he'd called me directly in my office. The truth was that if Lyle did go to the Council, they'd almost certainly make it a direct order. Lyle would lose face, but I'd lose a lot more. 'Fine.'

'You'll go?'

I didn't answer.

'Alex?'

'*Yes*, I'll go. Stop pestering me.'

'Excellent,' Lyle said. 'You know the gate location?'

'Yes.'

'And the time.'

'Yes.'

'You'll be sure to be punctual? It's very important—'

'Thank you, Lyle,' I said. I cut the connection before he could respond.

Anne looked up. 'Didn't go well?'

I sat back with a sigh. 'I'm really not in the mood for this.'

'Why do they want you there anyway?'

'Wish I knew,' I said. People think that being a diviner makes this kind of thing easy, but it really doesn't. Being able to look into short-term futures doesn't help much when it comes to revealing long-term plans, and when it comes to politics, pretty much *everything* is long-term plans. 'Best guess is that Levistus is hoping to use Morden's fall to involve me, but I don't know exactly how.'

Anne stretched, put down the papers and stood up. 'Sounds as though I should come along for this one.'

'It's probably nothing.'

'Oh, come on,' Anne said. 'Are you going to try to keep me away from everything? Richard isn't there this time.'

'I guess you're right,' I said. Morden had had some interest in Anne as well, but that was a long time ago. Besides, I could use someone to watch my back.

'Why did Lyle make such a big deal about you being on time?'

'It's just how he is,' I said. 'You know how big Light

mages are on protocol. If you're late for anything, they take it as a deliberate insult.'

'Okay.' Anne paused. 'Wasn't it supposed to be at two-thirty?'

I picked up the report I'd been looking over. 'You don't want to rush these things.'

14

At exactly 2.55 p.m., Anne and I stepped through the gateway into San Vittore. The gate linking our world with the bubble realm closed behind us.

There were two people waiting for us in the anteroom, a man and a woman. The man had been talking into a communicator, but as we entered he stopped what he'd been saying. 'Never mind,' he said. 'They're here.' He dropped the communicator into a pocket. 'Verus. I see you were delayed.'

'Yes, sorry about that,' I said pleasantly. 'Busy afternoon.' Which was two lies for the price of one. I'd carefully calculated the waiting time so that it was long enough to be a clear insult, but short enough that I could pass it off as an accident.

'So you finally showed up,' the woman said.

'Yes, I did.' I smiled at her. 'So what can I can help you with?'

The two mages in front of us were Barrayar and Solace, the aides to Levistus and Sal Sarque. Of the two, I was most familiar with Barrayar. He's slender, a fraction under medium height, dresses in expensive suits and has a polite, pleasant manner that gives away nothing at all of what he's actually thinking. Underneath, I knew him to be calculating and dangerous. He'd been Levistus's aide for something near to ten years, and he hadn't kept his job by being incompetent.

Solace was the newer of the two, a replacement for Jarnaff, the mage Richard had killed last year in the Vault. She's pale-skinned with mousy brown hair, and a particular look – slim but slightly pouchy – that I've learned to recognise. It's a popular thing among Light mages to get life magic treatments where the life mage alters their physiology to give them the traits of being fit and athletic without them having to exercise. It kind of works, but once you know what to look for, it's a lot like putting up a sign that says 'easy target'. Given Sal Sarque's background, I didn't know why he'd gone for someone like that for his aide, but maybe his options were limited. In any case, I was pretty sure she was at least tangentially connected to the assassination attempts I'd been dealing with since last year.

As if that weren't enough, I knew from asking around that there were a couple of Keepers present to be security for the negotiations. One of them had been approved by Levistus, while the other was Caldera, meaning that by my count, pretty much every mage occupying this facility other than Anne either disliked me, wanted me dead or both. This was not shaping up to be a pleasant visit.

'Well,' Barrayar said. 'Since you're here, I suggest we get started.'

Solace gave Anne a narrow look. 'Why is *she* here?'

'Mage Walker is my aide,' I told her.

Solace curled her lip. 'You mean she's your bodyguard.'

'She's filled that role at times,' I said. A lot of mages assume that me keeping Anne as my aide is kind of the equivalent of a short guy owning a giant German shepherd. I don't do much to discourage it – being underestimated can be useful. 'Shall we?'

We passed through into the anteroom. Security screenings hadn't got any more convenient since my last visit.

'. . . drugs or drug-related items or paraphernalia,' the guard droned on, 'flammable or corrosive liquids, alcohol in any form, poisonous or infectious materials such as pesticides, insecticides, cyanides, laboratory specimens or bacterial cultures, and are you carrying any gas or pressure containers including but not limited to aerosols, carbon dioxide cartridges, oxygen tanks, Mace, pepper spray or liquid nitrogen?'

Anne looked at the guard. 'Oxygen tanks?'

'Just answer the question already,' Solace said irritably. She and Barrayar had already gone through and were waiting on the other side of the scanner.

'No,' Anne said.

'Are you carrying any cameras or other photographic devices, mobile telephones or other communication devices . . .'

Is it me, Anne asked, *or does Solace have something against me?*

It's not just you, I said. I'd kept our mental link open through the dreamstone.

Do you think she was the one who sent those men to my flat?

The one who made the decision? I said. *Probably not. But involved in some way . . . I'd put it around seventy/eighty per cent.*

'About time,' Solace told Anne as she finally made it through the scanner.

'Why do you even care?' I asked her. 'It's not as if you need us.'

'Your presence is required by law,' Barrayar said.

'Really?' I said. 'So you won't mind if we accompany you while you're questioning Morden?'

'That won't be necessary,' Solace said quickly.

I gave the two of them a look.

'Verus, I'd appreciate it if you didn't make this take any longer than necessary,' Barrayar said. 'We'll call if we need you.'

I shrugged. 'I'm sure you won't have any trouble finding us. You never have before.'

Barrayar and Solace turned and headed for the wing where I'd met Morden last time. *Did you actually want to be there when they talked to Morden?* Anne asked.

Just wanted to see how they reacted. I turned to the guard. 'You have somewhere we can wait?'

The guard looked at me unsmilingly. 'We don't have waiting rooms.'

'You have interview rooms.'

'Those are reserved for official use only.'

I gave the guard a look. 'How big an issue do you want to make out of this?'

'That took *way* too much effort,' I said as Anne closed the interview room door behind us.

'They're Light mages,' Anne said. She gave me a glance. 'Clear?'

The interview room was bare and inhospitable, with a single table and three not especially comfortable chairs. There was one door and no windows. 'We're clear,' I said. I gestured at the left wall. 'That's a viewing port. One-way glass: looks opaque from this side. But there's no one in the other room and the cameras are out in the corridor.'

'So we wait?'

'We wait.'

Anne pulled out a chair. I stayed standing, leaning against

the wall. 'What do you think they're going to be saying to Morden?' Anne asked.

'Trying to see if they can get him to spill some sort of secret in exchange for his life,' I said. 'I doubt it'll work. If Morden hasn't cracked yet, I don't see why this would do it.'

'Unless he's been saving something up.'

I nodded. 'I wish I knew what Morden's game was. Ever since he surrendered last year, none of what he's done has seemed to make any sense. I know how smart Morden is – he wouldn't be doing all this if he didn't have a plan. But I can't figure out what it is, and it's bothering me.'

'Do you think he really is trying to be a martyr?'

I raised my hands helplessly. 'It almost feels like it, doesn't it? It's like he's daring the Council to kill him. But I just can't square that with what I know of what Morden believes. Risking his life, sure. He's no coward. But sacrificing it just to make a point?'

'Either way, it doesn't seem good news for us.'

'Yeah, the way this has worked out, it's played right into Levistus's hands. Now he gets to remove Morden and probably me as well. He won't be able to get rid of us straightaway, but once I'm off the Council, he can just pass another resolution to get me arrested again and there's precious little I can do about it.'

Anne stretched, looking around. 'I hope those two aren't spying on us.'

'They're not,' I said. Being on the Council teaches you to be pretty good at spotting surveillance. 'Could always switch to mental if you're worried.'

Anne shook her head. 'I like talking to you the regular

way. And it's nice not to have to wait for you to start the conversation first.'

I had to smile at that. 'You seem like you've found ways around that.'

'I haven't really,' Anne said. 'You know how many times I've tried to say something and found that the link's been broken and I'm just talking out loud in my own head?'

'Okay, but *some* of the time you can talk to me first.'

'No, I can't.'

'You just did,' I said. 'Ten minutes ago, at the security scanners.'

'That doesn't count,' Anne said. 'You're the one holding the link open. If I'm paying close attention I can tell, but it's really easy to forget and start talking when you can't hear me.'

'Technically you're still the one starting the conversation.'

'Okay, okay,' Anne said. 'I still don't think it really counts.'

We sat in comfortable silence for a little while. I find being around Anne relaxing these days. 'What about the Tiger's Palace, then?' I asked.

'What do you mean?'

'You definitely spoke to me first then. I figured it was just a case of you getting more practised with it.'

'Well, it's easier for me to control what I'm thinking when I do that with you, sure, but I still can't actually open the link. If you don't reach out first, it's like I'm just calling where no one can hear.'

'I did hear though.'

'Only because you spoke to me first,' Anne said. 'Out when you were in the queue, remember?'

'No, I mean when we were inside.'

'You hardly spoke to me at *all* when you were inside,'

Anne said. 'I was really worried. I had no idea what was happening.'

'We were a little busy.'

'You're not making me feel any better.'

'And anyway, it wasn't "hardly at all". I was checking in with you all the time.'

'You called me *once*,' Anne said, 'when you wanted to check that the person you were looking at was really Vihaela. After that, nothing. I had to call Vari to get any idea what was going on, and all he did was tell me to stay away and hang up.'

'Oh, come on,' I said. 'You're seriously exaggerating now. What about the running back-and-forth during the fight? From the sound of it, you might have had more of an idea of what was going on in that building than we did. You were practically commentating the fight from the stands.'

'I know my lifesight's good, but it's not *that* good,' Anne said. 'It was way too chaotic in there with all the patterns.'

'Then what about when you were telling me to get away from where I was standing?'

'What do you mean?'

'After Vihaela did her power-up thing,' I said. 'You warned me away from her, then you were telling me to get off the floor.'

Anne frowned. 'When?'

'I know your memory isn't that bad,' I said. 'What about when you were saying that Vihaela's signature had changed? "*A lot less human and a lot more powerful*" — wasn't that how you put it? You're seriously telling me you can't remember that part?'

Anne gave me a confused look. 'I'm not sure what to tell you,' she said. 'But Alex, I promise. I did *not* say anything like that, not through the dreamstone, and not any other way either. After that first conversation I didn't talk to you at all. The next time I saw you was when I got into the club after the battle was over and we met up face to face.'

I stared at Anne. She looked back at me, clear-eyed and sincere. I'm pretty good at telling when people are telling me the truth, and I was one hundred per cent sure that Anne was being honest.

An icy chill started down my spine, growing stronger with each passing second. 'Then if that's true,' I said slowly, 'who was I talking to?'

Anne changed.

An odd expression crossed her face, and she looked at me, lips parted, as though she were about to say something, then her eyes unfocused and her head drooped. A moment later her head came up, and this time there was a very different look in her eyes. When she spoke, her voice was stronger, layered with exasperation. 'You just had to make this difficult, didn't you?'

I held very still. Alarm bells were going off in my head, but I didn't let anything show on my face. 'Anne?' I said carefully.

'You could say that,' Anne said. 'Here, see if this jogs your memory.'

Black tendrils emerged from under Anne's clothing, twining across her hands, her face. She stood, and wings of darkness unfolded, filling the room from wall to wall. All of a sudden she seemed taller, looming over me. Her eyes as she looked down were the same reddish colour, but there seemed to be something else layered over her, looking down on me from a second set of eyes.

I scrambled back, the chair going over, nearly falling to

the floor. My back hit the wall and I opened my mouth to yell.

'Ah-ah,' Anne said. 'Trust me, you really don't want to do that.'

I swallowed. 'Who are you?'

'Come on, Alex,' Anne said. 'Don't play dumb. You know *exactly* who I am.'

I did. The black tendrils playing around Anne's face were distracting, but I recognised the mannerisms, the way of speaking. I'd seen it before, in Elsewhere. But right now, what was *really* scaring me, making my breath catch and my thoughts turn to horror, was something else. The shadowy black aura around Anne was blurry but very distinctive, and it was the same one that had been surrounding that figure that I'd seen on Friday at the Tiger's Palace.

'It wasn't Vihaela,' I said, my voice unsteady. 'It was you.'

'Ding ding!' Anne smiled. 'See, I knew you were fast enough to keep up. Now before you do anything hasty, sit down and take a breath. Because there are some things you really want to hear.'

I stayed standing, staring at her. I'd faced this other Anne in Elsewhere, but back there I'd been fairly certain that she couldn't hurt me, at least not seriously. Here was another story.

'What have you done with her?' I said. I managed to keep my voice level this time.

'Relax,' Anne said. 'Nothing she hasn't done to me. Actually, *exactly* the same thing she's done to me.' She cocked her head. 'Why so tense? Feeling a little threatened?'

I didn't answer.

'Oh, all right.' Anne glanced from side to side at the

wings curling around her. 'I guess they are a little intimidating, aren't they? Let's dial it back a bit.' There was no sound, but the black shadows around her faded, the tendrils sinking back into her skin. In a moment, she looked like a normal girl again . . . almost. There was still something different in her eyes, a hint of something larger behind her. She sat down, smiling at me. 'Now. I'm sure you're thinking of yelling for help, or maybe using a communicator or that dreamstone. You're not going to do any of those things.'

'You think you're fast enough to stop me?'

'Yes, actually,' Anne said. 'But if I'd wanted to, I'd have done that already. No, the reason you aren't going to call for help is that if you do, then once the story comes out, Anne's going to be executed.'

'She . . .' I began to say, then stopped.

'Oh good, you're catching on,' Anne said. 'I mean, the two of you have had enough trouble keeping the Council off your back as things are. How do you think they're going to act when they find out that she was the one who kicked the collective arses of that Keeper team up one end of the Tiger's Palace and down the other? Not too happy, don't you think? And that doesn't even come close to how pissed they'll be about what I'm *about* to do.'

'That wasn't her.'

'Oh?' Anne raised her eyebrows. 'That's going to be your defence, is it? "It wasn't her fault, it was her split personality." How do you think that's going to play, Alex?'

I couldn't think of anything to say. It had been hard enough to keep Levistus and his allies from getting us prosecuted for crimes when we were innocent. Keeping us safe from prosecution when we were *guilty* . . .

'And don't forget yourself!' Anne said. 'You were the one who sponsored Anne, remember? You picked her as your aide, and you brought her along here today. Somehow I don't think the Council are going to be the forgiving types when it comes to this kind of thing, do you?' Anne leaned back and smiled. 'So you're going to stay there and keep very quiet. Because the only chance you have of staying alive – not to mention keeping *her* alive – is for this to stay our little secret.'

'Are you serious?'

'Why not?' Anne said. 'They bought it last time, didn't they?' Black shadows flowed over her skin, turning her into a dark silhouette, just like the one I'd seen at the Tiger's Palace, and the tone of her voice shifted. 'Obviously Vihaela found a way into this prison somehow. Who knows what tricks those Dark mages have.' The shadows pulled away to reveal Anne's face once again. 'I mean, it fooled *you*.'

I should have seen this coming. All the pieces had been there. When I'd seen that black shape at the Tiger's Palace, I'd noticed that it was exactly as tall as Vihaela. I just hadn't made the connection that with the shadow adding a couple of inches, it was also exactly as tall as *Anne*. And with 'Anne' telling me that it was someone else . . .

'This would have been so much easier if you hadn't insisted on talking about it,' Anne said. 'If you'd been a typical man and just communicated in grunts, everything would have been fine. But no, Anne has to pick the one guy whose idea of a casual conversation apparently involves checking their memories for inconsistencies.' Anne shrugged. 'Oh well, I was getting bored anyway.'

'How did you do it?' I said. 'You took her over at the

Tiger's Palace, I can see that now. But how come she didn't figure it out?'

'You aren't the only one who's been learning new tricks,' Anne said. 'It's not too hard to cloud someone's memories once you know how. Only works if you're very close, but obviously that's not really a problem for me, is it? After everything was over, I gated back to where Anne had been hiding and left her with a bunch of confused impressions of waiting around outside for the fight to finish.' Anne raised an eyebrow at me. 'I was surprised that didn't tip you off. You really thought she was going to just sit things out? One way or another, she was taking part in that battle. I just made sure she made an impression.'

'So what's the big plan?' I said. 'What do you want?'

'What do you think I want, Alex?' Anne leaned across the table to look at me, and she wasn't smiling any more. 'It's my turn to drive.'

'What are you going to do to her?' I said quietly.

'A better question is what *you'll* do. You see, once we're done with this conversation, I'm going to walk out this door. And you're going to make absolutely sure that everyone thinks that I'm Vihaela. Because if the Council finds out, I think we both know what's going to happen.'

I did know. We'd be totally and irrevocably screwed. There was no way the Council would have any mercy on us, not for this. It'd make Levistus's attempts to kill us look like a friendly warning. 'Here's an idea. How about you turn back into normal Anne and don't tip them off?'

'Sorry, not on the cards,' Anne said. She glanced past me at the wall. 'Well, fun as this is, I've got a schedule to keep.'

'Why?' I said. 'I thought you could do whatever you want now. That's the idea, isn't it? Getting your freedom?'

'Unfortunately I did have to make some deals.' Anne stretched, rising to her feet. 'But I've got high hopes that you'll help me out with that.'

'What kind of help?'

Anne started to answer, then frowned, looking at me. 'Wait. You're trying to keep me talking, aren't you? Buying time to think of something?' She shook her head. 'You *are* good at that. I guess you've never actually tried it on me before.'

Uh-oh. I tried to think faster. 'Look. If you want to get out of here, you'll need my help. You aren't going to be able—'

'Sorry, Alex,' Anne interrupted. 'Like I said, I'm on a schedule. And I don't want you hurt, but I'd really rather not having you running around messing things up. So . . .'

I saw the attack coming, but there wasn't anywhere to run. Blackness surrounded me, pulling me under.

It felt as though I was running through deep water. Anne was somewhere ahead of me, and I was trying to catch up with her, but my legs were heavy and slow and I was falling further and further behind.

'Get up,' Luna told me.

'I'm trying,' I tried to say.

'Staff to the guard station.' Luna said. 'You need to get up.'

'I know. Give me a second.'

Luna crouched in front of me. 'Facility lockdown. Report.'

'What does that even mean?'

Luna leaned in close. '*Get up.*'

My eyes snapped open. Light stabbed into them and I squinted, twisting my head. I was lying on my side in the interview room; one of my arms was numb from where my head had been lying on it. Aside from me, the room was empty.

Through the closed door, I could hear a rising and falling siren. A female voice was speaking calmly over a public address system. 'Facility lockdown. All staff report to the nearest guard station. Facility lockdown. All staff report to the nearest guard station.'

I pulled myself to my feet, staggered and grabbed at the table to stop myself from going over. My head ached and my limbs felt heavy and sluggish. *Anne. Where did she go?* I reached for the door handle, got it on the second try, and pulled it open.

The siren was still going. It sounded like it dated from World War II, and it was loud as hell. I heard a scrabbling sound and turned to look.

The corridor met another one to form a crossroads just a little way down, and a guard had just backed out into my view. He had a radio in one hand and had been shouting something into it, but as I watched he dropped it with a clatter and scrabbled for his gun. He levelled it and got off two shots before something came around the corner and opened him up in a spray of blood.

It all happened almost too fast to follow. The guard was screaming, wrestling with *something* that seemed to be all shadows and sharp edges, then he was on the ground and there were two of the things on him, claws ripping and tearing, blood spattering on the floor. The screams died away in a wet throaty sound and his hands clutched and went still. The things kept mauling his body, then their heads snapped up to stare at me.

I froze. I couldn't figure out what I was looking at. They

looked vaguely humanoid, thin and spindly, but their bodies and limbs seemed to be made of solid shadows that twisted in the light. They looked almost translucent, but there was blood clinging to their claws, and eyeless faces stared into mine. I reached instinctively for a weapon, found nothing. The security screening. *Shit.* I looked into the future, searching for their attack path, ready to dodge.

Then the nearer one sniffed at the air, and futures in which it attacked flickered and vanished. It hissed, and one after another the two of them turned and slipped away down the corridor, leaving a bloody trail behind them. In an instant I was alone but for the guard's torn body.

I shook my head. Too much was happening. What the hell *were* those things?

I moved to the guard's body, and one look was enough to confirm that he wasn't getting up. I took his gun, saw a ring of keys on his belt, took those too. The siren was still going, the recorded voice was still playing, and now that I listened, I could hear shouts and screams echoing down the corridors. I wished uselessly for my armour. I'd come today expecting politics, not something out of a horror movie.

I didn't know what was going on, but something told me that whatever it was, it was going to involve Morden. I remembered the route to his cell from my last visit and took off at a jog. I could hear sounds of combat from all around, but my divination showed me a path clear of danger. I found another dead guard two corridors down, and a blood trail indicated where someone had been attacked but managed to get away. The shadow creatures, whatever they were, were still prowling the corridors.

I came to a security gate. One of the keys from the guard's ring fit the lock and I opened it, letting it clang shut behind me. I could hear the sound of combat from up ahead, and it was getting louder. I hurried around the corner and stopped, looking at the scene ahead.

I'd reached the guard post just ahead of Morden's cell. The last time I'd been here it had been staffed by mantis golems, but now the golems were lying sprawled on the floor, their eyes lifeless and dull. Two guards were lying there as well, though unlike the bodies I'd seen in the corridors, they bore no marks.

There were three people still upright – Barrayar, Solace and Caldera – and they were engaged in combat against more of those shadow things. Caldera was at the front, fighting hand-to-hand, while Barrayar was watching her back. Solace was behind them both, hiding in the corner. The shadows threw themselves at Caldera, claws ripping and tearing, but their strikes slid off her skin as though it were stone. Caldera fought slowly and deliberately, taking her time to line up each punch. The shadows might look insubstantial, but they were obviously solid enough to be hurt: each of Caldera's blows sent them staggering. Barrayar was holding back, a barely visible blade of force held low and out of sight. One of the shadows tried to attack Caldera from behind, and Barrayar killed it almost too fast to see, his blade gutting it from stomach to throat.

I'd arrived at the tail end of the fight. There were only three of the shadow things left, and as I watched, the number became two, then one. The last of the creatures lunged at Caldera, hissing, and she smashed her fist right through its head. The decapitated body hit the floor, twitching, and Caldera whirled on me.

'Whoa!' I held up my hands. Caldera's blood was up and I didn't want her seeing me as a threat. 'Easy!'

'What the hell are you doing here?' Caldera snapped.

'What do you think? What the hell *are* those things?'

'How the fuck should I know?'

There were half a dozen of the shadow creatures lying on the floor, but as I looked, I saw that they were dissolving. Pieces of their bodies were flaking away, disappearing into the air. As I looked more closely, I saw that there were eight or nine bodies, not half a dozen; the ones I'd missed were already mostly gone. Soon there'd be nothing at all.

'Summoned creatures,' Barrayar said. He was kneeling over one of the ones he'd killed. 'They're discorporating now that the effect is broken.' He looked at me. 'Did you and Morden plan this?'

'No!' I said vehemently. 'I have no idea what's going on. I thought Morden was with you!'

Barrayar looked aside. 'Solace?'

'He wasn't here,' Solace said reluctantly. 'He came from the interview room.'

They haven't figured it out. I said a silent prayer of thanks. It's the way that Light mages think – in Barrayar's and Solace's minds, it was only Council members that were the players. It hadn't occurred to them to suspect Anne. Caldera, though . . .

But Caldera had other things on her mind. 'Is Morden still here?' she demanded of Solace.

Solace was looking down the corridor towards the airlock leading to Morden's cell. 'Yes,' she said uneasily. 'But there's something in there with him. Another – or two – I don't like this.'

'You said it was Vihaela?' Solace asked Barrayar.

'I only had a brief look before the door closed,' Barrayar said. 'But it looked very much like the reports from the Tiger's Palace.'

'Wonderful,' Caldera muttered. 'What do you think those creatures are? Some side perk of whatever item she's using?'

'I would imagine so.'

'They're coming,' Solace said suddenly. 'Two mages – no, three – no, two . . .'

'Would you make up your mind please?' Barrayar said.

'We should fall back,' Solace said. She took a few steps away, placing Barrayar and Caldera between her and the airlock doors. 'Report to the Council.'

'Communications are out,' Barrayar said curtly. 'By the time we made it outside, they'd be on our heels.'

'Then we should call for backup . . .'

Caldera gave Solace a look of contempt. 'Will you shut the fuck up?'

Solace drew herself up. 'You can't talk to me like—'

'What Caldera is trying to say,' Barrayar said, 'is that we are all there is. If anyone is going to prevent Morden's escape, it will be us.' He turned back towards the airlock. 'Let's see how this unfolds.'

Solace's voice rose. 'They're coming!'

There was a creaking sound as the wheel on the airlock door spun. I knew from my last visit that that door was supposed to be impossible to open except from the guard post we were standing at right now; apparently it wasn't *that* impossible. The wheel came to rest with a click and the door swung smoothly open.

Shadow creatures flowed out, filling the corridor. There were at least a dozen, but it was the figure following them that my eyes fixed on. A black shadow, opaque but recognisably feminine, slim and deadly-looking. The face was a black mask, but I could just make out the gleam of two reddish eyes. 'Oh look,' Anne called out. 'Welcoming committee.'

Now that I knew what I was looking at, I wondered how I'd ever mistaken the shape for Vihaela. It was the same height, yes, the same rough proportions, but the movements were Anne's. Even the voice was recognisable – it was deeper, distorted by the shadow, but the accent, the manner of speaking, was the same. Surely Caldera and the others would see it. They'd never paid Anne much attention, but now that I knew what to look for, it was so obvious—

'Mage Vihaela,' Caldera said coldly. 'You're under arrest. Stand down.'

'Are you really expecting that to work?' Anne moved out of the way. 'Oh, and by the way, I've brought an old friend.'

Morden straightened as he stepped out into the corridor and swept his eyes over us with a smile. 'Barrayar,' he said. He was dressed in his full regalia, complete with his chain of office. 'And Verus and Solace. Quite the convention.'

'Morden,' Barrayar said coolly. 'You're looking well, all things considered. I hope you aren't expecting to breeze out of here.'

'Actually, I am.' Morden began to stroll down the corridor, Anne at his side. The shadow creatures slunk out of the way. 'Please don't make too much of a fuss. I'd prefer to do this the easy way.'

'You wish,' Caldera said.

'Come on, Caldera,' Anne said. The shadows hid her face, but I could imagine her smile. 'Didn't we do this once already?'

Caldera made as if to answer, then hesitated. 'Caldera, Barrayar,' I said quietly. 'I don't think we're winning this one.'

Caldera didn't turn around. 'Shut up.'

'No, I'm serious,' I said in a low voice. I was pretty sure that either Morden or Anne could take on all four of us at once. Both of them together wasn't even worth considering, not to mention the shadow things, which were crowding the corridor behind Morden and Anne, watching us with hungry eyes. 'We *really* don't want to—'

'Shut *up!*' Caldera's voice rose to a snarl. 'Okay, Vihaela. You want to take on the Council, you're going to have to start by going through me.'

Anne tilted her head. 'Okay.'

With Caldera blocking my vision I couldn't see what happened, but it was over so fast that I'm not sure I would have caught it anyway. Caldera started to cast a spell, Anne moved, there was a flash of magic — life mixed with something else — and Caldera gave a grunt and rocked back slightly as if she'd taken a punch. Then she hit the floor like a ton of bricks. I stared down at her, then up at Anne, still standing next to Morden. She'd barely moved. Darkness twined around her right hand as she tilted her head at me, and somehow I knew she was still smiling.

'Do we have another volunteer?' Morden asked.

Barrayar let out a slow, measured breath. 'Solace, Verus,' he said over his shoulder. 'Back up, please.' He reached down to grab one of Caldera's arms and moved to the side. Caldera must have been twice Barrayar's weight and more, but he dragged her to the wall without apparent effort. I followed his example.

'You're just going to let them go?' Solace demanded.

'I'm not *letting* them do anything,' Barrayar said in irritation. 'They've won this round.' He looked at Morden and Anne. 'Whether they'll make it out of San Vittore alive is another matter.'

'We'll take our chances,' Morden said. 'I'm glad you've decided to be sensible about this.' He walked past us, Anne at his side. As he did, he glanced at me. 'Here you go, Verus.' He tossed his chain of office in my direction.

I caught it left-handed. My right hand was still holding the guard's handgun, which so far was doing me about as much good as it had him. 'What are you expecting me to do with this?' I asked. 'Hold onto it until you get back?'

'No, I rather think my time on the Council has come to an end,' Morden said. 'Feel free to return it to the rest of the Council. Or don't.'

Morden and Anne walked away down the corridor. The shadow creatures didn't. They formed a semicircle in the guard post, pinning us against the wall. 'Um, Morden?' I said, raising my voice. The Dark mage and Anne were almost around the corner. 'I think you're missing your entourage.'

Morden gave a brief glance back at us. 'Oh,' he said. 'They're not mine.' He gave me a wave. 'Goodbye, Verus. Nice of you to visit.' He and Anne turned the corner and were gone.

Barrayar, Solace and I were left alone, standing over Caldera's unconscious body, facing a small army of shadow monsters. I tried to count them and stopped at twenty. They stared at us with blank white eyes. They weren't making any move to follow Morden and Anne. In fact, I had the feeling that they were just waiting for them to get out of earshot. 'This,' I said to no one in particular, 'has been a really shitty day.'

'Thank you for the commentary,' Barrayar said. I had to give the little bastard credit: his voice was as cool as ever. 'I don't suppose that given your position under Morden, you've learned any way to deal with these creatures?'

'Barrayar, I hate to break this to you,' I said. 'But you know how you and Levistus have been telling everyone that I'm a traitor and a Dark mage, and that I'm working with Morden and know all his plans? It's not actually true.'

'So you have no idea what these things are.'

'Not a clue.'

'Well,' Barrayar said. 'That would seem unfortunate for both of us.'

'They're getting closer!' Solace said from behind us. She'd somehow managed to position herself between us and the wall.

She wasn't wrong. As I looked around, I realised that the shadow things were inching towards us. If I looked straight at them they'd pause, but each time I did, the ones on the other side of the semicircle would creep forward a fraction. 'Thank you, Solace,' Barrayar said. 'I noticed.'

'Well?' Solace said. 'What are you going to do about them?'

'Solace,' I said without taking my eyes off the creatures surrounding us. 'I have to say, out of all the Light mages I've met in my life, I think you might be the most irritating.'

'So how many of these things can you take on at once?' Barrayar said conversationally. 'Because I suspect we have maybe sixty seconds before they force the issue.'

'Well, I can probably take two, and you can take four, and maybe the last fourteen will spontaneously unsummon themselves.'

'Is that likely to happen?'

'No.'

The semicircle had contracted to half its size. 'Screw this,' I announced suddenly. 'Don't take this personally, but if I'm going to die in here, I'm not doing it with you and Solace for company.'

'Is there some other company you'd prefer?'

'I'm going to go after those two and chase them down,' I said. 'They're getting further and further away while these things waste our time. You can follow me or stand your ground, I don't much care which.'

'And how exactly——?' Barrayar began, right before I launched myself into the middle of the shadows.

I'd had a lot of time to look at the futures of what would happen if I came into close quarters with these things, and one thing I'd noticed was that I wasn't going to die straightaway. Plenty of futures in which I got slashed or cut up, but none where I got my guts torn out the way that guard had. Given how many other people they'd killed so far, that had made me wonder why.

And the best answer I'd come up with was that they weren't trying to kill me at all. Anne had had more than enough chances to finish me off if she'd wanted to. She could have done it at the Tiger's Palace, and again while I was in the interview room. But she'd left me alive, and now that I thought about it, I was pretty sure she'd told her summoned pets to do the same. Those two creatures that I'd run into earlier had backed off once they'd figured out who I was. Either that other Anne didn't want me dead, the real Anne still had some influence over her actions or Morden and company had plans that involved me being alive. I didn't know which it was, but I was going to take advantage.

I went through the shadow creatures in a rush, only fighting when I had to and leaving my sides and back unguarded. One got in my way and I shot it through the face, but the others fell back, hissing. The back of my neck was tense and all my instincts screamed against leaving myself open like this, but it was over in seconds and space opened up before me. I sprinted around the corner and slammed the security gate closed behind me with a clang of metal. A flurry of shadows and claws hit the gate about two-tenths of a second later, but they were too late. I was through.

I backed off, watching the shadow things hiss and tear at the metal. I could sense force magic from behind and I knew that Barrayar was fighting. I had mixed feelings about him, Solace and Caldera being left in their current position, but since I had no further ability to affect the battle one way or the other, my feelings didn't matter very much. Perhaps I'd drawn off enough of the things to give them a chance. For now, I had bigger problems.

I sprinted down the corridors of San Vittore, chasing Morden and Anne. The prison was silent; the alarm had shut off and I couldn't hear any movement from down the halls. I made it back to the entrance room to find it deserted, the scanner offline. The gateway focus was inactive, but from the residue I could tell it had been used recently. I activated it and stepped through, back into our world, and found myself facing the business end of ten sub-machine-guns.

There was a Keeper leading the squad, one I vaguely knew — his name began with a D. 'Who else has come through here?' I demanded.

'Why are you—?' the Keeper began.

'I don't have time for this.' I stalked forward, ignoring the weapons pointing in my direction; they wavered as the Council security men holding them started to have second thoughts. 'Morden has escaped. Did he come through here? Yes or no?'

'How did—? No. What's going on?'

'Shit,' I muttered. The bubble realm was supposed to be gate-locked so that the only way to leave it was via this point. Apparently Morden and Anne had found a way around that too. I pointed back the way I'd come. 'The prison's getting attacked by some kind of summoned monsters. They're not a match for a Keeper, but a good fraction of the guards are dead and the survivors need help. Take your men in there.'

The Keeper held his ground. 'Orders are to secure the entry point.'

I stepped closer and leaned in towards the Keeper, eyes narrowed. 'Men are dying in there. Very soon now, calls are going to go out summoning the Council for an emergency meeting to figure out what to do about this clusterfuck. When that happens, people are going to start looking for someone to blame, and a Keeper who ignored direct Council orders and sat on his arse when he could have helped will make an *extremely* good scapegoat.' I switched my glare to the squad behind the Keeper. 'That goes for the rest of you as well. *Move.*'

Anger flashed across the Keeper's face, then he took a breath and looked aside towards his men. 'We're moving out. Get the others in here.'

I walked past and out. I got sidelong looks but no one tried to stop me. Plans were running through my head. Where would Morden have gone? His mansion . . . no, too obvious. It was the first place the Council were going to check, and besides, Onyx was there. If I were in his place, I'd go to some sort of staging point, somewhere in another country, to make pursuit harder. I knew I wouldn't be able to guess all the places Morden could have gone, but Anne was another story. I might be able to intercept her, catch up . . .

. . . and what? Even if I could catch Anne, what could I do? I'd seen how easily Anne had handled Caldera. What was I going to do differently?

But even as I asked that question, I knew the answer. I couldn't match Anne in a fight, but there was a way for me to face her on even footing. I changed direction and started walking, pulling out my phone and hitting the signal to alert Luna and Variam. I knew there wasn't much time.

15

Luna and Variam got my message and called one after the other. I told them to meet me in the Hollow and that I'd explain everything there. My Council communicator and my work phone were starting to light up with calls from Light mages. I ignored them all – I'd figure out about what lies I needed to tell them later, assuming there was a later.

Luna and Variam arrived in the Hollow less than two minutes after I did. 'What's going on?' Variam said as he let the gate close behind him. 'The whole Keeper net was just starting to light up when I—'

'Anne's been possessed,' I said. 'The jinn's back and it's not going away.' I told them the story quickly and succinctly, leaving nothing out. Luna's mouth was open by the time I finished.

'Wait, that was *her?*' Luna said. 'In the Tiger's Palace?'

'Yes, and if we can't get to her, she's going to stay like that.'

Variam looked a lot less surprised than Luna. His expression was grim. 'What can we do?'

'I need the two of you to get to Anne's new flat,' I said. 'You can take my stone to get through the wards if you don't have your own. Find that tracer focus and use it. She's been pretty good about keeping it supplied with fresh blood.'

'What if she's got there first?' Variam asked.

'She hasn't,' I said. 'I've checked. She'll get around to it eventually, but right now she's going to be busy and this other Anne isn't really the conscientious type. You should have at least an hour.'

'But when we catch up with her, then what?' Luna asked. 'If she decides she's not coming quietly . . . well, the way you're describing it, I'm not sure we'd win that argument.'

'We wouldn't,' I said. 'And it won't be all three of us.'

'Why?'

'Because you're not going to be fighting Anne,' I said. 'I am. You're right: there's no way we can beat her in a fight, not physically. But I'm not going to be there physically. I'm going to enter Elsewhere, go into her mind, kick that jinn out and wake the real Anne back up again.'

Luna and Variam stared at me. 'Can you *do* that?' Luna asked.

'Only chance we've got,' I said. 'I'll stay in touch with you two through the dreamstone. I need you both to get a fix on Anne and be ready. As soon as I give the word, use the tracer to gate to her location, grab her and get her back here.'

'Wait,' Luna said. 'How is that going to work?'

'We have to do this in exactly the right order,' I said. 'You can't engage Anne first, because she and the jinn will wipe the floor with you. But if I do manage to pull this off, the most likely result is that she'll be left unconscious. Either way, while I'm attacking in Elsewhere, her physical body will be vulnerable.'

'I get that,' Variam said. 'But I can see one big problem. What if she's in Richard's mansion or something?'

'Then . . .' I hesitated. 'We'll improvise. I probably don't need to tell you this, but this is dangerous. Really dangerous. I don't think that Anne would kill either of you, but anyone else who might be there . . .'

'Yeah, like that's anything new,' Luna said. 'We'll figure something out.'

'Wait,' I said. 'There's more. You can't let anyone else know about this. Anyone. What Anne just did today has earned her a death sentence three times over. Even the most lenient members of the Council will execute her without a second thought. Our only chance is to shut this down before anyone finds out what really happened.'

'Got it.' Luna ran for where she stores her gear.

Variam didn't follow, not straightaway. 'What if it doesn't work?' he asked me.

'Then we're screwed. Which part do you mean?'

'You going into Elsewhere and un-possessing her.'

'Then . . .' I tried to think of an answer and came up blank. 'I don't know.'

Variam looked at me for a second. 'If you can't deal with this, someone else is going to have to,' he said. 'You understand that. Right?'

'I know,' I said. Variam nodded and went after Luna.

There was no time to wish them luck; every minute mattered now. I hurried to my cottage and lay down on my futon, not bothering to undress. The dreamstone glinted on the side table and I reached out to it, pulling myself into sleep. The world faded away.

I opened a gate and stepped through into Anne's Elsewhere.

The dreamscape felt . . . different. The forests and greenery were the same, but the sky above was clouding, on its way to overcast. A cool wind was blowing through the leaves, and in the distance I thought I heard the cry of some wild animal. I set off for the tower, moving swiftly.

As I walked, I ran through what Arachne had taught me about combat in Elsewhere. It wasn't something we'd practised, not yet, but she'd explained the theory. According to Arachne, most mages are terrible at fighting in Elsewhere, because the rules of this place go completely against what they're used to. When most mages fight, their instinct is to use physical force, because in their world, that's what works. And the fluidity of Elsewhere makes that easy. You want to throw a fireball? If you're in Elsewhere, then anyone can do it, no fire magic required. You'd prefer a weapon? Swords, guns, lightsabers, nuclear bombs . . . anything you can think of, you can make.

Of course, with a blank cheque like that, you know there's going to be a catch, and in this case the catch is that none of the weapons really *do* anything. Weapons are dangerous because they can damage your body, and in Elsewhere, you don't *have* a body. To an observer it might look as though I was walking through the forest, but what they were seeing was a projection, shaped by my unconscious. If someone jumped out and stabbed me, it wouldn't affect me unless I believed that it would, and even then, it'd be more uncomfortable than dangerous. I didn't have a heart to pierce or blood to spill; nothing that happened here could touch my body, which was lying safe back in the Hollow.

But just because my body was safe didn't mean that the rest of me was. Mental attacks can reach you in Elsewhere just fine. It's not just direct attacks that are the worry either: your body being safe doesn't help much if you can't *find* it again, and it's very possible to become lost in Elsewhere, leaving your body an empty husk. The good news was that I didn't think Anne would have any more idea than I did about how to do either of those things. A mind mage would be far more dangerous in this situation, but Anne's a life mage, and that other Anne had those same memories to draw upon. She'd be used to ending fights by touching her enemies and disabling them. I was fairly sure that when she tried that on me and found that it didn't work, it would throw her for a loop.

But the jinn was another story. I know what Anne's magic can do and what its limitations are. I knew practically nothing about the jinn's powers, except for a nasty feeling that they were very, very large. I knew that it was restricted in its ability to affect the real world – it needed a willing host. I *didn't* know if the same rules applied here. If they didn't, then this trip could turn very bad very fast.

I reached the black-glass walls surrounding Anne's tower and hopped over, landing in the courtyard. The window at the top of the tower beckoned, but I didn't want to go there, not yet. Instead I walked towards the tower. A cold breeze swept across the stone, ruffling my hair as I reached the smooth walls. There was no door. I reached out to place my hand flat against the wall and a passage opened. I walked inside and it sealed behind me.

The interior of the tower was hushed and gloomy. The corridors were lit with the same white sphere lamps that I remembered, but as I watched, one of them flickered and went out. Even the ones that were still glowing seemed to be dimmer, or perhaps it was because the black walls and floor soaked up the light as it was cast. Despite the silence, the tower didn't feel empty. It felt as though something was waiting for me.

I needed some way to find out where Anne was. I picked a door at random and opened it to reveal an empty room with a stand at the far end that held an oval dressing mirror. I walked over and touched the mirror, sending a thread of magic into it.

The mirror swirled and darkened. An image became visible in the glass, clear at the centre and fuzzy at the edges. I was seeing a picture of the inside of a living room: wooden tables and a white sofa with a cross-beamed roof. Something about the architecture made me think of Spain, or maybe Morocco. Arched windows gave a view out onto a sun-drenched garden, and from outside I could hear the buzz of cicadas.

Morden was standing in the middle of the room, and he was dressing. The clothes he'd been wearing in San Vittore were lying neatly folded on a chair, and he was in the middle of donning a black button-up shirt. 'Why?' he said, without turning around. 'Was this not what you were expecting?'

'Where are all your underlings?' It was Anne's voice, and I nearly jumped. It sounded as though it were coming from over my shoulder. The timbre was different, deeper; it was her voice, but strange somehow. 'Let me guess – they ran out once you got thrown in prison?'

'I don't need bodyguards, Anne.'

'Could have fooled me.'

I still couldn't see Anne . . . *oh.* It was Anne's eyes I was seeing through. It made sense, but it was kind of inconvenient. I wondered what the chances were of her pulling out her mobile and bringing up Google Maps. Probably not very high.

Anne's viewpoint shifted, as if she'd crossed her arms. 'So what's your next move?'

'Did Richard not tell you?'

'What, you think we were exchanging texts?' Anne said.

'Memory clouding only does so much. I think Anne *might* have got suspicious if she saw his name on her mobile.'

'In that case, you should be happy to see him.'

Anne paused. 'He's coming here?'

Morden finished buttoning his shirt and smoothed it down. 'We'll be meeting at a neutral location.'

'I wasn't told.'

Morden glanced at Anne. It was unnerving seeing him apparently looking straight into my eyes. 'You don't seem entirely pleased.'

'Yeah, you could say that.' I couldn't see Anne's expression, but her voice was a lot less friendly. 'I'm guessing he's bringing his retinue, right? *And* his items.'

'He won't be unprotected, if that's what you're asking.' Morden tilted his head. 'Is there a problem?'

'You bet there's a problem. I'm not here so that I can be his slave girl.'

'That's not the intention.'

'You think I'm an idiot?' Anne asked. 'I was the one who found that dreamstone, remember? I know what it does. If he's coming, that means he wants me as well.'

'Was that not the arrangement?' Morden asked. 'I admit I've been a little out of the loop of late, but I was under the impression that you were intending to accept Richard's offer. The same one that he gave you in Sagash's shadow realm three years ago.'

'Yeah,' Anne said. 'I saw what happened to the last girl who took him up on a deal like that.'

'Deleo's circumstances were . . . particular to her.'

'Bet he says that to everyone.' My view of Morden swayed as Anne shook her head. 'No deal.'

Morden picked up a coat and slung it over his arm,

turning to Anne. 'Then are you intending to go back to Verus?'

'I'm okay with helping Richard,' Anne said. 'But it's going to be on my terms. I'm not interested in being another Deleo. More like Vihaela.'

Morden studied Anne, tilting his head. 'Ambitious.' He quirked his lips in a smile. 'Quite different from your other self. You should bear in mind that Vihaela did not attain her position for free. She brought a great deal to Richard's cause, and she has not sat idle since.'

'I just broke you out of prison. I think that earns me some credit.'

'Don't let your newfound power go to your head, Anne,' Morden said. 'Remember, that power is not yours. It is the jinn's. And the jinn does not serve you.'

My viewpoint moved as Anne shrugged. 'Yeah, well, Richard still needs me if he wants his jinn to do anything, doesn't he? Otherwise that ring of his is just a pretty piece of jewellery.'

'Then why don't you explain that to him yourself?'

Anne looked at Morden silently.

'No?' Morden said. 'I hadn't expected you to be timid.'

'You going to try to force me?' Anne said.

'Richard and I are not Sagash,' Morden said. 'We prefer willing servants. If you wish to go your own way, then I will not stop you. But have a care. Without Richard's influence, you will find that jinn considerably less tractable.'

'I'll take my chances.'

Morden picked up his old clothes and left the room. Anne's viewpoint swivelled as she looked over her shoulder. Something about the movement made me wonder if she could sense she was being watched, and I touched the mirror quickly. The image faded and went dark.

I hurried out of the room, and as I did I reached out to Luna. It was a little harder, opening a mental link from here, but I'd had plenty of practice, and Luna's one of the people I can reach most easily. I came to a spiral staircase and began to climb, and as I did I felt the touch of Luna's mind. *Luna, it's me. You found the tracer?*

We did, Luna answered instantly. *Blood's fresh; we're ready to go. But Vari's worried that as soon as we do, Anne'll sense it.*

She might, I admitted. I really didn't want to bet against Anne's powers right now. *She's out of the country. Couldn't get a fix on where.*

We can handle that. Who else is there?

Morden, but he's leaving. I get the feeling he and Anne don't trust each other very much.

What about our jinn problem?

Yeah, that's going to be the tricky part, I said. The stairs kept going up; I climbed them as I talked, taking them two at a time. I didn't have to worry about getting tired, not here. *One thing I've found out. I don't think other-Anne is actually controlling that jinn. At least, not completely.*

Then who is?

She said something about a ring, I said. *It must be the same one that Richard took from the Vault, the one the jinn's bound to. He's using that and the dreamstone to influence it. Other-Anne has her own deal with the jinn, but it doesn't seem like she controls it completely either. Remember when we thought that it was just the jinn possessing Anne? It's looking like more of a triangle. There's Richard, there's Anne's dark side and there's the jinn. None of them have full control, and each of them needs the other two to get what they want. Unfortunately, I'm pretty sure that if there's one thing all three of them can agree on, it'll be that they want to keep Anne possessed.*

Then figure out a way to make sure they don't get what they want!

Working on it. Be ready to move as soon as I give the word.

We already are, Luna said. *Oh, and Vari says to step on it.*

'Thanks for the advice,' I muttered, cutting the connection. I wondered what Anne was doing in the outside world. What I really needed was a portable version of that mirror . . .

Then I smiled. *But this is Elsewhere, isn't it? If I want it . . .* I held up my hand, and a small hand mirror appeared in my grip. I concentrated on it, focusing a thread of magic into the glass. The mirror darkened . . . and stayed dark.

I frowned and tried again. Same result. *Is it not working?* I was pretty sure it should be. Maybe something was stopping it . . .

. . . or maybe it was working just fine, and this *was* what Anne was seeing. I didn't like that idea. *Enough climbing. I need to find her.* As I thought that, I looked up and saw a landing with a door. I opened it and stepped through.

The room on the other side was vast. Circular walls curved away to the left and right, with cylindrical pillars. The pillars went up and up, disappearing into the shadows, so that the ceiling, if there was one, was lost in darkness. Everything was made of the same black glass, and the white lamps on the walls and pillars seemed small and feeble against the gloom. The room should have been too big to fit into the tower, but then it was Elsewhere.

At the centre of the room was a dais, and mounted on the dais was a crystal sphere, maybe eight or ten feet wide. The sphere was nearly opaque but I thought I could make out an outline of something within. I walked out through the pillars towards it, my footsteps echoing in the stillness.

A voice spoke from behind the columns. 'I had a feeling it was you.'

The shadows moved and Anne stepped out. One look was enough to tell me which Anne. She was wearing a black dress that left her arms and shoulders bare; its hem trailed on the floor as she walked towards me. Her gaze was locked onto me, and she did not look happy. 'You should not be here.'

'First you complain about being left alone; now you get upset when I visit,' I said. I kept my voice casual, but inwardly I was keyed up. This was it. 'Make up your mind.'

Dark Anne's eyes flashed. 'You're too soon. You'll ruin everything.'

I reached out through the dreamstone to Luna. *Luna. She's in here with me. Go get her.*

All right, Luna said. *We're going in.*

'Ruin everything?' I said. 'What do you think's going to happen when the Council finds out what happened today?'

'Then you'd better make sure they don't, hadn't you?' Dark Anne took a step closer, her eyes hard. 'Now I'm only going to say this once. Get out.'

I met her gaze and spoke clearly and slowly. 'That's not going to happen.'

We faced each other across the black-glass floor. 'I could have killed you any time I wanted,' Dark Anne said. 'You want to make me start reconsidering that?'

'Oh, I'm sure you could,' I said. 'Out there. You're about to find that Elsewhere is a little different.'

'This is *my* Elsewhere,' Dark Anne said. 'I created it.

Everything in this place, every stone, every leaf on every tree, they're here because I made them. You think you can face me here?'

'You didn't create this place,' I said. 'It was the real Anne who did that. And you know what? I don't think you're capable of changing it. If you could, you'd have done it already. All you can do is hold it together, and from what I've seen, you're having trouble even managing that.'

Anger flashed across Dark Anne's face. 'I *am* the real Anne.'

'There's still a chance to work this out,' I said. 'Give her back control. Because if you don't, then I have the feeling that when she wakes up, you are not going to like what she's going to do to you.'

'Wake her up?' Dark Anne's lip curled. 'Come and try.'

'Fine by me,' I said, and strode towards her.

Dark Anne didn't hesitate. The real Anne probably would have, would have stopped to wonder why I'd walk into arm's reach against a life mage, but this Anne wasn't the type to stop and think. Her hand came out, green light kindling.

I caught Dark Anne's arm at the wrist. I felt the pressure as her spell tried to attack me, but it was no more than pressure. This might be Anne's Elsewhere, but the closer she came to me, the harder it was for her to exert her will. It was like forcing two very powerful magnets together; the closer they came, the greater the resistance. The spell slid off, and I swung her away behind me. Dark Anne staggered, then caught her balance, looking at me in confusion.

I'd already made it to the sphere. Now that I was close enough, I could see that within it was a black stone slab. Another Anne was inside, this one dressed in white, laid out with her arms by her sides. Her chest didn't rise or fall, but somehow I had the impression she was sleeping.

'What the hell . . . ?' Dark Anne ran at me.

I caught her wrist again without turning to look. Again her magic reached out, trying to attack me, with the same result.

'Stop it!' Dark Anne struggled. 'Let go!'

'Did you make this?' I asked her. 'Doesn't seem like your style.'

'Let GO!'

I released Dark Anne and she jumped back out of range. 'Don't take this the wrong way,' I told her, 'but I'd like some other company.' I wondered how tough that crystal was. *Only one way to find out.* A giant weapon appeared in my hands, somewhere between a scythe and a pick, glowing blue-white. The haft was about ten feet long and the curving blade was as tall as I was. In the real world I wouldn't even have been able to lift it off the ground.

'No!' Dark Anne said. 'Don't—!'

I took an overhand swing, focusing my will into the tip of the blade.

The point struck the crystal and the sphere rang like a bell. I'd been willing the blade to cut through, and as it struck I felt my will slam into something, like a blade scraping off bone. It felt like running into a brick wall. The scythe jarred out of my hands, vanishing as it touched the floor, and I staggered back.

'Idiot!' Anne shouted. 'Are you trying to get us killed?'

I started to answer, then trailed off. All of a sudden I could sense another presence in the room, something stirring. I thought I saw movement out of the corner of my eye and whirled, but there was nothing.

I turned, looking around. The great room felt hushed, waiting. I couldn't see anything in the columns around us. Up above, the roof faded into darkness. The gloom made it hard to see, but I was sure I was being watched. I looked up, frowning. Something about the shadows around the roof felt wrong. There could be something hiding up there . . .

The shadows in the roof moved.

Oh. My eyes went wide. *That's not a roof.*

The jinn stirred and looked down at me.

Looking at the jinn felt like something out of a dream: you have an impression, a sense, but you don't see it, not exactly. I had a vague impression of a body, a towering shape going up and up, but it was cloaked in darkness. Or maybe not darkness; it wasn't black, or any other colour, but something that made my eyes shy away and refuse to focus. The best comparison I can think of is what you see when you close your eyes, black and grey and specks of not-quite-light, all mixed together.

'Just stay quiet,' Dark Anne said, her voice low. 'If you don't—'

The jinn struck.

I leaped aside, jumping thirty feet to land on the other side of the sphere. For one instant I had a confused impression of two images at once, the jinn looming overhead as an incorporeal cloud and yet also swinging a blow downwards like a giant, then the strike landed. There was a ripping noise like enormous bedsheets being torn apart, and a section of floor just . . . vanished. All of a sudden there was a jagged twenty-foot hole. Below was nothingness – instead of the room below, I could see an endless void and distant stars.

Dark Anne staggered, putting a hand to her head. I summoned up the scythe again and struck at the sphere a second time, focusing harder. Again I felt my will slam up against the barrier, and this time a bright spike of pain went through my head.

'Stop it!' Dark Anne shouted. 'Both of you!'

The jinn struck again. One of the columns was cut off at its base, the gigantic pillar toppling like a falling tree. The part of it that fell through the floor vanished; the rest crashed into the floor. The room trembled, seeming to flicker briefly in and out of existence.

I straightened up from where I'd landed on the far side of the room. I wasn't sure why I was still alive. The amount of power the jinn had to be putting into these attacks was insane, so I didn't know why it was having so much trouble landing a hit . . .

Wait. That's it, isn't it? The jinn was *too* powerful. Out in the real world, Anne could focus and direct its magic, but in here it was like a battleship trying to blow up a tuna fish.

Of course, the tuna fish isn't going to win that battle either. I needed to get through that sphere, but how? I had the nasty feeling that if I kept attacking, I would break before it did. The dragon had told me that if I tried to sever the link between Anne and the jinn, it would destroy me. I needed a better plan.

The jinn threw some kind of attack at me that I'd never seen before; I couldn't tell what it would do and didn't hang around to find out. My jump took me out of range and an instant later the whole section of the room in which I'd been standing seemed to distort and vanish. Looking back at Dark Anne, I saw that she was standing in front of one of the holes in the floor, concentrating. As I watched,

I saw the floor reassemble itself, the void turning back into smooth black stone.

Another attack came above, then another. Each time I managed to dodge without understanding why or how. It wasn't my precognition that was helping me here: it was my sense of Elsewhere. Somehow I could feel the movements, like ripples in water. But those same movements gave me some sense of the jinn's strength too, and it was terrifying. There was no way I could even think about attacking something like that.

But if I couldn't fight this thing, what else could I do? I looked around, searching for an edge. Dark Anne was trying to split her attention between me and the damage to the room. She seemed to be trying to repair the tower, but the jinn was destroying it faster than she could patch the holes. There were gaping voids everywhere now, and beyond them I could see a strange star-filled sky that hurt my eyes. Only the sphere at the centre and the tiny patch of floor seemed to be undamaged, and that made me pause. Why would that part be untouched . . . ?

Because she's the one thing the jinn can't destroy. That was it, wasn't it? I couldn't drive the jinn out of this place. But Anne could.

'Get out of here!' Dark Anne shouted at me. 'You're going to get us killed!'

I reached out through the dreamstone, trying to reach Anne. I could see her right there, lying inside that sphere, and my thoughts arrowed straight towards her—

—and came up against something. There was a barrier there too, softer and more porous, but just as strong. I tried to force my way; it felt like trying to punch through a mattress.

The jinn loomed over me. I couldn't make out its eyes or its gaze, but somehow I knew that I had its attention. There was a shift in the room as it gathered its strength, but no blow fell. This time it was something new.

The crystal sphere on the dais darkened and became opaque. The room around me seemed to vibrate, shimmering at the edge of my vision, then it began to fade, the walls and columns unravelling into nothingness.

A wave of instinctive panic shot through me, the fear of falling. The floor beneath my feet was fading to nothing, a starry abyss below, and frantically I concentrated on my footing, willing it to hold. It hesitated, then solidified – but only for a few feet. I was standing on a tiny island floating in space. Looking around, I saw that Dark Anne was on her own little island off to my right, but it was the only piece of the tower remaining. We were alone in an endless void.

I tried again to push my thoughts through to reach Anne's, and again I failed. The barrier wasn't hard, but it seemed to gather strength the more deeply I forced it. I thought fast: in the Tiger's Palace I'd managed to send a message without establishing a full mental link. Maybe I could do that again. I tried to amplify my thoughts, imagining that I was shouting at Anne through a megaphone. *Anne! Can you hear me?*

No response. For a moment though, I could sense something; a half-awake presence, stirring. *Wake up. It's Alex. Wake up!*

The jinn struck again. This time there was nowhere to go, and I froze. *Can't dodge, it's going to kill me—*

'Alex!' Dark Anne shouted.

I jumped. Behind me the platform was wiped from existence, and I focused desperately, imagining a landing pad. There was resistance, and for one heart-stopping moment I was sure I was going to fall for ever, then my feet came down on a new platform, smaller than the last.

'Just *go*!' Dark Anne shouted at me. It was disorientating, looking at her floating in the void on her tiny island. Even a few minutes ago she would have scared me; now, she was one of the most familiar things here.

Anne, the jinn's here and it's trapping you. You're a prisoner. You have to break free. I strained to make out a response, but there was nothing. I didn't know if she could even hear me.

'If you keep fighting this thing it's going to kill you!' Dark Anne shouted.

'Then help!' I shouted back. 'If there's anyone who should be on her side, it's you!'

'Like hell I will!'

The jinn sent some kind of wave outwards. I felt myself thinning, growing misty; without knowing how or why I grounded myself, making myself more solid. Even diffused, the jinn's power was terrifying and I had to struggle to stabilise myself. Out of the corner of my eye I saw Dark Anne stagger. *Anne*, I called at the sphere. *You don't have much time. You're being sealed in. If this keeps up I don't know what's going to happen to you, but it'll be bad. Either you'll be a prisoner for ever, or it'll destroy you completely. If you want to live, if you want to be free, wake up and break out of there!*

Nothing. I couldn't sense any response. Maybe she was so far gone she couldn't hear . . . no, she'd responded that first time, I'd felt it. Why wasn't it working now?

'Listen to me, Alex.' Dark Anne came walking towards me and the platform grew outwards to accommodate her, materialising beneath her footsteps and fading away behind. I didn't think she noticed; her eyes were fixed on me. 'For years she's been out there, getting to live and be happy, while I've been shut away in the dark. Now it's my turn, and you want to put everything back the way it was? She goes back to being in control, and I go back to being locked in this tower?' Dark Anne shook her head. 'No. Not this time.'

I looked into Dark Anne's eyes and I knew she meant it. She might not want me dead, but if I tried to imprison her again she'd fight me with everything she had—

Wait. That's it. I'd been urging Anne to break free, to fight and survive. But those were the motivations that powered *this* Anne. She'd been born out of anger and desperation and the will to survive. And that wasn't what Anne was, not at her core.

Say the right words . . .

Anne, I called. I didn't try to amplify my thoughts this time; instead I made them clearer, more focused. *Come to us. We need you.*

'Time to run, Alex,' Anne said. 'Come on, isn't that what you do? When you can't win, you run and live another day. Used to piss me off, but I'll give you credit, you're not dumb. You don't fight losing battles.'

I thought about what running would mean. Dark Anne staying in control, with the true Anne, the one I cared about, locked here in stasis. I wouldn't get another chance at this. The jinn would reinforce the prison and I'd never reach her again . . .

I reached out to Anne one last time. It was getting harder to get through; whatever the jinn was doing, it was sealing her off from mental contact as well. *Please wake up. I don't want to go back to our world without you.* A breath. *I love you.*

No answer. The jinn loomed over me and I could sense that it was gathering power for some new kind of attack. I couldn't see what it was and I didn't know if I'd survive this time.

'It's over, Alex,' Dark Anne said. 'Just do the smart thing and—'

Power flared from the sphere.

With a keening crash, the crystal shattered. Thousands of shards flew outwards, and with them came a wave of white light, washing over us. In an eye-blink it was gone . . . and so was the starry void. The tower room was back once again, columns rising up to the ceiling, sphere lights glowing clear and bright.

Dark Anne was standing just a little way to my side, her eyes wide with shock. And at the centre of the room, standing on the dais, was another Anne, dressed in white with shoulder-length hair. Green light glowed around her, and as I watched, she looked up at the jinn.

The jinn loomed above her, a towering shape that hurt my eyes and twisted the senses, as tall as the room and more. In contrast Anne looked tiny, a doll-sized figure at the centre of a vast open space. But the light shining around her was stronger than the darkness ahead.

'I told you not to come back,' Anne said. She didn't raise her voice, but it echoed around the room.

The jinn stared down at her. If I strained I could almost imagine that I could hear words, whispers at the edge of hearing.

'Your contract is with her,' Anne answered. 'Not with me.'

The jinn drew itself up. The eye-twisting aura around it seemed to die, but the darkness grew. For a moment I thought I could see it: a humanoid figure, impossibly slender and tall. It reached for Anne, one long arm stretching out and down.

Light blazed, green and white. The jinn recoiled, and Anne took a step forward, a leaf-green aura glowing around her. 'Your invitation is revoked,' she said clearly. 'Now *get out of my head.*'

The jinn struck down, and Anne rose up to meet it.

The room shook. Light exploded outwards, forcing me to shield my eyes. I couldn't see or hear what was going on; I could sense that it was a battle, but one I couldn't reach or affect.

And just that fast, it was over. The light winked out and I lowered my hand, looking around. Anne was still there, standing in the centre of the room . . . but the room was different. The shadows were gone; where the lights had been weak and dim, they now shone clearly, illuminating the walls and ceiling. I looked for the jinn and saw no trace of it. The oppressive feeling had lifted.

Anne looked around. She saw me and a smile touched her lips, then her gaze fell upon the other Anne, and the smile faded. 'You,' she said. And never had I heard her voice contain such venom.

Dark Anne stared back at her.

'I am *done* with you.' Anne walked straight towards her shadow, her eyes set. 'Do you have any idea what you've done today?'

Dark Anne looked back at her, defiant. 'You deserved it.'

Anne came to a stop in front of her. The two Annes stared at each other, light and dark mirrors. 'How long would you have kept me like that?' she said. 'How long would you have used my body to go on a rampage?'

'How long would I have kept *you*?' Dark Anne said. 'How long have *you* kept *me*?'

'Because I had to!' Anne shouted. 'I saw everything you did and I thought it had to be a nightmare, because even you couldn't be that bad. But it was real! Dozens of people are dead, Morden's escaped and the Council is going to blame it all on *me*!'

'Well, that's what you get, isn't it?' Dark Anne said. 'You wanted to be the one to live in the outside world. You get to deal with that as well.'

'Deal with that?' Anne said. 'No. I'm dealing with *you*.'

Manacles sprang up from the floor, latching onto Dark Anne's wrists. She looked down in shock, tried to pull away; behind her, an armchair materialised out of the floor. The chains on the manacles began to retract, drawing her backwards.

'No!' Dark Anne shouted, struggling. 'Don't you dare!'

'Letting you run free in this tower was a mistake,' Anne said.

The chains withdrew into the arms of the chair, locking Dark Anne's wrists in place. Two more manacles locked around her ankles, pulling them apart to the armchair's corners. 'You can't do this!' Dark Anne shouted. 'You need me!'

'To do what?' Anne asked. 'To fight? I'm learning to do that on my own.'

'How long do you think you can—?' A metal band locked around Dark Anne's neck, pulling her against the back of the chair.

'How long?' Anne walked forward and leaned in close, staring into her twin's eyes. 'However long I have to. Because you are not getting out.'

The floor underneath the chair opened and it began to slowly descend, disappearing into a black pit. There were no stars in the darkness this time. Dark Anne struggled furiously. 'You can't keep me like this for ever!' she shouted at Anne. 'You think you can just forget about me? You remember how that worked last time?'

Something about that struck a chord. 'Anne,' I said. 'Wait.'

Anne turned to me, and the expression on her face was not welcoming. 'You do not get a vote in this.'

'What if there's another way?'

'I don't care,' Anne said. 'This isn't your choice to make. And I'm making sure this doesn't happen again.'

I hesitated. I looked down at Dark Anne, disappearing into the darkness, and felt a moment's pity for her. But then I remembered the guards I'd seen massacred at San Vittore. They'd just gone in to work to do their jobs, and they'd been torn apart by summoned monsters. Maybe Dark Anne did deserve some sympathy, but her victims deserved a lot more.

The chair vanished from sight, and the floor began to close over Dark Anne, but her voice floated up from the pit, high and furious. 'I won't be here for ever! You hear me? I'll be—' The floor sealed and her words were cut off.

Anne let out a long breath, then turned to me. 'Thank you,' she said simply. Then she closed her eyes and slipped to the floor. I darted to catch her, but she was already fading, turning to mist. In an instant she was gone. I was alone in the room.

I reached out through the dreamstone. *Luna. Report.*

There was a moment's wait, agonisingly long, then I felt Luna's thoughts, strong and clear. *We've got her.*

I closed my eyes, feeling a wave of relief wash through me. *We won. Anne's herself.*

Good. We're heading home.

I took a last look around the black chamber, now silent and empty. I knew that the other Anne was somewhere beneath me, locked away, and that still wasn't something I was fully comfortable with. But Anne was in control again and the jinn was gone, and I knew we were lucky to be walking away with as much as we had. I turned and created a door that would take me out of Elsewhere and back to the waking world.

16

It was later that evening.

'What I can't figure out,' Luna said, 'is what she was doing in New Zealand.'

We were in Dr Shirland's living room. The quiet room felt strange after everything we'd been through that day. I'd changed my clothes, but my muscles still remembered the battle in San Vittore, and my mind the weird brain-twisting fight in Elsewhere. But here, nothing seemed to change. Dr Shirland's cat was sitting with his paws tucked beneath him in the exact same armchair he always used.

'She wanted somewhere private,' I said. It was just me and Luna in the room at the moment. Variam was outside making calls, while Dr Shirland was with Anne in the consulting room. Anne had still been unconscious when we'd brought her in, and Dr Shirland asked not to be disturbed. That had been almost two hours ago. 'She was going to join Morden and Richard eventually, but she didn't want to meet them unprepared. She thought that they'd take the opportunity to capture her.' I shrugged. 'She was probably right.'

'It was pretty scary going through that gate,' Luna admitted. 'I know you're good with your predictions, but you've told me enough times that they're not perfect. I mean, bodyguards would have been one thing, but if someone like Vihaela had been there . . .'

'Anne wouldn't have trusted Vihaela to watch her while

she slept,' I said. 'It's always the weakness of Dark mages. They're just as much a threat to each other as they are to us.'

'So why New Zealand?'

'Anne sensed me watching her when she was talking to Morden,' I said. 'As soon as he left, she must have gated away. The description you and Vari gave me sounded a lot like a bay in New Zealand that the two of us visited when we were on the run. I guess she wanted somewhere safe and secluded, and that was the first place she thought of.'

The sound of the front door closing made us both look up. Variam was talking out in the corridor, his voice muffled. '. . . yeah,' he was saying. 'So they aren't calling us in? . . . Okay . . . Yeah, that makes sense . . . Okay, I will. Later.' He opened the door to the living room and stepped in, slipping the communicator into his pocket.

'So?' I asked. I couldn't keep the tension from my voice.

'I'm not making any promises,' Variam said. 'But so far? I don't think they've figured it out.'

Luna let out her breath in a long whistle. 'You sure?' I said.

'I asked two different Keepers. They haven't put your name out, or Anne's.'

'What if they're just waiting to jump on us with everything they've got?' Luna asked.

'That's what I've been checking,' I said. I'd been leaving the room with Luna at ten-minute intervals, path-walking to look for signs of danger. So far – *so far* – there had been nothing. But it would only take one person asking the right questions, one Council Keeper getting an inkling of what had really been going on . . .

'So you're really going to bluff it out?' Luna said. 'Pretend it wasn't you?'

'If I can.'

'Jesus.' Luna shook her head. 'Anne gets possessed by a jinn and summons up a whole army right in the middle of a Council prison, and come tomorrow, you're going to just walk into the War Rooms like nothing happened?'

'What choice do I have?' I said. 'We can't admit to it. We can't put up a defence, not for something like this. Actually, I don't think we'd even get the chance to *make* a defence. They'd kill us before we opened our mouths.'

Luna grimaced but didn't argue. 'What happens when they go through the recordings?'

'Anne and Morden trashed the control room on the way out,' I said. 'The cameras didn't have digital backups. Apparently they were still using CDs. And the wards over San Vittore will make it really hard to use timesight.'

'They can still break through if they look in the right place,' Variam said.

'I know,' I said with a sigh. I'd seen Sonder penetrate shrouds before. 'But I'm not sure they *will* be looking in the right place. They'll suspect me because I'm Junior Council. But if I can convince them that I didn't know anything, then it won't occur to them to look at Anne.'

'That feels like a really flimsy thing to stake your life on,' Luna said.

'Actually, he might be right,' Variam said unexpectedly. 'It's how the Council thinks. The way they see it, Anne's not even a real mage. They won't think she's important.'

'That still leaves a lot of people who know,' Luna said. 'Vihaela, Morden, Richard . . .'

'Who are all on the Dark side of the fence,' I said. 'We

just have to hope that the spectacularly crappy lines of communication between the Light Council and everyone else work in our favour for a change.'

Luna and Variam didn't say anything, but I knew what they were thinking. It was a *horribly* weak protection.

Footsteps out in the corridor made all three of us look up. Dr Shirland opened the door, stepping through.

'So?' Variam said before either Luna or I could speak.

'Anne is well,' Dr Shirland said, shutting the door behind her. 'The jinn is gone.'

Luna sighed in relief. 'Is it going to last?'

Dr Shirland sat down in one of the armchairs. The cat opened a drowsy eye to look at her, then stretched and went back to sleep. 'Theoretically.'

'Theoretically?' I said.

'This isn't a situation I've seen before,' Dr Shirland said. 'But as far as I can tell, Anne has gone through a mental realignment that has greatly diminished her shadow's influence. It will not be able to take her over again unless something changes.'

'What kind of change are we talking about?' I asked.

'Up until now, whenever possible, Anne has attempted to solve her issues alone,' Dr Shirland said. 'This has placed her under a great deal of mental pressure, and the strain and isolation was a large factor in enabling the jinn to possess her as it did. She was able to break its possession because, at the key moment, she was *not* alone.' Dr Shirland looked between us. 'The three of you are the people in the world she most trusts and depends on. If she's to prevent this from happening again, she will need your support.' Her eyes rested on me as she said the last sentence.

'It can't come back?' Variam demanded.

'Not as things are now.'

'What if she tries using the jinn's magic again?' Luna asked.

'That would be absolutely disastrous,' Dr Shirland said. 'The nature of a jinn's magic is such that the more its bearer uses it, the more influence the jinn can exert upon the bearer. At first, Anne was able to banish the jinn herself. This time, she needed your help. If it happens again, it might very well be irreversible. She can*not* use these powers again.'

'Can I see her?' I asked.

'Yes,' Dr Shirland said. 'She's resting but—'

I was already through the door. Behind me, I heard Variam starting to ask Dr Shirland something else.

The room down the corridor looked like a consulting room, with a chair and a flat couch. A window looked out onto the back garden, but I only had eyes for Anne, sitting on the couch with her head drooping. She looked pale, and there were dark circles under her eyes. She managed a smile when she saw me, but it faded almost instantly.

I started towards the chair, changed my mind and sat on the couch by her side. 'How are you doing?'

'I'm okay,' Anne said. She didn't say *for now*.

I looked at Anne. She didn't meet my eyes. 'Will you keep being okay?' I asked.

Anne let out a long breath. 'That's the question, isn't it? I feel like I am. Dr Shirland thinks I am. But that was what I thought before, and that didn't work out so well, did it?'

'We know how it happened,' I said. 'We can stop it from happening again.'

'Can we?'

'Yes.'

Anne still didn't look at me. I felt the futures flicker, then settle. She'd been about to say something, but I hadn't seen what . . .

Except I knew what she'd been about to say. She'd been going to ask me about what I'd said in Elsewhere. But she hadn't, and something told me that if I didn't raise the subject, she wouldn't either. A part of me – the same part that had been making the decisions about Anne for a long time – liked that idea. After all, this was a bad time to bring this up. Anne had just recovered from a traumatic and dangerous experience. Better to wait for things to calm down . . .

. . . *which is never going to happen.* I'd known Anne for five years, and we'd faced every kind of threat imaginable, from Light mages to Dark mages to magical creatures, trying to attack us or capture us or kill us or torture us or all of the above in various orders. After this danger there would be another one, and then another, and then another. Our lives weren't safe and they never would be, and that little voice that kept telling me to wait hadn't been prudence, it had been fear. And maybe if I hadn't spent so long listening to it, things wouldn't have gone so badly wrong today.

I couldn't change what I'd done. But I *could* learn from my mistakes.

'You're thinking about what I said in Elsewhere,' I said.

Anne did look up then. Her eyes searched my face.

'And the answer's yes,' I said. 'I meant it.' *Funny, my heart wasn't beating this fast against the jinn.*

Anne was still watching, as if waiting for something. I could path-walk, figure out what the results would be if . . .

Screw it. I leaned in to kiss her. I did it slowly enough that Anne could easily pull away.

She didn't.

After what felt like a long time but probably wasn't, I pulled back.

'This is a bad idea,' Anne said. She sounded short of breath, but she didn't draw away from my touch. 'I'm dangerous.'

It was hard to keep myself from smiling. It wasn't to do with anything Anne had said – I just felt light-headed. 'So are the rest of us.'

'Not like this. Richard wants me. What happened today could happen again. Just by being near me— Wait, what's so funny?'

I stopped laughing long enough to answer. 'Half the reason I never brought this up was because I was afraid *you'd* be in danger from being close to *me*.'

'I'm serious!'

'So am I,' I said. 'We're always going to be in danger and that's never going to change. I'm through wasting time.'

Anne looked me right in the eyes. 'Do you really want to take on everything that this'll mean? All the mistakes I've made, all the enemies I have? Everything that's wrong with me?'

'Yes,' I said. 'And I decided that a long time ago. It just took me until now to say it out loud.'

Anne kept looking at me, then tears glittered in her eyes and she leaned forward to rest her head against my chest.

I stroked her hair. In a little while, we'd go back to the living room to rejoin our friends. And after that, we'd have all of our other problems to deal with. There was Richard, and Morden, and the jinn, and Levistus, and the rest of the Council, and more others than I could count, not to mention Anne's other self. None of those things were going away, and I didn't know if I would be able to deal with them all. But right now, for the first time that I could remember, I was happy.

Let's see what tomorrow brings.

Look out for, Fallen, *book ten
in the Alex Verus series!*

extras

www.orbitbooks.net

about the author

Benedict Jacka became a writer almost by accident, when at nineteen he sat in his school library and started a story in the back of an exercise book. Since then he has studied philosophy at Cambridge, lived in China and worked as everything from civil servant to bouncer to teacher before returning to London to take up law.

Find out more about Benedict Jacka and other Orbit authors by registering for the free monthly newsletter at www.orbitbooks.net.

if you enjoyed
MARKED

look out for

THE FIFTH WARD: FIRST WATCH

by

Dale Lucas

In the cramped quarters of the city of Yenara, humans, orcs, mages, elves and dwarves all jostle for success and survival, while understaffed watch wardens struggle to keep the citizens in line.

Enter Rem. New to the city, he wakes bruised and hungover in the dungeons of the fifth ward. With no money for bail – and seeing no other way out of his cell – Rem jumps at the chance to join the Watch.

Torval, his new partner – a dwarf who's handy with a maul and known for hitting first and asking questions later – is highly unimpressed with the untrained and weaponless Rem. But when Torval's former partner goes missing, the two must learn to work together to uncover the truth and catch a murderer loose in their fair city.

ONE

Rem awoke in a dungeon with a thunderous headache. He knew it was a dungeon because he lay on a thin bed of straw, and because there were iron bars between where he lay and a larger chamber outside. The light was spotty, some of it from torches in sconces outside his cell, some from a few tiny windows high on the stone walls admitting small streams of wan sunlight. Moving nearer the bars, he noted that his cell was one of several, each roomy enough to hold multiple prisoners.

A large pile of straw on the far side of his cell coughed, shifted, then started to snore. Clearly, Rem was not alone.

And just how did I end up here? he wondered. *I seem to recall a winning streak at Roll-the-Bones.*

He could not remember clearly. But if the lumpy soreness of his face and body were any indication, his dice game had gone awry. If only he could clear his pounding head, or slake his thirst. His tongue and throat felt like sharkskin.

Desperate for a drink, Rem crawled to a nearby bucket, hoping for a little brackish water. To his dismay, he found that it was the piss jar, not a water bucket, and not well rinsed at that. The sight and smell made Rem recoil with a gag. He went sprawling back onto the hay. A few feet away, his cellmate muttered something in the tongue of the Kosterfolk, then resumed snoring.

Somewhere across the chamber, a multitumbler lock

clanked and clacked. Rusty hinges squealed as a great door lumbered open. From the other cells Rem heard prisoners roused from their sleep, shuffling forward hurriedly to thrust their arms out through the cage bars. If Rem didn't misjudge, there were only about four or five other prisoners in all the dungeon cells. A select company, to be sure. Perhaps it was a slow day for the Yenaran city watch?

Four men marched into the dungeon. Well, three marched; the fourth seemed a little more reticent, being dragged by two others behind their leader, a thickset man with black hair, sullen eyes, and a drooping mustache.

'Prefect, sir,' Rem heard from an adjacent cell, 'there's been a terrible mistake . . .'

From across the chamber: 'Prefect, sir, someone must have spiked my ale, because the last thing I remember, I was enjoying an evening out with some mates . . .'

From off to his left: 'Prefect, sir, I've a chest of treasure waiting back at my rooms at the Sauntering Mink. A golden cup full of rubies and emeralds is yours, if you'll just let me out of here . . .'

Prefect, sir . . . Prefect, sir . . . over and over again.

Rem decided that thrusting his own arms out and begging for the prefect's attention was useless. What would he do? Claim his innocence? Promise riches if they'd let him out? That was quite a tall order when Rem himself couldn't remember what he'd done to get in here. If he could just clear his thunder-addled, achingly thirsty brain . . .

The sullen-eyed prefect led the two who dragged the prisoner down a short flight of steps into a shallow sort of operating theater in the center of the dungeon: the inter-rogation pit, like some shallow bath that someone had let all the water out of. On one side of the pit was a brick oven in which fire and coals glowed. Opposite the oven was a burbling fountain. Rem thought these additions rather ingenious. Whatever elemental need one had—fire to burn with, water to drown with—both were readily provided. The floor of the pit, Rem guessed, probably sported a couple of grates that led right down into the sewers, as well as the tools of the trade: a table full of torturer's implements, a couple of hot braziers, some chairs and manacles. Rem hadn't seen the inside of any city dungeons, but he'd seen their private equivalents. Had it been the dungeon of some march lord up north—from his own country—that's what would have been waiting in the little amphitheater.

'Come on, Ondego, you know me,' the prisoner pleaded. 'This isn't necessary.'

''Fraid so,' sullen-eyed Ondego said, his low voice easy and without malice. 'The chair, lads.'

The two guardsmen flanking the prisoner were a study in contrasts—one a tall, rugged sort, face stony and flecked with stubble, shoulders broad, while the other was lithe and graceful, sporting braided black locks, skin the color of dark-stained wood, and a telltale pair of tapered, pointing ears. Staring, Rem realized that second guardsman was no man at all, but an elf, and female, at that. Here was a puzzle, indeed. Rem had seen elves at a distance before, usually in or around frontier settlements farther north, or simply haunting the bleak crossroads of a woodland highway like pikers who never demanded a toll. But he had never seen one of them up close like this—and certainly not in the middle of one of the largest cities in the Western world, deep underground, in a dingy, shit- and blood-stained dungeon. Nonetheless, the dark-skinned elfmaid seemed quite at home in her surroundings, and perfectly comfortable beside the bigger man on the other side of the prisoner.

Together, those two guards thrust the third man's squirming, wobbly body down into a chair. Heavy manacles were produced and the protester was chained to his seat. He struggled a little, to test his bonds, but seemed to know instinctively that it was no use. Ondego stood at a brazier nearby, stoking its coals, the pile of dark cinders glowing ominously in the oily darkness.

'Oi, that's right!' one of the other prisoners shouted. 'Give that bastard what for, Prefect!'

'You shut your filthy mouth, Foss!' the chained man spat back.

'Eat me, Kevel!' the prisoner countered. 'How do *you* like the chair, eh?'

Huh. Rem moved closer to his cell bars, trying to get a better look. So, this prisoner, Kevel, knew that fellow in the cell, Foss, and vice versa. Part of a conspiracy? Brother marauders, questioned one by one—and in sight of one another—for some vital information?

Then Rem saw it: Kevel, the prisoner in the hot seat, wore a signet pendant around his throat identical to those worn by the prefect and the two guards. It was unmistakable, even in the shoddy light.

'Well, I'll be,' Rem muttered aloud.

The prisoner was one of the prefect's own watchmen.

Ex-watchmen now, he supposed.

All of a sudden, Rem felt a little sorry for him . . . but not much. No doubt, Kevel himself had performed the prefect's present actions a number of times: chaining some poor sap into the hot seat, stoking the brazier, using fire and water and physical distress to intimidate the prisoner into revealing vital information.

The prefect, Ondego, stepped away from the brazier and moved to a table nearby. He studied a number of implements—it was too dark and the angle too awkward for Rem to tell what, exactly—then picked something up. He hefted the object in his hands, testing its weight.

It looked like a book—thick, with a hundred leaves or more bound between soft leather covers.

'Do you know what this is?' Ondego asked Kevel. 'Haven't the foggiest,' Kevel said. Rem could tell that he was bracing himself, mentally and physically.

'It's a genealogy of Yenara's richest families. Out-of-date, though. At least a generation old.'

'Do tell,' Kevel said, his throat sounding like it had contracted to the size of a reed.

'Look at this,' Ondego said, hefting the book in his hands, studying it. 'That is one enormous pile of useless information. Thick as a bloody brick—'

And that's when Ondego drew back the book and brought it smashing into Kevel's face in a broad, flat arc. The sound of the strike—leather and parchment pages connecting at high speed with Kevel's jawbone—echoed in the dungeon like the crack of a calving iceberg. A few of the other prisoners even wailed as though they were the ones struck.

Rem's cellmate stirred beneath his pile of straw, but did not rise.

Kevel almost fell with the force of the blow. The big guard caught him and set him upright again. The lithe elf backed off, staring intently at the prisoner, as though searching his face and his manner for a sign of something. Without warning, Ondego hit Kevel again, this time on the other side of his face. Once more Kevel toppled. Once more the guard in his path caught him and set him upright.

Kevel spat out blood. Ondego tossed the book back onto the table behind him and went looking for another implement.

'That all you got, old man?' Kevel asked.

'Bravado doesn't suit you,' Ondego said, still studying his options from the torture table. He threw a glance at the elf on the far side of the torture pit. Rem watched intently, realizing that some strange ritual was under way: Kevel, blinking sweat from his eyes, studied Ondego; the lady elf, silent and implacable, studied Kevel; and Ondego idly studied the elf, the prefect's thick, workman's hand hovering slowly over the gathered implements of torture on the table.

Then, Kevel blinked. That small, unconscious movement seemed to signal something to the elf, who then spoke to the prefect. Her voice was soft, deep, melodious.

'The amputation knife,' she said, her large, unnerving, honey-colored eyes never leaving the prisoner.

Ondego took up the instrument that his hand hovered above—a long, curving blade like a field-hand's billhook, the honed edge being on the inside, rather than the outside, of the curve. Ondego brandished the knife and looked to Kevel. The prisoner's eyes were as wide as empty goblets.

Ingenious! The elf had apparently used her latent mind-reading abilities to determine which of the implements on the table Kevel most feared being used on him. Not precisely the paragon of sylvan harmony and ancient grace that Rem would have imagined such a creature to be, but impressive nonetheless.

As Ondego spoke, he continued to brandish the knife, casually, as if it were an extension of his own arm. 'Honestly, Kev,' he said, 'haven't I seen you feign bravery a hundred times? I know you're shitting your kecks about now.'

'So you'd like to think,' Kevel answered, eyes still on the knife. 'You're just bitter because you didn't do it. Rich men don't get rich keeping to a set percentage, Ondego. They get rich by redrawing the percentages.'

Ondego shook his head. Rem could be mistaken, but he thought he saw real regret there.

'Rule number one,' Ondego said, as though reciting holy writ. 'Keep the peace.'

'Suck it,' Kevel said bitterly.

'Rule number two,' Ondego said, slowly turning to face Kevel, 'Keep your partner safe, and he'll do the same for you.'

'He was going to squeal,' Kevel said, now looking a little more repentant. 'I couldn't have that. You said yourself, Ondego—he wasn't cut out for it. Never was. Never would be.'

'So that bought him a midnight swim in the bay?' Ondego asked. 'Rule number three: let the punishment fit the crime, Kevel. Throttling that poor lad and throwing him in the drink . . . that's what the judges call cruel and unusual. We don't do cruel and unusual in my ward.'

'Go spit,' Kevel said.

'Rule number four,' Ondego quickly countered. 'And this is important, Kevel, so listen good: never take more than your share. There's enough for everyone, so long as no one's greedy. So long as no one's hoarding or getting fat. I knew you were taking a bigger cut when your jerkin started straining. There's only one way a watchman that didn't start out fat gets that way, and that's by hoarding and taking more than his fair share.'

'So what's it gonna be?' Kevel asked. 'The knife? The razor? The book again? The hammer and the nail-tongs?'

'Nah,' Ondego said, seemingly bored by their exchange, as though he were disciplining a child that he'd spanked a hundred times before. He tossed the amputation knife back on the table. 'Bare fists.'

And then, as Rem and the other prisoners watched, Ondego, prefect of the watch, proceeded to beat the living shit out of Kevel, a onetime member of his own watch company. Despite the fact that Ondego said not another word while the beating commenced, Rem thought he sensed some grim and unhappy purpose in Ondego's corporal punishment. He never once smiled, nor even gritted his teeth in anger. The intensity of the beating never flared nor ebbed. He simply kept his mouth set, his eyes open, and slowly, methodically, laid fists to flesh. He made Kevel whimper and bleed. From time to time he would stop and look to the elf. The elf would study Kevel, clearly not simply looking at him but *into* him, perhaps reading just how close he was to losing consciousness, or whether he was feigning senselessness to gain some brief reprieve. The elf would then offer a cursory, 'More.' Ondego, on the elfmaid's advice, would continue.

Rem admired that: Ondego's businesslike approach, the fact that he could mete out punishment without enjoying it. In some ways, Ondego reminded Rem of his own father.

Before Ondego was done, a few of the other prisoners were crying out. Some begged mercy on Kevel's behalf.

Ondego wasn't having it. He didn't acknowledge them. His fists carried on their bloody work. To Kevel's credit he never begged mercy. Granted, that might have been hard after the first quarter hour or so, when most of his teeth were on the floor.

Ondego only relented when the elf finally offered a single word. 'Out.' At that, Ondego stepped back, like a pugilist retreating to his corner between melee rounds. He shook his hands, no doubt feeling a great deal of pain in them. Beating a man like that tested the limits of one's own pain threshold as well as the victim's.

'Still breathing?' Ondego asked, all business.

The human guard bent. Listened. Felt for a pulse. 'Still with us. Out cold.'

'Put him in the stocks,' Ondego said. 'If he survives five days on Zabayus's Square, he can walk out of the city so long as he never comes back. Post his crimes, so everyone sees.'

The guards nodded and set to unchaining Kevel. Ondego swept past them and mounted the stairs up to the main cell level again, heading toward the door. That's when Rem suddenly noticed an enormous presence beside him. He had not heard the brute's approach, but he could only be the sleeping form beneath the hay. For one, he was covered in the stuff. For another, his long braided hair, thick beard, and rough-sewn, stinking leathers marked him as a Kosterman. And hadn't Rem heard Koster words muttered by the sleeper in the hay?

'Prefect!' the Kosterman called, his speech sharply accented.

Ondego turned, as if this was the first time he'd heard a single word spoken from the cells and the prisoners in them.

Rem's cellmate rattled the bars. 'Let me out of here, little man,' he said.

Kosterman all right. The long, yawning vowels and glass-sharp consonants were a dead giveaway. For emphasis, the Kosterman even snarled, as though the prefect were the lowest of house servants.

Ondego looked puzzled for a moment. Could it be that no one had ever spoken to him that way? Then the prefect stepped forward, snarling, looking like a maddened hound. His fist shot out in front of him and shook as he approached.

'Get back in your hay and keep your gods-damned head down, con! I'll have none of your nonsense after such a bevy of bitter business—'

Rem realized what was about to happen a moment before it did. He opened his mouth to warn the prefect off—surely the man wasn't so gullible? Maybe it was just his weariness in the wake of the beating he'd given Kevel? His regret at having to so savagely punish one of his own men?

Whatever the reason, Ondego clearly wasn't thinking straight. The moment his shaking fist was within arm's reach of the Kosterman in the cell, the barbarian reached out, snagged that fist, and yanked Ondego close. The prefect's face and torso hit the bars of the cell with a heavy clang.

Rem scurried aside as the Kosterman stretched both arms out through the bars, wrapped them around Ondego, then tossed all of his weight backward. He had the prefect in a deadly bear hug and was using his body's considerable weight to crush the man against the bars of the cell. Rem heard the other two watchmen rushing near, a flurry of curses and stomping boots. Around the dungeon, the men in the cells began to curse and cheer. Some even laughed.

'Let me out of here, now!' the Kosterman roared. 'Let me out or I'll crush him, I swear!'

Rem's instincts were frustrated by his headache, his thirst, his confusion. But despite all that, he knew, deep in his gut, that he had to do something. He couldn't just let the hay-covered Kosterman in the smelly leathers crush the prefect to death against the bars of the cell.

But that Kosterman was enormous—at least a head and a half taller than Rem.

The other watchmen had reached the bars now. The stubble-faced one was trying to break the Kosterman's grip while the elfmaid snatched for the rattling keys to the cells on the human guard's belt.

Without thinking, Rem rushed up behind the angry Kosterman, drew back one boot, and kicked. The kick landed square in the Kosterman's fur-clad testicles.

The barbarian roared—an angry bear, indeed—and Rem's gambit worked. For just a moment, the Kosterman released his hold on the prefect. On the far side of the bars, the stubble-faced watchman managed to get the prefect in his grip and yank him backward, away from the cell. When Rem saw that, he made his next move.

He leapt onto the Kosterman's broad shoulders. Instead of wrapping his arms around the Kosterman's throat, he grabbed the bars of the cell. Then, locking his legs around the Kosterman's torso from behind, he yanked hard. The Kosterman was driven forward hard, his skull slamming with a resonant clang into the cell bars. Rem heard nose cartilage crunch. The Kosterman sputtered a little and tried to reach for whoever was on his back. Rem drew back and yanked again, driving the Kosterman forward into the bars once more.

Another clang. The Kosterman's body seemed to sag beneath Rem.

Then the sagging body began to topple backward.

Clinging high on the great, muscular frame, Rem realized that he was overbalanced. He lost his grip on the cell bars, and the towering Kosterman beneath him fell. Rem tried to leap free, but he was too entangled with the barbarian to make it clear. Instead, he simply disengaged and went falling with him.

Both of them—Rem and the barbarian—hit the floor. The Kosterman was out cold. Rem had the wind knocked out of him and his vision came alight with whirling stars and dancing fireflies.

Blinking, trying to get his sight and his breath back, he heard the whine of rusty hinges, then footsteps. Strong hands seized him and dragged him out of the cell. By the time his vision had returned, he found himself on the stone pathway outside the cell that he had shared with the smelly, unconscious Kosterman. The prefect and his two watchmen stood over him.

'Explain yourself,' Ondego said. He was a little disheveled, but otherwise, the Kosterman's attack seemed to have left not a mark on him, nor shaken him.

Rem coughed. Drew breath. Sighed. 'Just trying to help,' he said.

'I'll bet you want out now, don't you?' Ondego asked. 'One good turn deserves another and all that.'

Rem shrugged. 'It hadn't really crossed my mind.'

Ondego frowned, as though Rem were the most puzzling prisoner he had ever encountered. 'Well, what do you want, then? I can be a hard bastard when I choose, but I know how to return a favor.'

Rem had a thought. 'I'm looking for work,' he said.

Ondego raised one eyebrow.

'Seeing as you have space on your watch rosters'— Rem gestured to the spot where they had been beating Kevel in the torture pit—'perhaps I could impress upon you—'

Ondego seemed to appraise Rem honestly for a moment. For confirmation of his instincts, he looked to the elf.

Rem suddenly knew the strange sensation of another living being poking around in his mind. It was momentary and fleeting and entirely painless, but eminently strange and unnerving, like having one's privates appraised by the other patrons in a bathhouse. Then the elf's probing intellect withdrew, and Rem no longer felt naked. The elfmaid seemed to wear a small, knowing half smile. Her dark and ancient eyes settled on Rem and chilled him.

She knows everything, Rem thought. *A moment in my mind, two, and she knows everything. Everything worth knowing, anyway.*

'Harmless,' the elfmaid said.

'Weak,' the stubble-faced guardsmen added.

The elf's gaze never wavered. 'No.'

'You don't impress me,' Ondego said, despite the elf's appraisal. 'Not one bit.'

'No doubt I don't,' Rem said. 'But, by Aemon, sir, I'd like to.'

The watchman beside Ondego leaned close. Rem heard the words he whispered to the prefect.

'*He did get that brute off you, sir.*'

Ondego and the big watchman continued to study him. The elf now turned her gaze on the boisterous prisoners in the other cells. A moment's eye contact was all it took. As the elfmaid turned her stone idol's glare on each of them, they fell silent and withdrew from the bars. Bearing witness to the effect the elf's silent, threatening stare had on those hard, desperate men made Rem's skin crawl.

But, to his own predicament: Rem decided to mount a better argument—he certainly couldn't end up in any more trouble, could he?

'You're down two men,' Rem said, trying to look and sound as reasonable as possible. 'That man you were beating and the partner he murdered. Surely you can give me the opportunity?'

'What's he in here for?' Ondego asked the watchman.

Rem prepared himself to listen. He was still trying to reason that part out himself.

'Bar brawl,' the stubble-faced watchman said. 'The Bonny Prince here was casting dice with some Koster longshoremen. Rolled straight nines, nine times in a row. They called him a cheat and he lit into them.'

It was coming back now. Rem remembered the tavern. He'd been waiting for someone. A girl. She hadn't shown. He'd had a little too much to drink while waiting. He vaguely remembered the dice and the longshoremen—two tall fellows, not unlike the barbarian he'd just tussled with in the cell.

He couldn't recall their faces, or even starting a fight with them . . . but he did remember being called a cheat, and taking umbrage.

'I wasn't cheating,' Rem said emphatically. 'It was just a run of good luck.'

'Not so good,' Ondego said, 'seeing as you're here in my dungeon.' To the guardsmen beside him: 'Where are the other two?'

'Taken to the hospital, sir,' the big man said. 'Beaten senseless by the Bonny Prince here.'

'And a third Kosterman, out like a light on my dungeon floor. What is it with you and these northerners, boy?'

Rem shrugged. 'Ill-starred, I guess.'

Ondego seemed to appraise Rem anew. Three Kostermen on their backs was bold, and he couldn't deny it. 'Doesn't look like much,' the prefect said, as if to himself, 'but he can hold his own in a fight.'

Ondego was impressed with Rem—no thanks to the stone-faced watchman laying that damned 'Bonny Prince' label on him. Rem guessed that Ondego's grudging respect might work in his favor.

'I don't like being called a cheat,' Rem said, 'first and foremost because I don't cheat. Ever.'

Ondego nodded toward Kevel, limp in his chair. 'Neither do we,' he said.

'So I see,' Rem answered.

A long silence fell between them.

'Get him on his feet,' Ondego said. 'We'll try him out.'

Without another word, the prefect left.

Rem looked to the tall man. He felt a smile blooming on his face, then suddenly felt the pain of his brawl the night before. A swollen, split lip; a bruised nose; at least one missing tooth, far back in his mouth; the taste of old blood.

The big man offered a hand and yanked Rem to his feet. Upright, Rem swooned for a moment, his vision briefly going black again before finally clearing.

'Don't look so pleased with yourself, my bonny boy,' the stubble-faced watchman said. 'You've no idea what you're in for walking the ward.'

Enter the monthly

Orbit sweepstakes at

www.orbitloot.com

With a different prize every month,
from advance copies of books by
your favourite authors to exclusive
merchandise packs,
**we think you'll find something
you love.**